Will she surrender to the tall, dark king of the desert?

Captivated by the Sheikh

Three seductive and passionate romances from three beloved Mills & Boon authors!

Captivated by the Sheikh

ANNIE WEST

SUE SWIFT

MEREDITH WEBBER

MILLS & BOON

All the characters in this book have no existence outside the imagination of the auth... ... ... same name or nam... they ... ... known or unkno...

All Ri... part in... ... ... whole or in ... ... Harlequin Enterp... ... thereof may not be ... ... electronic or mecha... ... information retriev... ... ... publisher.

This b... ... of trade or otherw... ... ... the prior consen... ... ... than that in which ... ... is condition being i...

® and ™ are trademarks owned and used by the trademark owner and/or its licensee. Trademarks marked with ® are registered with the United Kingdom Patent Office and/or the Office for Harmonisation in the Internal Market and in other countries.

First published in Great Britain 2010
Harlequin Mills & Boon Limited,
Eton House, 18-24 Paradise Road, Richmond, Surrey TW9 1SR

CAPTIVATED BY THE SHEIKH
© by Harlequin Enterprises II B.V./S.à.r.l 2010

For the Sheikh's Pleasure, *In the Sheikh's Arms* and *Sheikh Surgeon* were first published in Great Britain by Harlequin Mills & Boon Limited in separate, single volumes.

For the Sheikh's Pleasure © Annie West 2007
In the Sheikh's Arms © Susan Freya Swift 2003
Sheikh Surgeon © Meredith Webber 2005

ISBN: 978 0 263 88114 1

05-1110

Printed and bound in Spain
by Litografía Rosés S.A., Barcelona

FOR THE SHEIKH'S PLEASURE

BY
ANNIE WEST

Annie West spent her childhood with her nose between the covers of a book—a habit she retains. After years preparing government reports and official correspondence she decided to write something she *really* enjoys. And there's nothing she loves more than a great romance. Despite her office-bound past she has managed a few interesting moments—including a marriage offer with the promise of a herd of camels to sweeten the contract. She is happily married to her ever-patient husband (who has never owned a dromedary). They live with their two children amongst the tall eucalypts at beautiful Lake Macquarie, on Australia's east coast. You can e-mail Annie at www.annie-west. com or write to her at PO Box 1041, Warners Bay, NSW 2282, Australia.

To my friend Vanessa: a talented writer and a girl who knows the value of best-quality chocolate. Thanks for the unexpected supply that powered this story.
I owe you!

CHAPTER ONE

THERE she was.

Arik adjusted the binoculars a fraction to bring her into clearer focus.

A slow smile stretched his mouth as the early light limned her figure with gold.

Surprising to realise how disappointed he'd been just moments ago, thinking she wouldn't arrive. She'd become the highlight of each tedious day as she appeared on the beach, a lone, perfect Aphrodite with her long rippling hair, her delicious curves and her air of innocent allure.

Even at a distance of five hundred metres, the sight of her tightened each muscle in his lower body, turned his blood sluggish as his heartbeat slowed to a heavy anticipatory thud.

He lowered the binoculars and scrubbed his hand over his face.

Hell! What had he come to? Six weeks in plaster and he was reduced to playing the voyeur. Maybe he should have accepted one of the offers of feminine companionship he'd received while he recuperated.

But he'd been impatient to get this leg healed. He didn't want any fawning women around, fussing over him and nurturing false hopes of domestic bliss, staying here in his home. He'd seen the look in Helene's eyes just a couple of months ago and had known immediately it was time to end their relationship.

A pity. Helene was clever and witty, as well as sleekly seductive and with an appetite for sex he found rare in a woman. Their time together had been stimulating, satisfying and fun. But once she'd started dreaming about happily-ever-after, it was over.

He worked hard and played hard, seeking out women who'd enjoy the fast-paced ride with him. He wasn't into breaking hearts.

No, what he needed now was a diversion, a short, satisfying affair that would keep his mind off the frustration of being cooped up here.

He lifted the binoculars again and was rewarded with a sight that made him lean forward, elbows braced on the parapet.

His golden girl had put up her easel, positioned for the view along the beach to the next rocky headland. But, instead of concentrating on her paints, she was unbuttoning her shirt.

Arik's heart jolted in expectation. Yes! Her hands skimmed quickly down the shirt, then she shrugged it off, revealing smooth shoulders and arms and a curvaceous body that made him want to discard the wheelchair and hobble down to help her undress. Slim at the waist but full-breasted: she'd be a delicious handful, he decided as he watched her bend to strip off her trousers. A ripe peach of a *derrière*, invitingly curved hips and slim shapely legs.

Just as he'd suspected. A woman worth knowing better.

He watched her walk down to the waves curling in on the sand. Saw her pause as the water frothed about her ankles. It would be warm, caressing her skin. The current in this part of the Arabian Sea kept the temperature inviting.

His gaze roved appreciatively down her back, her legs and up again to the swell of her breasts as she turned. Abruptly her chin lifted and she stared straight up at him, as if she could make him out among the shadows on the long terrace.

A *frisson* of something shot through him.

Recognition? No, that was impossible.

And yet the illusion that their eyes met and held for one, two, three long pulse beats was strong enough to jerk him out of his complacent speculation.

He lowered the glasses and stared at her. But already she'd turned away, stepping out into the shallows till the waves lapped around her dark one-piece swimsuit.

She'd look better in a bikini.

Or best of all, nude.

He watched as she waded out further, then, with a sinuous shallow dive, swam out with an easy stroke into the bay. He leaned back in his seat, relieved to see she was clearly at home in the water. There'd be no need for any emergency rescue.

She swam for twenty minutes then waded ashore. The first rosy light of dawn had dissipated as the sun rose higher and brighter. It lit her to perfection, slanting off a body that made him itch to be rid of the full-leg plaster and down on the sand beside her. Close. Touching. Learning the texture of those smooth limbs, her scent, the taste of her skin against his lips, the sound of her sighs as she surrendered to pleasure.

Heat roared through him, a blaze of wanting so strong he shifted in his seat, fully aroused and impatient that he couldn't get what he wanted immediately.

If they'd been alive a hundred years ago, he could have snapped his fingers and had her brought instantly before him. It was a shame some of the old ways had died. There were definite drawbacks to the march of progress. To being a civilised man. Especially when there was something utterly *un*-civilised about the feelings this woman sparked in him.

Who was she? Where was she from? With that long swathe of blonde hair she was no local.

He leaned back in the chair as he contemplated the possibilities.

A girl: gorgeous, alone, tempting.

A man: bored, frustrated and intrigued.

Another smile curved his lips. He wasn't the sort to sit and wonder. He was all for action and that was exactly what he planned to get.

Soon—very soon—he'd satisfy his curiosity about her. And more…

Rosalie tucked her hair behind her ear and critically surveyed her landscape. After days of effort she'd made pathetically little progress. Despite every attempt, the scene still eluded her. She'd sketched the outline of beach and headland, attempted a watercolour and toyed with oils. But nothing had worked. Nor had the photos she'd taken captured the spirit of the place, the sheer magic of it.

The translucent ripple of the early morning tide, the impossible blush-pink of the fine-grained sand marking the long crescent of beach, the sheer vertical drop of the blue-shadowed headland, like a brooding sentinel. And the Moorish fantasy of angled walls, perfect arches and deep terraces that comprised the ancient ochre-coloured fort dominating the cliff line.

From the first morning she'd rounded the point and discovered this bay, she'd felt the unfamiliar fizz of excitement, of anticipation in her veins. It had taken her by surprise. A sensation she'd never thought to experience again.

The stark beauty of the place had made her long to paint once more. And surely it was inspirational enough to reawaken her long-neglected talent, coax and inspire her into achieving something at least passably encouraging.

It had given her the courage to open the art supplies her mother had smuggled hopefully into the luggage.

But years of inactivity had taken their toll. Whatever artistic talent Rosalie had once aspired to, it would clearly take more than this spectacular scene to reawaken it.

Perhaps she'd lost it for ever—that joyous gift of translating what she saw into something worth keeping on canvas.

Three years ago she'd accepted the loss with a sullen stoicism. It hadn't even distressed her, given the fact that her whole world had shattered around her. Three years ago she hadn't *wanted* to paint any more. It had been left to her family and friends to fret over the change in her.

But now, to her surprise, something, a tentative hope, a flutter of excitement, had flared into life. Only to be extinguished by disappointing reality.

She ripped the page from her sketchbook in disgust. There was something missing.

Her lips curved in a cynical smile. *Talent, obviously*.

But something else too, she realised as she scrutinised the view. Despite the rolling surge of waves on the shore and the slow whirl of a falcon high over the cliff ahead, the scene lacked life.

She stood and stretched her cramped muscles.

It didn't matter. She couldn't do it justice anyway.

She was no artist. Not any more. She firmed her lips to counter the sudden absurd wobble of her chin as devastation rocked her.

Stupid, stupid, to even hope to regain what she'd lost. That part of her life had gone for ever.

She sucked in a deep sustaining breath. She was a survivor, she'd dragged herself out of fear and fury and grief and got on with living. More than that, she'd found peace and joy in her new life. A happiness she'd never thought to experience. She was a lucky woman. What did it matter if she'd never be an artist?

But her hands trembled as she gathered her gear, carefully stowed each item in her bag. Somehow the truth was harder to bear now after that brief surge of hope and inspiration.

She wouldn't walk this way again and torture herself with what she couldn't have. Instead she'd concentrate on other things. Sightseeing in the quaint old coastal town with its souk and its minarets. Maybe take a trip into the desert. Get back into swimming each day and finally open the paperback mystery she'd brought on her holiday.

She'd forget the haunting beauty of the deserted bay and its *Arabian Nights* fortress.

Her bag was almost packed when something, some distant sound or flash of motion, made her look up.

At the far end of the beach something moved. Something that resolved itself into two shapes, white-gold in the early light. Shapes that moved towards her with a steady pace, then plunged suddenly towards the sea.

Rosalie stared, recognising the beasts now. How could she not, since her brother-in-law was an enthusiastic breeder of horses? These two weren't just any horses; they were Arabs, finely proportioned with arched elegant necks and a sure gait. A colour somewhere between palest dove-grey and white, she decided as they approached, dancing a little as a wave coursed in around their hooves.

She heard a whinny and saw one toss a long mane. The man on its back leaned forward as if speaking to it, his dark hair ebony against the equine paleness. She saw the horse's ear flicker back, its head turn a fraction.

It was hard to tell where man ended and beast began. He wore white: trousers and a loose long-sleeved shirt, the neck open to reveal a V of dark bronzed skin. There was no saddle and he sat with the easy grace of one who'd grown up on horseback. His powerful shoulders and long frame seemed at odds with the lazy grace of his hands—one on the reins and one holding the second horse's lead.

Without any perceptible direction from the rider, both horses wheeled as one and picked their way through the shallows towards deeper water.

By the time they were fetlock-deep, Rosalie had her sketch-book in her hands, automatically following the graceful curve of necks and powerful haunches, such a contrast to the lean hard lines of the man with them. He was in profile now and for an instant her hand faltered at the pure masculine beauty of him. Too far away to read the details of his face, but even from here there was something arresting about the tilt of his head, the angle of his nose, the long, burnished column of his throat.

Her heart beat faster as she stared, imprinting impressions on her mind as her hand flew across the paper, desperate to get down the sense of what she saw.

And while she focused on the trio, now deep in the water, she realised that this was precisely what she'd needed to complete the wider landscape. Something living, vibrant and beautiful to breathe energy into the scene.

Over the rush of the waves another sound reached her— the man's deep voice, murmuring what could only be Arabic endearments. The sound rippled across the water and right down into her chest, creating the oddest sensation of loosening warmth deep within her. Then he laughed, a low sound, rich as dark chocolate, and the hairs on the back of her neck stood on end. She shivered, aware of the tightening of her muscles and sudden tension in her spine. But she dismissed it and sketched faster.

Too soon they turned and headed back to shore. They'd be gone before she had a chance to capture even part of what she was trying to achieve.

Frantically Rosalie hunched over her work, trying to catch something of the bond between rider and animal that made them move as one.

It took a few moments to realise they'd turned towards her rather than back the way they'd come.

Details caught her attention as they approached: the faint jingle of harness, the flare of equine nostrils as the horses scented her, the quickening pace, the rider's bare feet, strong and well-shaped. And the way his sodden trousers clung to him, revealing long muscled thighs; even his thin cotton shirt had been liberally splashed, become translucent in places where it caught his skin. Hard planes, flat belly, a ridge of muscle.

Rosalie stopped sketching and lifted her gaze higher.

He was watching her. His eyes were narrowed a little against the angle of the sun but she could see they were liquid-dark and piercing. She sat straighter, barely aware of her rapidly thumping heart. She must have got carried away by the excitement of working again.

But as she met his look she wondered, just for an instant, if it was artistic fervour that notched up her pulse, or something else.

Impossible. Her mouth pinched automatically. There *was* no other explanation. Not for her.

Nevertheless, she couldn't deny he had the sort of face any woman would love to look at. Or any artist.

His body was supple yet powerful. He looked to be around thirty, a study in latent vitality. The breeze ruffled his hair, making it spring with the hint of a curl. His face was long and lean, with exotic, high cut cheekbones. His nose, slightly aquiline, spoke of power and energy, but those angled brows and hooded eyes belonged in a bedroom.

Hastily she looked away, reaching down to pick up the crayon that had fallen to the ground.

Perhaps he was angry that she'd taken his likeness. She hadn't thought of that. She had no idea how the locals would react to her work. Now she wondered about Q'aroumi protocols—whether she should have asked permission first.

She felt the intensity of his regard even while she fumbled in the sand.

'*Saba'a alkair.*' His voice was low and even more attractive up close.

'*Saba'a alkair,*' she replied, thankful that she at least knew how to say good morning in Arabic. 'I hope you don't mind…' She gestured to the pad before her and then realised, flustered, that he might not understand her. 'Do you speak—?'

'I speak English,' he answered before she completed the question. 'You like our scenery?'

Rosalie nodded, tilting her head up to meet his scrutiny and unable to look away. His eyes were so dark she couldn't distinguish iris from pupil. It must be a trick of the early morning light. Close up she knew his eyes must be dark brown, but from here the illusion was of lustrous, fathomless black. She hadn't realised it could be so enticing.

'The view from here, it's spectacular.' Her voice was high and breathless. She strove to control it. 'In the morning light it's perfect.'

'You will show me your work?' His voice had the faintest trace of an accent, softening the consonants. Rosalie felt a shimmer of response deep inside her to its cadence.

An instant later she registered the fact that his question had sounded more like an order, for all it was softly spoken.

'Am I trespassing?'

He shook his head and she noticed the way his black hair, slightly long at the back, brushed and curled over his collar. Even his hair was invested with an aura of vibrancy.

'What would you do if I said you were?' His mouth lifted up at one side in a half-smile that tugged at something deep inside her.

'I'd leave, of course.'

Which was exactly what she should do anyway. She couldn't understand her hypersensitivity to this man. It was unprecedented. Unsettling.

She got to her feet, stumbling a little as she caught her balance after sitting engrossed in her drawing.

'Then it's a good thing you're not trespassing.' The half-smile widened and Rosalie stood, transfixed for a moment by the effect. Who'd have thought a man with all that power and...yes, authority in his features, could look so charming and—?

'Nevertheless, I should be on my way.'

'Without letting me see your work?'

It would be churlish to refuse. And though her scribbling was nothing like the work she'd once achieved it would be no worse than that of a raw beginner.

She took a step towards him, then paused, unsure of those two horses. This close they looked large and spirited, as if they might shy or, worse, bite.

'No need to fear. Layla and Soraya have excellent manners. They bite no one, not even the hand that feeds them.'

'And that's you?' she asked as she edged closer.

'It is. But that's only one of the reasons they love me, isn't it, my sweets?' He leaned down as he spoke and the horses whickered in response. Then he urged his mount forward and suddenly Rosalie found herself surrounded, a mare on either side. Warmth engulfed her. A damp horsey smell that was somehow earthy and comforting. And something else, less tangible, that teased her nostrils. It intensified as he reached towards her sketch-book. Tangy, salt and spice: the scent of man.

Rosalie's nostrils flared and she took a step back, bumping into a horse. She looked up and met his hooded eyes. The gleam she read there disturbed her.

'Show me?' he murmured and again she felt his voice slip like a velvet ribbon across her skin. She frowned, uneasy and suddenly tense.

'Of course.' *Concentrate on the sketches*. Easier said than done when she was hemmed in, increasingly aware of...something. Something about him that jolted her out of her comfort zone.

She lifted the large sketch-book and flipped over a few pages. What she saw there arrested her, banishing unease and doubt in an instant. The first sketch, of the horses heading into the water, was raw, rough and spare but it caught precisely the effect she'd sought: their elegance of movement and proud bearing.

Without waiting for him to comment, she slid her hand under the page and flipped it over. Another sketch—that distinctive arch of the neck, the wide nostrils and dark eyes. Alive, real, better than anything she'd done in all these days of trying. Another sketch—a blur, a fleeting yet effective impression of movement and another, of horse and man moving centaur-like out of the water.

She caught her breath.

'You're very talented,' he said above her and she was so stunned by what she saw that she said nothing, only turned another page, to find herself staring at hands, his hands, long and square-knuckled and strong. The sharp outline of masculine shoulder, a hint of corded neck and decisive chin and, in the background, a couple of lines that somehow gave the impression of the castle on the hill.

'*Very* talented,' he said, breaking her absorption.

'Thank you.' In her surprise at what she'd produced Rosalie forgot to avoid his gaze and found herself looking up into the dark abyss of his stare. Even this close his eyes were black. How near would she need to be to discern their true colour?

'You don't mind me sketching you? The horses are so beautiful I couldn't resist.'

He leaned closer and she swallowed hard, wondering what was going on behind those unreadable eyes. That was no casual glance. It looked…assessing.

'I'm honoured you chose Layla and Soraya as your subjects.' Arik forbore to mention the drawings of himself. She looked skittish enough already, eyes wide and dazed as if she'd never seen a man before. Yet those sketches confirmed she knew how a man was made. Surely that appreciation of form and detail meant she had a strong sensual awareness.

Instantly anticipation fired his blood and he had to concentrate on schooling his expression to one of mild interest.

His first glance at her this morning had left him disappointed. She'd looked so young—far too young for what he had in mind. But as he'd ridden closer he'd been relieved to find her air of fragility wasn't due to extreme youth, though she had to be only in her early twenties. There was a firmness around her lush mouth, and more, a gravity in her eyes that told him she was no innocent.

His relief had been a physical force, washing over him in a wave that eased the tension in his shoulders.

'Do you prefer landscapes or living subjects?'

The way her eyes darted down to his torso, his hands on the reins, gave him all the answer he wanted, and an idea.

'I...both.' She closed the large pad and turned away, pretending to concentrate on Soraya, who was snuffling at her sleeve in hopes of a treat. But Arik saw the furtive glance his golden girl sent him from under lowered lids. How could he not when she had eyes as mysterious as smoke on water, a green-grey at once enticing and secretive? He felt that glance with the keenness of a blade, sharp and sure against his flesh.

He wanted to vault down to stand beside her. Close enough to enfold her in his arms and feel her warmth.

But, he admitted to himself, he was too proud. If he dismounted his stiff leg would mean he'd have trouble remounting again. He probably shouldn't be riding at all, not yet, but he hadn't been able to resist the temptation to meet her at last, no matter what the doctor's warnings.

He'd already noted her bare ring finger but it made sense to be sure. 'You're here on holiday?'

Slowly she nodded and then turned to stuff the portfolio into a capacious bag. 'Yes.'

'And your husband doesn't mind you venturing out alone?' If she were his he'd keep her close, knowing that with those stunning looks she'd be a magnet for any male not on his deathbed.

She paused, her hands gripping the bag so tightly he saw her knuckles whiten. 'I don't have a husband.' Her voice sounded muffled and he recognised strong emotion in her tone. A disagreement with the boyfriend about long term commitment? Disappointment seared through him.

'Your significant other, then. He doesn't mind?'

She straightened and jammed her fists on to her hips. Her eyes flashed green fire and he realised he'd hit a nerve.

'Your English is excellent.' It was almost an accusation.

'Thank you,' he said, watching her intently.

Eventually she shrugged and her gaze slid away. 'There is no man to object to anything I do.' There was something in her voice, a bitterness that caught his attention. 'I suppose that's unusual in a country like Q'aroum?'

'You may be surprised to learn how independent Q'aroumi women are.' His own mother was a case in point.

He smiled and saw with satisfaction that the attraction was definitely *not* one-sided. So all he had to do was give her the opportunity and soon he'd be enjoying the delights of her warm, willing body. Yet something about her air of caution, as if she were ready to flee at the slightest provocation, tempered his impatience.

'I will look forward to seeing you another morning.' He made as if to pull on the reins.

'You'll be back here tomorrow?' Her eyes were bright, her tone a shade too eager. It told him all he needed to know.

He shrugged. 'I hadn't planned to come here.' He paused, as if considering. 'You want to see the horses again? Is that it? You wish to draw them?'

She nodded. 'If you don't mind. That would be wonderful. I'd like…' She bit her lip and he silently urged her to continue. 'I'd like to paint the scene with them here. If it's possible.'

Taking candy from a baby. 'I suppose that can be arranged,' he said after making her wait a few moments. 'I could ask old Ahmed to bring them.'

Silence. She gnawed her lip, her hands clasped together in front of her.

'You won't be riding them?' she asked at last, lifting her eyes to his. He could tell how much the question cost her. There was satisfaction in making her wait, after the frustration she'd caused him.

'You would like to see me again?'

She blushed to the roots of her hair, her hands twisting together. She reacted like a virgin, confronting desire for the first time. But her eyes had already told him another story. She was more experienced than that. Still, the sight intrigued him. It really would be a pleasure, learning more about this woman.

'For the painting—if you wouldn't mind?'

Who could resist those wide eyes, the rosebud lips?

'I suppose I could ride here. If you really want me.'

The words pulsed in the silence between them. If she wanted him. He knew in the intense hush between them that she did, indeed, want him.

'How long would it take? The painting?' Better if she felt he was doing her a favour.

'A few days? Three, four mornings?' She couldn't conceal her excitement; it was there in her glittering eyes, the energy vibrating from every line in her body.

'Four mornings.' He paused. 'Very well. I will give you the mornings.' He couldn't prevent the smile that curled his lips. 'If you will give me the afternoons.'

CHAPTER TWO

THE afternoons? Rosalie blinked. Surely she was hearing things.

But, looking up into those lustrous eyes, she doubted it. The devil was there, lurking in the darkness and tempting her to do something stupid like say yes.

But yes to what?

It couldn't be what she thought. Could it?

'I'm sorry? What did you say?'

'I will give up my mornings until you have finished your painting if, in exchange, you spend the afternoons with me.'

Simple, his bland expression seemed to say, but his eyes told another story. Their brilliant glitter was too avid, almost hungry.

'I don't understand,' she said, edging away a fraction. Who was this man? Suddenly her sense of being crowded by him and his horses took on another, more sinister air. A chill shivered down Rosalie's spine as memories of the past she'd worked so hard to forget flooded back. The hairs on her arms rose and her mouth dried.

Her fear was intense, immediate and completely unstoppable.

His gaze bored into hers for a long moment, as if he knew what was going on in her mind. She saw his straight brows lift a fraction, his nostrils widen as if in surprise, and then the horses were moving away, parting to leave her standing alone. Without their warm bodies so close, the sea breeze seemed suddenly cool and she shivered.

'It's straightforward enough,' he said as he wheeled the mares round to face her. His voice dropped to a reassuring burr. She assumed it was reassurance she felt—that unfurling heat in her belly that welled and spread as he spoke. It couldn't be anything else.

'I'm recuperating from an injury and tired of my own company. Now I'm mobile again but under doctor's orders not to travel, while I do some physiotherapy and they check my recovery is complete.' He shrugged and the movement of those wide shoulders seemed unutterably weary, bored even. 'A few hours of company would take my mind off all the things I want to do but can't.'

Somehow she doubted he was a man who had to ask a stranger for companionship. Even now, her nerves still jangling from the adrenaline rush of tension, she felt the impact of his attraction. He radiated power and strength and something potently male. Something that made her aware of a small, hollow, yearning ache deep inside.

'I'm sure you have friends who—'

'But that's the problem,' he murmured. 'In my arrogance, my impatience to put all this behind me, I warned them off visiting until I was better.' His lips curled up in a rueful smile that made him look younger, more approachable. 'Call me proud, but I didn't want sympathy while I limped about.'

'Still, I don't think I—'

'I'm quite respectable,' he assured her. And the glint of strong white teeth in that beautiful aristocratic face told her he didn't usually have to vouch for his respectability. 'My name is Arik Kareem Ben Hassan. My home is here.' He gestured to the fortress hugging the cliff behind him.

Rosalie felt her eyes widen. He *lived* in that massive castle? Somehow she'd thought it must be a museum or national treasure or something. Not a house.

His easy assurance, his air of authority, and the way he handled those purebred horses, as if born to the saddle, made her suspect he wasn't a servant. And he spoke English so fluently he must have spent a lot of time overseas. So did he *own* the place?

'You can ask about me at your hotel if you wish. Everyone knows me—mention the Sheikh Ben Hassan.'

Rosalie's eyebrows shot up. A sheikh! Impossible that there could be two such stunning men, both with the same title, here in Q'aroum.

'But I thought the royal prince was the Sheikh.' Certainly that was how her brother-in-law was addressed, though to her he had always just been Rafiq, the gorgeous man who'd swept her sister, Belle, right off her feet.

The man before her shook his head. 'The prince is our head of state but each tribe has its own sheikh. My people live in the easternmost islands of Q'aroum and I am their leader.'

He sent her a dazzling smile that made her insides roll over. 'Don't worry.' Even from here she could see the mischief dancing in his eyes. 'Contrary to popular fiction, and despite the temptation, we do not make a habit of kidnapping beautiful blonde strangers for our harems. Not any more.'

Rosalie opened her mouth to ask if that had ever, really, been the custom, then realised she already knew the answer. This island nation was rife with exotic tales of plunder and piracy. Its famed wealth had grown centuries ago from rapacious attacks on passing ships. The Q'aroumis had long ago earned a reputation as fierce warriors who conversely had an appreciation of not only wealth but beauty. As a result their booty had, if legend were to be believed, included beautiful women as well as riches.

'But you have me at a disadvantage,' he continued. 'I don't even know your name.'

'It's Rosalie. Rosalie Winters.' She felt gauche standing here, hands clasped together as she lifted her chin to look up at the superb man controlling those fidgety horses with such lazy, yet ruthless grace.

Of course he had no ulterior motive in wanting her company. A man with his looks and, no doubt, wealth, wouldn't be interested in a very ordinary Australian tourist. He was bored, that was all, and no doubt intrigued to find someone on his beach.

'It's a pleasure to meet you, Rosalie.' His voice was deep and smooth, rippling across her skin and warming her deep inside. 'You must call me Arik.'

'Thank you.' She inclined her head and stretched her lips into a tense smile, panicked by the thrill of pleasure coursing through her, the impact of his smooth velvety voice.

'I look forward to our afternoons together,' he said and Rosalie's breath caught as his smile disappeared and his hooded eyelids lowered just a fraction. Her instant impression was of brooding, waiting sensuality. It should repel her—she knew it should—but somehow this man's casually harnessed male power and potent sexuality intrigued her.

She shook her head. Impossible. She'd learned her lesson well. Men and their desires were never to be trusted. She'd come to her senses as soon as he left.

'I'm sorry but—'

'You do not wish to spend time with me?' He sounded astonished, as if he'd never before encountered a refusal. His eyebrows rose in disbelief.

It would do him good to realise he couldn't smooth talk every woman he met.

'Thank you for the offer,' she said, conscious of the need not to offend, 'but I wouldn't feel comfortable alone with a man I didn't know.' That much was the truth. No need to explain that it was his potent maleness, combined with the gleam of appreciation she'd recognised in his eyes, that guaranteed she could never let herself trust him.

His brows levelled as he stared at her. His scrutiny was so intense she could swear it burned across her skin, invoking an embarrassed blush up her throat. She felt vulnerable, as if he saw too much of her fears and insecurities, as if his scrutiny stripped away layer upon layer of the self-protective armour she'd forged for herself.

'You have my word, Rosalie, that I would never force my attentions where they were not wanted.' He drew himself straighter on his mount, every line of his lean, powerful body and every muscle in his face rigid with outraged pride. His strong hands, so relaxed a moment ago, clenched hard on the reins and his horse danced sideways, rolling its eyes as if it sensed its master's displeasure.

Despite herself, Rosalie felt her blush intensify to a burning vivid crimson, flooding up and over her cheeks. But she stood her ground and met his haughty stare.

'I appreciate your assurance,' she said, consciously avoiding the use of his name and the intimacy that implied. 'And I apologise if I've offended you, but—'

'But you are right to be cautious with men you do not know.' He nodded and some of the tension left his face. His lips curved in a rueful smile. Once again she felt that throb of awareness between them. Unwanted but only too real.

What was happening to her? He was a chance-met stranger. Despite his good looks and his sex appeal, he should mean nothing to her.

'I do not wish to make you uncomfortable, but I have to admit I would appreciate your company. I'm obviously a bad patient, not cut out for solitude and quiet recovery.' Again that shrug of wide shoulders. 'We could perhaps visit some of the local sights, if that would ease your mind. There are always plenty of people about in the marketplace and the old city. We need not be alone.'

Now she really did feel awkward, as if she'd overreacted to the most innocent of requests.

'And,' he added with slow deliberation, 'the pleasure of your presence would count as suitable recompense for my assistance to your art.'

The sting in the tail, Rosalie realised, watching his shrewd eyes narrow assessingly.

She hesitated, bent and picked up her bulging canvas bag to give herself time to collect her thoughts. This man made her nervous, her damp palms and roiling stomach were testament to that. Yet the trembling sensation still tingling down her backbone in response to his last smile was proof of something more dangerous. Interest, awareness, excitement. That was what really worried her. The fear of the unknown.

On the other hand, there was her painting. The thrill of creative energy she'd experienced this morning was addictive, intoxicating. It promised something wonderful. She'd give almost anything to be able to work again. Maybe this painting would be the key she needed to resume her art. A key that she'd thought gone for ever. How could she pass that up? It could be her last chance to regain something of what she'd lost.

She drew a slow breath and met his eyes. 'Thank you. I'd appreciate seeing more of the island with someone who knows it so well.'

Simple, easy—she hadn't committed to anything dangerous. So why did she feel as if she'd just taken a step into the fraught unknown?

His smile was a blinding flash that stalled her breath in her throat.

'Thank you, Rosalie.' Her name on his lips sounded different: exotic and intriguing. 'And I promise that I will never do anything that you do not like. You have only to say the word if you object to something.'

Rosalie stared up at his satisfied expression, his relaxed pose, and wondered if she'd done the right thing. He looked too…smug, as if he'd got more out of the bargain than she suspected.

That had to be her perennially suspicious mind. She'd conditioned herself to be wary. Now she'd forgotten how to take people at face value. Perhaps this was her chance to rectify the balance, relax a little on her holiday and learn not to freeze up when she was with a man.

'Thank you…Arik. I'll look forward to seeing you tomorrow morning.'

Arik watched her turn and walk away, barefoot along the damp sand.

The sound of her soft voice saying his name, the sight of her lush mouth forming the word, had pulled the muscles tight in his belly. He felt a gnawing ache there, a greedy hunger that had grown in intensity once he'd come close enough to see her properly.

From a distance Rosalie Winters had been desirable, tempting and intriguing. Close up she was stunning.

Her eyes were wide and surprisingly innocent, more alluring than those of most women he met, with their consciously seductive glances that invited flirtation. Her skin looked soft as a petal, making him eager to experience it for himself. Her heart-shaped face, her perfect pink bow of a mouth and her rose gold hair, like gilt with the hint of a blush, were all superb.

Yet there was something else at the core of her attractiveness. Not her air of vulnerability—that had been a surprise and it had evoked in him a sudden surge of protectiveness so strong he'd wondered if he should shelve his plan completely. Turn around and leave her.

But he wasn't into self-denial.

Maybe it was the fact that she hadn't immediately tried to pursue *him*. He'd had women chasing after him since he'd reached puberty. He had to do no more than indicate his interest to have whatever woman he wanted. Even the discovery that he was a sheikh, a leader of his people, had failed to arouse anything more than mild curiosity in her. That news had, in the past, led to some women becoming almost embarrassingly fascinated. They were so busy fantasising about his sex life they had no concept of his real life: his responsibilities and his manic work schedule.

Not that he objected to the right woman taking an interest in his sex life.

At the moment Rosalie Winters was the right woman.

She was a new phenomenon: gorgeous, naturally seductive, but with no apparent awareness of her own devastating sex appeal. That air of innocence was incredibly alluring, even to a man who'd never been interested in deflowering virgins. For a moment he'd almost believed she'd never been with a man— till he read the knowledge, the wariness in her eyes. They told him she'd known at least one man far too well and had been disillusioned by the experience. Her caution had even, for an instant, verged on fear. And, with that realisation, searing pain had stabbed through him.

Who was she? How had she got under his skin so completely? And why did he feel that seducing her would be an unforgettable experience?

Arik was determined to uncover her secrets, would delight in discovering what went on in her mind almost as much as he'd enjoy possessing her sleek, ripe body.

She was a challenge unlike any he'd met. Already his blood ran hot in expectation of gratification to come. He would make her burn for him too, sigh out her desire for him, her need for fulfilment that only he could provide.

He watched her disappear round the rocks at the end of the beach. Not once had she glanced back. As if she'd known he sat here, watching her, anticipating tomorrow with barely concealed impatience.

He thought of his promise to her: not to do anything she didn't like. He grinned. Of course she'd enjoy what he had in mind. He was no untried youth, nor a selfish hedonist seeking nothing but his own release. He was a man who fully appreciated the pleasure a woman's satisfaction could bring. Whose lovers never had complaints about his ability to arouse and satisfy.

No, despite her caution, he was sure Rosalie Winters would never say the word that would prevent them both enjoying the ultimate pleasure together.

Rosalie paused at the headland. It marked the end of all that was safe. The point of no return. Far behind her lay the town, still slumbering in the dawn light.

Ahead lay the private cove with its ancient fort, and danger. She felt it in her bones. But what sort of danger? Yesterday she'd surely overreacted, overwhelmed by her excitement to be painting again and by her response to *him*.

She drew a deep breath. Did she really want to do this? All yesterday afternoon, while she was busy with Amy, her thoughts had returned to the man she'd met beyond this next headland: Arik Ben Hassan, and his invitation. He was a man unlike any she'd ever met.

Unbidden, a curl of excitement twisted low in her belly. The same sensation that had teased her all yesterday, reminding her that, despite the way she chose to live her life, and the needs she'd so long suppressed, she was, above all, a woman. With a woman's weakness for a man who epitomised male power, strength and beauty.

That had to explain her restless night. The disturbing dreams that had her tossing in her sleep. She'd awoken time and again to find her heart pounding and her temperature soaring.

The first time she'd put it down to stress. Her mother and Amy had left for the capital that afternoon to stay with Rosalie's sister, Belle, and her family. Originally Rosalie had planned to go too. She'd never spent the night away from Amy, not since her daughter was born, and the wrench had been just as hard as she'd expected. Not that Amy had been fazed—she'd been too busy looking forward to visiting the palace again and seeing her baby cousin.

It was Rosalie's mum who'd convinced her to stay. Maggie Winters had been thrilled to discover her daughter had taken her art supplies out during the early hours while Amy slept. She'd insisted Rosalie stay on for a few more days in the house Rafiq had arranged. The time alone would do her good, she'd insisted. Rosalie had never had a break from the demands of single parenthood. She needed time to herself and it would be good for Amy too, experiencing something different for a few days.

Her mother had been so insistent, but more, so upset when she'd planned to leave the island, Rosalie hadn't had the heart to persist. After all, she owed her mum so much. She was her rock.

Rosalie shuddered, recalling that day over three years ago when she'd stumbled from a taxi into her mother's outstretched arms. She'd been falling apart, shaking and nauseous, barely coherent in the aftermath of shock, but her mum had taken it all in her stride, not even pressing for details till Rosalie was ready to talk. And then it had spilled out—the Friday night date, the crowded party, the spiked drink and Rosalie waking in a strange bed to the realisation she'd been assaulted. Raped.

Even now the memory made her feel ill.

She knew it was her mum's loving support that had given

her the courage to put the past behind her and create a new life for herself. Especially since her new life included Amy, legacy of that disastrous night.

Yet, despite the progress she'd made, the wonderful fulfilment of motherhood and her determination not to look back, she knew her mum secretly fretted over her.

Was it any wonder Rosalie hadn't admitted that her attempts to rekindle her artistic skills were an abysmal failure?

Until yesterday, that was. It had all come together then, the sure light touch that had been her trademark in the days when she'd dreamed of making a name for herself as an artist.

Even then she'd been tempted to turn her back on what could be a false promise. Far safer to travel with her family to Q'aroum's capital than take a chance on the unknown. Who knew whether she really *could* paint?

And was she up to dealing with a man like Arik Ben Hassan? A man who probably had the world at his feet and who on a whim had decided he wanted her company. Given her background, she was the last person to keep him amused with casual small talk and witty observations, if that was what he expected.

He hadn't a clue about her. And that was the way she preferred it. Especially since he'd invaded her thoughts, even her dreams, in the twenty-four hours since she'd met him. He was dangerous to her peace of mind. To the delicate balance of her life.

But he was the key to her art. At least for now, until she worked out whether yesterday had been a fluke or a new start.

She hitched her bag higher on her shoulder and made herself walk on.

He came to her like a prince out of a fairy tale—strong, silent and commanding. The epitome of maidenly longings, Rosalie decided, trying to make herself smile to unwind the tension coiling tight in her chest.

It didn't work.

The sight of him: tall and devastatingly attractive, this time in lightweight beige trousers and another white shirt, weakened her knees. Closer he came, the muffled thud of hooves a vibration on the sand more than a sound. The wind caught his shirt and dragged it back, outlining the lean strength of his torso and wide, straight shoulders. The gleam of dawn gilded his face, throwing one side into deep shadow that accentuated the remarkable angles of his face, drawing the eye to those stunning cheekbones and the severe angle of his jaw.

Rosalie swallowed hard, then reached for the water she'd brought. She was parched, her mouth dried by the sight of him and by the sudden longing she experienced. A yearning that was strange and new and appalling.

This was a mistake. A disastrous mistake. But it was too late to leave. He'd seen her the moment he'd ridden down on to the beach. And she had too much pride to turn tail now and leave him wondering why she was scared of him. Especially when she didn't know the answer to that herself.

'*Saba'a alkair*, Rosalie.' His face was gravely courteous as he inclined his head, his voice the deeply seductive tone she remembered from her dream. She shivered.

'*Saba'a alkair.*'

'Your pronunciation is excellent.'

'Thank you.' No need to tell him she'd learned her few words of Arabic from her brother-in-law, another local and a man of immense patience with her faltering efforts.

'You slept well?' His scrutiny was intense, sweeping over her like a touch, so the blood heated beneath her skin.

'Thank you, I did,' she lied. 'Only one horse today?' She was eager to change the subject.

He shrugged, drawing her attention once more to the spare power of his torso. She wished she could look away.

'I thought one would be enough for your purposes. But if you want—'

'No, no. That's fine.' It was the magic between rider and mount that she wanted to capture. She turned away, as if to busy herself with her gear, but a sudden movement made her turn back. It was him, Arik, swinging his leg over the horse and dismounting.

'What are you doing?' The words were out before she could stop them. She heard her squeak of horror echo even now as the silence reverberated between them.

His eyebrows tilted up as he looped the reins in his hand. 'I thought that was obvious,' he said and took a single long step closer.

Rosalie had thought him impressive on horseback, imposing enough to dominate any scene. But that was before he stood close to her, enveloping her with his air of re-strained power. She felt his heat, detected again his spicy natural scent, and more. As she angled her chin up to meet his eyes, she experienced something else, something primal and powerful, a spell that kept her rooted to the spot. She watched him with widening eyes as her pulse thudded a quickening tattoo.

This close she could see his skin gleamed with health, his mouth was slightly crooked; when he smiled it curved up more on the left. And his eyes—she couldn't believe it! Even from less than a metre away, they were black as night, gleaming with humour as she struggled to find her composure.

'It's traditional here to seal a bargain with a gesture of trust,' he murmured, 'and our agreement is important to me.'

The flutter of panic in her stomach transformed into an earth tremor of mixed horror and anticipation as he leaned closer. He couldn't mean to—

Strong fingers closed around her right hand, she felt the scrape of calluses as he cradled it in his, then he firmed his grip.

'We always shake hands on a deal here, Rosalie.' His words were low, soft, making her lean even closer to hear.

His gaze, dark and unfathomable, held hers and she felt a sensation of weightlessness. For a long moment the illusion held as she stood, enthralled by the heat and promise in his eyes.

Then common sense reasserted itself. She straightened her spine. 'Of course.' She nodded, hoping to seem businesslike. Just a handshake. She could cope with that.

But, even as she reassured herself, he lifted her hand in his, held it just below his lips so she felt the rhythm of his breath hot on her skin. She blinked.

'But with a lady, a handshake is not enough.'

Was that glitter in his gaze laughter or something else?

No, it wasn't laughter. She just had time to realise it was something more dangerous when his mouth brushed her skin. The kiss was warm, soft and seductive. Her breath hitched as their gazes locked. His eyes were pure black. Black as night, dark as desire. Inviting, beckoning. A blaze of flame licked through her abdomen, igniting a flare that grew and spread like fire in her bloodstream.

She shuddered as his lips caressed her skin, pressing more firmly and somehow, impossibly, finding an erogenous zone on the back of her hand. Her chest heaved as she gasped for oxygen. He paused so long that she felt warm air feather across her skin as he exhaled once, twice, three times.

At last he lifted his head, but the stark hunger in his face made her want to turn tail and run back the way she'd come.

CHAPTER THREE

Now he knew. Her skin tasted sweetly addictive, its texture as smooth as cream against his lips. He wanted to bend his head again and lick her hand, turn it over and lave her palm, drawing her flavour, rich as wild honey, into his mouth.

He wanted to set his tongue against the frenetic pulse he felt fluttering at her delicate wrist, kiss her arm, her sensitive inner elbow, take his time in working his way to her collarbone, her throat, awash now with a tide of rose-pink. Then her lips.

His hand tightened around hers as his gaze dropped to her mouth, a perfect Cupid's bow of feminine invitation. Her lips parted just a fraction, as if in unconscious invitation, and the storm of longing notched up inside him.

Never had he experienced need so instantaneous, obliterating all else. It was like a roaring, racing conflagration swirling almost out of control.

And all he'd done was kiss her hand! Even the scent of her, like the perfume of dew on rosebuds, was enough to test his self-possession.

His heart pounded against his ribs, adrenaline surged in his bloodstream, inciting action. His every sense clamoured for fulfilment. Here. Now. On the hard-packed sand where the sun's early rays would light her body to gold and amber for his delectation.

He snagged one rough breath. Watched her eyes widen and realised his grip had firmed too much. Another breath and he loosened his hold, still unwilling to relinquish her hand.

But she tugged it away, slipped her fingers from his and cradled them with her other hand between her breasts. The unthinking gesture pulled the soft cotton of her shirt tight and his breath seized in his lungs as he eyed the outline of her bra.

'A handshake would have done,' she whispered, her voice shaky.

Arik almost laughed at the absurdity of it. She was chastising him for being too forward in kissing her hand. How would she react if she knew he was hard with need for her? That just the sight of her plain bra beneath that prudish high-buttoned shirt and the taste of her against his lips made him hot with desire?

But his laughter fled as he looked in her eyes and saw the confusion there. Confusion and…trepidation?

She was scared of him, his golden girl?

Instantly he took a half pace backwards, watching the way her dilated eyes seemed to focus somewhere near his chin as her breathing slowly evened out.

She looked as if no man had ever kissed her hand. More, as if the dance of desire between the sexes was something new to her.

Impossible. Surely in Australia men were men enough to pursue a beauty as delicate and enticing as this one. It still amazed him that she was alone, no male hovering close to guard against intruders.

'I see our customs are different to what you are used to. I meant no offence.'

He wondered if she'd be satisfied with that explanation. Surely even an innocent would realise that a formal kiss on the fingers was completely different from the sensuous introduction they'd just experienced. Or maybe she'd ignore the fact, pretend it hadn't happened.

She nodded, turned her head away to stare at the glow of light on the horizon. 'Of course. I understand.'

He was right—she was avoiding the truth.

But he'd achieved his aim. She was *aware* of him now. Not just as a distant figure on horseback to be captured in paints, but as a man. Flesh and blood. Her agitated breathing, the quick sidelong glance at him, the way she bit down on the corner of her mouth, all affirmed it.

The first step towards his goal. He smothered a smile and turned towards Layla, saddled this time so he could mount more easily with his stiff leg.

'Where do you want me?'

The question caught Rosalie by surprise and her mouth rounded in an O of shock. Faint colour warmed her cheeks and Arik held his mouth tight so as not to betray his satisfied grin. So, it had been more than just an introduction for her too. That was a guilty expression if ever he'd seen one. Obviously she *did* want him.

Now it was just a matter of getting her to admit it.

Rosalie put her hand to her back and stretched out the stiffness there. She'd sat too long, absorbed in her work, and now her muscles protested.

She looked at the canvas before her and fought down bubbling excitement. It was too early to tell. Far too early to know if this would be anything worthwhile. *But*, a tiny part of her wanted to crow, it was promising. Definitely promising. Certainly far better than her faltering attempts earlier in the week.

After her tension when she'd begun this morning, she thought she'd never be able to settle down and work. She'd been strung taut like a bow, wary of the knowing light in Arik's eyes, the flagrant desire she read in his face, and scared to betray the secret answering yearning that spiralled deep inside her.

That had taken her completely by surprise, even after yesterday's encounter and last night's restless dreams. She'd experienced nothing like it. Even in the days when she had been young and innocent. Her teenage fantasies had been about romance and happy endings. They'd never been raw with the force of untrammelled physical desire.

It had been like a surge of white-hot electricity, the arousal she'd felt as Arik had taken her hand in his, moved his lips against her skin and made her want…him. The jolt of energy had arced deep inside her, straight to her womb where the aching emptiness had been like a throbbing pain.

No one had said it would ever be like that.

'You're happy with what you've done?' She looked up to find him leaning towards her from the back of his horse. There was a safe distance between them now but it wasn't enough. Rosalie suspected that with this man there would never be enough distance for her to feel secure.

'It's not bad,' she said cautiously, turning away from his regard.

He saw too much, she knew that already. Though not, she hoped, nearly as much as she wanted to hide from him.

'And so we're finishing for the morning?' The question was straightforward, but it held a note of something unsettling.

'Yes.' She nodded. 'All finished for now.'

'Good.' He nudged his horse away and dragged something from his pocket—a cellphone. As Rosalie started tidying up her supplies she heard his voice, low and warm, as he spoke in his native tongue. She loved the lilt of it, the fluidity, and her hands slowed as she listened.

She remembered the teasing sound of his voice yesterday, as he'd chivvied the horses. A thrill skittered down her spine as she imagined him speaking, his tone intimately caressing, pitched for her alone.

Appalled at herself, she began to shove her gear away with

more force than prudence. She couldn't believe her wayward imagination. *Never* had she fantasised about a man in this way. She shook her head, wondering what had changed. This instant overwhelming attraction was terrifying. It was the sort of attraction that she guessed led to one-night stands.

For an instant the horrible irony of that thought struck her, but she shoved it aside. She had no time for self-pity. The past was gone.

But that still left her way out of her depth.

Five minutes later she was packed, all except her easel and canvas, when the rumble of an engine made her look up. It was a four-wheel drive approaching over a stony track from the ridge above. Arik was already riding to meet it.

As she watched, a couple of men got out and, following his instructions, began unloading something from the back of the vehicle. Soon it began to take shape, high on the beach, as a large canvas awning. No, a tent, with one side open, facing the sea.

Arik walked towards her, his naturally long stride shortening almost imperceptibly on each second step. His damaged leg. The realisation brought a crazy rush of sympathy for whatever pain he'd suffered.

Rosalie shook her head. What had got into her? She'd known the man a little more than a day, if she could be said to *know* him.

'If you permit, I'll have your work taken to my home and brought along tomorrow morning at first light. That way you won't have to carry it each day.' He paused, then added, 'I will personally vouch that it will be handled appropriately. My mother is an amateur artist and my staff understand that it is more than their lives are worth to damage a work in progress.' His smile was charming, robbing his words of any threat.

'I…of course. That's very thoughtful of you.' Pointless to assert that she didn't want it leaving her hands. That she'd feel safer with the canvas in her own keeping. Was she supersti-

tious enough to fear that without it in her possession she
might lose this second chance?

Reluctantly she nodded and followed him to the vehicle,
where he'd tethered his mare. She clutched her tote bag close
as he stowed first the portable easel and then her canvas in the
rear of the four-wheel drive.

The men had finished setting up the tent and nodded as
Arik spoke again to them in their own language. Then one of
them turned and said with a bow, 'I will look after your
painting, miss. It will be safe with me.'

She only had time to smile and nod her thanks before they
were on their way, one in the four-wheel drive and the other
leading the mare up the track, leaving Rosalie alone with Arik.

Her heart thumped an uncomfortable rhythm and she told
herself not to be stupid. She'd been alone with him for hours.
But somehow this was different. No easel to hide behind. No
horse to demand his attention.

Silently she followed him to the tent. It was far too large
for a beach shelter—a dozen people could easily have stood
inside it.

But then this was far more than a shelter from the sun, she
discovered as she rounded one side and found herself looking
in. It was—luxury. A jumble of rich colours and fabrics, from
the patterned floor coverings to the sumptuous pile of cushions
heaped on the floor. A low folding table with a round brass
top gleamed in the centre of the space and on it, incongruously,
sat a huge vacuum flask. A cool chest stood beside it, making
Rosalie wonder suddenly if there was any food in it. She'd
been working solidly for hours and now she was starving.

'You would like some refreshment?' Arik's deep voice said
beside her.

'Yes, thank you.' She avoided his eyes and watched as he
bent to collect something from just inside the tent. A copper
ewer, soap and a linen towel which he folded over his arm.

'Here.' He held out the soap to her. She took it and held out her hands while he poured a steady stream of warm water over them. She inhaled the fragrance of sandalwood as she lathered and washed, then handed him the soap and rinsed her hands.

Rosalie reached for the finely woven towel, trying not to touch his arm. There was something too intimate about the situation, for all he stood as still and unthreatening as a statue. The warm soapy scent rose between them, but this close to him she recognised his own unique fragrance: male skin and just a hint of sea salt and horse.

She breathed in deeply and held out her hand for the ewer. 'Let me.'

She kept her eyes down, away from his. Instead she found herself watching his strong, well-shaped hands as he soaped them, sliding one against the other slowly and thoroughly. Rosalie stared.

She'd drawn countless hands over the years. Had sketched them relaxed, fisted, holding various objects. Just as she'd sketched naked models with never a flicker of emotion.

But standing here, watching those long powerful hands slide together, seeing the corded muscles and sinews of his forearms where he'd rolled back his sleeves, Rosalie found herself swallowing hard as excitement stirred deep inside her.

He put down the soap and she tipped more water over his hands, his wrists, wishing she could reach out and trace their tensile strength for herself.

He reached for the towel she'd draped over her arm, barely brushing her shirt with his fingers. She almost sighed with relief when she could step away, put a precious pace or two between them.

'Thank you, Rosalie.' His voice broke the silence between them and she darted a look up at him. His eyes were unreadable, the obsidian-black that she still couldn't believe. She wished she could read his thoughts. Then, as his nostrils widened a fraction, his mouth curled up in a half smile, she was suddenly glad she couldn't. No doubt she was totally transparent in the way she reacted to his sheer maleness. But she couldn't help herself.

That was what scared her most. Her reaction to this man.

'Do you usually picnic in such style?' She tried not to sound too impressed and the words came out accusing.

He shrugged and motioned for her to enter. 'If I'm entertaining I prefer that my guests are comfortable and well taken care of.'

Rosalie just bet he did a lot of entertaining. Especially of women.

She hesitated, aware once more of how isolated they were. There had been no one else on the beach all morning. And in the tent they'd be out of sight even from the windows of the fortress on the hill. She eyed the tumble of cushions on the floor and wondered what he had in mind for their afternoon together.

'Ahmed will be back in an hour to clear away the remains of our meal,' Arik said from beside her. 'Then I thought we might drive into the town and do some sightseeing.'

'That sounds lovely, thank you.'

See, it's just company he wants. Someone to talk to. You've grown too suspicious.

Nevertheless, she felt uneasily as if she'd committed herself to far more than lunch as she slipped off her shoes and stepped into the tent. The soft fabric beneath her feet was sheer decadence. The colours, the textures, even the scent was exotic, like something out of an Arabian fantasy. Just like the man at her side: the epitome of absolute male strength and sensuality. It was all too easy to picture him in flowing robes with a scimitar in his hands. Or in a bed with silken sheets where some dusky beauty kept him occupied.

'Please.' He gestured towards the pile of cushions. 'Make yourself comfortable.'

Gingerly she moved forward, averting her flushed face. She settled herself on a large cushion, resisting the temptation to flop back and let her tired body relax on the luxurious pile. Nevertheless, she felt some of the stiffness seep out of her as she tucked her legs into a comfortable position and looked out at the fabulous coastal scene before her.

Beside her, but not too close, Arik settled with a single easy movement of graceful power. He didn't crowd her and her breathing eased a little. But then, she supposed it wasn't his style to crowd a woman. She was sure that with his looks and obvious wealth he was usually fending them off instead. He'd have no need to do anything but smile and women would flock to him.

Surely she'd mistaken his intense expression earlier. She'd read raw hunger in his face but maybe she'd been wrong. Perhaps she'd just assumed that was what he felt—a mirror of her own sudden longing. She'd been so overcome by the stifling sensation of heat when he'd kissed her hand that she hadn't been able to think straight.

After all, why would he be interested in someone as ordinary as her? She wasn't glamorous or chic. She was a working mum. How much more mundane could you get?

'Coffee?'

'Thank you.' The scent of it as he opened the flask was heavenly, reminding her that she'd been too nervous this morning to have more than a glass of water and a piece of toast before she left the house. She watched him pour the hot coffee and decided it was better to concentrate on her surroundings than on her growing fascination with those magnificent hands.

'This—' she gestured to the interior of the tent '—is amazing.' Only now did she notice the tiny side table with its bowl of full velvety roses. She'd assumed the scent was some sort of rose essence sprinkled on the gorgeous cushions.

'Not too over-the-top for you?' One eyebrow tilted and

there was a gleam of humour in his dark eyes as he handed her a cup of coffee and gestured towards milk and sugar on the table before her.

She shook her head, permitting herself a tiny answering smile. 'It's more luxurious than what we have back home.' Which was a towel and maybe an old beach umbrella for shade. 'But it's lovely. And the coffee's wonderful. Thank you.' She sighed as the rich liquid slid down her throat.

Arik watched her eyes close for a moment as she savoured the coffee.

Even with a tiny smudge of paint high on her cheek, her cotton shirt creased and her long hair slipping from the ponytail that secured it, she was temptation personified. That creamy-soft skin, a pale gold that showed each delicate blush, and those eyes, hauntingly erotic. The sensual curves designed for a man's pleasure. And her long ripple of hair the colour of a dawn sunburst. All too easily he could visualise those strands spread across the pillows behind her as she lay beneath him, an invitation to his touch.

He itched for her. Burned for her.

But she wasn't ready. She wasn't like his usual women: eager and flirty, sometimes too eager.

Rosalie Winters was different. She was ripe for him, he'd easily read her body's unconscious signals. But her mind was another matter. This was a woman who did not give herself lightly.

Yet he knew instinctively she'd be worth waiting for. This time it wouldn't be about almost instant gratification. For once he was willing to delay. With Rosalie he was discovering that anticipation was part of the pleasure.

'So where is home? What part of Australia?'

'Queensland. In the north east.'

'I know it, or part of it. I've dived on the Great Barrier Reef.'

Her eyes widened. What had she expected? That he'd never left his island home?

'That's where I come from. A small town on the coast just north of Cairns.'

'You're blessed with beautiful country.'

She looked out across the bay. 'And so are you.'

'Thank you.' Despite the fact that he spent most of his time elsewhere, Q'aroum was his home. Her simple compliment pleased him.

'And have you always lived near Cairns?'

She shook her head and he saw the rose-gold strands of hair snag on her shirt. 'I lived in Brisbane once.'

'For work?' Her reticence intrigued him. He was accustomed to women demanding his attention, vying for his interest.

'I was only there for a year. To attend art school.' She kept her gaze fixed on the sea but he saw the way her mouth tightened, her lips pulling flat.

Not a good experience, then. He wondered what had happened. His curiosity about her grew with every passing hour.

'You didn't like the city life?'

She shrugged, leaving her shoulders hunched and defensive. 'It didn't work out.'

There was a wealth of pain in her voice and he decided against prying. But he'd give a great deal to know what had caused her such hurt. A man, he supposed. Only a failed relationship could cause such pain, or so his friends told him. He'd never had any such problems.

'And now you live on the coast and work as an artist.'

She shot him a glance he couldn't decipher and shook her head once more. 'I work part-time in a child care centre. I decided against art as a career.'

'I understand it's a very difficult field in which to make a living. But with your talent that must have been a difficult decision.' Obviously she loved her art. She'd been so totally absorbed in it this morning that he'd been piqued at how little attention she'd paid him—as anything more than a necessary part of the scene. It was as if nothing else had existed for her.

She laughed, a short, hard sound that held no humour, dragging at something deep inside him.

'I didn't have much choice in the matter.'

Another look at her face and he decided against pursuing the issue, for now.

'And you like working with children?'

Her face softened. She was so easy to read, and yet she was still an enigma. 'I love it. Working with little ones puts your life in perspective.'

'I can see you're looking forward to becoming a mother yourself one day.'

She turned and snared him with those smoky-green eyes. Her mouth widened into a smile that lit her face. 'I'm already a mother. My little girl, Amy, is two and a half.'

Arik felt his stare harden as her words sank in, something, some strong emotion, balled in his gut, drawing each muscle taut to the point of pain.

He turned away to refill his cup, desperately gathering his control about him.

Fury, that was what it was.

His frown turned to a scowl as he recognised the emotion, hard as a knot, inside him. Anger. And jealousy.

The idea that she'd carried another man's child, had *belonged* so intimately to another, burned deep, eating like acid.

The intensity of sensation shocked him. Shook him out of his complacent belief in himself as an easygoing man. There was nothing easygoing about the churning turmoil in the pit of his stomach. It was a surge of pure old-fashioned covetousness. Envy that some other man had enjoyed what he so wanted.

Arik couldn't believe it. He'd never been jealous in his life!

'My congratulations,' he murmured, trying to concentrate on pouring the coffee. 'Does she look like you or like her father?'

So absorbed was he in mastering the roiling mass of his jealousy that he almost missed her hesitation.

'Everyone says she looks like me.'

He turned back and offered her the flask of coffee, but she shook her head.

'She must be a very pretty little girl, then.' Even that was enough to heighten the glow in Rosalie's cheeks. As if she wasn't used to receiving such compliments.

Were Australian men so clumsy, then? Or, the thought suddenly emerged, had she been avoiding them? Had she been burned by the relationship with her daughter's father so that she shied away from men?

That was a definite possibility, given her skittishness. Arik filed away the thought for later consideration. 'Your daughter isn't with you?'

Rosalie shook her head. 'My mother's looking after her this week. I'm by myself for now.'

Arik worked hard to keep the satisfaction from his face. Alone for the week. And perhaps a little lonely? Perfect.

Rosalie watched as he unpacked their lunch from the coolbox. It was a relief when he'd ceased his questions and begun to explain the dishes his cook had prepared. Not that he'd probed. Yet with him she felt defensive, as if she didn't trust him not to use the information against her.

Ridiculous! How could he? She hadn't said anything particularly personal. Just the bare bones of her life. And yet…she'd sensed a purpose behind his questions, as if he weren't just making small talk.

Arik Ben Hassan was too unsettling for her peace of mind.

Was that why she hadn't come clean about exactly who she was? The sister-in-law of the sovereign prince of Q'aroum.

She'd automatically shied away from the fact, eager to preserve her anonymity. Everywhere she and her mother went in Q'aroum, they'd been treated with such formal courtesy once people discovered their connection to the ruling family. It was nice to be just plain Rosalie Winters again.

Even now it seemed bizarre, her sister marrying into royalty. But it had taken just an hour spent with Rafiq, on his first visit to Australia, for her to understand why Belle had fallen for him.

Strong, protective, handsome and, above all, completely besotted with his new wife. The sort of man Rosalie could have fallen in love with herself.

The sort of man who was as rare as gold at the end of the rainbow.

She shot a sideways glance at her host, cataloguing the noble profile, the lean strength and easy grace of his actions.

Another stunningly attractive man. Yet, she sensed, a completely different personality to her brother-in-law. She couldn't imagine Arik settling down with just one woman. Those heavy-lidded eyes with their knowing, teasing gleam indicated he enjoyed the good life too much. No doubt he had the money and free time to indulge any whim. Why should he take life seriously?

She watched him unpack the platters and bowls of tempting local dishes—salads, dips, sesame bread and cold meats. All perfect. All exquisitely presented. Even for a man with his own private chef, surely this was no ordinary picnic?

'Arik?' His name sounded too good on her lips. She wished she hadn't used it. Especially when he turned round to her, that tempting half-smile tugging at his lips and changing his face from imposing to sexy.

'What is all this?' Her gesture encompassed the luxurious setting as well as the feast spread before her.

'A picnic lunch?' There was a twinkle in those dark eyes that almost made her smile, despite her wariness.

She shook her head. 'No, it's more than that.' She hesitated, wondering how big a fool she was about to make of herself. But she had to know. 'Please. I'm not into games. Exactly what is it you want from me?'

The humour faded from his eyes in an instant, replaced by a brooding severity she hadn't seen before. It caught her by surprise.

So did his hand, reaching out and enfolding hers. His touch was light but firm, his flesh warm and enticing. She sucked in a breath.

'Exactly?' His thumb stroked over hers, sending a shiver of excitement straight to her secret feminine core. 'I would like to know you better, Rosalie. *Much better.*' Another stroke of his thumb made her tremble.

'I want to become your lover.'

CHAPTER FOUR

ROSALIE wrenched her hand away. Dismay lit her face.

And something else. A dazzling instant of connection that told Arik he was right. She too felt the surge of desire between them. She wanted him and it scared her. He read vulnerability in her eyes, in the twist of her lips.

'No!' Her eyes boggled. 'I mean—'

'You're not interested in a short romance?'

She shook her head and long strands of rose gilt swirled around her neck. 'No. No, I'm not.'

His eyes narrowed as he took in her clenched fists, the rapid rise and fall of her breasts, her stormy eyes.

If he were a sensitive soul his ego might have been bruised by her vehemence. Instead he saw beyond her rejection to the inner pain she couldn't conceal. There was *something* there. Some deep-seated fear that made her deny him, and herself, the pleasure they would find together.

For an instant, impatience, pique at the unprecedented rejection, threatened to swamp him. Then sense reasserted itself. Much as she denied it, Rosalie was ripe for him. She couldn't conceal her body's eagerness. Or the way her eyes devoured him when she thought he wasn't aware.

He'd need time to thaw her shell of ice. But then, didn't he have time on his hands? She was a delectable challenge, yet with patience he'd triumph over her caution. He knew it. And victory would taste like paradise.

The certainty of her surrender added piquancy to the situation. Maybe he was jaded by easy conquests. The knowledge that he'd need his wits as well as charm to seduce her merely fired his determination to have her.

He would play a waiting game. *For now.*

'I apologise for embarrassing you, Rosalie.' Her eyes were huge in her face. 'Forgive me.'

She swallowed down hard. He watched the convulsive movement of her throat and tried not to wonder how soft her skin would be there. How tender the spot under the corner of her jaw, and further up her neck, just below her ear.

'That's it?' Her brow furrowed. 'You don't mind?'

'I'd rather you took a different view. We would find much pleasure together.' Pink bloomed in her cheeks, darkened and spread, as he held her gaze.

Her blushes delighted him. The illusion that she was virtually untouched, untutored in the realms of sexual passion, held a strange appeal. He wondered if the blush extended down across her breasts to her peaked nipples.

'You asked what I wanted and I told you. But as you don't want an affair, let us concentrate on our lunch.'

'As simple as that?' Disbelief echoed in her tone.

'As simple as that.' It was a good thing she didn't know how badly he wanted her. How intense was his desire. How eagerly he anticipated her eventual capitulation.

'But surely…' Frowning, she shook her head again as if to clear it. 'It would be better if I left.'

'Not at all. I'm looking forward to your opinion on our local fare.' He turned to reach for a plate.

'Still, I should go.' She made to rise and Arik fought the impulse to snare her hand.

'And your painting? You wish to leave that too?'

That stopped her in mid-movement, her expression
arrested. But only for a moment. 'That's all right. I wasn't sure
it would turn out well anyway.'

'You're a very bad liar, Rosalie. Has no one told you that
before? Of course it's good. It's more than good.' He knew
enough to understand Rosalie Winters had real talent.

'Nevertheless—' the jut of her chin sharpened '—it's only
a painting. It's not worth…'

'You think I ask you to prostitute yourself for the sake of
a painting?' Okay, so he'd used her art to get close to her. But
pride rebelled at her idea that he'd blackmail her into bed. The
doubt in her eyes fuelled his anger, tightened the muscles
across his neck and shoulders.

'I am not quite as needy as *that*, Rosalie.'

'I didn't mean to insult you.' Her voice was a muffled
whisper, yet she met his eyes. 'But I don't know you.'

Curtly he nodded. Women needed to protect themselves.

'Let me assure you, on my word as sheikh of my people,
I would never force you into intimacy. If my own scruples
aren't enough, remember I'm a public figure. Any wrongdo-
ing on my part would swiftly become widely known.'

He watched her troubled face and, for a moment, wished
he hadn't told her what was on his mind. It was too soon.

'I have never taken what was not freely offered.' He paused,
letting her weigh his words.

Her eyes, shadowed and doubting, held his. He was losing
her. The sudden appalling notion crowded his brain and he felt
as if someone had punched him hard in the gut.

The intensity of his reaction didn't make sense. For all her
intoxicating allure she was just a woman. There would be
plenty of those when he returned to his normal life. Women
eager and impatient for his attention.

Why did his heart thud harder as he waited for her to say
goodbye?

'I *would* rather finish.' Her gaze slid from his as she half turned to watch the waves shushing in on the beach. 'But it wouldn't feel right, knowing you want more.'

He shrugged as relief hummed through him. 'Men often look and want. But we don't always get what we desire.'

His experience was different; he made it his business always to get what he wanted. No need to tell her that.

Her head swung round and their eyes met. He felt the impact in his tightening lungs. He wanted to thread a hand through the shimmering silk of her hair and pull her close. He wanted to taste her, not her hand this time, but her lips: lush, ripe, inviting. He wanted to explore her body, discover the places that triggered delight and ecstasy.

Slowly he exhaled. Patience. It would take time to breach the barrier of her distrust. She was as flighty as a newborn colt. Easily scared.

He summoned a smile and held out a plate. 'Let's enjoy lunch before it spoils. I will bring my horse to the beach each morning while you paint. In the afternoons we will view the local sights. Simple. No strings attached.'

Simple, he'd said.

Rosalie stared out the window of the four-wheel drive and knew this was anything but simple. All afternoon as they'd toured the old town, she'd struggled against the force of his personality, his magnetic attractiveness. Against desire and a burgeoning curiosity that undermined her determination to keep her distance.

She was losing the fight.

She should have left him at the beach. No matter that she *wanted* to feel it again, that rush of excitement when he looked at her with such searing intensity.

Perversely, it was his anger that had made her stay. The fury in his jet-dark eyes. Arik Ben Hassan had been genuinely outraged at the suggestion he might force his attentions. Pride had made his head jerk up, his eyes narrow in flashing denial and his hands curl into fists.

Rosalie wondered if the idea was outside his code of ethics. Or was it the hint that he might need to coerce any female to succumb to him? No doubt he cut a swathe through women with his looks and air of lazy sensuality.

Either way, she'd known with absolute certainty that he wouldn't use force. He might tempt and persuade, but he'd respect her wishes. She was safe: while she wanted to be.

The thought sent a skitter of feral excitement down her spine. Did he guess how she felt?

'I like the way the new buildings in the city blend in with the old,' she said abruptly, conscious that the silence had lengthened between them as he drove.

'I'm glad you approve. Planning sympathetic redevelopment has been a major issue for us.' His smooth voice drew her skin tight and tingling.

'You're involved in the planning?' She cut him a curious sideways glance.

He shrugged broad shoulders as he manoeuvred round a tight curve. 'I am the Sheikh. It is expected.'

She'd seen that amazing house, the obvious wealth he commanded, but hadn't considered the responsibilities of his position. Silly, considering what she knew of her brother-in-law's punishing workload.

'I suppose your official duties keep you busy.'

'Busy enough. But my work often takes me away.'

He had a *job* too? She'd imagined him living the good life, flitting from city to city, and woman to woman.

His dark eyes danced as he turned to her. His lips curled up in a smile that made her insides liquefy. How did he do that with just one slow, sexy grin?

'You're surprised I work?' He turned back to the road.

'I…suppose I assumed that you didn't need to.'

He nodded. 'But inactivity does not suit me. I couldn't loll about growing fat and idle.'

He'd never be fat. He had too much vigour. Even in repose his lean body was a study in power and leashed energy. She blinked and watched the road rather than let her gaze drift appreciatively over him.

'What sort of work do you do?'

'I manage a resources enterprise.' His deep voice sent a trickle of warmth down her spine.

'An oil company, you mean?'

'Oil and other things. We invest in renewable energy too. We're even experimenting in generating electricity from the sea.'

'You're not content to make your money from oil?' She'd heard Q'aroum had enough reserves to maintain it as one of the world's wealthiest states for generations.

'We're an island nation, Rosalie. We have a vested interest in combating climate change and rising sea levels. Besides, a man needs a challenge.'

His tone hinted that he wasn't just talking about power generation. Or maybe it was the sudden wide white grin that slashed across his face as he shot her a look.

She felt the whole impact of his personality focused on *her*. It was a tangible thing, a potent force. There was a rushing in her ears, like water flooding past, blocking the sound of nearby traffic. The late afternoon sun seemed to dim as she stared back at him, aware of her skin prickling on her neck and her lungs squeezing tight.

She had to be careful with this man. The feelings he evoked were too much. Too potent. Too new. Too tempting.

'I'll have you back to your hotel soon.'

She opencd her mouth to explain that she wasn't staying at a hotel and then snapped it shut. Better if he didn't know she was staying alone in the house Rafiq had organised.

Arik had been a perfect gentleman all afternoon. Yet there was a restlessness about him, an edginess that warned her he wasn't as easygoing as he seemed. Something simmered behind that relaxed expression. Self-preservation cautioned her against revealing where she was staying.

'Thanks,' she said as they approached one of the two hotels on this coastal road. 'You can drop me here.'

'I'll see you to your door.'

Rosalie sucked in a deep breath. 'I'd rather you didn't.' He stopped the car and regarded her through narrowing eyes, his brows rising.

'You're not exactly incognito.' She remembered the excited pleasure with which he'd been greeted wherever they went. 'So I'd rather go in alone.' She wondered if he saw through her subterfuge. It was true as far as it went. She *didn't* want to draw attention to herself.

'Very well.' He inclined his head. 'We will not court gossip.' Then he got out and fetched her canvas bag from the back while she fumbled with her seatbelt.

His hand was warm and hard as he helped her out. A tremor shot up her arm at his touch, ripping right through any illusion that she was impervious to him.

'Thank you for the pleasure of your company, Rosalie.'

He lifted her hand to his lips. Her eyelids flickered as he pressed a kiss there. A jolt of something very like lightning speared through her. The swirl of reaction in her abdomen grew to a spiralling twist of aching emptiness.

It lasted an instant, only that. But it was enough to jolt Rosalie back to her senses.

She tugged back her hand as if stung. That empty yearning feeling was too real, too powerful to be safe.

'Until tomorrow, then.' His eyes were fathomless, deep as the night and just as impenetrable.

Rosalie turned away. Tomorrow, if she had any sense, she'd take the first flight out from here.

She was late. Arik narrowed his eyes against the slanting rays of dawn light and stared down the beach.

Had he erred yesterday? Should he have pressed his advantage when he'd read the need so clear in her eyes?

No. He'd given his word he'd respect her wishes. She was nervous, fighting to resist what was between them. As if she could push back the inevitable flood-tide of desire.

He wondered at her naïvety. Their attraction had been instantaneous, so urgent and all-consuming that even he, with his experience, couldn't ignore it. It was a constant fire in the blood, a gnawing hunger in the pit of his belly. He felt wired, restive and alert. Sleep was elusive, replaced by hours imagining her in his bed. Or naked, almost anywhere: in the window seat of his room, on a silk-covered divan or down here on the fine-grained sand.

The only way out was to assuage this need for mutual satisfaction. His lips curved in a taut smile. *Prolonged* mutual satisfaction.

Rosalie had much to learn and he would enjoy contributing to her education. Anticipation hummed through him, tightening his groin, his thighs, his hands on the reins. He nudged Layla till she gathered herself into a thudding gallop. The thunder of her hooves teamed with the beat of blood in his ears: heavy, urgent, racing.

They reached the point and there was Rosalie, walking from the next beach. Arik reined in, watching her falter to a stop. Her stance was wary, as if she were in two minds whether to scurry back to the safety of her hotel.

Eventually, as he'd known she would, she resumed her stride towards him. He should be pleased. Triumphant even.

He had her now, he knew. Or close enough that, with a little effort, he could have what he wanted from her.

Yet the emotion filling him wasn't triumph. It was fury. At the unprecedented level of his earlier disappointment. At the unadulterated relief that swept him now, making him for a few moments light-headed.

Since when had he been dependent on any woman? Pleasure, companionship, mutual enjoyment—that was what he sought from the women in his life. But this raw, visceral need that threatened all sense of proportion? That *drove* him with the force of pure compulsion? This wasn't right.

He watched her approach, her head up to meet his gaze, a gesture at odds with the defensive way she clutched that bag to her. Arik felt a surge of unexpected protectiveness.

But it was overborne by anger that she should unsettle him so. He was aroused to the edge of pain just watching her. And his indecisiveness as he'd debated ringing her hotel had been uncharacteristic. He was *too* needy.

Lust had never been like this. It *shouldn't* be like this. It had always been a pleasure to be savoured. Now for the first time, desire was a blood-deep craving. As if more was at stake than the pleasure of a woman's body. As if he felt far more than physical need.

Arik clenched his jaw at the absurd notion, angrier still at that flight of fancy. He urged his mount forward.

Rosalie wished she'd stayed away. What did it matter if her painting remained unfinished? Or if she never saw him again? She knew now that with effort she would paint. And as for her reaction to *him*…better to ignore that.

Yet like a moth to a candle she was drawn against her will along the beach. With every step she'd known this was dangerous, the sort of impetuous act she'd always avoided.

But then, a demon inner voice taunted, *where did playing safe get you*? She'd been perennially sensible, so cautious with men, and look where that had landed her!

She clasped her bag closer, wondering yet again how big a mistake she was making.

Then she saw him, a study in masculine grace and arrogance as he sat his magnificent Arab mount. Instantly she had her answer. Error or not, she couldn't have stayed away. The rapid-fire tumult of her pulse, the constriction of her lungs, the swirling heat all told the same story. She *had* to be here. Owed it to herself to discover what it was about this man that spoke to her innermost being, to the self she'd kept hidden for years now. The self that, at nineteen-and-a-half, had been brutally silenced, locked away by the force of grief and hate and despair.

More than three years had passed and suddenly that other Rosalie Winters, the one who'd secretly yearned for fantasy and adventure, was back, slipping under her guard.

She gritted her teeth and resumed walking. Foolish she might be, but she'd never again be the unthinking innocent she'd been at nineteen. She'd learned her lesson well. If she took any chances they'd be on her terms.

Nevertheless, as Arik's horse plunged close, its hooves lifting high to a resounding rhythm, she couldn't repress a thrill of mixed trepidation and excitement.

'I thought you weren't coming.' His deep voice held a note of accusation as it rumbled in her ear.

'I almost didn't,' she replied, annoyed as he circled. Man and beast together were awesomely beautiful—as he knew. He probably stayed up there so she could admire him.

That was the sort of man he was, she reminded herself, ignoring yesterday's revelations. She squashed the fact that he worked hard despite his wealth. Easier to deal with Arik Ben Hassan if she could peg him as a rich playboy.

Yet she followed his every move with hungry attention. He

was so vibrantly male, so attractive. Her imagination hadn't embroidered a single detail. He was devastating.

'You would have reneged on our bargain?' His expression was severe, as if no one ever had the temerity to inconvenience him.

Rosalie stepped away, preferring not to dwell on the fact that he could read her so easily. 'It's only a temporary arrangement. I wouldn't have thought you'd mind.'

He swung the mare round to walk beside her. 'I'd have minded very much,' he murmured and, despite her best intentions, Rosalie found herself looking up into midnight-dark eyes. Tension pulsed between them, the sizzle of unspoken connection that had no parallel in her experience.

'Then you should be pleased that I'm here after all.'

For two heartbeats he held her gaze, then the shadows fled. He smiled and something tumbled over in her chest at the zap of magnetism between them.

'And so I am, Rosalie. Very pleased.' His voice dropped to a deep sultry murmur that reverberated in her bloodstream, tingled through her body and awakened every nerve-ending.

Why, oh why, hadn't she stayed away?

Because you've never felt so incredibly alive as you do here, with him.

'You're not having second thoughts, are you?' He dismounted to stand beside her on the sand. With only a metre between them the space seemed too intimate.

'Perhaps. Should I?'

He shook his head and reached out, his fingers closing around hers, hard, warm and strong. It felt so right.

'No.' He tugged gently, bringing her closer. She saw herself reflected in his eyes. 'I will never hurt you. You have my word of honour.' Her thudding heartbeat echoed the pulse throbbing at the base of his neck. 'Trust me?'

She hesitated. She had nothing but his words and her instincts to guide her. Yet there was no doubt in her mind.

'Yes. I trust you, Arik.'

'Good.' A spark of emotion flared in his eyes, his hand tightened around hers and a wave of excitement washed over her. His gaze snared hers and her breath crammed in her throat at the intensity of his expression. 'You know what I want, Rosalie, but that must be your decision.'

She shook her head. 'But I've told you that I won't—' Her words ended on a hiss of indrawn breath as he lifted her hand to his mouth and pressed a kiss to the back of it.

'Perhaps you may change your mind.' His mouth moving against her skin was subtly erotic. She stiffened her spine against the need to slump in a wanting heap at his feet.

Now was the time to turn away and make her excuses. She wasn't sophisticated enough to play these provocative games of seduction. 'I'm not sure…'

Her words petered out into a sigh as he turned her hand and planted a tender kiss on the centre of her palm. A kiss that sent shockwaves of heat spearing through her. Her knees trembled at the force of them.

'Nothing is sure,' Arik murmured, caressing her with his lips as he spoke. 'Can we not simply enjoy each other's company for a few days and see where it leads us?'

To perdition, probably. Rosalie sucked a huge breath into her starved lungs, but it wasn't enough to restore her equilibrium. Not when his hot breath hazed her skin and his lips hovered a bare centimetre from her throbbing pulse.

She tugged her hand free and whipped it behind her back, terrified she might beg him to kiss her there again.

'You'll be disappointed.' She might be desperate for his caresses, but she wasn't completely foolhardy.

'Then so be it.' His smile gave nothing away.

The morning disappeared rapidly once Rosalie focused on her work and not the insidious twist of excitement low in her belly, testament to Arik's lethal attraction. But now and then, as she looked across the beach, his head would lift, his eyes meet hers and she'd feel the heavy throb of awareness in the crisp morning air.

Too soon the morning was over. Her canvas was taken to Arik's home. They'd eaten lunch and now they were alone in the opulent marquee that passed for a beach shelter. For all their small talk about art and local sights, Rosalie was acutely conscious of their isolation. The undercurrents eddying in the lengthening silence unnerved her.

She shot him a look, relieved to find that for once his attention was elsewhere. He seemed absorbed in the view of sea and sand, the distant blue shadow of an island.

His profile was arresting, etched with stark, sure lines comprising a whole that was more than handsome. There was intelligence in his high brow, or perhaps that was because she'd learned how perceptive he was. His eyes were piercing, unsettlingly so when they rested on her. His mouth—there was something innately sensual about the curve of his lips—the way it quirked readily into a smile that invited shared laughter. Or pleasure.

Her stomach dipped. He was a man who understood physical pleasure. It was obvious in the way he caressed her hand, the sensuous light in his eyes when he spoke of desire. His look held a promise of gratification. And, if she wanted, he could share that knowledge, that expertise with her. She had only to say the word and Arik would take her to places, to pleasure, so long denied her.

The knowledge was heady, tempting. Frightening.

How could she even consider his proposition?

Because you're lonely. Because there's something missing in your life. Because there's something about this man that overrides a lifetime's caution and makes you long for the passion you've never had.

She looked at him and she felt hot. Her skin prickled as if it no longer fitted. Her lungs couldn't process enough oxygen. There was a tingling, heavy sensation inside that kept her on edge, an aching sense of emptiness.

Suddenly his eyes were on her. Dark and gleaming with a heat that scorched her skin to a fiery blush. He knew what she felt, she realised in amazement.

He understood.

She read the reflection of her own burgeoning need in the haunted expression of his eyes. In the tic of a pulse at his jaw. Even the compressed line of his mouth mirrored the confused tension pulling her body taut.

His lips curved up in that sexy crooked smile but there was no humour in his gaze this time.

'You feel it too.' His voice was low and sure, sending a ripple of reaction through every nerve. 'You feel what's between us, don't you, Rosalie?'

She shook her head in denial. But she couldn't pull her gaze from his. It was as if some force trapped her.

'There's no need to lie,' he said and there was a glimmer of amusement in his look. 'You won't be singed by a bolt of lightning for admitting the truth. There's nothing shameful about desire between a man and a woman.'

Rosalie's breath caught high in her throat as his words echoed through her head. *Desire.*

He was right. That was exactly what she felt. Raw, unadulterated desire for the man before her. She shivered.

'But I'm not interested in becoming some playmate to keep a rich man from boredom.' It came out in a rush.

His stare hardened to a laser-bright glitter, keen and cutting. She'd gone too far. His face drew tight with repressed anger, accentuating his aristocratic bone structure. The pulse at his jaw raced to a frenetic beat.

She'd blurted out the first thing that came into her numbed

brain. But in this part of the world men called all the shots. Automatically she shrank back, expecting an explosion of outraged fury.

'You Australians believe in directness, don't you?' One dark brow winged up at an arrogant angle. Then he frowned, as if noticing her shuffled withdrawal.

Instantly his expression of stifled fury eased, replaced by a watching stillness.

'There's no need to be afraid to express your opinions.' His voice was calm but there was no mistaking its harsh rasping edge. As if he battled for self-control.

His eyes held hers and she knew he meant it. Relief relaxed her muscles. 'I'm sorry,' she said, wondering how he'd read her sudden fear. 'That was insulting.'

'You should not apologise.' His words cut across hers. 'You spoke the truth as you saw it.'

They stared at each other across the narrow space and once more Rosalie could have sworn he understood her confusion and fear. Understood far too much.

'I regret that you see my interest as cheapening.' He paused, as if the word left a sour taste. 'I have always regarded my love affairs as liaisons between equals.'

What could she say? Embarrassment flooded her but she could survive that. She'd survived much worse.

'Though I suppose,' he murmured, 'in this case it would be an unequal relationship.'

He was admitting it? Surely no man was that honest.

'After all, the power is squarely in your hands.'

'I beg your pardon?' Surely she was hearing things.

He shrugged those impressive shoulders. 'Don't be naïve, Rosalie. I want to become your lover.' His voice dropped so low that she felt it resonate deep inside, creating a hollow, wanting ache. 'I've said I won't do anything you don't want me to. I'd stop at a single word.'

His eyes were so bright now they seared her.

'So that means *you* have all the power in this relationship. You can ask for what you want. *Whatever* you want. And I'll give it to you.'

There was no mistaking the look on his face. Sex. That was what he was talking about.

'But,' he continued, 'you only have to say no and I'd be obliged to stop.'

Rosalie drew in a shaky breath, aware of moist heat blossoming across her skin. She bit her lip, striving for control against the illicit thrill coursing through her.

She shouldn't want him. She didn't need any man. Especially one as self satisfied and knowing as this one.

But that didn't prevent a surge of excitement. She could ask for whatever she wanted. As much or as little as she chose and he'd respect her wishes. She'd be safe.

'That wouldn't be right or fair.' Her voice was breathless, unsteady. 'It'd be better if I left.' But how would she find the strength to walk away and not look back?

'I never took you for a coward, Rosalie.' His deep voice fell like a stone in the silence between them.

She jerked her head around. 'Just because I don't want to play these games doesn't make me a coward.'

'Doesn't it?' Again one superior eyebrow lifted in query. 'Then what are you afraid of, if not yourself?'

Rosalie sucked in a breath. She wasn't afraid. She was cautious. He was far beyond her league.

Why then, did the idea of intimacy with him appeal so much? Why this excitement at the notion of exploring those sensations and cravings she'd so long repressed?

Her mother had hinted it was unhealthy for her to avoid personal contact with men as much as she had. What would her mum say about the unrelenting forces building within her right now? The temptation to say yes?

'I'm not afraid,' she lied.

'Good.' He leaned towards her till her whole world was encompassed by the brilliance of his dark eyes, the strength of his powerful shoulders blotting out the view and the warmth of his body reaching out to her.

'It's not fear I want from you, Rosalie.' His words were warm against her cheek. But he came no closer. An invisible barrier remained between them. The protection of his promise. Power rested solely in her hands.

Black, burning eyes met hers. The flare of his nostrils told her he registered it too—the faint musky aroma. The scent of arousal. From her skin? From his?

And yet he didn't move.

'Ahmed will bring the four-wheel drive soon,' he said.

Rosalie swallowed and swiped the tip of her tongue over her bottom lip. His gaze flickered and held.

'Is there anything you want before he arrives?' His words were barely audible over the thunder of her pulse.

'No. Nothing.' Yet her voice sounded like a sigh of wind, an echo of the soft waves on the beach.

'Are you sure?' he whispered.

She bit her lip to prevent herself from saying anything stupid. Arik was seduction on two legs and she had precious few defences against him. 'No,' she muttered again.

'No, you don't want anything? Or no, you're not sure?'

He was close enough for her to feel encompassed by the sheer strength of the man. His hands were planted on either side of her hips, his fingers splayed across the rich fabric of the carpet. His chest was like a wall, pressing her back, despite the fact that he didn't touch her. His gaze held hers, like a bird enmeshed in a net.

'I…' The words died in her throat as she realised what she wanted. What she *craved* from him.

'A kiss, perhaps? Just one to satisfy your curiosity?' His

mouth curled up in a smile that stopped her pulse for a beat. 'Surely you've wondered what it would be like, just a simple kiss between us?'

If only he'd looked smug she'd have been able to summon the will-power to push him away. But there was only the glow of invitation in his eyes. The temptation to pleasure in his curving lips.

'Yes,' she heard herself whisper on a sigh of surrender. 'I've wondered.'

'Good,' he murmured. 'In that we are equals.' His smile faded. 'Relax, Rosalie. You are safe with me.'

He leaned even closer, paused with his mouth an infinitesimal fraction away. He waited long enough for her to absorb the scent of his skin, adjust to the power and heat of his body almost touching hers, for her to taste his breath on her lips and to want more.

Then he slanted his mouth over hers and the world disappeared into a whirling blur as he took her mouth with his.

CHAPTER FIVE

SHE kissed like a virgin.

Her lips were soft, pliant, clinging as he brushed his mouth against hers. Yet when he opened his mouth to slide his tongue along her lips she shivered, retreating a little.

So sweet. So enticing. He leaned closer, careful to keep his hands firmly on the floor. This time when he invited her to open for him, her lips moved against his, mimicking the gentle persuasion of his caress.

Instantly a surge of blood shot simultaneously to his head and his groin. A jolt of fire ignited in his belly, blasting his careful restraint to smithereens.

But somehow he managed to contain the compulsion to ravish her mouth, to pull her close to his needy body and plunder her depths.

He coaxed her mouth open, increasing the pressure slowly. Her breath was fresh and warm, her lips like satin, the scent of her skin heady and arousing. There was no artifice about her, not even so much as a manufactured scent. Yet her delicate kisses, her seemingly untutored response, had him clenching his fists against the impulse to throw caution and restraint to the winds and simply take what he wanted.

He'd never known such fierce need. He *had* to have her. Every atom of his being screamed for her. She was a temptress such as he'd never known before. A houri who seduced not with practised arts but with a tentative, natural eroticism that was unsurpassed in his experience.

What had he got himself into?

He pressed closer, his kiss more demanding. She melted against him, her sigh a muffled surrender in his mouth and instantly his blood thrummed an imperative to conquer. To take.

Yet he mustn't touch. Not this time. This time he had to go slowly, not scare her into headlong retreat. She was skittish enough as it was. If he touched her the way he wanted to, palmed her breasts, learnt the firm curves of her body, discovered her secret femininity and tasted her flesh with his tongue, he wouldn't be able to call a halt.

Instinctively he knew she needed time.

He wondered how long he could hold out before the visceral need that gnawed at his vitals overcame the last of his scruples.

He pressed closer still, the peaks of her breasts grazing his chest for an instant, sending a judder of erotic sensation straight to his groin. His erection was a heavy fretful ache that surged into full-blooded readiness. A groan of pain, of thwarted need, rose from his chest but he ignored it, fisting his hands tighter till the circulation ebbed and his fingers ached.

He'd started this and he owed it to Rosalie, as a man of honour, not to finish it here and now with a quick frantic coupling, no matter the cost to his fast-shredding self-control.

Arik was all she'd dreamed he'd be. And more. The dance of his tongue against hers, languorous and innately seductive, the taste of him on her lips, the scent of his warm skin so close—it was a heady combination that blasted any logic right out of her brain. The sheer bombardment of physical pleasure assailing her senses made her dizzy.

She wondered how it would feel if he wrapped his arms

around her and drew her close to the aggressive heat of his body. She longed to know. Could almost imagine the heavy weight of his strong torso against hers.

Rosalie shifted, edgy with an aching, empty sensation that would only be satisfied with more. More of Arik. More of the magic he created just with his lips and tongue against hers.

He pushed closer, still not close enough, and she almost sighed with relief as she felt the soft luxury of piled cushions behind her. He adjusted the angle of his mouth slightly, giving even better access to hers, and she knew with a faint last coherent thought that surrender wasn't so bad after all.

If only he'd touch her, lift his palm to her face and stroke her there, as she longed to be touched.

But, despite the intensity of their meshed mouths, of the spiralling desire between them, he took no further advantage. Only their mouths met and held, in a kiss that contained all the potent intoxication of pure need.

The pressure built inside her until she could ignore it no longer. She lifted her hands, tentatively skimmed them between his heaving solid chest and her over-sensitive breasts, up to his shoulders. Her hands lingered there indecisively till she heard a sound like a low growl in her ears, felt him shudder against her hands.

Without thought she responded to his primal maleness, the raw sound of his desire. She cupped the heated skin of his neck, revelling in the hint of racing pulse she discovered, the smooth, enticing sensation of his flesh against her hands.

She speared her fingers up through his hair. It was like rough silk to her touch. She cradled his skull as she drew him closer. But still it wasn't enough. It would never be enough.

The primitive rhythm pulsing in her blood, drumming in the dark, hidden core of her body urged her on. She needed more.

Then Arik moved.

Not in against her body as she craved. Instead he pulled

back, ending the kiss so suddenly that her eyes snapped open and she lost the comforting sensual darkness.

What had happened?

Her lips were swollen, throbbing with the force of his mouth against hers. Her breasts were full and heavy, her body weighted with a languor she didn't recognise. She blinked, trying to bring him into focus. Trying to engage her brain.

He breathed deeply, as if starved of oxygen, and she felt his breath on her sensitised skin. Maybe that was why she felt dizzy, she was panting as if she'd run a marathon.

Her hands still held him close. The sensation of hard bone and flesh and soft hair beneath her hands was exquisite. She saw her raised arms, her hands clutching him and realised, muzzily, that she should let him go. But her brain couldn't seem to conjure the appropriate command.

She stared up at him. His was the strong, burnished face of seduction. The epitome of every secret, scandalous desire she'd ever harboured. His lips were fuller than before, from the taste of her. The knowledge sent a thrill of excitement straight through her. His eyes gleamed brighter than ever under those heavy hooded lids, as if he understood her yearning. His high cut cheekbones and the strong lines of his jaw, even the slashing angle of his nose, seemed more pronounced, as if the flesh had been pared back to reveal only stark desire.

If sensual need had a face, it was here: bold and utterly captivating.

Against him, against her own rising need, her defences were crystalline: transparent, brittle and easily splintered. She felt them crack and shatter under the heat of his flagrantly wanting gaze. But it was the force of her own desire that finally destroyed them. The knowledge that, however wrong, however dangerous, *this* was what she wanted. *This man.*

The epiphany was instant and complete. For all her fear,

her caution, her longing for a safe secure life, she couldn't escape the truth.

She wanted Arik. In the most elemental way a woman could want a man.

She should have been embarrassed, swimming up out of her sensual haze to discover that she'd succumbed so completely to him. That, without lifting a finger, he'd enticed her back to lie before him in a pose of wanton invitation. With his mouth alone he'd coaxed her into a new reality, where all that mattered was the present, the all-consuming hunger for sensual pleasure.

Later, she knew, she'd wince at the image of her hands clutching him close, a symbol of her complete abandonment.

If he'd been less trustworthy, if he'd taken advantage as he so easily could have, she might not be lying here fully clothed. The thought created a twist of horror deep in her belly. She'd invited trouble when she'd lost control. But, amazingly, Arik had retained his. He hadn't faltered in his promise of a kiss only.

Her eyes widened as she stared into the impenetrable blackness of his gaze. He wanted her. He'd spelled it out more than once. Yet he'd taken no more than she'd agreed to. Despite the fact that he could have plundered her for so much more than a kiss. Despite the fact that she'd wanted him pressed against her, his hands on her body, his arms pulling her close.

Her brow furrowed as her foggy brain worked through the implications. Her hands grew lax and slid down his neck, past the iron-hard tendons and scorching heat of his shoulders. The heavy thud of his heart pounding against his chest reinforced the knowledge of his arousal and her hands dropped away.

Even in the sudden delirium of her new-found physical desire, she would have called a halt—eventually, but probably too late, if he'd decided she was willing.

She could barely believe she'd let herself go so far.

He could have pushed her even further into intimacy. Could have taken all that he wanted with very little persuasion.

Yet he hadn't.

She stared up at him, the throb of her racing pulse deafening in her ears.

He was a man of his word, she realised.

Against all the odds she'd found a man who could be trusted, even against his own urgent desires.

After the dark phantoms that crowded her past, that should be impossible. *A man she could trust.*

Rosalie's chest tightened suddenly as if constricted by metal bands. Her breath sawed in her lungs and a ball of burning emotion rose in her throat. She tried to swallow it down, combating the searing ache at the back of her eyes.

Stupid to be upset now, when everything was all right. She was safe, after all. Unharmed. Untouched, but for the heady caress of his mouth against hers.

Yet the sharp pain of unharnessed emotions accelerated rather than dwindled. She gulped down hard on the knot of sensation as she blinked against her blurring gaze.

'Rosalie?' His voice was rusty, harsh. 'What's wrong?'

She shook her head. She couldn't speak. And no way could she explain the surge of emotions churning within her: the relief and incredulity, the self-disgust and remembered pain. There was more too, a tumble of pent-up feelings that had more to do with the past than with what had just happened. Somehow their kiss, the intimacy between them, had unleashed the demons she'd kept at bay for so long.

Rosalie bit her lip and turned away. She felt him move to give her more space. He probably thought she was off her rocker! To get teary over a kiss. A first class mind-blowing kiss, but still, as far as he knew, just a kiss.

She planted her hands against the richly patterned carpet of the floor and tried to concentrate only on what she saw. On the delicate whorls of colour in the stylised pattern of flowers and tendrils in the silk and wool. Flowing lines, clear ruby tones with a fine tracery of azure and cream and indigo. Buds and leaves and arabesques of gold.

'Rosalie.' His voice was lower this time, husky and deep. She felt it roll across her shredded nerves, soft and powerful as the surge of the tide.

Even his voice had the power to seduce!

'I'm sorry,' she murmured, finding her voice at last. 'I just felt a little…faint,' she lied. How else could she explain the unstoppable force of raw emotion that had hit her, just when she was at her most vulnerable? She couldn't explain it to him. She could barely understand it herself. She just knew that she'd experienced something…wonderful. And it wasn't just Arik's expertise at kissing or the taste of mutual enjoyment. It was the tentative rekindling of faith in another.

It had been a long time coming. Until today she'd never thought it would happen.

And it was overwhelming.

She lifted a hand and surreptitiously wiped away the tears that had overflowed on to her cheeks. With her shoulders hunched and her back to Arik, she hoped he wouldn't notice. But she doubted he'd miss anything. His eyes were as keen as an eagle's. Which meant she had to brazen it out.

'Here.' She looked down to see his squared hand hold out a gilt-edged glass to her. 'Drink this.'

It was tropical fruit juice. Cold, sweetly tart and refreshing. The everyday act of sipping and swallowing helped. So did the immediate sugar boost. Slowly she drained it.

'Thanks.' She held the glass out, darting a glance at his set face, and then away from his intense scrutiny.

'Are you ill?' Arik took the empty glass and placed it on the table. 'Do you need a doctor?'

She shook her head and the wispy tendrils of bright hair

swirled round her face, framing features that were only gradually regaining some colour.

'No, I'm okay.' Her lips quirked up in a perfunctory smile that tugged at something in his chest. 'I just felt a little…'

'Faint,' he finished for her, angry at the frustration of knowing he wouldn't get the truth from her now. Worried for her. Whatever had happened, she wasn't going to trust him with it. But of one thing he was sure: Rosalie Winters hadn't been on the verge of a faint, however stunning their kiss. He'd still been reeling from the impact of her mouth opening like a flower beneath his, the sensation of her warm, seductive body relaxing into complete abandonment beneath him, when he'd seen the look on her face.

Tears, that was what he'd seen. Tears and a flash of something he couldn't pin down. Surprise? No, it had been stronger than that. Amazement? Horror?

Surely not. He could vouch for the fact that no woman he'd kissed had ever been horrified by him.

And that kiss had been completely mutual, after those first few moments when she'd hesitated. No way could she have faked that reaction. She'd been perfect. Responsive; almost innocently seductive and eager. So eager that he'd been tested to the limit, reining in his burgeoning lust. No woman had ever tasted that good or felt so inviting. And it hadn't been the piquancy of their almost-caress, of knowing he shouldn't, couldn't trust himself to hold her and stop at a single kiss.

No, there was something…different about kissing Rosalie Winters. Something that left him with a gnawing, unsatisfied hunger deep inside. Hunger for her body. But for more too—for her smiles and her confidence.

He stared at her averted profile, lost for an explanation as to why this woman affected him so. Yet this wasn't the time to fathom it out. There was something wrong. Badly wrong.

'Would you like me to take you back to your hotel?' He

hadn't known he was going to make the offer until the words spilled from his mouth. It wasn't what he wanted. What he wanted was a repeat of that kiss. And to explore a little further, to hold her in his arms and learn the secrets of her body. Taking her back would put an end to those plans. And yet it mattered more to him that she recover from whatever had upset her.

Just as long as it wasn't him. What would he do if he discovered it was *he* who'd made her cry?

'Thank you, but I'm all right. It was just a passing thing.' She flashed him a look from stormy grey-green eyes that cut right through him. He'd give so much to see the shadows fade from her face.

'I'd rather go sightseeing—' she paused and drew in a shuddering breath '—if the offer still stands?'

Arik knew a moment's uncharacteristic indecision. Instinct told him he should press for more information, uncover whatever it was she kept hidden, for he knew it was important. But selfishly he wanted to spend the afternoon with her. If he pushed for answers then she could take flight and leave.

'Of course the offer still stands. On one condition.'

Her widening eyes met his. He watched the tip of her tongue slip out and moisten her lips and wished he'd bargained for another kiss. The effect she had on his body was overpowering and immediate. Even now, worried about her, he was hard with lust.

'What's the condition?'

'That if you feel faint again I take you straight to a doctor.'

Her smile this time was genuine and its impact hit him hard in the solar plexus.

'Thanks, Arik, but I'm sure I'll be okay.'

Watching her lips shape his name had to be one of the most erotic things in the world. Especially now, when her mouth was swollen from kissing him. The taste of her was still in his mouth, an addictive flavour that heightened his appetite for her. He stared at her lips a moment longer, wishing the old custom of wearing a face veil still prevailed. It was too distracting watching her mouth, inviting and lush, and not being able to take it again.

'Come.' He rose to his feet and held out an imperious hand to her. 'I hear the four wheel drive. It's time we were on our way.'

For an instant she hesitated, her eyes on his outstretched arm, and then she reached out and let him fold his hand around hers. Good. The trust was there still. Arik ignored the rush of relief he felt as he tucked her hand into the crook of his arm and led her outside. She was where he wanted her and that was what counted.

Late sunlight slanted down into the broad courtyard and glinted off Rosalie's hair. As the afternoon had progressed and she'd become more engrossed by what she'd seen, she'd forgotten to push the strands back from her face or catch them up into her usual ponytail. Now her hair was a rose-gold halo, framing her delicate features. The perfect foil for her clear skin and lush pink mouth.

Arik leaned against a stone pillar, arms crossed as he watched her. It had taken a while but gradually the shadows had disappeared from her face. The tense grey glint of her eyes had faded, replaced by a deep jade-green as she'd forgotten whatever it was that had caused her so much pain.

He'd learnt that much about her, that her mood could be gauged by the shade of her eyes. Storm-grey for pain or anxiety. Green for pleasure.

Her eyes had glittered green as she'd stared up at him after their kiss. He could have drowned in those depths, had felt the rising tide of need tugging him closer so he could lose himself in her. It had only been the glint of sudden tears that had halted him.

There'd been pain there. And it bothered him that he didn't

know why. Could it have been their kiss? No. It had felt too right. Something from the past, then? He sensed that Rosalie Winters was a woman of secrets. And he knew an overwhelming urge to lay them all bare, uncover her mysteries and conquer her fears.

He'd been right to bring her here. She'd been at home almost from the moment of introductions. Obviously art had a language all of its own for most of the artists here had only rudimentary French or English and Rosalie's Arabic, though surprisingly well accented for a beginner, was basic. Yet she'd made herself understood. In fact he'd been superfluous after the first half hour. He'd retired instead to take tea with the director, to discuss the school's progress and its finances. Despite the funding arrangements that ensured the place ran smoothly, there were always more worthy initiatives for Arik's money to sponsor.

'It's getting late,' he murmured eventually, closing in behind Rosalie where she crouched beside a young mosaic maker. Her gaze was focused on the nimble play of the girl's fingers as she selected another tiny glass tile, fitting it delicately into the pattern.

At first Rosalie didn't hear. It was only when he let his hand settle on her shoulder that she looked up and brought him into focus.

'I'm sorry; have I taken too long?'

He shook his head. 'Not at all. It's a pleasure to see your enthusiasm. But the school will be closing soon and you'll want to phone your daughter.'

'It's *that* late?' She gave her watch a stunned glance. 'I hadn't realised.' Immediately she turned to the young woman beside her and, in a mixture of English and halting Arabic, expressed her thanks and good wishes. The girl smiled and told her how much she'd enjoyed sharing her work.

It took time to say their farewells but eventually they left, walking through the courtyard gates and out to the vehicle. Arik glanced at the lowering sun. Too late to suggest going elsewhere and he knew Rosalie would again reject an offer of an evening meal together. She was too wary about being alone with him. In fact, after her reaction to their kiss, he wondered if she'd find some excuse not to meet tomorrow.

'Arik?' Automatically he stopped at the sound of his name on her lips. Her voice was soft and tentative and a jolt of ice speared him at the thought that he'd been right. She was going to renege on their arrangement.

She stood beside him, her head just topping his chin, and he experienced a fierce urge to pull her close and not let her go, no matter what her objections.

'You didn't tell me that you funded the art school.'

He frowned, nonplussed at her words. Of all the things she might have said, that was the least expected. The frozen shard in his chest began to thaw as he relaxed.

'What makes you think I do?'

'One of the instructors mentioned it when he was showing me around.' She paused, staring up at him. 'You don't mind me knowing, do you? It's such a brilliant idea, fostering young talent and at the same time providing an education for kids whose families find it difficult to support them. I think it's great.'

He shrugged, repressing his annoyance that his role in the enterprise had been raised. It wasn't a secret; after all, he was involved in lots of schemes to support his people. 'I didn't bring you here to impress you with my work as a benefactor. I simply thought that, as an artist, you'd enjoy seeing the work of other talented artists.'

'And I *did*. It was wonderful. Especially the ceramic painters and the mosaic makers.' Her eyes shone with an enthusiasm that made her face glow. Her hand grasped his forearm, but he guessed she didn't notice.

He did. He felt the imprint of each finger through the cotton of his shirt, the warmth of her palm, and wanted more. The craving for her touch against his bare flesh was so strong he wanted to tear his shirt open and plant her palm against his chest. Right here, right now, in the lengthening shadows of the school grounds, he wanted her hands on him, stroking, clinging as he embraced her.

'I'd love to try mosaic work. But I don't know anyone with that sort of expertise at home to teach me.'

'You could learn here. Stay a little longer. There'd be no objection to your taking tuition here.'

Her head tilted back and her bright eyes met his. The force of their impact sent heat sparking through him.

'It's tempting but, no, I couldn't. I have responsibilities.'

Her daughter. Of course.

Suddenly the prospect of their short relationship ending, as it naturally would, loomed on the horizon, far too close. The thought unsettled him.

Could it be that he wanted more than a few days with Rosalie? More than the pleasure of her body for the time it took him to recuperate and resume his normal routine?

'Perhaps during another visit, later?'

She hesitated for a moment. Long enough for him to be appalled at how he hung on her answer. Did her presence mean that much to him?

'Maybe one day,' she said at last, slipping her hand away. 'In the meantime I need to work on my painting skills. I'm so rusty.'

'Then it's a good thing you have time in which to work on them.' He gestured for her to precede him towards the gate. 'We will meet at the same time tomorrow?'

'Yes, same time tomorrow.' Her voice was light and breath-less, as if she were nervous. But that didn't bother him. She intended to meet him again, despite her... *faintness* earlier. His bloodstream fizzed in anticipation.

Whatever had happened to make her wary, Rosalie Winters kissed like a woman blind to everything but him. And he intended to capitalise on that enthusiasm. Very soon.

When she had interrogated inside her, Rosalie. Where blazed the bitter unfulfilled to everyday to, but that As the interested to curtain to conversation, her own...

CHAPTER SIX

ROSALIE looked around the huge room with its magnificent view over the sea and knew she'd stepped straight into a world of wealth that most people never experienced.

There was nothing gaudy or ostentatious here but Arik's home was imbued with the luxury only serious money could buy. Generation upon generation of riches and privilege. And hard fought battles, she realised, noting the pair of antique muskets mounted over an arched doorway. They were decorated with the finest silver embossing, making them fit weapons for a sheikh.

'It's breathtaking,' she said, turning slowly around. And it was. From the spectacular panorama along the coast to the superb silks of hand woven rugs and tapestries. From the fine-grained leather of low modern lounges to the high vaulted ceiling tiled in a mosaic the colour of lapis lazuli, complete with a sprinkling of golden stars.

'It pleases me that you approve of my home.' Arik was his usual urbane self as he watched her take in her surroundings. His eyes were unreadable, his tall body relaxed. Again she wished he wasn't quite such a perfect host. She longed for a glimmer of the passion she'd seen in him two days ago. That she'd felt in the erotic caress of his mouth against hers.

Heat burned across her cheeks at the memory and she swung round towards the wide terrace that hung out over the cliff.

The memory of Arik's kiss. She'd been unable to put it from her mind. Or forget her reaction to it.

She'd gone to the beach the following day, half nervous, half secretly thrilled at the thought of him kissing her again. This time he'd pull her close in his arms, let her feel his strong body against hers, alleviate her burgeoning curiosity to know his touch.

She'd gone expecting another lesson in seduction from this man who was obviously a master of the art. She hadn't even considered not going—and that was the most telling thing of all. Despite her past, despite the fact that she hadn't trusted a man in years, the need to see Arik again, to be with him, overrode all else.

Perhaps, as her mother promised, time *did* heal. Maybe she was ready to take a chance on life.

Rosalie stared through the plate glass doors to the terrace and, beyond that, the vivid aquamarine of the sea.

It had been a momentous thing for her, deciding she wanted what Arik offered: the chance to experience passion, to ease the unceasing hollow ache deep inside her that told her she wanted a man—wanted *him*. That had been a revelation of her own femininity. Proof that she really *had* moved on from her troubled past.

In the long ago days when she'd indulged in daydreams she'd pictured a future with a man by her side. Someone she could rely on, who'd love her always. But times had changed and she knew that what Arik offered was perfect for her now: a way to explore her feelings, assuage these new found sexual cravings in safety. For he would be tender. He could be trusted.

And he was experienced enough to teach her all she longed to know. She shivered and crossed her arms at the thought of what she wanted from Arik.

Too bad he'd obviously changed his mind.

She was ready for more. But now he behaved like a perfect distant gentleman. He avoided so much as touching her hand, had clearly pulled back from intimacy. Dully she'd wondered if she'd kissed so badly that he'd decided she was no longer worth the effort of seducing. It wouldn't surprise her.

But he was a man to whom a promise was important and it seemed he was determined to stick to their bargain. Lunch yesterday had been a short affair. Then in the afternoon he'd driven her round part of the coast road, pointing out towns, historic sites and scenic vistas that should have caught and held her imagination. But she'd been too deep in disappointment to care.

How did you tell a man you wanted him to make love to you? Was it really that simple? And what if, like Arik, he'd clearly decided he was no longer interested?

Last night in her lonely bed had been the worst. She'd been so edgy she hadn't slept. Even after a long phone chat with her mother and Belle. Even after a relaxing bath. All that had achieved was to remind her that her body was…aroused. Ready for Arik's touch.

Heat scalded through her. Even now, after a second morning of polite decorum from Arik while she'd painted, she couldn't banish her craving for him. It was shaming, this relentless need, the breath-stealing suspense as she watched his every move and hoped he'd reach out to touch her.

Sensual awareness had come late to her and she hadn't yet mastered the art of controlling it. Why else was she standing here, breathless with the forlorn hope that even now, after two days of scrupulous distance, Arik might continue where their kiss had left off?

Blindly she groped for the door handle, swung open the glass door and stepped out. She needed air. She needed sanctuary. She'd been an idiot to agree when Arik had suggested they lunch at his home today. What she really needed was to get away while she had some shred of self-respect left.

She leaned heavily on the stone balustrade, her fingers gripping tightly, her chest constricting as she fought for control.

Laughable, wasn't it? Finally to decide to take up Arik's seductive promise of a no-strings affair and then to discover the option was no longer on offer. She shook her head miserably. Just another of life's disappointments.

In the overall scheme of things, this surely didn't rate such profound regret.

'Rosalie?' He stopped just a pace behind her and saw the tension stiffen her spine when she realised he was so close. The sea breeze fanned her hair and he shoved his hands deep in his pockets rather than reach out and fondle the silken tresses.

'It's a magnificent view. You're so lucky to have this.' Her gesture encompassed not only the beach far below but the ancient fortress that was his home. Yet he was more interested in the high uneven tone of her voice and in her averted profile.

She was doing it again, shutting him out.

Damn it! After two days of superhuman restraint, he deserved more. He'd read the pain so clear in her expression after their kiss and he'd respected her need for space. It had almost killed him, reining in the drive to claim her. To bind her close in his arms and not let her escape till he found satisfaction. That kiss, a mere taste of her treasures, had only titillated.

He needed more. Far more.

What had begun as an idle amusement had become a raw compulsion. He'd recognised her wariness, her fear, and gone slow. But he'd seen the hot desire in her unconscious responses and now it was time to act.

'Yes, extremely lucky.' He took another step towards her, close enough to feel the heat she generated and hear the hasty breath she sucked in. 'My ancestors fought long and hard to win this territory and keep it safe for their people.'

'And now you enjoy the benefits.'

Still her head was averted. Was she afraid of what he might read in her face? The thought spurred him. He leaned forward and placed one hand on the balustrade beside hers. There was a neatness to it—her hand, small and delicate, yet, he knew, clever and capable, beside his own. She'd be like that all over: skin pale and soft, dainty and feminine. In his mind's eye he could picture his own darker, larger hand moving slowly across her bare flesh, sliding, caressing, discovering. He could almost hear her sighs as he located each sensitive spot on her body and claimed it for himself.

'I make it my policy always to enjoy the benefits on offer.'

Her head swung round then, her eyes wide and confused. Her lips parted and he wanted to duck his head and taste her. Instead he took a slow breath and reached for her hand. It slid into his unresistingly and he felt his mouth kick up in a tight smile of satisfaction.

'Come, Rosalie. Our lunch will be ready. You can admire the view later.'

She was silent as he led her into the house. Silent as he took her through room after room, giving her a potted history of the fortress-cum-palace that had been built by one of his ancestors hundreds of years ago. He had no idea if she took in his words; he barely registered them himself. He was more absorbed in the feel of her, hand in his, the proximity of her so close beside him as he took her deeper into the palace.

'Your home is huge,' she said at last as they approached the end of a long passageway.

He didn't tell her that they'd eschewed the public dining rooms, all three of them, in favour of a meal in his private suite. Even with his well-trained staff, he had no intention of being disturbed this afternoon.

His fingers tightened fractionally round hers, then released their grip as he gestured for her to enter his chambers.

'After you, Rosalie.'

For an instant her eyes lifted to his and he felt the now familiar jolt, like a bolt of electricity, sizzle through him.

Then she stepped over the threshold and into the suite. He fought to keep the anticipatory smile from his face.

Her exclamation of delight masked the soft click of the door closing behind them and he turned to see her standing in the deep semi-circular window embrasure that jutted out over the cliff-line. She reached out to brush her hand across the continuous round seat that lined it and then lift to the silk hangings, tied back to reveal the view.

His body thrummed an urgent message of need. He'd imagined her here so often, naked on that padded seat, or leaning back against the window frame, her bare arms outstretched invitingly towards him. The images were almost his undoing. Tension knotted his muscles and he felt the strain of imposing control in every cell of his body.

Deliberately he turned away and walked further into the sitting room, towards the drinks tray positioned beside one of the sofas.

'Would you like a cool drink?' he murmured in a voice rough with repressed desire.

'Yes, please.'

He glanced over his shoulder and found she'd moved, bypassing the circular table laden with food, and was investigating the large telescope positioned before the next window.

'You look at the stars?'

He shrugged, remembering the day—was it only a week ago?—when he'd first seen her through the telescopic lens. He'd known even then what he'd wanted from her.

'Or the ships at sea. There's a lot of activity in the shipping lane further off the coast.' He put ice in a couple of glasses, then filled them. 'I was in plaster with a broken leg and looking for any diversion. I'm not used to being cooped up.' He turned and offered her a glass.

'How did you do it? Break your leg, I mean.'

'An accident on an oil rig. It happens. But, fortunately, not often.' An explosion on a rig was disastrous. And this time it had nearly claimed the life of one of his men. If Arik hadn't realised in time and turned back to look for him as they'd been evacuating, they might have had a fatality on their hands instead of mere fractures.

'It sounds dangerous.' She looked up at him so seriously that he wanted to pull her close and reassure her. But he couldn't take her in his arms. Not yet.

'Most of the time it's no more dangerous than being on land. It was just a matter of bad timing.' He turned towards the table that almost filled the window embrasure. 'It looks like Ayisha has been busy.'

'Ayisha?'

'My cook. She seems to have decided we must be starving after our exertions on the beach.' From the corner of his eye he saw Rosalie start. He wondered if, like him, she'd been thinking of exertions other than riding and painting. The suspicion pleased him. 'I hope you're hungry.'

Personally he was ravenous. But not for food. At least the meal would force him to take his time and not ravish her immediately. 'Please, take a seat.'

He watched Rosalie settle on the wide padded seat beneath the windows and then pushed the round table in closer, within easy reach. He slid in beside her, close but not touching, and placed his untouched drink on the table.

The food was delicious. Subtly spiced, fragrant with herbs and unnamed spices, melting in the mouth at each bite. And yet Rosalie found it almost impossible to concentrate on the fare before her.

Instead it was the man at her side who took all her attention. Surreptitiously she watched his strong hands reach for dishes, lift covers, offer delicacies. A shiver slid across her skin as his fingers brushed hers. She loved his touch, had secretly

dreamed of it all over her body. Now the sight of his hands
mesmerised her into a haze of fascination and longing. She
wanted to reach out and draw Arik's hand closer, close it over
her breast so she could feel its strength against her softness.

Rosalie swallowed down hard on a morsel of grilled fish
and tried to concentrate on the meal.

She listened to his stream of small talk that reinforced the
leisurely tempo of the meal. But there was no way she could
relax. As each moment passed the tension in her stomach
notched harder, tighter.

Arik passed her some rice flavoured with apricots, raisins
and almonds.

'This is one of Ayisha's specialities and I can recommend
it. Would you like some?' The flash of his smile stole her
breath and she found herself nodding, even though her throat
had closed and she doubted she'd be able to swallow properly.

'Here,' he murmured, his voice dropping to a low, husky
pitch that seemed to reverberate right through her, 'tell me
what you think.'

He lifted a fork laden with fluffy rice and held it out. Eyes
as dark as her own midnight longings looked back at her and
she felt something loosen and give way, deep inside her.
Restraint? Caution?…Fear?

Obediently she opened her mouth, catching the flicker of
expression in his eyes, unable to place it. She was too wrapped
up in the…intimacy of having this man feed her to even try.

Taste exploded in her mouth—sweet, nutty, a perfect blend
of flavours. But it was his gaze that had her attention. It was
a palpable force, warming her skin, holding her still, waiting
for his next move.

Finally she swallowed. 'It's delicious.'

'Good.' His one-sided smile sent a surge of pure longing
through her. 'Have some more.'

Again he held out the fork. Again he watched her open her

mouth and accept the food. And once again she saw a ripple of something in his expression. Something at odds with the easy, relaxed pose of his big body and the slow smile on his face.

Hurriedly she chewed and swallowed. 'Thank you. But no more.'

He raised one lazy dark eyebrow in enquiry. 'You've had enough?'

Silently she nodded.

'Ah, then we come to my favourite part of the meal.'

Something about the low burr of his voice, the infinitesimal strengthening of his accent, made gooseflesh rise on her skin. She shivered.

'Really?'

He inclined his head, still focused on her in a way that made her conscious of the heavy beat of her pulse, the miniscule distance separating them.

'Dessert,' he said. 'I've always had a weakness for sweet things.'

The words were innocuous. But not the way he said them. She *knew* he wasn't merely discussing food. His very look was an invitation: flagrant, tempting.

Now was the time to leave. To say she really needed to be going. That she'd changed her mind and wanted to go home. Or that she had a headache. Anything to get her out of here, where this man's ability to seduce with a look, a word, was the most potent force she'd ever known.

She could do it. She knew she could. If she wanted to.

'I…'

'Yes, Rosalie?' He leaned a fraction closer—close enough for her to inhale the scent of his skin: hot, male, musky.

She licked her lips. This was her chance to escape back to safety. Arik wouldn't stop her; she knew that with absolute certainty. She could scurry away to her private refuge from the world, turn her back on temptation and rely on the lessons of fear and caution she'd learned in the past three years. They would protect her from hurt.

'I like dessert,' she whispered after a long pause.

Immediately she was rewarded with the bright blaze of his smile, radiant with approval.

'And you shall have it, Rosalie.' His voice was lower, throatier than before, and she started when he reached for her hand, raised it to his mouth and placed a single kiss to the back of it. His thumb stroked her sensitive skin and she shuddered as awareness prickled through her, from the sensitive tips of her breasts to her neck, her thighs and deep in her womb.

He turned her hand and pressed a kiss to her palm, let his tongue lave its centre, and a jolt of something white-hot and stunning burst through her. She felt a clenching deep inside as every nerve reacted. Automatically she tugged her hand, trying to break his grip, but he simply smiled and held both her hands in his.

'There is no need for haste. We have all afternoon.'

Then he released her hand and reached out to a platter at the centre of the table.

'Would you like some fruit?'

She stared at the plate, her mind slow, still catching up after the effect of Arik's smile on her nervous system.

'I…yes. Thank you.' Her throat was dry, her voice cracked. She took refuge in a gulp of her iced juice as she frantically tried to get a grip on her churning emotions.

Had she done the right thing? Was she regretting the impulse to stay?

She waited for the icy finger of fear to trail down her spine, for the churning regret to unsettle her stomach.

But all she felt was a hot eagerness. An avid expectation that soon, very soon, she'd be in Arik's arms. She bit down on the small secret smile that curved her lips at the thought.

No, she had no regrets.

'Peach?' he offered and she turned her head. He held up a neat sliver of fresh fruit to her. It smelled like summer and it tasted like sunshine as she let him slip it between her lips. There was the faintest brush of his fingers against her mouth and then his hand was gone.

Her lips tingled from that fleeting touch.

'Aren't you having any?' she said as he held out another piece to her. This time his touch lingered against her mouth a second longer. Time enough for her to take in the slight salt tang of his skin and feel the passing caress of his thumb against her bottom lip.

Heat bloomed deep inside. Darts of sensation shot through her, pulling her straighter in her seat, eager for his next offering.

'That depends,' he said, letting his gaze slide from her face to her hand, grasping the edge of the table in a white-knuckled grip.

Depends? Rosalie looked from her hand to Arik and then to the neatly sliced peach on the plate before her.

It depends on me she realised with a thrill of daring. Tentatively she reached out and picked up a wedge of fruit. It was ripe, slippery with juice, and her fingers trembled.

Did she really mean to be so…provocative as to feed him?

She took a slow breath, trying to regulate the rhythm of her racing heart. But when she looked up into his fathomless eyes, her pulse pounded harder than ever. His gaze was so intense that she felt it graze her features, brush over her throat and linger on her lips.

Rosalie offered him the fruit, the tremor in her hand so pronounced that she was barely surprised when he closed his fingers around hers while he slid the peach into his mouth. He chewed, swallowed, smiled, and then licked the juice from her fingers.

A shudder of pure longing swept through her. Her nipples peaked, pebble-hard against her bra as she watched him suck the sticky sweetness from her thumb, her forefinger. Incendiary heat shot straight to the pit of her belly and to the moistening core of her desire.

Oh, my.

'Delicious,' he whispered in a throaty voice so deep it resonated within her.

Still holding her hand, Arik selected another segment of peach and held it to her lips. This time he didn't draw his hand away and she had to slip it from between his fingers. Heaven! It tasted of him. Or did he taste of the fruit? His thumb pressed against her bottom lip and she slid her tongue along it, watching the glimmer of anticipation in his eyes. Cautiously she parted her lips a little wider and took his thumb into her mouth, sucking the sweetness from it.

The searing pleasure in his expression reflected her own excitement, told her this was a mutual delight.

That was a heady realisation. For the first time she felt a thrill of power, knowing she could affect him so.

He might be the master at this, but even the novice had something to offer.

She reached for another piece of fruit and felt an unravelling, unsettling sensation as she watched him eat from her hand, then use his tongue to swipe up the juice on each of her fingers.

Her eyelids drifted down on a wordless sigh. She felt…everything. Her skin had grown so sensitised that even the lap of his tongue over a fingertip, the caress of his lips on her palm, was enough to seduce her into ecstasy.

'Rosalie.' At the sound of his voice she opened her eyes and found him leaning closer, offering her another piece. Obediently she took the segment but she was clumsy and juice dribbled from her lips.

He still held her hand in his so she lifted her other one to wipe away the moisture. But she was too late. Already he'd moved, tilting his head to catch the droplet of juice with his tongue.

She shuddered at the sensual impact of his mouth on her

flesh, smoothing along her chin. She felt his breath on her, scented him in her short, urgent gasps and shut her eyes against the dizzying onslaught of awareness. He kissed her jaw line, the corner of her mouth, across the sensitive spot beneath her ear that sent arrows of heat to every nerve in her body.

Her head lolled back as he pressed his lips to her throat, evoking the most exquisite sense of abandonment. If he put his hands on her now she'd welcome his touch. Revel in it.

And then, suddenly, he was gone. Rosalie opened her eyes to find him watching her, so close that she had only to lean forward a little to bring her lips to his.

For a heartbeat she stalled in thought, wondering, wishing. And in that instant Arik moved, shifting back in his seat and half turning away.

Panic shot through her. Had he changed his mind? He must *know* she wanted him. She sat up straighter just as he turned and held out a small damp cloth.

His expression was tight, almost hard, as he wiped the cloth across her chin and then her hands, removing the last sticky traces of peach. Then he flung the linen on to the table and fixed his eyes on hers.

What she saw there stole her voice. Gone was the laid-back insouciance she'd come to expect from Arik. The teasing half smile. Even the enigmatic stare.

Now his face seemed cast in hard bronze, drawn tight with the force of a compulsion he couldn't hide. On any other man that look would have frightened her.

On Arik it excited her.

'It's time,' he said, reaching out and enfolding both her hands in his. 'You've decided, haven't you, Rosalie?'

He paused, awaiting her response. Words were beyond her, so she nodded.

'Good.' Already he was drawing her to her feet. 'At last we will be lovers.'

CHAPTER SEVEN

THE light sea breeze from the open windows cooled Rosalie's flushed cheeks as he drew her through the arched doorway into his private domain. His bedroom was large, light and airy. At the centre of the back wall was a low bed, wide and sumptuous with its richly patterned coverlet. That was where Arik led her, slowly, inexorably, till it lay before them, a blatant invitation to pleasure.

She swallowed hard, faced with the reality of her desire. Did she have the nerve to go through with this?

But then Arik's hands were on her, gently compelling, drawing her down to the bed, and there was the promise of heaven in his touch. The lure of long-denied fulfilment. Of joy. Rosalie sank down beside him, leaning in against him without a second thought. For now it was her body responding, not her mind. She acted on instinct alone.

Their kiss was perfect. Growing passion tempered by a fierce restraint she sensed in him. And this time it wasn't just a meeting of lips and tongues. As he slanted his head to gain better access to her mouth, she felt his hands skim over her. Even through her clothes his touch ignited a desire that sparked and seared. Over the bare skin of her face and neck, across her shoulders, her back, her arms, down her sides and back up to her face. Wherever he caressed her he left a trail of sizzling excitement. It burned across her skin, coiled hard and tight inside her, till she was on fire, desperate for something to assuage the raging need.

Then the welcoming heat of his big body encompassed her, the hard strength of bone and taut muscle.

Automatically she clung to him, revelling in the sensation of his torso pushing her down into the soft mattress. Breathlessly she registered the way his broad chest flattened her breasts, but there was no pain, only a growing edginess, a delicious awareness tingling through every centimetre of her. She wanted to rub herself against him, explore his hard muscled form with her hands, her lips, her body.

She wanted to imprint herself on him and to feel his flesh against hers. She wanted…

'Rosalie.' His deep throaty murmur against the corner of her mouth was enticing, seductive. Did she hear it or feel it? His lips brushed her own, caressed the sensitive corner of her mouth, dipped down to the pulse point low on her neck, and she arched up involuntarily, gasping with delight.

The impact of that kiss reverberated to every pleasure point in her body. There was effervescence in her blood, a surge of energy so strong she felt almost faint with it.

'I've waited so long for you,' he whispered and now she felt his hands move, deftly unbuttoning her shirt.

She opened eyes she hadn't realised she'd closed and stared up at Arik. He was breathtaking, each severe line of his face, each angle and plane contributing to a whole that was compelling. He was handsome, beautiful even, in a hard, ultramasculine way. But it was the inner fire, the spark of his personality, and of his desire, that overwhelmed Rosalie. There was a single-minded intensity about him that would have scared her a week ago.

Now she revelled in it.

She wanted Arik so much. *Needed* him. His expression:

eyelids hooded, nostrils flared, mouth a taut line, made something leap inside her.

Then she registered the caress of cool air as he spread wide the sides of her shirt, baring her from the waist up to his gaze.

His eyes lingered on her bra, tracing its curve over her breasts. His gaze was smoky with desire.

'You are beautiful, Rosalie.' He lifted a hand and feathered his fingers along the upper edge of her bra.

She jolted at the unexpected intensity of that light touch. Her breath was a gasp of pure pleasure. Without thought she arched her back, silently begging him to repeat the gesture.

'And so exquisitely responsive,' he murmured as he again stroked the upper curve of her breasts and her eyes fluttered shut.

His tone was appreciative, knowing. It reminded her for an instant of the gulf of experience between them.

'I'm not protected,' she blurted out, then bit her lip as a fiery blush rose in her cheeks.

'Of course it will be my responsibility to protect you, little one.'

His gentle tone persuaded her to open her eyes. His gaze met hers and suddenly the embarrassment she'd felt a moment before was gone. She took a slow breath, saw the way his expression flickered at the deep rise of her breasts, but forced herself to go on.

'I don't have much…' *Experience*, she'd been about to say. But then she'd been pregnant, had given birth. He wouldn't understand. And she didn't want to enter into long explanations, not now. 'It's…'

'Been a while?' he finished for her, his gaze piercing. 'Don't worry, Rosalie. Once learned, the lessons of love aren't forgotten.'

That was what she was afraid of. Maybe she'd better tell him. She opened her mouth reluctantly but he forestalled her.

'Between us, little one, it will be easy.' His deep voice was reassuring and his slow smile reminded her that she could trust him. His eyes glowed with an excitement that matched her own. Could she ask for more?

Again his hand traced the outline of her bra, then dipped lower to find and tease her nipple through the cotton fabric.

She sucked in her breath in a hiss of surprised delight. Who'd have guessed such a touch would make her feel…?

'Perfect,' he murmured as he lowered his mouth to hers. 'It will be perfect with us.'

Then there was no more thinking. No more worries. No embarrassment. There was only the hot dark velvet of his kiss, the rising excitement as his hand grew heavier, more demanding at first one breast and then another.

She could grow addicted to Arik's touch. So sure, so sensitive. Her body clamoured for more, pushing up against his hand, his body, relieved and yet unsettled at the weight of him over her. It was what she wanted, but it wasn't enough.

When he drew back a fraction, her hands clung to his shoulders, her mouth throbbed from the passion that had soared between them. A passion reflected in the blaze of his eyes and the heave of his chest with every breath he took.

The last lingering shadow of doubt fled. She knew this was right.

'I want to touch you, Rosalie.' Arik was surprised at how steady his voice sounded. He teetered at the edge of his control, fiercely resisting the relentless urge to rip her clothes away and bury himself quick and deep in her soft waiting warmth.

He'd known urgent desire before, had more than enough experience to be able to temper his urges to ensure his partner was satisfied. Until now. The intensity of each sensation, the effect of watching Rosalie come alive at his touch, breathless and eager and somehow vulnerable, was something completely new to him.

His body felt as if it were on a rack, stretched almost to breaking-point by the weight of restraint placed upon it. Each muscle and sinew was stretched to the limit. But there was no alternative. He remembered the instant of doubt he'd seen in Rosalie's face and knew he had no choice but to love her slowly. Even it if killed him.

Gently he pushed her shirt from her shoulders. She shrugged out of it and he tossed it away.

'Touch me,' he ordered, hungry for the feel of her against his bare skin. For a moment she didn't move and then, slowly, so slowly he wanted to reach out and yank her hands against his chest, she reached up to him. Her fingers fumbled with a button. And then another. And then her hand slipped into his shirt, right over the spot where his heart pounded its message of hunger and painful control.

His eyes closed as he absorbed the sensation of her hand across his chest.

'More,' he demanded. The gentle exploration faltered and then, a moment later, her fingers worked his shirt buttons again. This time quickly, nimbly, and he sucked in a breath of relief. Another hurdle passed.

He waited till his shirt hung open, then shrugged his shoulders and shook it away. Opening his eyes, he found her staring, absorbed, as if committing to memory the sight of his bare torso. The look in her eyes did dangerous things to his ego. He felt like a hero, a god, not an ordinary man, when she looked at him like that.

She moved her hands over his chest, up and across, then circled down over muscles that spasmed at her touch. His arms trembled at the effort of remaining still under her caress.

'You're beautiful,' she breathed.

'No, Rosalie. But you are.' He couldn't resist the lure of

such temptation any longer. He reached out and slid his hand behind her, making short work of her bra clasp, drawing her plain white, ridiculously seductive bra away in his hand.

There was a hiss of frantic breath. A moment of stunned appreciation, and then he was touching her, stroking his index finger under the curve of her full, luscious breasts, up between them, then down and across the rose-pink nipples that tightened into buds at his touch.

She was exquisite. Perfect. And the little tremors vibrating through her at his caress were delicious proof of her incredible sensuality.

He palmed one breast, felt its weight in his hand, smiling at the exact fit. Hadn't he known she'd be just right? His fingers tightened on that sensitive bud, twisted just a fraction, and her whole body jolted.

It was as if she'd been waiting just for him. The thought was ridiculous, but an inviting fantasy, one he couldn't quite shake.

Her breath came in shallow pants, the sound of it igniting a heat deep in his loins. He was hard with desire, had been since lunch, when he'd tasted her in his mouth, had invited her to taste him. But now he'd reached a point where control was almost impossible. He let himself move across her body, insinuating his thighs between hers till he lay cradled against her, his erection throbbing its intent.

He didn't know if he could hold out much longer. But then he looked into Rosalie's face and read the stunned blankness there. She wanted him, but something, the furrow of surprise on her brow, gave him pause.

So he did what he'd wanted from the first—lowered his head to her breast. The fresh scent of her rose in his nostrils and her velvet-soft skin was a living caress against his chest.

He kissed her nipple, holding her tight in his arms as she almost came up off the bed in response. It was as if he'd triggered an earthquake deep inside her. The shudders echoed through her as he laved her breast. When he took her nipple in his mouth and sucked, her moans grew frantic. Her hands clenched against his skull as he tasted her sweetness, then moved to her other breast.

Restlessly her legs shifted against his and he allowed himself the luxury of pushing down against her, feeling her intimate heat against his erection, even through their clothes.

Soon.

His control was shredding, spinning away as his pulse thundered louder in his ears.

'Arik,' she whispered, 'please…'

Without thought his hand arrowed to the button on her trousers, the zip, pushing it down. He lifted himself a fraction from her as she tilted her hips and he stripped the cotton material down her thighs—enough to give him free access to the place he most wanted to be.

'Please,' she whispered again and he planted his palm between her thighs, pushing up against her sensitive core.

'Arik!' Her voice had a husky, sensual quality he loved, but when he raised his head to see her face he wondered if it was panic or delight he read on her features.

'Shh, it's all right, Rosalie. Just relax.' Her blind eyes turned to his and gradually focused. A jab of something that had the force of lightning struck right through him, making his heart leap.

Her hands slid down to cradle his neck. They were unsteady, shaking but warm and gently sensuous as they massaged his stiff muscles.

He searched her most secret place, circled and found the point he was seeking. She was hot, wet, ready.

'Arik? I don't—'

'Trust me, Rosalie.' Whatever her past sexual encounters, it was clear her experience hadn't included much pleasure.

The realisation brought anger. And a deep protectiveness, a need to ensure this was absolutely right for her.

She opened her mouth to respond as he stroked her slowly, surely, and suddenly she gasped. The light tremors that had been racing through her body became shudders. She bucked up against his hand with a force that belied her small frame. And her gaze clung to his—jade-green, brilliant and intoxicating. He could drown in that gaze, watching her come apart just for him. The thrill of it, of her body arching into his, the sound of his name on her lips again and again as she sighed out her delight, was better than anything that had gone before.

Her eyes drifted shut as the last of the vibrations subsided. His own body was on fire, desperate for release, after the heady sensations of Rosalie's climax. He slid his fingers between her legs and another aftershock racked her.

So incredibly sensual.

Gently he leaned down and took her mouth with his. Her response was instant, her lips opening to his, even though her movements were slow, languorous. He delved deep into her mouth, allowing himself the freedom he hadn't yet had with her body.

She moaned and tilted her head towards his, her fingers spreading out over his shoulders. Automatically his lower body pressed in against hers, right into the hot centre of her, and light spun behind his eyelids at the sensations of pleasure coursing through his body.

Their kiss held a different, richer quality now as she responded to his lead with a ready sultriness that urged him to deepen his caresses. The taste of her was designed to drive any man out of his senses. And the way she held him tight with her hands, the way her luscious body cushioned his, accepting and matching the insistent push of his erection against her, made his head spin.

At last he drew away, far enough that her hands broke their

hold and slid slowly, provocatively down over his chest. Her eyes were closed, her lips plump and pink with the force of their passion. A wash of colour spread across her breasts and up her cheeks, highlighting her delicate features. She breathed deeply and for a moment he was riveted by the sight of her perfect breasts, rising and falling. Hair like dawn gold flared across the silk coverlet, softer and more enticing than any man-made fabric.

Who was this woman who'd appeared out of nowhere just days ago? Who'd taken over his life? Absorbed his every waking hour and burrowed deep into his emotions?

She was a miracle.

He pushed himself up and away on his arms, then knelt to strip the last of her clothes from her. The heady scent of female arousal registered in his nostrils, inciting him to move more quickly.

It was the work of a few moments to remove her clothes, and his own, and reach for the protection he'd promised her.

Rosalie's world had tilted completely off its axis. She'd spun crazily out of control in Arik's arms as he'd brought her to a juddering, mind-blowing climax. It had been all red-hot light and heat, searing her body till she'd thought there'd be nothing left of her but ashes. Only Arik, his gaze holding hers, his body anchoring her to the spot, had brought her back to something like safety again. If it hadn't been for the link between them she felt she might have died from pure ecstasy.

His dark eyes had been the only real thing in her consciousness, other than the impossible burst of fire in her blood.

And now she felt…she squeezed her eyes shut, trying to give a name to the sense of wellbeing, of effervescent excitement that filled her, but she couldn't.

Her body was weighted, yet tingling with life. She stretched, registering for the first time the slide of the luxurious coverlet beneath her body. Her bare body. Arik had peeled away the last of her clothes just a moment ago.

Rosalie snapped open her eyes, anxious now that she couldn't feel him against her. But when she located him she swallowed hard.

He stood beside the bed, feet planted wide in a stance that was utterly masculine. He was naked, gloriously so, his dark olive skin the perfect foil for his athlete's body. Every taut muscle and powerful curve was bare for her to see. She stared, fascinated, at the fuzz of dark hair across his pectoral muscles that narrowed and disappeared as it descended. He'd make a wonderful study for an artist. Magnificent proportions, latent power and pure energy from every angle.

But she couldn't view Arik with an artist's dispassionate eye. She'd lost that objectivity.

Instead she dragged in an unsteady breath at the image of rampant male libido before her. He thrilled her. And frightened her.

He was fitting a condom. Rosalie swallowed again, her mouth suddenly dry. Surely it would break...it couldn't possibly...but it did. She felt her eyes widen.

He looked up and smiled at her, a tight, lopsided smile that nevertheless had the power to unravel some of the spiralling tension inside her.

'Rosalie,' he murmured as he took a single stride to the bed and knelt above her. 'My beautiful golden girl.' He raised her limp hand in his and kissed the palm, nipping at the fleshy part of it till a spear of heat arced straight from her hand to her womb.

How magnificent he was: so at ease in his flesh, each movement economical yet with an innate grace. The dark bronze of his body was in contrast to her own paler skin and as he lay down beside her she was fascinated by the sight of his large long-fingered hand splaying possessively across her body. Who'd have thought anything so simple could be so erotic?

Butterflies swooped in her stomach at the spreading sensation of warmth deep inside her. She felt his leg brush hers, the hair on his thigh wiry and tickling. Then he bent his head and planted a kiss at her navel.

Seismic waves spread out from the point of contact, making her shiver. The sight of his head bent over her so intimately made her conscious again of the moist heat between her legs. The empty, needy sensation.

He nuzzled her belly, planted a string of kisses across to her hip and set the butterflies dancing again inside.

She shifted uneasily, aware of a renewed urgency in the signals her body was sending to her brain.

He lifted his head and smiled, a knowing smile if ever there was one.

'You like it when I kiss you here?' He dropped his mouth once more to her waist, her stomach.

She reached out and tried to pull him up, edgy again and unsure of herself. She shouldn't feel like this again, surely.

'You don't like my kisses?' His tone was teasing but his face was set in harsh lines of desire. The flame of arousal was hot in his eyes.

She opened her mouth to answer, but something stopped her: a knot of hard, tight emotion that blocked her throat. He was so gentle, so tender. He treated her as no man ever had before. Heat glazed her eyes and she shook her head.

'Rosalie?' His tone was abrupt as he levered himself higher, the better to see her face.

For answer she wrapped her arms round his shoulders and lifted her lips to his, opening her mouth and giving herself up to the ecstasy that beckoned. Giving herself to *him*.

For a long moment he held himself rigid above her. Then, as her tongue danced against his and her hands swept in wide circles down over his back, he settled closer. She revelled in the smooth texture of his skin against her hands, and in the sensual friction of his chest hair brushing her breasts. It was…arousing. The press of his large body against hers was an exciting weight. She felt the hot, heavy throb of him between her legs and fascination mingled with trepidation.

'Rosalie,' he murmured against her mouth. 'You drive me wild with wanting.' Now their kisses were more urgent and the caress of his hands heavier, more possessive. He gripped her hips and pushed forward and she felt the hard length of him intimately against her. Instinctively she tilted her hips up towards him and he growled deep in his throat. 'You're a houri sent to bewitch me.'

He raised one hand to her breast, squeezing gently, and she let out a cry of excitement as a flaming arrow of sensation shot through her body. Above the drumming in her ears and the rocking tension in their almost-joined bodies, she heard the whisper of his deep voice in her ear. He spoke in his own language, a lyrical intonation of syllables that flowed like music around her. The words were soothing yet somehow un-settling, urging her closer as he rocked harder against her.

All she knew was him. The clean, earthy fragrance of his skin, the taste of him on her tongue, the feel of him everywhere, and still that yearning, aching sensation that couldn't be denied.

She barely noticed when he moved, hooking his arm under her thigh and lifting her leg up and over him. But she *did* register the pressure as he pushed between her legs, nudging up against her, into her.

She froze, absorbed in the sensation of him filling her.

Arik drew back a fraction. She had an impression of flashing dark eyes surveying her, then his head dipped to her breast and all capacity for coherent thought fled. His tongue was on her. His mouth. His teeth. She cried out, a muffled shout of bliss, and cradled him closer, arching her back as he wrought his magic on her body once more.

There was nothing but Arik and the dazzle of stars behind her closed eyelids.

But then, suddenly, there was more. One single, smooth, never-ending surge of movement drew him forward, impossibly filling her. She opened her eyes to see him poised above her, his face almost unrecognisable from the tension that held him so tight in its grip.

For an instant there was no movement but the rise and fall of their chests, each breathing deeply, struggling to find equilibrium.

'Lift your other leg, sweetheart.'

Slowly she complied, and then it seemed automatically he slid forward a fraction to rest deep within her. Rosalie's eyes widened.

'That's it, little one.' His kiss was a reward, a glorious, sensuous caress that made her bones melt, even as he moved again, rocking against her.

It felt…it felt…wonderful.

Rosalie slid her hands over the bunched muscles of his shoulders and down to wrap her arms around his back, to hold him close as he pushed forward again. There was something sparking between them, something that made her rise up to meet his next thrust and the next: eager, ready for him.

Their tempo increased, their bodies grew hot, slick from excitement and exertion. Rosalie felt again the welling, tingling sensation in her blood. She heard her pulse roar in her ears, heard Arik's breathing. Then his mouth closed over hers, his tongue thrusting deep even as he rocked into the centre of her being.

She tasted him, dark and rich. Scented his skin. She was part of him, his body sliding with hers, drawing her into a whirling, rushing storm of glorious commotion.

And then it came—a crashing wave of fulfilment, breaking over both of them. Desperate, she clung to Arik like a lifeline in a stormy sea. He was the one solid reality as her world shattered, bursting apart in a conflagration that shook her to her core. She had no words to express what she felt, only knew it was beyond her expectations, her hopes, even her fantasies.

And the fact that it was Arik gathering her close in strong arms that trembled with the force of their climax, holding her as if he'd never let her go, was most important of all.

How could this happen between two strangers?

It was far more surely than a union of bodies. It felt like a communion of souls.

Rosalie drew a deep shuddering breath, inhaling his heat and his musky scent.

Casual sex wasn't supposed to be this…perfect, was it?

What had she got herself into?

CHAPTER EIGHT

'THAT sounds like fun, Amy. What are you doing with Grandma tomorrow?' Rosalie shifted her grip on the phone as her daughter began a breathless description of her planned visit to puppies in the stables and a pony who took carrots from her outstretched hand. Obviously they were far more interesting to a toddler than the grandeur of the centuries-old palace where she was staying.

Though she had been impressed with Uncle Rafiq, the tall, smiling man who swept her up in his arms and swung her round till she squealed.

Rosalie's mum was right. Amy was having a great time with her family fussing over her. Not only that, but Rafiq's small army of royal servants were spoiling her too, apparently besotted by Amy's grin and sunny temperament.

The door to Rosalie's left opened and the smile on her face slipped a little as Arik came into the room. His gaze caught hers and that gleaming dark look made her mouth dry. Like her, he wore a long, loose robe. But, far from making him look effeminate, the outfit somehow accentuated the width of his shoulders, the whipcord strength of his body, his innate masculinity.

Just a single stare from this man sent a wave of heat roaring through her. She watched him pace into the room and her palms prickled in excitement as she remembered the way he'd loved her this afternoon. The world of sensual pleasure he'd opened up for her.

Finally, half an hour ago, he'd pressed a last bone-melting kiss to her lips before leaving her, saying she'd no doubt want to telephone her daughter. Only then had she realised the afternoon had sped by as she'd lain in his arms. Shame had washed through her, that it was he rather than her who'd remembered her responsibilities. That she'd been in danger of forgetting her call to Amy.

And now, just the sight of him made it hard to concentrate on Amy's chatter.

What sort of mother was she? Surely there was something wrong with her priorities. Nothing was more important to her than her daughter.

What was happening to her?

Arik didn't approach. He gave her a slow smile that sent liquid heat spilling down her spine. Then he disappeared through the door to the huge bathroom. It was a relief when he was out of sight and that sensual connection was severed.

An instant later she heard the sound of running water. She blinked, trying to bring her mind back to her call.

'I have to go now, Mummy. G'anma says it's time to hang up.'

'All right, sweetheart. You be a good girl for Grandma and Auntie Belle and I'll see you soon.'

'I will, Mummy. Bye, bye.'

'Bye, darling.'

Slowly Rosalie switched off the phone and put it beside the huge bed. Another sign of Arik's generosity, or more likely his enormous wealth. He didn't know Amy was actually in Q'aroum rather than at home in Australia. He would have assumed when he'd offered Rosalie the use of the phone that she'd be making an international call.

It only highlighted the difference between Arik's world and

her life of stretching to make ends meet. Despite persistent offers from Belle, Rosalie had been so determined to stand on her own two feet she'd accepted little financial help. The holiday to Q'aroum was an exception.

'You didn't need to end your call just yet.' Arik's deep voice interrupted her reverie and she looked up to find him framed by the doorway, watching her.

The look in his eyes made her shiver. Or perhaps it was remembered delight. She'd never experienced that incandescent burst of joy, that absolute sense of oneness with another person in her life. Arik had been all her fantasies rolled into one—strong, passionate and indescribably gentle. She felt as if she'd unwittingly given up part of herself to him through the act of making love. At the time it had seemed right—more than that, it had seemed perfect. Now the idea created a niggle of unease deep inside her.

She was in danger of getting in too deep. It was one thing to think in terms of a holiday fling with a gorgeous man: a safe way to experience passion and then move on, back to her ordinary life, her curiosity satisfied.

But this was something else altogether. It was as if an unseen link stretched between them. Even now she felt it tightening, tugging at her as he strode over to the bed.

She looked up into his black eyes and knew it was an unwinnable battle, trying to remain unmoved by him. He was in her blood, in her very bones. Somehow she'd absorbed him into herself. She had an overwhelming fear that now she'd never be the same again. Never be whole without him.

'Your daughter is well?' He smiled down at her and the melting rush of desire in the pit of her stomach commenced again.

'She's having a ball.' Rosalie ignored the breathless quality of her voice, swallowing hard at the excitement humming through her, just being close to him again. 'She's with her aunt and uncle and my mother. I suspect she's being spoiled rotten.'

Arik's grin was a flash of white in his dark face. 'That's as it should be. Every child deserves to be spoiled a little by their family. And it will take her mind off being away from you.'

Rosalie tilted her head, registering his words. Most men she knew wouldn't consider it from that angle. They weren't so sympathetic to the needs of others, would barely give a thought to what a little child needed.

But then, she'd never met a man like Arik before. So utterly, devastatingly male but compassionate too.

'You speak as if you've got some insight into it,' she said, suddenly curious to know more about him. In so many ways she knew him intimately: his character, his passion, his body. But she knew next to nothing about his life.

He shrugged. 'I'm an only child but I have a large, loving extended family. My childhood was spent learning discipline and responsibility from my father, and being indulged by almost everyone else. We Q'aroumis are especially fond of children, you know.'

'And your mother?'

'Ah, my mother is a woman of strong passions.' His dark eyes flashed. 'It was she who taught me to follow my heart. She believes that you can achieve whatever you set your heart on, so long as you never give up.'

Arik leaned close, his intense expression making her feel suddenly vulnerable. Something akin to apprehension skittered through her as she looked up, up at him. The stark planes and angles of his face were more pronounced in the late afternoon light, emphasising his strength and the slightly exotic cast of his features.

He's a stranger, whispered a voice in her head. *A man you barely know, and yet you let him—*

No! She knew Arik in the ways that counted. Knew his integrity, his caring. She knew exactly where she stood with him. They'd made a bargain. She was perfectly safe.

And yet…when he stared at her like that it made her wonder.

'Come.' He stepped forward and slid his hands beneath her, hauling her up into his arms. Automatically she clung to him, her hands linking round his neck. Her heart thudded to a quickening beat, just being in contact with him again. She revelled in the now familiar heat of his body against hers.

'Where are we going?'

His black gaze held hers in a look that made the blood rush to her face and anticipation sizzle in the pit of her stomach.

'Enough talking for now, Rosalie.' He shouldered his way through the open door and into the enormous bathroom.

Her eyes widened as she took in the octagonal room. On four sides huge windows gave out on to the spectacular cliff top view. And in the centre, right below the domed gilt ceiling, was the largest bath she'd ever seen. It was sunk into the floor, half filled with steamy water and bubbles. Sandalwood scented the air and something else—some fragrance that was heavy and lush.

Her racing heartbeat slowed to a lazy expectant beat. Then he was putting her down, letting her slide, inch by tantalising inch, down his body. Like her he was naked beneath the robe. And somehow the fact that they were both fully covered only enhanced the sensuality of the experience. The slide of hot silk against her flesh. The press of his hard body, ridged with muscle and flagrantly aroused, yet covered in the finest cotton, was even more erotic than seeing him naked.

Rosalie's mouth was dry as she found her footing. Her hands were linked around his neck. She tightened her hold, drawing his head closer while she rose on tiptoe.

'No.' He shook his head. 'Not yet.'

Her expression must have revealed her disappointment for he lifted one hand to her mouth, pressed his thumb against her bottom lip till she opened for him, and she tasted him, warm and salty on her tongue. Heat burst in the pit of her belly and down her legs, till she trembled where she stood.

'Soon,' he promised. Then, with one swift movement, he bent and gathered the silken skirts of her gown in his hands, skimming the fabric up her legs. Up and up till she felt the whisper-soft afternoon breeze on her thighs, her stomach, her breasts.

She watched the play of muscles in his upper arms as he flung the gossamer-thin robe to the floor.

Now his hands brushed against her, feathering up her legs, over her buttocks, her hips, her waist, to her breasts, heavy with the weight of desire. Moist heat pooled between her legs as she looked deep into his eyes. They were glazed with an excitement that matched her own.

Cotton bunched in her fingers. She lifted the weight of his robe, scrabbling a little as the fabric shifted. Underneath the material she felt tantalising traces of his body—the heavy weight of his muscled thigh as she bent low, the angle of his hip-bone and the ridged muscles of his abdomen. There was a hiss of breath as she shoved the robe higher, her hand sliding across his chest. Then he bent his head, allowed her to draw the garment off him and toss it away.

A weight settled on her chest, pressing down, making it hard to breathe as she skimmed his body with her gaze.

He was magnificent.

'If you look at me like that, this will be over before it's begun.'

She slanted a look up at his face. He seemed to be in pain, so great was the tension there. Had she done that to him? Her presence? Her body? It was a heady thought.

'Get in the bath, Rosalie, and I'll join you in a moment.' His voice was soft, a whisper. But he'd lost his smooth tones. Now his words were rough, as if something grated deep inside him. The sound was a primal message of barely restrained hunger that fed her excitement.

Quickly she turned and stepped into the deep bath, luxuriating in the feel of warm water sliding against her bare skin. In the knowledge that Arik would be with her soon.

He almost groaned aloud as he watched her descend into the foam. That peach-ripe *derrière*, the long, long legs, the indentation of her waist, so small he could almost span it with his hands. He fumbled, rolling on the condom. His whole body was shaking, throbbing with the force of his desire.

She turned, her eyes wide as she watched him lower himself into the bath, reminding him that, for all her enthusiasm and her natural sensuality, Rosalie was a woman of little experience.

The shock on her face as they'd become one, the wonder in her expression as she'd scaled the heights of passion, the hesitant way she'd embraced him at first…it had almost been like making love to a virgin.

The experience had been new to him. Far too quickly he'd become hooked by the thrill of surprising her, of teaching her about her body's own sweet secrets. And when she'd reciprocated, caressing him, moving with him, it had been as if together they'd ignited dynamite. The explosive force of their joint climax had deserved a Richter scale warning.

He was a man who enjoyed women. Enjoyed sex. He was a man of some experience. But nothing, ever, had matched the sheer ecstasy of making love to Rosalie Winters.

He'd wanted her again almost immediately. Even now he couldn't say how he'd managed to tear himself away long enough for her to recover and to phone home.

It would be the challenge of a lifetime to take this slow. She was temptation personified. She looked at him with those huge green eyes, her lips pouted and pink, her nipples teasing him, just peeping up through the bubbles when she moved. Involuntarily he throbbed in response, just at the sight of her.

He turned and wrenched off the taps, wishing he could

turn off his libido, or at least slow it down long enough to wrest control.

'Come here, Rosalie.' He lifted a hand in invitation and immediately she slid along the seat that edged the deep bath. Her hand rested in his and he drew her closer. He felt her hip beside his and immediately turned to claim her, one hand at her neck, as he slanted his mouth over hers, the other wrapping round her waist.

She was unique. He'd only known the taste of her for a few days and yet he craved it more than food or drink. She tilted her head back, allowing him better access to her mouth, and he took it, delving deeply, possessively, as he pressed her slippery form against his. He thrust a thigh between hers and felt the little jitter of reaction race through her body.

He smiled against her mouth. She was so ready.

When he cupped her breast in his palm she pushed against his hand, a sound like a hungry purr rolling deep in her throat. She slid against him, her hips circling, and he let his weight rest against her.

If he wanted he could take her now. With one swift movement he could possess her. Fierce heat pumped in his bloodstream at the thought of taking her hard and fast right now. Completion would be only seconds away.

But he held back. He wanted to give her more than a quick, hard coupling. And to do that he needed to hold out against the barbaric impulse to ravish. Somehow he had to find finesse. He needed to forget his own needs and—

Lightning struck to his heart as her small hand closed round him. He shuddered, surging forward into her intimate caress, unable to temper his hungry response. His tongue probed her mouth as he pushed against her hand, exulting in the sensation even as he recognised it wasn't enough.

'Don't!' The word was a low growl as he gripped her shoulders and leaned back. 'Don't touch me.'

'You don't like it?' There was no teasing lilt to her voice and her eyes were serious. Something hard knotted tight in his chest at the sight of her doubt, the way she bit down on her lush bottom lip as if afraid she'd done the wrong thing.

She genuinely didn't know what she did to him!

Breathing raggedly, Arik cupped her chin in his palm and felt her racing pulse flutter beneath her chin. He looked deep into her eyes, drawn by her honesty, registering her confusion.

'I love the feel of your hand on me, Rosalie. Too much.'

Her mouth opened in a delicious pout of surprise and Arik cursed the need for restraint. He dragged in an unsteady breath as desire warred with caution. 'That's the problem. That's why you have to stop.'

Instantly her hold on him tightened and another searing jolt of heat surged through him. He thrust against her, helpless to resist.

He drew in deep, scouring lungfuls of air and sought for strength. Strength to resist her.

His hand trembled as he gripped her wrist and drew her hand away, sliding his fingers through hers and holding her hand between them. With his other hand he reached down to cup her breast, squeezing gently till she sighed her pleasure. She moved restlessly against him, her body responding sinuously to his caresses. He took her mouth again and arrowed his hand down to the tender place between her thighs, exploring, probing, till she gasped and bucked into his touch.

'No!' She writhed against him, tore her hand from his grip. She planted her hands on his chest, pushing hard. 'No, Arik. Please.'

He looked down into her flushed face and knew a great tenderness for this remarkable woman. Whatever she wanted he'd give her.

'It's you I need,' she gasped. 'Please.'

How could he resist such an appeal? She shook against

him, her soft body against his iron-hard frame an invitation to pleasure. The knowledge of her desire was the strongest seduction of all.

With one sure movement he settled back on the tiled seat and swung her up till she straddled him, kneeling on the wide underwater bench. Next time, he promised himself. Next time he'd take it more slowly, tease her and tempt her and draw out each pleasure with infinite patience till she swooned with delight. Next time he'd be strong.

'Come down,' he whispered, his voice hoarse and unsteady as he cupped her breasts and leaned forward to draw her nipple into his mouth. The hiss of her indrawn breath was sweet, almost as sweet as the sensation of her velvety heat teasing his erection.

He sucked harder, tightening his hold, hearing her gasp. And then slowly, so incredibly slowly, she shifted, bearing down, allowing him the entry he craved.

It was death by degrees, ecstasy in such slow motion it must surely kill him. He slid his hands down to her waist, clamping hard and drawing her down lower, further till at last they were one.

Paradise.

He looked into her eyes and was lost. How could any woman be both seductress and innocent? She had the body, the erotic instincts of a wanton and yet she seemed so untutored, almost amazed at the sensations she aroused. He wanted to ravish her and yet protect her. Take her with the full force of the merciless need she awoke in him, and at the same time cherish her with gentle words and soothing caresses.

Then she moved, tilted her hips experimentally, and cogent thought fled. Arik let his hands slide down to the swell of her hips as he pushed up against her. Saw her eyes widen as a wave of pleasure hit them both.

'Arik? I…'

Her voice dwindled as the ripples of pleasure began deep

inside her. So soon, so strong that they tugged at him, loosening his control, making his hands slip as he moved against her, instinctively adopting the rhythm that they both needed. She moved with him and there was magic in their tempo, in the hungry slide of flesh into flesh, in the matched drum beat of their hearts pounding as one.

He'd never seen anything more magnificent than the blaze of ecstasy in her jade-bright eyes.

Completion came upon them hard and fast, obliterating everything in a rush of ecstasy so brilliant, so fantastic, that it should be impossible. It was endless, like the sound of her soft mews of excitement, like the roaring locomotive rush of blood in his ears, like his desire for her—building and never diminishing.

When at last it was over she slumped, boneless, against him, his arms wrapped possessively around her. His body was weak in the aftermath of a force stronger than anything he'd known and only one thought circled in his numbed brain. *Next time*. Next time he'd take it slowly. Next time he wouldn't give in to pleasure so fast. Next time he'd love her as she deserved to be loved...

Dawn light cast an amber-pink glow across the room, the wide bed, the man lying beside her, one arm stretched out to curve round her waist, holding her close, even in sleep.

All through the evening and the long night she and Arik had been together: touching, caressing. Even when she slept she'd merely dozed in his arms and had woken to find him alert and watching her, the heat of his gaze immediately firing her blood. She'd been wanton, eager and ready for his loving, an ever-willing pupil as he'd taught her about physical desire, and about herself.

She'd revelled in his tempered strength, his tenderness and patience.

She stared into his beautiful face, traced the planes of his jaw, the high angles of his cheekbones, the strong shape of his nose, the sensual line of his lips. Something tumbled over in her stomach as she remembered those lips on her body, exquisitely sensitive, roughly demanding, making her want things, do things, she'd never before dreamed of.

Her gaze drifted to the wide spread of his shoulders, his deep chest, where she'd nuzzled, feeling safe as never before in his strong embrace.

Again that sensation of heat churned deep inside her. But this time it didn't presage sexual desire, the urgent need for completion that Arik had taught her so much about. This was deeper, more disturbing.

Rosalie swallowed down hard on the constriction in her throat as she summoned the strength to face reality after a night so wonderful it rivalled fantasy.

She'd always known she wasn't the type to enjoy a casual affair. That had never been her style. And the traumatic events over three years ago had only increased her caution.

Yet she'd succumbed to Arik's seduction with barely a protest. She couldn't claim she'd been swept away in the heat of the moment. No, despite the force of her suddenly awakened physical longings, she'd made a conscious decision to accept what Arik offered. She'd wanted him, wanted the simmering passion that flared between them every time they were close. She'd wanted to satisfy her curiosity, learn about desire and sex and passion. She'd told herself that with Arik she was safe. He wouldn't take more than she wanted to give. He would treat her well.

And when it was over she could walk away, back to her real life, secure in the knowledge that it had been only a holiday affair, a moment's snatched pleasure in a life focused on rebuilding her future and raising her daughter. Nothing would change.

But it had.

She'd deceived herself.

Rosalie squeezed her eyes shut, breathing deep as she sought for strength. The warm, musky scent of his skin teased her, the evocative scent of sex. She opened her eyes to his face, relaxed in sleep yet so strong and now so dear. She'd been deliberately blind to the consequences as she'd given herself to him. Blind to the warning signals, ignoring danger with a single-minded determination to live for the moment.

Now she had to pay the price.

The circling sensation in her stomach turned to a twist of pain as she stared at him, memorising his unique features.

She wanted to lift her hand and stroke his face, feel the stubble darkening his jaw, tease his mouth with her own, nestle against the hard, warm wall of his chest where the fuzz of black hair would tease her breasts into tingling expectation of his loving.

But she daredn't. She understood her weakness now. That was one thing Arik had taught her well. She knew that once he took her in his arms she'd be lost. She'd succumb to the magic of his body against hers, the craving for him that even now was unabated. She'd never get away, not until he was ready to call a halt.

And by that time she'd be even deeper in his thrall. It didn't bear thinking about.

The truth was that Arik was far more to her than a casual partner. There was nothing casual about what she felt for him. There never had been. Instinctively she'd known it but she'd shunned the truth, hiding behind the facile argument that it was a short-term romance, easily ended.

Heat prickled at the back of her eyes as she looked for the last time at his face, imprinting it on her memory.

Better to go now. End this affair before he realised how she felt. She didn't think she could face his pity.

After all, their time was up, wasn't it? She'd finished her artwork yesterday. Had it only been then? Vaguely she remembered the sense of satisfaction, of pleasure at her achievement. Technically her agreement with Arik was over.

Did she have the strength to fight her own desperate longing and do what must be done?

CHAPTER NINE

'NO, SIR. I've double-checked. We've had no Rosalie Winters staying with us. No Australians at all in the last month.'

'All right, thank you for checking.' Arik severed the connection and drew in a deep breath.

Think, man. She wasn't at either of the beachfront hotels or the smaller guest houses. But she couldn't have vanished into thin air. Where could she have been staying?

His fist clenched more tightly on the crumpled paper. The rustling sound fuelled his anger.

What had she thought she was doing, leaving him such a note? Stilted phrases swirled in his head, indelibly printed there.

It's been wonderful…

Better if we didn't see each other again…

And finally, devastatingly: *Thank you.*

Thank you! As if he'd done her some small courtesy, a trifling favour that required acknowledgement.

His pulse throbbed furiously and his jaw gritted more tightly at the audacity of the woman's actions.

As if he was some casual acquaintance to be fobbed off with polite thanks! Or, worse, as if he'd served his purpose and could now be dismissed, left behind like some cheap souvenir she'd decided not to buy.

As if they hadn't been lovers. Lovers in a way he'd never

124 FOR THE SHEIKH'S PLEASURE

been with any other woman. Each moment with her had been so intense, so addictively exciting. He'd even learned to enjoy her abstracted silence as she'd focused on her painting rather than him. He'd delighted in her pleasure, had been moved by her appreciation of his country and enjoyed her quick wit almost as much as he'd adored her body.

They'd shared the best sex he'd ever experienced and he refused to be cheated of more.

How dared she leave him like that? No explanation. No possible reason to run from him like a thief in the night.

That was what she'd done—scurried away when he'd finally fallen asleep, as if she couldn't bring herself to face him. As if she were *ashamed* of the pleasure they'd found together, of the intimacy that had stunned him with its rare potency.

It was for him to feel shame that he'd let their liaison mean so much. He'd allowed Rosalie Winters to get under his skin in a way no woman ever had. With her apparent innocence, her sweet seductiveness, she'd been stringing him along all the time, using *him* and then running away. No doubt she was eager to share the story of her holiday romance with her friends.

Arik frowned. No, despite his fury, he couldn't believe that of her. She was no manipulator.

But then, what had gone wrong? Why her sudden flight?

He spun on his foot and strode out on to the balcony, staring down for the hundredth time at the beach below, unmarked by footprints since the last high tide. No sign of her familiar figure returning around the point.

Something hard and tight jammed up high in his ribs. A pain, an ache. A rough, burning sensation that made him want to reach out and strike something.

He would not allow it. Of course their relationship had to end at some point. He'd always known it.

But not yet.

Not now.

Not till he was ready.

An afternoon and a night with Rosalie in his arms had merely whetted his appetite for her, not sated it. Whatever bizarre notion she had about leaving, he'd persuade her out of it. Even if it meant postponing his return to work for a week or two—for long enough to have his fill of her.

He punched out the number for the local airport on his cellphone, then leaned on the parapet while he spoke to one of the administrators.

Within a few minutes he'd confirmed that Rosalie had taken a flight to the Q'aroumi capital within the last hour. She must have broken the land speed record to get there in time.

There were no more flights to the main island today but that was no problem; he could use his helicopter. And, besides, he knew there were no connecting international flights to Australia for a couple of days. Plenty of time to locate her and persuade her to return. It even fitted his schedule. He was due in the capital himself tomorrow afternoon for an official engagement.

Arik's mouth curved in a tight smile. When he found Rosalie Winters she'd soon beg for his lovemaking. He'd make sure of that. No more holding back. The time for caution had passed. Rosalie would feel the full, unfettered force of his passion. It would be a simple thing to convince her she'd made a mistake. After all, she was so satisfyingly eager for his touch.

He'd take his pleasure with her till the bright, flaming need burned itself out, as it inevitably would.

Then, only then, would he agree to end their affair.

He swung round and paced back into his room. First he'd find out which hotel she'd booked into and then he'd visit his errant lover.

His lips curved into a slow smile. He looked forward to persuading her to stay.

* * *

A day later Arik stared across the myriad of people filling the audience chamber in Q'aroum's royal palace. He felt as if an enormous unseen weight had slammed straight into his solar plexus. The air slid out of his lungs in a whoosh of shock. He could barely believe his eyes.

No wonder he'd found no trace of Rosalie at any of the hotels. Nor at the guest houses or private *pensions* that flourished in the city.

He hadn't understood how she'd vanished without a trace. Until now. Until he'd looked across the massive room to the royal family.

There were his cousin Rafiq and his cousin's wife, Belle, holding their son, Adham. The first birthday of the heir to Q'aroum's throne was the reason for this royal reception. Behind Rafiq and Belle stood an older woman in western dress who could only be Belle's mother. The family resemblance between the two women was strong. Even with her greying hair she was handsome, her face full of character.

And by her side, partly hidden from view, was another younger woman. The trousers and long-sleeved tunic she wore covered her figure but couldn't conceal it. Not when the jade silk skimmed voluptuous breasts, revealed a neat waist as she turned to talk to the man beside her. Not when Arik already knew every centimetre of that siren's body. Not when the feel of it, the scent of it, the taste of it, were imprinted on his brain.

Rosalie.

Her name echoed in his stunned brain as he viewed the scene.

There was no mistake. She had to be Belle's sister. Just look at the shape of those eyes, that mouth, that neat determined chin. Mirror images they weren't, but there was enough similarity to put the connection beyond doubt.

His lover was Rafiq's sister-in-law.

Arik sucked in a breath that shuddered through his oxygen-starved chest as he absorbed the implications.

She was related to royalty. More than that—she was, by marriage, a member of his own extended family. Rafiq, though by blood no closer than a second cousin, was like a brother to him. They'd grown up together, shared a bond that had strengthened as they'd weathered the early loss of parents: Rafiq's parents in a 'copter smash and Arik's father from sudden illness.

If he'd known who Rosalie was from the start he'd have put all thought of an affair from his mind. Not because he'd have wanted to, but because he would have had no choice. He was bound by familial ties, by custom, by the merest common courtesy, much less the respect he felt for Rafiq, not to seduce her into his bed.

Her connections made her eminently unsuitable for a short-term sexual liaison, no matter how willing she was.

Pain twisted deep in his chest as he remembered to breathe again. He dragged in more air.

There was no going back. What was done was done. His body already knew hers, knew and craved its sweet softness. And yet any chance of resuming their liaison had just been destroyed by the knowledge of her true identity.

Arik clenched his fists at his sides, feeling the burning need, the ravening hunger, still hot in his blood. He could have howled his frustration aloud, staring across the room at the woman who unquestionably he couldn't have.

By any calculation she was out of bounds.

The light caught her bright blonde hair as she tipped her face up and smiled at something Rafiq said. Instantly, unreasonably, Arik's blood boiled, searing his veins with futile jealousy. That she should share that smile, even that minor intimacy, with any man other than himself, fed his frustration.

He wanted her. More—he *craved* her. Even now, just

watching her across the thronged room, his body hummed its need, his groin tightening in sexual anticipation of the woman he'd already claimed as his own.

He hadn't rested since she'd left his bed. Instead he'd been haunted by the memory of her seductive body, her bright eyes, her gentle laugh and her sharp mind.

And now to discover she was untouchable…

It was more than flesh and blood could bear.

Was that why she'd kept her identity a secret? To string him along?

He shook his head, trying to clear it. No, Rosalie wasn't that calculating. Whatever the reason for her reticence, he was sure it wasn't that.

Across the room the crowd shifted, revealing another golden head in the group. The fluffy curls belonged to a little girl with the face of an angel and her mother's wide smile. Amy.

Arik stared, conscious of a queer hollow sensation in his chest as he watched Rosalie bend down to talk to her daughter. Something squeezed hard inside him as he watched the pair. The love between them was obvious, bright as day.

Suddenly, unbelievably, he felt an arrow of piercing discomfort, watching the intimacy between them. He breathed deep, deliberately unclenching his tight fists and spreading his fingers. He couldn't be jealous of her relationship with her daughter. That would be bizarre.

And yet…strong emotion gripped him tight around the heart as he watched the two of them and knew he was forever denied the intimacy he wanted with this woman. The intimacy he'd only just discovered and now yearned for with an intensity that threatened to unman him.

'Her name's Rosalie,' a female voice said beside him.

Startled, Arik swung round, silently cursing the possibility that his thoughts had been revealed on his face as he'd stood brooding.

But the woman hadn't spoken to him. She'd addressed her comment to another middle aged woman with a tight, sour face. The pair stood a little to his right, their heads bent together as they surveyed the crowd.

'Pretty enough, like her sister,' responded the other woman. 'But pretty is as pretty does, I always say. And there's more to that one than meets the eye.'

'Really?' The first woman lowered her voice. 'What have you heard?'

Arik held his breath. He'd been so discreet, at least in public, that no one should guess his private interest in Rosalie. And his staff were utterly loyal and discreet. They wouldn't have spread gossip about her. But had something leaked out? Something that might hurt her?

'Well, you see her little daughter? She doesn't have a father. He's not dead and there was no divorce. In fact—' the woman tilted her head closer to her friend '—I've heard that she refuses to name the father. If you ask me, that's just an excuse. She probably *can't* name the father. You know how young women are these days.'

'Unfortunately there don't seem to be enough fine, upstanding older women to provide an example to them.' The words were out of Arik's mouth even as he turned to confront the speaker.

He watched two pairs of eyes grow round, two mouths gape as the women looked up at him. Some savage inner self wished they were men, young and fit, so he could find a physical outlet for the blood-red rage that marred his vision and pumped in his arteries. It would take only the slightest provocation to tempt him to violence.

Slowly he drew breath, tempered his aggressive response.

'Surely it's Q'aroumi custom to be hospitable to newcomers?' he asked, arching a brow. 'It's a sad state of affairs when a stranger is subjected to malicious gossip by those who should know better. I wonder how our host would react if he heard such rumours spread under his own roof?'

Their reaction would have been comical if their offence weren't so great. He heard their apologies, their excuses, watched the embarrassment and chagrin on their faces as they scuttled away. But he felt no satisfaction.

Instead he wanted to take something in his bare hands and break it. Smash it. Pulverise it.

He raged at this impossible situation. He wanted Rosalie. He wanted her in his bed again but now he recognised he needed so much more. Above all he wanted to protect her, even from the harm he might do to her reputation among the more strait-laced of his people.

He set his jaw and swung round to face the royal party. His eyes narrowed.

It was time he paid his respects to his hosts.

Rosalie was talking to Amy when she heard him.

For a moment she thought she imagined it. The low liquid sound of his voice that brushed across her skin and sent a quiver of longing through her. It had to be a hallucination, a trick of her subconscious, to think Arik was here.

She bit down hard on her lip, summoning the resolve she'd tested to the limits in the last thirty-six hours.

Was it that long since she'd left him? The dull, persistent ache deep in her chest told her it was all that and more.

Then she heard him again. *Arik!*

She swung round, hampered by her crouching position, and almost collapsed in a heap.

It was him. Here. Only a couple of metres away.

He stood talking to Rafiq and Belle and, from the sound of it, they were old friends. Why hadn't she thought of that? As leader of his tribe, he was an important figure in Q'aroum. He was probably on the central government council that Rafiq had mentioned. And the way Arik and her brother-in-law were greeting each other, it was clear their relationship was more than one of formal protocol. There was genuine affection in their voices.

Rosalie's head spun as she tried to think through the implications. Had he seen her? Did he know who she was? And how was she going to face him again and pretend polite interest when the mere sound of his voice smashed straight through her defences? Already the warm liquid spill of desire swirled low in her body in eager anticipation of his touch.

Helplessly she stared at him. From this level she had an excellent view of his long, soft leather boots, hand-stitched and supple. Loose trousers in pristine white that just hinted at the strength of those powerful thighs beneath. A wide sash embroidered in reds and gold in place of a belt and, in it, the jewelled sheath and haft of a ceremonial knife. Shirt of finest linen, high-necked and adorned with the tiniest hint of gold stitching. A long pale cloak, flung back over his shoulders. A head scarf of purest white, bound in gold, that only served to emphasise the magnificent bronze of his strong neck and aristocratic face.

It was Arik, but Arik as she'd never seen him. Arik the sheikh, the nobleman. The stranger.

Realising her vulnerable position down on the floor, Rosalie stumbled to her feet, pulling Amy into her arms.

Her heart thudded out of control as, for an instant, she contemplated fleeing the room. Escaping before he saw her. But that was impossible. Already Belle was introducing him to their mother. Any minute now…

'And this is my sister, Rosalie. And her daughter, Amy.'

Eyes dark as the velvet night sky pinioned her. They blazed with an inner fire that somehow leapt across the intervening space and into her bloodstream. Heat scorched through her body, the familiar burn of desire.

But it wasn't just physical wanting that she read in his expression. She'd seen that and welcomed it before. This was something else. Something even stronger. More dangerous.

'Rosalie?' There was concern in Belle's voice but Rosalie couldn't drag her gaze away from the man who stared down at her with such intensity.

She'd opened her mouth, searching for the non-committal, polite words suitable for the occasion, when Arik spoke.

'Hello, Rosalie.' Just that. But in such a tone, his voice laced with dark honey, that there could be no doubt in anyone's mind that they'd met before.

In her peripheral vision Rosalie saw Belle shift suddenly. Beside her Rafiq stood, unmoving, watching.

And all the while Rosalie sought her voice, spellbound as much by the sight and sound of her lover as by the need that pulsed even now deep inside her.

'I didn't expect to see you here.' Was that anger in Arik's voice? She'd focused so much on her own need for flight that she'd barely considered how angry he might be at her sudden departure.

If she'd been stronger she'd have stayed and told him of her decision to leave. No doubt then he'd have shrugged and accepted her decision. After all, he was only interested in a short-term fling. It must be pique at her sudden departure that made his jaw clench so tight, his nostrils flare.

'Hello, Arik.' Her voice sounded rusty. She swallowed hard and took refuge from his searing eyes by turning to her daughter. Her arms tightened protectively around her.

'Amy, this is Arik.'

Her daughter's eyes were wide as she looked up into the dark face above them. For a long moment she considered him and then her face split into a wide sunny grin.

'Hello.'

'Hello, Amy. It's nice to meet you. I've heard lots about you.'

Rosalie turned back to see him smiling at her daughter. Gone from his expression was the heat, the hardness. He looked almost…gentle.

Something shifted inside her as she stared up at the man who meant so much to her, watching him bestow his winning smile on her little girl.

For a single insane instant Rosalie found herself wishing things were different…wishing for the impossible.

'You know each other?' Belle stepped forward and Rosalie saw the curiosity on her sister's face. That expression told her she wasn't going to escape without a detailed explanation. She'd better have her story ready for when they were in private.

'Yes.' Rosalie cleared her throat. 'We met on the beach one morning just before Mum and Amy flew over here to join you.'

'Just a single meeting?' Was that disappointment in her sister's voice or disbelief?

Rosalie slanted a look up at Arik but there was no help to be had there. His lips were closed in a firm line.

'No. More than that. I spent a couple of mornings painting a beach scene and Arik helped me. I mean—'

'Rosalie saw my horses swimming and wanted one in the scene she was painting. It was my pleasure to agree.'

'So you had Ahmed bring the horses down for Rosalie to paint?' Rafiq spoke for the first time, his voice cool.

Arik looked down into her face, his expression bland, his eyes blazing, and Rosalie wondered that she didn't catch fire from the heat he radiated. Could no one else see that incendiary spark in his gaze?

'No.' He shook his head slowly. 'I was at a loose end, unable to return to my normal routine. I took the horses to the beach myself for Rosalie to paint.'

He turned abruptly to meet Rafiq's gaze. There was a challenge in his expression and in the taut line of his jaw. He didn't move but suddenly Arik looked bigger, broader, the set of his shoulders almost confrontational.

Something passed between the two men in that silent moment. As if they held a wordless communication shared by no one else.

Then Arik's features relaxed and Rafiq smiled. He clapped a hand to Arik's shoulder. 'You're so proud of those horses of yours. Anyone would think they rivalled the ones in my own stable.'

'It's a good thing for you, cousin, that I have the good manners not to argue with my host. I will merely observe that it's clearly too long since you rode one of my horses.'

'Cousin?' Rosalie breathed out the word.

'Rafiq and Arik are related,' Belle answered, still watching her closely. 'I forget the specific details but they're family, as you can see.'

Rafiq was already suggesting a horse race to settle the issue of which were the better horses. But his smile was wide and his expression easy as he bantered with Arik.

'Yes. I see,' Rosalie whispered.

This situation was impossible. Bad enough to be pining for a man she couldn't have. To realise she'd made the biggest mistake of her life in succumbing to the charm of the one man who embodied all her secret fantasies. But to be forced to face him in the intimacy of her over-protective family circle, where everyone was obsessed with her welfare… It was unthinkable.

She breathed deep against the sudden sensation of the walls closing in around her. Trapping her. The conversation morphed into a low background buzz and a chill nibbled at her spine.

She hadn't felt this sudden sense of unreasoning panic in so long. Had hoped it was a thing of the past, like the worst of the nightmares.

'Rosalie. Are you all right?'

Arik's voice broke across her consciousness, shattering

her sense of isolation. Gratefully she looked up at him. His intent, encouraging look warmed her from the inside out. Her heart thudded painfully and life pulsed back into her chest. Automatically she shifted Amy up higher on her hip.

'Yes. I'm okay.'

'But you've been running around after Amy since dawn,' her mother said from beside her. 'It's time you had a rest.' She reached out her arms. 'Here, Amy, come and spend some time with Grandma.'

Reluctantly Rosalie let her daughter go. Without Amy held close in her arms she felt vulnerable, far too exposed to Arik's attention.

But she needn't have worried. Seconds later she was surrounded by animated discussions. Arik and her brother-in-law amicably disputed the rival claims of their stables. Her mother and Belle checked on little Adham, the birthday boy, fast asleep in an ornate gilded cot. They debated how long before he woke and whether Belle could slip him away for a quiet feed. Amy suggested they offer him ice cream and peaches, her current favourite foods.

Rosalie listened to their voices and the amorphous noise rising from the wider crowd and longed to be alone with her thoughts.

She lasted through another hour of introductions and light chat, of official speeches in honour of Adham and of watching Amy while she played with some new found friends. Then, finally, Rosalie noticed people beginning to say their goodbyes. She could leave now without feeling she was breaking up the special occasion.

With a murmured word to her mother, she led Amy away and down the labyrinthine passages of the old palace. Her daughter was almost out on her feet with excitement and lack of her usual daytime nap, so getting her ready for bed took far less time than usual.

Soon Amy was sleeping soundly and Rosalie looked out at the darkening night sky. Strangely, she felt lonelier than she had in years, even standing here, listening to her daughter's soft breathing.

He'd done this to her. *Arik.*

He'd unsettled her, made her yearn for so much that she couldn't have, especially from him.

That sense of claustrophobia haunted her. She wanted to be outside where she could breathe deeply and banish the remains of those old haunting fears.

Five minutes later she stood on an ancient stone balcony jutting out from the citadel bastion, looking out over the sea. A glow of sunset pink rimmed the horizon as the sky darkened from azure to indigo.

Rosalie sighed her relief. She'd found this quiet spot on her first visit. Something about the view and the solitude always invigorated her, helped her to think.

What would she do if Arik decided to stay and spend time with his cousin? She wasn't due to leave Q'aroum for several weeks and she'd arouse suspicion and worry her family if she left early. Yet she didn't think she could manage to treat him as a polite, amiable acquaintance. Not while her body and her soul burned for so much more.

But what alternative did she have?

She was leaning out over the parapet, her hands planted on the stonework, when something made her stiffen.

The sound of the massive old door dragging shut behind her.

'Hello, Rosalie,' said the low, sultry voice that haunted her dreams. 'I thought I might find you here.'

CHAPTER TEN

ROSALIE spun round to face him and he realised with despair that she looked more gorgeous than ever. Her tunic top was wrinkled on one side where Amy had clung and her hair was rumpled, as if tiny fingers had played with those rose-gold strands. Her eyes were huge, her lips parted.

Arik liked her this way—slightly mussed. As if she'd come straight from his bed. Or was just going there.

Muscles spasmed tight in his belly and groin at the thought. The inevitability of his reaction only fuelled his anger. He crossed his arms over his chest and waited. He was looking forward to hearing her explanation.

'I wasn't expecting to see you here.' Her voice was light and breathless, as it had been back in the audience chamber. No wonder her family had watched them closely. She'd sounded so obviously like a woman hiding secrets.

'Weren't you?' He stared down at her. 'You expected me to remain at home, satisfied with that farcical note you left me?' Fury bubbled up inside him as he remembered the trite little missive. She hadn't even thought him worthy of a face-to-face explanation!

She shook her head. 'I didn't know you were coming to the reception.'

'If you'd been honest with me, Rosalie, I'd have told you

my plans. I had no idea you were part of Rafiq's family or that you'd be here yourself.'

'I *was* honest with you!' Her hands clasped together yet her chin tilted up provocatively. 'I never lied.'

Slowly he shook his head, pacing forward and finding raw satisfaction in the way she shifted, half stumbling back against the balustrade.

'You lied by omission, Rosalie. And you know it.' He scowled down into her face, challenging her to disagree. 'You must know we'd never have become lovers if I'd known who you were. Is that why you kept the truth from me?'

Her gaze slid from his and she half turned towards the sea. 'Of course not. I didn't plan to have an affair with you. That was *your* idea.'

'So why didn't you explain who you are? Why hide the truth unless you had an ulterior motive?'

He stepped closer, near enough to inhale her soft, enticing scent on the salty evening air. His nostrils flared and his chest rose as he breathed deep. Only yesterday he wouldn't have hesitated to reach out and pull her to him, nuzzle the pressure point at the base of her neck, taste her sweetness on his tongue as his hands divested her of those exquisite, unnecessary clothes.

Such a difference a day made!

Now he resisted her because she was forbidden to him. Yet his body thrummed with desire so potent, so keen that it was torture standing so damnably close to the paradise he knew he could find in her arms.

'I just wanted to be…me, I suppose. I didn't want the fuss that goes with being linked to royalty. It's important for me to be independent.' She shrugged and her hands spread before her as if pleading for understanding. 'Anyway, I don't see that it matters. It wasn't important.'

'*Not important!*' His voice was a barely muted roar as he recalled the shaft of searing pain that had speared through him, transfixing him as he'd walked into the audience chamber and recognised her. The shock of recognition and thwarted desire had paralysed him in mid-stride.

How could she claim her true identity wasn't important when it was all that kept him from scooping her up into his arms and ravishing her right here, right now, against the sun-warmed stones?

Had she no conception of the intensity of his hunger for her?

She couldn't be that naïve. Not after what they'd shared. She had to know how he burned for her even now.

At last her eyes rose to his. In the fast-gathering gloom they looked sombre.

'You didn't need to know all about me,' she countered, her voice tight and bitter. 'You wanted me in your bed, that's all. You don't need to know every intimate detail about someone for that. And that's all there was between us, Arik. Sex. A casual affair—no strings attached. That's all there could ever be.'

Seconds ticked by as he exhaled. There was a rushing roar in his ears as his blood pumped faster. His fingers bit into his arms through the layers of his clothing as he fought the impulse to snatch her close and shake her till she recanted.

He breathed in so deeply that his chest ached.

He frowned, stunned to register such outrage at her words. Surely she was right. Sex was all he'd had on his mind at first. But now...

Now it wasn't enough.

His frown tilted into a scowl at his confused thoughts. It should be simple. Hers was the sort of logic he'd used time and again himself over the years. And yet somehow, *now*, it was flawed.

'You have a very low opinion of me, of men, if you think there's no more to us than the need for a quick lay. Didn't our time together tell you anything about me? Don't you know there's more to me than my libido?' His voice was clipped, staccato with rage.

After all the patience, the tenderness he'd shown with her, he was sullied by her accusation.

If she'd been right then he'd have seduced her that first day, as he knew he could have, ignoring her protestations and her caution, using his body and her weakness for it, to get what he wanted. It would have been fast and furious and fantastic. But not as mind-numbing as the exquisite lovemaking they'd eventually shared.

He stalked to the balustrade and gripped the stonework so hard that it bit into his palms. He was furious with her for the implied insult. And with himself for the knowledge that she'd been all too correct in her reading of his original motives. He *had* wanted nothing more than her sensuous, delightful body against his.

He lashed out furiously, remembering the malicious gossip he'd heard at the reception. 'Or is it *you* who can't bear the thought of sharing with a man? Of trusting one? Is that it, Rosalie? Are you scared of what might happen if you open yourself?' He turned and fixed her with a glare. 'Is that what happened to Amy's father? Did you tell *him* it was only about physical need?'

Her raw gasp was loud in the throbbing silence. Her eyes were glazed with shock as she stared up at him. Instantly he regretted his words. It was his frustration speaking. He'd never felt such a flood of unrestrained wrath. She was a soft target for his anger, but he knew he should direct his fury at himself.

She slumped against the balcony rail as if her knees had given way and Arik stepped towards her, ready to catch her close as guilt seared him. But her outstretched hand barred him. That and the anguished twist of her mouth as she sucked in another laboured breath.

'No! Don't.' She shook her head so that her unbound hair swirled round her face.

He watched as she braced herself on the stonework, her gaze fixed on the sea. Even from this angle, in the fading light, he could read the bitterness in her tight mouth.

It was the hardest thing he'd done, holding back from her when she was in such a state. Even harder than resisting her sensual allure.

'Maybe you're right,' she said at last in a voice he didn't recognise. 'Maybe it's me that's the problem. Do you think so?' She turned her head to meet his gaze and the sight of her drawn face made his gut clench.

She turned away again, fixing her eyes on the distant horizon. When she finally spoke her voice was cool, uninflected, as if all emotion had faded away. 'But you're wrong about Amy's father. It wasn't like that.'

'I know, Rosalie. I—'

'You *can't* know. You have no idea.' She paused and drew a deep, shaky breath. 'So I'll tell you. Confession is supposed to be good for the soul, isn't it?'

Part of him wanted to reach out and fold his arms about her. To tell her there was no need to share a past that was so obviously painful to her. But he kept quiet. For his baser self wanted to hear it all. Even though he couldn't have what he wanted from her again. Even though she was taboo. Even though just standing here with her tested his self-control to the limits.

'A few years ago I left home and moved to Brisbane,' she said in a voice devoid of colour. 'I'd saved enough to go to art school there. I had no scholarship but I found a part time job and a tiny flat. I had dreams of becoming an artist.'

Her voice wobbled and searing heat pierced his chest at the sound of her pain.

'I suppose I was gullible in those days. Too trusting. I took people at face value and I was so thrilled to be learning about art that I didn't have much time for anything else.' She paused so long that he thought she wouldn't go on.

'I'd never even had a boyfriend. Not a real one. You could say I was a late bloomer when it came to interest in the opposite sex.' She laughed then, the sound mirthless and grating.

Arik's hands clenched white-knuckled on the stonework as he forced himself to listen and not gather her close. There was such distress in her voice.

'And then, in my second semester in Brisbane, there was a guy.' Her breath eased out in a long sigh. 'He was…different. Even the way he looked at me was different; it made me feel…special.'

Arik cursed himself for a fool, forcing her into these memories. He didn't want to hear about her past lovers. Yet he couldn't tear himself away.

'At first he didn't seem to notice me, not properly. And then one day he asked me out. He was going to a party that night and he wanted me to go too.' She was breathing faster now, her words coming quickly.

'It was at a big two-storey house. A mansion. I'd never been inside a place like it. There were so many rooms. And people everywhere. Lots of shouting and music. People having a good time.'

Arik moved closer, concerned at the way her breath came in rough pants. At the clipped unnatural rhythm of her voice.

'Rosalie? You don't have to—'

'I had a cocktail and we stood out on the balcony, a huge group of us, talking about art and galleries and our prospects for the future. It was great…' Her voice petered out and Arik saw her close her eyes.

'It was great to start with. But then I started to feel sick. Woozy. Someone suggested the drink had been a bit too strong and I needed to lie down.' She swallowed down hard.

'I don't even remember making it off the balcony. I just remember someone supporting me, holding me. And then, nothing.'

The silence was thick between them, taut with the weight of her memories and his sudden sense of foreboding.

She opened her eyes and clasped her hands on the railing before her.

'When I woke it was morning.' Her voice wobbled so much that she had to stop. Her shoulders heaved and then she angled her chin up, staring out at the darkening sea. 'When I woke I was naked. The bed was a tangled mess and I was…bruised. I'd been raped.'

Arik heard her words ring out defiantly and felt something whack into his abdomen. A sensation of swooping distress. Of helpless rage.

For long minutes silence throbbed between them.

'Did you press charges?' he asked when he eventually found his voice.

She shook her head. 'I had no idea who was responsible. Whether it was the guy who took me there or someone else. And I felt…soiled; all I wanted to do was get home. Get away. I couldn't face the prospect of an investigation. All those people being questioned. All of them finding out.'

'It wasn't your fault, Rosalie.' The words emerged through his gritted teeth. The fire in his belly, the adrenaline in his bloodstream needed an outlet. He wished he'd been there to deal with the scum responsible. His fury was blood-hot. Violent.

Instead he turned and, with infinite gentleness, drew her into his arms. He held his breath, waiting for her to protest, to shrink away. It felt so incredibly good when she didn't. At least she trusted him to comfort her.

'I know it wasn't my fault.' Her voice was muffled against his chest and her face buried in his shirt. The heat of her breath on his body eased just a fraction of the desolate emptiness he felt. 'But I wasn't strong then. Not like now. I was scared.'

His arms tightened around her, gathering her against him. He wished he could wipe the pain from her mind. Hell! He wished he'd never opened his mouth. He'd been so ready to fling thoughtless accusations.

'And then I found out I was pregnant.' There was more pain in her breaking voice than he'd ever heard. He tucked her close under his chin and rocked her against him.

'It's all right, Rosalie.'

'It is now,' she whispered. 'At first it wasn't. At first I didn't want the baby. I thought she'd just remind me of what had happened. But then, when she was born, it was different. I love her so much. She's a part of me and I'll never let anything come between us.'

She sniffed and drew back in his arms. Reluctantly he released her as she stepped away. Cool air replaced her warmth against his chest.

His arms felt empty without her.

'Amy's all I need in my life.' She lifted her face to look at him and he could make out the shimmer of tears glazing her eyes. The sight twisted pain through his chest, clamping down on his roughly pulsing heart.

'But when you offered me…passion, I couldn't resist. I was curious. I wanted to find out for myself what it was like. I wanted to know, to have what I'd never had before.'

In all his life Arik had never felt such a heel. In the face of her trauma, her need for solace, his own physical desire was a shallow thing, his scheme to get her into his bed shamefully selfish.

He stared down at her, seeking some sign of animation in her blank face. But there was nothing. No pain, no regret, no emotion at all. The sight of that nothingness brought piercing sorrow. He felt the rusty taste of raw emotion in his throat, the salt tang of distress that he hadn't tasted since childhood with the loss of his father. His chest felt tight and full as if his heart were about to burst out of his body.

'What we shared was wonderful,' Rosalie whispered in a voice devoid of all emotion. 'Thank you, Arik. But it's time for me to get back to my *real* life. To my responsibilities and my daughter.'

Her words had the ring of finality, like metal slamming down, echoing endlessly into emptiness.

She moved away from him, slipping silently out of his reach like a ghost.

The wooden door grated on its hinges as she left.

And then there was nothing but the shushing of the waves on the shore far below and the voice of his conscience castigating him for a thoughtless, selfish brute.

CHAPTER ELEVEN

FOR the first time in years Rosalie slept late next morning, waking groggy and thick-headed to bright sunlight and the sound of birdsong.

Surprisingly, she hadn't tossed and turned, replaying memories in her mind, reliving old fears and pain. Nor had last night's confrontation with Arik kept her awake. It was as if both mind and body had finally shut down, allowing her a night's respite from the emotions that plagued her.

Instead, as she'd eased into slumber, she'd remembered the strong curve of Arik's arms around her. The solid masculine heat of his body against hers as he held her close. The steady thump of his heart beneath her cheek as she'd let herself lean into him. The comfort she'd drawn from his concern and his protective embrace.

That had been enough to dispel the old anxieties that had once stalked her nights.

She'd felt drained, exhausted and, finally, at peace.

But now, stretching in the bright morning sun, Rosalie realised that peace had been an illusion.

It was still there, nagging at her, refusing to be silenced: the truth she'd been avoiding for days.

The fact that she'd fallen in love.

Even now, just acknowledging it to herself, her heart gave a little fluttery thump.

She'd given in to temptation, had entered into an affair despite her better judgement, and look what had happened.

She was in love with Arik Ben Hassan.

A man she'd only met last week.

The man she knew intimately.

A man who was arrogant and proud and expected always to get his own way.

The man who'd been tender and gentle and who'd tempered his urgent need in the face of her fears and caution.

A man who had the sensual expertise of a true sybarite. A man whose past was littered with mistresses and filled with luxury.

The man who'd made her feel as if she were the centre of his world. As if no woman could compare with her.

A man with the wealth to enjoy life as a carefree playboy, in a world far removed from the harsh realities of her own life.

The man who worked hard, not because he needed to, but because it was his duty to support his people. And because he'd never be content to live aimlessly.

The man who made her *feel* so much.

She turned and buried her face in her pillow as the burning tide of despair welled in her.

She wanted the impossible. She wanted him to want her, to feel just a tiny spark of the love she felt for him.

She wanted the fairy tale.

But it was out of the question. She'd been a passing fancy. A woman to while away the hours till he returned to his fast-paced life. He'd told her a little about his world—the travel, the busy schedules. No doubt he'd been at a loose end for all those weeks, recuperating at home. She'd been an amusing interlude to alleviate the boredom.

Now he was angry that she'd left him high and dry. He

wasn't accustomed to women deserting him before he was ready to say goodbye.

She remembered the imposing angle of his high cheekbones, the plane of his jaw, the quirk of his mobile mouth, the sensual intensity of his sizzling regard, and knew he must spend his life fighting off would-be lovers. That was why he was annoyed—because he was used to calling the shots.

With his devastating charm, his sensational body and his wealth, Arik was a man who got his own way. Every time.

It was pique that had driven him to confront her last night. Pique and curiosity.

She swallowed down on the knot of bitter memory filling her throat.

Well, she'd satisfied his curiosity. She'd told him about her past. And she remembered only too well the look of horror on his shadowed face. It had wiped the anger and the remnants of lust from his expression.

Now he knew her for what she was: a woman permanently damaged by a past she couldn't change. A woman who battled every day to build a positive life for herself and her daughter. Who couldn't rely on romantic dreams.

Abruptly she sat up and pulled her hair from her face.

That was one thing she knew about: independence.

Her father had walked out on the family when she was just a kid, breaking her heart. His desertion had made her draw in upon herself, living in a sheltered fantasy world where everything turned out all right in the end. She'd been reserved, introspective, finding hope and reassurance in her art. Then even that had been stolen from her when she'd been abused and assaulted. She'd almost given up the struggle then, knew her mother had worried for her very survival. But then Amy had come along and with that her own salvation.

Rosalie had become a mother and from that point had worked with dogged determination to drag herself out of the quagmire of fear and misery that haunted her. The future was hers to build for herself. For her and Amy.

That was all she needed. Her independence. The love of her daughter, her family.

And now, miraculously, she had her art again too. The power that had been denied her in the darkest days of despair had been given back to her.

She didn't need a man to be whole.

Rosalie flung back the covers and glanced at the other bed in the room. It was empty. Amy had already left for the stables and her early morning visit to the puppies.

For a moment anxiety speared through Rosalie, then she realised Amy would never be alone, not here. She suspected the servants actually waited, on watch for the little tot to appear. Amy would have at least one of the stable hands and probably more, looking after her.

Nevertheless, Rosalie swung her legs out of bed quickly. She'd feel better when she was with Amy. And her daughter would keep her busy enough that, with luck, she wouldn't have time to think about Arik.

She'd never see him again. No way would he come back to the palace to see Rafiq while she was here. It would be too uncomfortable for him. No doubt he was already planning his next trip to the Far East or the new offshore oil rigs he'd mentioned.

How long would it take the pain of her lost hope to ease?

Giggles echoed through the dim building as Rosalie entered the vast stable. Instinctively she turned towards the direction of her daughter's laughter, only to pause at the sound of a deep voice, murmuring something she couldn't catch. It slipped like warm treacle across her skin, drawing a ripple of reaction from her.

Arik! She'd know his voice anywhere.

That shivery sensation in the pit of her stomach, the way

her nipples budded and tightened and her short uneven breathing: they were all dead giveaways.

What was he doing here? He should have returned home now, surely? Little Adham's birthday celebration was over and there was nothing more to keep him here, especially after what she'd told him last night.

But there was no mistaking the timbre of that voice.

She sagged back against the wall, her knees quivering and her pulse racing. She could no more persuade herself not to react to him than she could fly. Arik was like a lodestone, tugging at her senses, drawing her inevitably towards him.

All the more reason to get away as soon as she'd collected her daughter.

Rosalie straightened her shoulders and lifted her chin. Her hands were clammy and she tucked them into the pockets of her jeans. Then she stepped forward with what she hoped was an air of casual curiosity.

'If I lift you, you have to promise not to shout or wave your arms around,' said Arik in a voice that melted something vital inside her. 'Okay?'

''Kay.' Amy's voice was breathless with excitement and Rosalie automatically quickened her pace.

'There,' said Arik. 'Hold your hand out like this. Steady. Let her come to you. If you move suddenly you'll scare her and we don't want that, do we?'

'No. We don't want that,' Amy solemnly repeated.

Rosalie reached the stalls at the end of the building in time to hear Amy giggle shrilly and see her daughter held high in Arik's arms, totally absorbed in the sight of an enormous mare, leaning out from her stall towards her.

'She tickles!'

'Yes, I know, she's breathing on your hand,' Arik explained, 'sniffing to see if you have any food. Would you like to feed her?'

'Yes!'

'Yes, *please*, Amy.' It was her mother's voice correcting Amy from Arik's other side.

'Yes, *please*.'

But from here Rosalie saw only her daughter, focused totally on the horse, and Arik, the strong lines of his face softening as he looked down at Amy.

A twist of something almost like pain circled low in Rosalie's stomach, seeing the gentle approval on his hard, handsome face. Seeing her precious daughter held so protectively in his powerful arms. It pulled her up short just as she reached them.

'Then you may feed her since you ask so nicely. Here you are.' Arik passed Amy a piece of apple. 'No, not that way. Keep your hand flat and Saki will take it from you.'

He held Amy's hand steady in his own so the mare could snuffle up the treat. 'That's it. Perfect! Have you done this before?'

'No. Never!' Amy's voice was excited. 'Again! Please?'

'Of course you may. You fed her just right.'

'Can I ride her? Auntie Belle and Uncle Rafi ride.'

Instinctively Rosalie opened her mouth to intervene but it wasn't necessary. Arik was already answering.

'When you're old enough, perhaps you can ride.'

'When's that?'

'When your mother says so,' Arik responded. 'Here's some more apple you can give to Saki. Are you ready?'

'Mm hm!' Amy concentrated on balancing the apple on her palm, giggling when the mare daintily extracted it from her hand.

'Wait till your mother sees how well you do this,' said Arik. 'I know she'll be impressed.'

'I certainly *am* impressed.' Rosalie pasted a tense smile on her face and walked up to the group, careful to keep her attention on Amy, not the man who held her.

'Mummy, Mummy, did you see?' Amy swung round so fast that she startled the mare who jerked her head away. Instantly Arik turned his shoulder, putting himself between Amy and the animal.

'I saw, sweetheart. You've done very well. I think Saki must like you. Have you thanked Arik for letting you feed her?'

'Thank you,' Amy said with a wide grin as she looked up at him.

Rosalie saw a flash of expression on Arik's dark face, then he smiled back. 'You're welcome, little one.'

'Arik has been entertaining Amy for the best part of an hour.' It was Rosalie's mother speaking as she moved round to greet her. 'First with the puppies, then a visit to the peacock house and now a tour of the horses.'

Amy nodded vigorously and Rosalie watched her golden curls bob and swirl against the pale blue of Arik's shirt. If she moved her gaze a fraction she'd meet his eyes. But that was best avoided. She focused instead on the deeply tanned column of his throat.

'That's very kind of you—'

'It was entirely my pleasure. Amy is delightful.' He raised his hand to untangle a curl that had caught on his shirt button. Rosalie watched his long fingers deftly dislodging the long strands and swallowed hard.

Unbidden memories rushed back. Of him stroking the length of her own hair, down over her shoulders and breasts, of him lifting the strands to his face and inhaling, telling her she smelled like sunshine and roses. Of his hands spearing through her hair as he held her close, tilting her head as he kissed her: passionately, endlessly, addictively.

Rosalie bit down on her lip, trying to break the spell of evocative memory that blindsided her.

'It's time to come inside now, Amy, and have some breakfast.' She held out her arms.

'Arik too?' Amy asked as she tumbled forward into her arms. Startled, Rosalie lifted her eyes to his, wondering what he was thinking. But once again his dark gaze was impenetrable. She saw a flicker of warmth but no more. Just a long steady look that made her tremble at the realisation of how close he stood to her. Close enough to reach out and stroke her cheek. If he'd wanted to.

'Sorry, Amy,' Arik answered, 'I'm going out. I promised your uncle Rafiq I'd try out one of his horses this morning. I'm going for a ride. Perhaps another morning we could breakfast together.'

'You're staying here?' Rosalie couldn't help it that the words sounded brusque.

Arik inclined his head, one eyebrow tilting up towards his hairline. 'That's right. Rafiq invited me to stay some time ago. Initially I thought I wouldn't be able to remain as I had another…commitment.' Sudden fire blazed in his eyes as he looked down at her and Rosalie felt the heat scorch right through her.

'But my plans have altered. I'll be here for at least a week.'

For a long moment his gaze held hers and her throat dried at the banked heat she saw there. Then he swung away with a nod to her mother and a blinding smile for Amy. 'I'll see you ladies later.'

A week. A week in the same house as Arik! Rosalie braced herself against the intense turmoil of emotions that rocked her. Fear, pain, anger…and excitement? No. She couldn't be so stupidly self-destructive as to welcome the opportunity to see him again. Not when the sight of him tore at her heart with razor claws.

She was in a daze as she walked back to the palace with her mum and Amy. She listened to their chatter and nodded and smiled at the appropriate times, but all the while she was aware of a deep sinking feeling in the pit of her stomach.

Arik would be at the palace for a whole week. And the look on his face told her he didn't intend to avoid her. How could she survive so long without giving herself away? Without betraying the depth of her feelings for him? Without tumbling into his arms and begging for just one more embrace? One final caress before they parted?

'And such a pleasant man too,' she heard her mother say. 'I had no idea you'd met someone while you were out painting.' She paused as if awaiting a response.

Rosalie shrugged and lifted Amy higher on her hip. 'It didn't seem important at the time.'

Liar.

'I didn't think I'd see him again.'

'And now you have. What a nice surprise for you both.'

Rosalie shot her mum a sideways glance. There was far more to that observation than trite chat and those penetrating blue eyes were fixed on her intently. Her mother had always seen far too much, especially where she was concerned. The stress of the last few years meant that Maggie Winters kept a close protective eye on her younger daughter.

Rosalie knew her family had watched her and Arik with avid curiosity last night. No doubt they'd spent the evening speculating on the relationship between them for, despite her best efforts, she'd failed miserably in her attempts to appear as a polite stranger to him.

She'd seen the significant looks pass between her mum and Belle. Thank goodness they hadn't realised precisely how well *acquainted* she and Arik really were.

Rosalie shrugged. 'I don't suppose I'll see much of him. After his conversation with Rafiq last night, I gather he'll spend his time in the stables.'

But that was where she was wrong.

Over the days that followed it seemed Arik was everywhere she turned. He didn't overtly follow her but his presence was unavoidable. He was treated as one of the family, which meant sharing mealtimes. That was a torment she couldn't escape, not unless she wanted her eagle-eyed sister and her mum to worry that she was unwell.

Every morning when she took an insistent Amy to the stables to visit the animals, he was there, just in from a ride or chatting with Rafiq about horse-breeding. And every morning he'd stop what he was doing to spend time with Amy.

The sight of her little girl, so eagerly seeking his company, and he, so patently good with kids, made her feel dangerously soft and mushy inside. He'd make a great father one day. When he finally decided it was time to settle down with one of his glamorous society girlfriends or maybe a royal princess.

But it wasn't only in the early mornings that he invaded her peace. It seemed that, wherever she wandered when Amy was asleep, there he was: in the heavily scented tropical garden, chatting with her family, reading newspapers in the library or doing laps in the magnificent azure pool.

More than once she'd stopped there, hidden in the shadows, her heart in her mouth as she'd watched him power the length of the pool, then turn with a supple jackknife and plough back down the lane. The water rippled from his broad shoulders, his dark hair plastered to his skull and the curve of his rising arms made her itch for her crayons so she could capture the sheer energy of him on paper.

The sight of him enthralled her—and not just because he'd make a perfect model. Her interest in his magnificent physique was much more *personal* than that.

She spent more and more time in her room or playing alone with Amy, till her mum started to question whether she was all right and she was forced to make an appearance and join the family party.

Which inevitably meant being with Arik, for he was one

of the family. He and Rafiq had grown up together, had shared a lifetime's experiences. Even her sister, Belle, had a soft spot for him. He'd been one of Belle's first friends in Q'aroum and the sight of her and Arik, laughing together, was enough to turn Rosalie's mood sour.

Rosalie's feelings when she saw the two of them together confounded her. She couldn't be jealous of Belle. She knew her sister was head over heels in love with her own handsome husband. But that didn't stop the green-eyed demon of jealousy popping up when Rosalie saw how close Belle and Arik were, how comfortable together. There was an ease between them that she would never share with him.

How much she longed to be able to relax in Arik's company. Enjoy his wit and his conversation without feeling guilty because she wanted what she shouldn't, couldn't have. No matter how many times she told herself to be strong, it was impossible to stifle her hopeless yearning.

Worse still, her family patently approved of him. Who wouldn't? He was courteous, amiable, attentive, a great conversationalist, but a man who listened as well.

Rosalie sighed. He was so darned near perfect! Even his single-minded determination to get what he set his mind to was a plus. Belle called it strength of character and described how much he'd done to stimulate investment and research in alternative energies, the multitude of community support programmes he'd initiated and his energetic plans for local reform.

Rosalie wondered what her sister would say if she knew he'd turned that formidable focus on to the task of seducing her kid sister. Even now she shivered at the forbidden memory of his hot, hungry gaze and his possessive touch.

If Rosalie had to listen to her family sing his praises much longer she thought she'd explode!

It wasn't that she disagreed with them. He *was* a most remarkable man. That was precisely the problem. She didn't want to be reminded again and again of what she couldn't have. Each day, each hour was torture, not knowing when or how they'd be flung together again. Time and again at meals she found herself trapped next to him at the table, overwhelmed by the sensations his proximity aroused.

Aroused.

Now there was a word that said it all. No matter how often she told herself the affair was over, she couldn't dispel the secret shivery excitement of her betraying body. She only had to hear his dark velvet voice, scent his skin as he leaned close to pass her something or feel his eyes on her across a room and her body jangled with excitement. Ready. Waiting. Wanting.

It infuriated her almost as much as it scared her. Would she ever get over her feelings for him? Finally, devastatingly she'd fallen in love. And now she wondered if there was any way out. Surely she wasn't doomed to suffer this maelstrom of longing and despair for the rest of her life?

If only she could escape. Get away from the stress of pretending to enjoy herself when all the while she yearned desperately for the man who was so patently beyond her reach. The keenness of her pain caught her breath, especially when she turned suddenly to see him watching her, his face brooding and his eyes shuttered.

What went on behind that mask of control? Was he still angry with her? Or did he remember only her ugly story of violence and lost innocence? Did he pity her for what she'd suffered? The idea snagged at her wounded ego.

Either way it didn't matter. Her future was set. Soon she'd return home and take up the threads of her real life. She wouldn't allow herself to yearn for the impossible.

CHAPTER TWELVE

ROSALIE slipped through the door of her suite and into the wide passage. Amy had settled down for the night with one of the maids to watch over her and Rosalie didn't want her to wake. It had taken ages to get her daughter to sleep, partly because she was so excited, seeing her mum dressed up in un-accustomed finery.

Rosalie smoothed the satiny fabric of her new dress down over her hips, feeling the sensuous slide of it against her skin. It was a beautiful gift from Belle, with its delicately embroi-dered neckline, close-fitting bodice and the ultra-feminine swirl of long skirt. Just the sort of dress Rosalie would never have chosen for herself, but perfect for tonight's formal party.

That was one thing Rosalie would never envy her sister. She might have a gorgeous, loving husband, an adorable baby, the career she always wanted and a blessed life in a fairy tale palace, but the downside was the weight of public duty. This was the second formal reception at the palace in a week. Thank goodness Rosalie had no official role and could blend into the background.

She started down the corridor, hurrying a little despite the unfamiliar high heels, knowing she was late. At the first corner she turned left and straight into the arms of the man coming towards her.

This passageway was in unfamiliar darkness, but she knew immediately it was Arik. The grip of his hands on her arms, the subtle teasing scent of his skin, the familiarity of his body—all were unmistakable. As was her instant reaction. Her lungs emptied of air in a sudden rush and a tickle of awareness spread across her skin. Deep within her that insidious coil of desire twisted into life.

'You can let me go.' Was that her voice, breathless and uneven? She stepped back and his hands fell away.

In the gloom she couldn't make out his expression but she felt his gaze on her face. She lifted her chin.

'What's happened to the lights?'

'That's why I came to get you. Rafiq and Belle are already entertaining the first guests.' In contrast to her voice, his was calm and even. 'You remember the workmen rewiring this older section of the building today? Well, it seems they haven't quite fool-proofed the new circuits. The next few corridors are blacked out and it may take a while to locate the problem.'

Of course. There could be no personal reason for him to search her out. Yet her pulse hammered in her throat when she stood so close to him.

It was the first time they'd been alone together since the evening she'd revealed the secrets of her past.

Is that what he was thinking about as he stood unmoving, his head inclined towards hers? Tension stiffened her shoulders, gripped her chest in a vice that snatched her breath.

Not his pity. Not that!

She sidestepped his looming bulk and paced forward into the darkness. Now her eyes had adjusted she saw silvery light ahead, moonlight spilling in through the high windows.

He fell into step beside her and she felt the warmth of his body press close. His hand reached for hers and folded it in the crook of his elbow. She faltered and would have stumbled but for his support.

'Stay by me, Rosalie. That way there'll be no mishaps.'

'But I can see my way well enough!' She tugged to be free, a useless effort since he kept her clamped close to his side. She felt the fine cotton of his shirt beneath her fingers, the fleeting caress of his long cloak against her bare ankle. And his heat. How could she have forgotten the intensity of the warmth that spread from his muscled body, teasing her even through their clothes?

'You're safer with me.'

'I'm perfectly capable of walking unsupported!'

His pace slowed and, perforce, hers did too. 'You find my presence so objectionable?' His words were crisp, deliberate, yet she couldn't decipher that particular inflection. Was it anger?

'Is that why you continually avoid me?' Now he stopped and turned towards her, his shoulders blocking the bright slabs of moonlight from view.

'I don't avoid you. I—'

'Don't lie, Rosalie. You're very bad at it.'

She sucked in a stunned breath and stared up into the darkness that was his face. What did this man *want* from her? Surely he was grateful she hadn't played the clinging vine? That she hadn't embarrassed them both in front of her family and his cousin.

Just as well he didn't have a clue how much the façade of disinterest cost her. Even now pain was welling inside.

'Let me go, please. I prefer to walk alone.' She couldn't help the tremor in her tone, but at least she sounded calm.

For answer he swung round and pulled her forwards, pacing fast down the corridor. 'And I prefer that we take this opportunity to talk. *Alone.* Whenever I come near you, you scurry away. You continually find excuses to put distance between us.'

Rosalie's jaw dropped. 'There's nothing to talk about. It's over between us,' she hissed, stumbling a little as his pace lengthened and he tugged her towards the dark side of the corridor.

'Nothing to discuss?' His voice grated, a harsh whisper just above her ear. Then he lunged to one side, thrust open a door and tugged her into a darkened room.

'What are you doing?' Nerves made her voice thin.

'Making sure we're alone.'

Emphatically she shook her head. 'No! Belle and Rafiq are expecting us. We need to go now.' There was nothing left to say to Arik. Nothing she *trusted* herself to say.

'No one will miss us. And it's past time we sorted this out.'

Rosalie stepped back into the gloom, straight into the back of a padded sofa. 'There's nothing to sort out. We had an affair. It's over. Now we go our separate ways.'

He paced closer, a threatening bulk looming blacker than the shadows of the moonlit room. She bit her lip and stood straighter, her fingers digging into the upholstery behind her.

'You cannot be so naïve as to believe that, Rosalie.' His voice had the seductive quality of rich, dark chocolate, his accent suddenly more pronounced, its lilt making her stomach dip in unwanted excitement.

'It's the truth!'

The truth.

What *was* the truth about him and this woman?

She was like wildfire in his blood. He wanted her in his bed; in fact, he craved her anywhere he could get her, with such a driven need that he was in perpetual torment. He couldn't put her out of his mind, no matter how sternly he reminded himself of the barriers between them. Yet, despite the consuming rush of lust, his need was greater even than that. He wanted to hold her, comfort her, protect her. Her pain was his, he *felt* her hurts in his blood, his bones, his very marrow. It was as if he'd absorbed her anguish into himself. No wonder he felt ripped asunder every time he remembered the fresh pain he'd caused her with his thoughtless words the other night.

What did it mean?

This was beyond even his experience. And if there was one thing he could claim, it was experience of women.

All he knew was that he couldn't drag himself away as he was duty-bound to do. He was like some damned satellite, orbiting, coming tantalisingly close to a bright, beckoning star and then veering off into darkness again.

It couldn't go on. This situation had to be resolved.

'We need to talk, Rosalie.' Somehow he'd sort this out, break the unseen ties that bound them so he could do what he must and walk away from her.

She shook her head and her long unbound hair swirled around her head. In the gloom it rippled like silver, but he knew it to be the colour of gold, warm and silkily seductive to the touch.

His hands clenched as he resisted the impulse to reach out and slide his hand down those tresses, over her shoulder and her breast. Too dangerous. He needed to keep a cool head.

But already she was moving away, heading for the door.

He spun round as she reached for the handle.

'No!'

She ignored him, tugging the door towards her.

His splayed hand slammed down on the heavy wood just above her shoulder, thrusting it shut.

'Arik. Open the door, please. I want to leave.'

He heard the waver in her low voice and almost relented. The tension came off her in waves and he had to repress the urge to comfort her as he wanted to, with her tucked in against his chest and his arms holding her tight. This close he could smell the fresh scent of her skin, the sunshine smell of her soap, sparking intimate memories.

He couldn't afford to be sidetracked.

'We need to talk, Rosalie. That's all.'

There was a flurry of movement as she spun round to face

him. Her pale face looked up into his. He heard her breaths, short and sharp, and his pulse quickened. With his arm still holding the door shut, they stood far too close for clear thinking. But he couldn't move away. Not yet.

'Don't you listen?' The words were harsh, rising on emotion. 'There's nothing for us to discuss. It's over. Done. Finished. There's nothing between us any more, Arik.'

Some tiny voice in his mind told him she was lashing out to protect herself. But the sound of it was drowned by the urgent clamour of blood pounding in his head. By the surge of molten fury that suddenly gripped him.

Finished! She had to be kidding.

He'd tried all damned week to end this torment. To do what had to be done—to turn his back on her. And yet something held him back.

Never before had he found it impossible to do his duty.

He raised his other hand to her cheek, let the back of his fingers brush feather-light over her warm flesh.

Her sigh, stifled as she snapped her mouth shut, echoed the deep, slow, satisfied release of air from his own lungs. He'd wanted to reach out to her all week. Now, as his hand turned and he palmed the soft skin of her cheek, he wondered how he'd resisted for so long.

'It's not over, Rosalie. Not while there's *this* between us.'

'It has to be!'

Her hair caressed his hand as she shook her head. Her fingers were warm, supple and inviting as they closed on his hand, slid down to his wrist. But then suddenly she was tugging, trying to pull his hand away. Her grip grew more urgent and he allowed her to raise his hand a few centimetres from her face.

'This is your ego talking, Arik. You just don't want to admit it's over because *I* was the one who left *you*.'

Her words struck him with the force of a blow. For he knew

instantly that once that might have been the case. Once he might have felt his masculine pride had been dented by her ending their affair.

But this was something else. This was something—more.

His breathing snagged as the force of what he felt rocked him. It blasted through him like an explosion of red-hot lava. Good intentions, common sense, his careful plans, all obliterated in a scorching blaze of raw emotion.

'So there's nothing between us.' He didn't recognise the hoarse voice as his own. But nor were these aggressive, blatantly possessive instincts familiar as he looked down into her pale face.

He gathered her wrists in his hand and yanked them high over her head, hearing her hiss of surprise as if from a distance. He let his other hand trail over her face, his thumb pressing against her lips, parting them as his fingers cupped her cheek.

The air sizzled with static electricity. If there were a naked flame here Arik thought he'd ignite. Just the touch of her flesh against his, the warmth of her breath on his hand, had him burning up.

He opened his mouth to accuse her of lying, when her tongue, warm and wet and flagrantly seductive, grazed his thumb.

He groaned as the fire in his belly shot straight to his groin. That single caress brought him to instant, rampant readiness. His whole body stiffened and shook as she sucked his thumb into her mouth. Darts of fire speared into his belly, his chest, his legs. Instinctively he widened his stance, locking his knees against the ripples of desire shuddering through him.

In the shadows his eyes met hers. They were huge, staring up at him unblinking, inviting. Capitulating.

He didn't remember releasing his hold on her wrists but he must have for her breast was soft and pouting beneath his touch. Her fingers cupped his other hand at her mouth, slid up his wrist, then further, along his arm and back again. Her movements were restless, edgy, feeding the raw desire that surged within him.

Arik let his hand slide from her mouth, over her chin, her delicate bare neck, past the frantically racing pulse to her collar-bone, her other breast.

His mouth twisted in a tight smile as she pushed forward into his hands, filling them with her luscious feminine bounty.

'You still need me.' His voice grated out of his dry throat. 'Don't you, Rosalie?'

Her eyes closed as he squeezed her breasts and he watched her head loll back against the door, her neck curving in an erotic, inviting arch.

He lowered his head, allowing himself to be engulfed in the hot, heady scent of her, and licked the warm skin at her collar-bone.

She shuddered and he slipped his hands round her, tugging her close.

'Yes.' It was a sigh of a word, barely audible.

'Say it, Rosalie,' he demanded as he nuzzled the gossamer-thin silk of her bodice. He needed to hear her admit it. His lips closed over one thrusting nipple and he sucked hard. She bucked in his arms, her hands braced on his shoulders, her fingers digging into him. Deliberately he drew her close, flush against the iron hardness of his lower body.

'I need you, Arik.' It emerged as a desperate sob that incited immediate action. His hands moved automatically, scrabbling at her long skirts, thrusting them up so he could anchor himself against her.

Of course it wasn't enough. His chest heaved, his breathing coming too fast as he fumbled at his trousers.

Her hands were on him now, distracting him as they attacked his shirt, wrenching buttons undone till he felt the warmth of her palms against his skin.

Yes!

Finally he was free of the restricting clothes. He reached out to her, found the delicate wisp of fabric barring his entry to paradise and tore it away in a single ripping tug.

Hot, soft flesh, the graze of silky hair, moist heat. His breath stopped in his lungs as he explored her intimately, felt her body jerk against his hand, heard her breath stop on a gasp of excitement.

No time now for words. For finesse. Arik knew only the instinct for fulfilment. To take this woman and claim her as his own. Incontrovertibly. Undeniably. Completely. In the surest way a man could claim a woman.

'Please, Arik.' Her arms were wrapped around him, drawing him to her.

He closed his hands on the curve of her waist, dimly aware of a primitive satisfaction at the way the neat indentation fitted his grasp. He lifted her up, pushing her back against the door and positioned himself right…there.

Her legs wrapped round him, tugging him closer. And now Rosalie anchored her hands at the back of his neck. Her fingers splayed through his hair.

It took just one decisive thrust, long and sure and perfect, to take him home.

The world stood still as he dragged in a breath, dimly aware that he ought to slow down. He should—

'Yes!' Her voice was the merest echo of sound in his ear, yet it shattered the last of his faltering control. Every muscle tensed, flexed as he bucked against her, surging high and deep and hard.

Arik's lips moved against the delicate curve of her ear as he described to her in an unbroken stream of words how good she felt. He told her exactly what he intended to do with her as he thrust into her again and again.

The flow of Arabic became slower, less fluent, broken, as

their bodies moved together, found a frantic, urgent rhythm that took control of them, gripped them and pounded them together against the door.

Rosalie welcomed him, pulled him tighter, further, till the world spun and colours flared and their rhythm raced out of control. Ecstasy. A barrage of exquisite sensation. It could have been the end of the world and Arik wouldn't have cared. For here, now, in his arms, he held all that he needed.

He pulsed hard inside her, the very essence of him flooding deep within her, filling her. And he knew that, beyond everything, this was *right*.

He held her, slumped and panting, against his chest as the last tremors died away. It hurt to breathe, the oxygen scoured his lungs, but he didn't care. He never wanted to let her go.

But all too soon her splayed hands were pushing at his chest. Her legs unlocked their intimate hold and she was wriggling, trying to slide down to the floor. Her long hair hid her down bent head, but he could hear her uneven breathing, feel her body's shivers in the aftermath of ecstasy.

He smiled, stepping back and lowering her. Even now the sensation of her delectable body easing down past his sated one brought the promise of future pleasure.

When she stood on her own feet he held her close for a moment before releasing her. Better to keep his hands to himself while they talked. Even after that cataclysmic orgasm, he didn't trust his libido around this woman. Her ability to arouse him, and to satisfy him, was unprecedented.

He was adjusting his clothes, trying to make himself look respectable again, when a sound froze his blood. Two sounds. The huge door creaking open almost drowned out the other noise, but not quite. Rosalie's anguished sob was enough to still his rapidly beating heart. His chest constricted painfully at the sound of her despair.

'Rosalie—' He reached for her but she was already hurtling away down the corridor. He stumbled over something—a pair of discarded shoes—and lost the opportunity to grab her.

Even so he would have pursued her if he hadn't heard the sound of her crying: raw and heartfelt. That stopped him in his tracks as surely as a spear through the chest.

He'd done that to her. With his demands, his violent passion, his insistence on getting his own way.

He *knew* how much Rosalie had been through. The rape, the fear and despair. How much she'd suffered. He'd sworn he'd keep his distance, just reason with her.

Yet there'd been no reason in his actions. He hadn't shown a shred of gentleness just now. He hadn't made love to the girl. He hadn't persuaded or seduced.

He'd demanded and ravaged.

Searing heat suffused his face as he recalled the desperate battering beat of his body slamming into hers, his hands tight and uncompromising on her delicate flesh as he'd slaked his lust with raw passion. No finesse. No tenderness.

It had been the most perfect sexual union of his life. And he'd been so sure it had been the same for her. But had he really bothered to find out?

All she'd wanted from the moment she'd cannoned into him was to get away. Surely she deserved to be left alone now.

Mechanically he buttoned his shirt, fastened his trousers, put her shoes neatly to one side. But as he bent he saw something pale on the floor. A scrap of white.

His fingers touched lace and automatically closed on the fabric. He couldn't leave Rosalie's underwear there, torn and tell-tale, to be discovered by one of the maids. Instead he shoved the scrap into his pocket, knowing a self-loathing so deep it stifled his breath.

How could he atone for what he'd done?

Could he ever make this right?

* * *

Fifteen minutes later, when he finally returned to the large reception room, Arik was conscious only of branding guilt. It was like a physical mark on his flesh, reminding him of his hubris. No plan had emerged from the seething mass of emotions and guilt. He felt punch-drunk on the enormity of what had just happened, and the unforgivable damage he'd inflicted on Rosalie.

He was barely aware of the colourful crowd closing in round him as he strode across the marble floor, intent on finding Rafiq and giving his excuses. He needed to be alone to sort this out.

His stride broke as he had to stop and skirt a middle-aged couple stepping across his path. His gaze flickered towards them as he heard a voice he recognised. Immediately he wished he hadn't. The man was a stranger to him but the woman he knew. She'd been the one spreading poison about Rosalie, just a week ago in this same room.

Automatically Arik halted, a sixth sense warning him of the need to beware.

Blood still pounded in his ears. That and the cacophony of voices had deafened him to any single conversation. Until now. Whispered words trickled into his ears, snatches half-masked by the crowd's hubbub.

Déjà vu.

'Bold as brass she was…but no husband, not that one…what damage she'll do to the reputation of the royal house…'

This time Arik was almost prepared for the salacious character assassination. And yet the woman's audacity was stunning. To speak so of Rosalie, here in the palace.

Last time he'd acted purely on gut instinct when he'd confronted the malicious gossip, hadn't even thought before the words were out of his mouth.

This time he stopped, absorbing the full impact of the ugly innuendo like a sickening body blow.

Out of the mind-numbing mass of half-formed thoughts

and guilty speculation that had plagued him since Rosalie had run away, certainty emerged. Absolute, bone-deep certainty. It came upon him in an instant of blinding insight, sudden and satisfying. He almost smiled his relief.

Instead he stuck his hands on his hips, planted his feet wide and looked down his nose at the plump pair wandering into his path. It was the fat husband who noticed him first, looking up, his jaw sagging his horror. Then the wife, her face paling and her words petering out as she took in the look on Arik's face.

Over their heads Arik caught an impression of decisive movement and looked up to see Rafiq striding purposefully through the crowd.

Too late, cousin. I'll handle this once and for all.

Arik stared down at the pair before him. He didn't bother to lower his voice. He had a point to make and the more that heard the better.

'I'd advise you to keep a still tongue in your head, woman.' She flinched at his tone, but he barely noticed. 'No one talks like that about the woman I plan to marry.'

CHAPTER THIRTEEN

'YOU haven't asked me my intentions.' Arik met his cousin's eyes, knowing how much it cost Rafiq to keep his own counsel on this matter. After all, Rosalie was by marriage one of his womenfolk. It was Rafiq's duty to protect and care for her, especially when confronted with the man who'd seduced her and risked her public reputation.

Rafiq's expression was sombre in the early morning light. 'As if I don't know you as well as I know myself.' He paused, his look assessing. 'And it seems a night of contemplation hasn't changed your mind.'

Arik shook his head. A few sleepless hours hadn't altered the fundamental problem.

His cousin smiled then, a taut, quick curve of the lips. 'You know she's as stubborn as her sister? Totally independent?'

'I know.' Neither voiced the other issue: the fact that Rosalie Winters would hate Arik for what he'd done to her. He'd put her in an untenable position. The knowledge was like acid, eating away at Arik's conscience.

'I can give you probably fifteen minutes. But longer than that I can't promise. Belle won't want to let her out of her sight.'

Arik nodded. The window of opportunity was pitifully small. But it would have to do.

Both men turned at the sound of voices approaching across

the manicured lawn. A group emerged from the palace: Belle
carrying little Adham, Amy skipping ahead, Mrs Winters and,
in the centre, as if shielded by her relatives, Rosalie, looking
pale and tired.

Something squeezed hard in Arik's chest as he took in the
bruised shadows beneath her eyes and the droop of her shoulders. Guilt flagellated him, tearing at his flesh and seizing
his breath.

'Uncle Rafi! Arik!' It was Amy who spotted them first,
swerving away from the women and racing towards them
across the grass.

Arik felt a hand on his shoulder and then Rafiq strode
away towards his family. For the first time in his life Arik felt
a pang of pure envy, watching Rafiq's pace quicken as he
neared his wife and baby son. He saw Belle pause, reach out
a protective arm towards her younger sister. But then Maggie
Winters, her mother, was somehow between her daughters and
urging Belle away, towards Rafiq.

Arik frowned. What did that gesture mean?

Then his mind clouded as he stared into Rosalie's huge,
pained eyes. Even from here he could guess that they were
grey rather than green. The colour of storms and anguish.

His breath rattled in his chest.

He'd done that to her.

Rosalie stumbled to a halt at the sight of Arik, tall and lean
and utterly gorgeous, bathed in the golden glow of morning.
He stood at the entrance to the stables, watching her. Her
blood quickened. Despite everything, despite a night of
silent admonition, she couldn't prevent her tell-tale reaction.
The sheer excitement the sight of him generated in her
betraying body.

It didn't matter that he only wanted her for sex. Had only ever
felt lust for her: raw and primitive and barbarically glorious.

Her body didn't care. Just look at the way she'd responded to him last night. She'd been hungry for him, wanton and more than willing in her craving for him. Just the caress of his hand on her face, the scent and sound and feel of him standing so close to her in the dark had stripped away every defence, every last shred of control. She'd *invited* him to take her. She'd revelled in their urgent, almost violent coupling, up against a door of all places!

It had only been afterwards, when it had been too late, that she'd realised what she'd done. She'd thrown away her self-respect for steaming sex in the dark.

Heat scorched her cheeks as she dropped her gaze. But she couldn't hide from the truth. Despite everything, it was excitement that skittered through her body.

She bit her trembling lower lip. When would she learn to control these primitive emotions? The stupid, pointless yearning for a man who didn't need her?

Jerkily she lifted her chin, refusing to be cowed, only to see Amy veer past Rafiq and, straight as an arrow, catapult into Arik's arms.

Something hard and sharp jolted deep inside her at the sight of her precious little girl swung high in the arms of the man Rosalie needed to avoid at all costs. The man who could seduce her without trying, who held her heart in his hands and didn't even know it.

Seeing the pair together was a heartbreaking travesty of her hopeless, self-indulgent dreams—of Arik returning her love, wanting her, even accepting her daughter as his own.

'You'd better go with Amy to check on the pups,' said her mum's voice near her ear. 'You know she won't settle till she's seen them. We'll go on ahead to this picnic breakfast Rafiq has organised.'

Rosalie looked over to the picturesque pavilion where Rafiq's servants had carried platter upon platter of food.

Already Rafiq and Belle were walking ahead, deep in conversation, Rafiq with his arm wrapped lovingly around his wife.

Rosalie stifled a sigh. She had to face Arik some time. Better to do it with Amy there to keep things in perspective. Maybe this time she could persuade herself that she didn't care. That it had been no more than a meaningless holiday romance.

One day, surely, she'd come to believe it.

Her gait was stiff, her shoulders cramped with tension as she approached the stables. She could feel his eyes on her, hot as a brand, but she managed not to flinch.

'Are you ready to see the puppies, sweetheart?' Perhaps if she looked only at her daughter and avoided Arik's gaze, she could get through this.

'Uh huh.' Amy nodded vigorously and wriggled to be put down. But then, to Rosalie's horror, she reached up a hand to Arik and another to her.

Beside her she sensed Arik stiffen, clearly appalled at the unconscious intimacy of Amy's gesture. But then, a second later, Rosalie saw his strong, long-fingered hand engulf Amy's. Rosalie reached for her little girl's other hand, telling herself not to think about the picture they made. The strong, handsome man, the gorgeous little girl and the woman who loved them both. Almost like a family.

Rosalie swallowed down on the bitter taste of self-indulgent tears. She needed to stop this now! She was too strong for this. She'd never have survived the last few years if she'd allowed herself to languish in self-pity.

So she stifled the sob that rose in her throat and plastered an overbright smile on her face.

'Just a quick visit this time, Amy. Everyone's waiting to have breakfast with us.'

'Yes, Mummy.' But already Amy's attention was absorbed elsewhere as she knelt in the straw of the first stall, surrounded by a wriggling, furry mass of chubby pups.

Which left Rosalie standing alone with—

'Rosalie.' His voice was low, devastating in its ability to awaken needs she tried so firmly to repress. 'I need to tell you—'

'There's nothing to say,' she hissed, automatically edging aside.

'You're wrong, *habibti*—'

'Don't call me that!' Rosalie swallowed down a lump of pure emotion. No matter how easily the endearments came to him, she couldn't bear to have him call her sweetheart. Not when she knew it meant nothing to him.

For answer he reached out and grasped her hand in his. She tugged, desperate for some space between them, but she couldn't match his superior strength. Not without an undignified tussle that would draw Amy's attention and her curiosity.

His hand was warm and hard, engulfing hers in a hold that restrained and yet seemed almost caressing.

She had to get a grip and stop imagining things!

'So what is it you need to tell me?' She darted a savage look up at his shuttered face and then away. Even in her sudden anger she didn't trust herself to look at him.

'Last night—'

'I'd rather not talk about that.'

'Last night,' he continued, his voice terse and curiously devoid of expression, 'when I reached the reception, I discovered someone gossiping.' He paused and she heard him breathe deeply. 'About you.'

She jerked round to face him. What on earth was going on?

'About me?' She shook her head. Of all the things he could have said, this was the least expected. What sort of gossip could there be about her?

His eyes, hooded and darkly gleaming, held hers. 'About the fact that Amy has no father.'

Rosalie felt something plummet through her chest. Emotion. Indignation. Anger. Disbelief.

It was unbelievable!

'That's no one's business but my own,' she said through her clenched jaw, unable to credit the sort of maliciousness that would make an issue of that. Then she realised she wasn't at home any more. She was in a foreign country. A country where the customs and expectations were different to her own.

Nevertheless, *she* had nothing to be ashamed of!

'I have to tell you that I made it my business.'

'How?' Rosalie stilled as the hairs on her nape prickled. Only now did she begin to notice the tension humming through his big body and the rigid set of his broad shoulders. Something was very wrong.

There was silence for a long moment and Rosalie heard the thrum of her heartbeat, loud and heavy.

'I announced that you were under my protection. That we were going to wed.'

There was a sudden whooshing sound that had to be the air rushing from her lungs. His hand tightened on hers as her knees threatened to buckle and she swayed.

In front of them, totally oblivious to the bombshell Arik had just dropped, Amy giggled as one of the puppies stood up on its hind legs and licked her chin.

Rosalie stared, trying to bring her whirling thoughts into order. It was impossible. Unbelievable.

'You had no right.' She swung round and looked up into his stern, impenetrable face. He looked forbidding, his expression harsh, his nose arrogantly hewn, his jaw solid and uncompromising. Like a man carved of stone or shaped of unyielding metal. His eyes glittered bright as obsidian and just as hard.

'It was my duty to protect you.'

'Your *duty*!' Her voice rose on a screech of disbelief that made Amy look up for an instant.

'You *have* no *duty* towards me,' Rosalie whispered when she was in control of her voice again. What did he think she was? Some helpless weakling in need of a protector? 'I can fight my own battles.'

'And if I want to fight them with you?'

She shook her head, tugging to pull her hand from his grasp. For answer he reached for her other hand, holding her steady so she couldn't escape without drawing Amy's attention.

'Don't be absurd! I'm nothing to you.'

'You keep saying that.' His mouth twisted up in a smile that looked as if it hurt. 'And yet you're the woman I plan to marry.'

If he hadn't been holding her, Rosalie knew she would have slumped to the floor as her knees liquefied in shock. She stared up into his brooding face, but there wasn't a flicker of emotion to be seen there. Not even a flash of humour.

'That's not funny.' There was a quiver in her voice and she gulped, trying to get control of her voice-box.

'No, Rosalie. It's not funny.'

'You can't be so…antiquated as to expect me to marry you just to stop some stupid gossip.'

He tilted his head as if considering her words.

'You don't care what people say about you? About Amy?'

'Of course I care. But I'm not going to let some malicious tattle force me into anything so absurd as marriage.'

'So you see the idea of marriage to me as absurd?' His deep voice resonated with an inflection she couldn't identify. Something that twisted her insides into a knot of hard distress.

'I…' She floundered for a suitable lie.

'As wife of the Sheikh you would be beyond such recriminations. You would be respected. Revered even.'

She couldn't believe her ears. He was talking as if it were even remotely feasible. Her and him. Man and wife. She choked down on welling emotion, blinked back the haze of useless tears that threatened. Even in this ridiculous situation she couldn't divorce herself from her secret, utterly absurd yearning—for his love.

'It's academic,' she murmured brokenly, looking down at his strong hands holding hers. 'It's not going to happen.'

'Rosalie.' His fierce whisper made her head snap up. 'I *want* to marry you.'

She shook her head. This had gone beyond a joke. She knew him to be supremely self confident, sure of getting his own way. But he was an honourable man too. He could be tender and patient. He shouldn't treat her like this.

'Don't lie to me, Arik. It doesn't matter. Truly. I'll survive a bit of gossip.'

If he'd looked severe before, the stark, aristocratic cast of his features made him look utterly unapproachable now. His fingers tightened their grip till the blood pulsed heavily in her hands.

'You couldn't be happy living with me? Living here in Q'aroum?'

Rosalie squeezed shut her eyes. It was too much, being offered such temptation. Of course she could be happy here. She'd be in seventh heaven if Arik loved her as she did him. But that wasn't within the realm of possibility. Not even to someone who'd spent her early years perfecting the art of fantasising.

She'd learned her lesson well since then. She lived in the real world. She faced the truth, no matter how harsh. Rosalie snapped her eyes open.

'There's no question of us marrying. It would have been better if you'd said nothing last night.' For surely he'd put himself in an invidious position, announcing a marriage that wasn't going to happen. It was *his* reputation he should worry about, not hers.

'You will not marry me?'

It was too much. Even for a woman who'd resolved not to show how much it hurt. Rosalie tasted blood on her tongue. She ducked her head, unable to meet his shuttered gaze any longer.

'Don't! Please, just…don't.'

'Rosalie? *Habibti*.' His arms came round her, tugging her resisting form close till she stood in his arms, felt the generous heat of his body encircling her.

Numbly she shook her head. The whole idea was crazy.

'I'm going home to Australia soon, anyway.' No matter what outmoded ideas prevailed in Q'aroum, they didn't apply in Australia.

'Then I shall follow you.'

What? Stunned, she looked up into his face. Never before had he looked so grim.

'I don't understand. Why would you—?'

'If that's where you are, then that's where I'll be. You should know by now that I'm a man who doesn't give up when he wants something.' He looked down at her and this time she saw a flicker of strong emotion on his features.

'I want you, Rosalie. And I intend to have you.'

'No!' What sort of game was this? 'It's over, Arik. I don't want an affair. I can't go on like this any more.'

'Nor can I, little one. This is tearing me apart.' His hand cupped her cheek, his thumb brushing across her lips in a caress that made her quiver deep inside.

'I love you, Rosalie Winters. I want you for my wife.' His lips quirked up in a smile that looked painfully tight. 'I want an affair with you that will last our whole lives.'

She stared. She'd seen his lips form the words. She'd *heard* the words. But they couldn't be right.

'There's no need to lie, Arik. There's no need to be gallant.'

'Gallant? To my shame, that's one thing I haven't been with you, *habibti*. I've been short-sighted, selfish. A slave to desire.' His hands pulled her close, sliding restlessly over her in long, urgent caresses that moulded her to his hard length.

'I thought I knew what I wanted. Thought I knew it all. What a fool I was!' He lowered his head to nuzzle her cheek, her ear, caress her neck with his lips till her head swam and darts of sweet sensation jetted through her. 'I had no idea. None at all.'

'You love me?' The words finally emerged from her rusty throat.

'I *adore* you, Rosalie. Your passion, your beauty, your seductive body. But so much more than that. It's your spirit, your stubborn, gritty, honest strength of character.' He pulled back just far enough to look her in the eye and what she saw in his face made her blink.

'You're beautiful on the inside as well as the outside. I've never met a woman like you. So gentle, clever and patient. So strong. I planned to seduce you into my life but it was you who did the seducing. I couldn't get you out of my mind. Even when you ran away. Even when I discovered who you were. I was honour-bound to leave you alone and yet still I couldn't turn from you as I should.'

His eyes, blazing with dark fire, held hers and, despite her caution and her distrust, a tiny flare of excitement flickered to life in the frozen recesses of her heart.

'What I feel is stronger than duty or honour. It has nothing to do with shabby gossip or convenience.'

Rosalie's heart was doing somersaults in her chest. Her whole body shook as she strove to understand. To be sensible.

'But you don't want a wife.'

'I didn't *plan* to take a wife yet. I was content with my life as it was. Until I met you. You turned my world upside down.' His caresses grew slower, his voice deeper, and Rosalie's body responded immediately. She felt as if she were melting.

'I wanted you for sex,' he whispered in a voice that rumbled, low and seductive, right through her. 'I thought I knew how it would be between us, Rosalie. But I was wrong. It was you who taught me. About honesty and about a yearning stronger even than lust. About love. Being with you was so different from being with any other woman.'

The weighted heat of his hands on her body drew the last of her strength away, lulling her into ecstasy and submission. But still she resisted.

'No! I'm just a novelty to you. That's all. I'm different to the other women you've…had.' He'd probably revelled in his role of teacher, in her patent lack of sensual knowledge. No wonder he was intrigued. But that would pass.

His hands tightened almost painfully. 'Is your self-confidence so bruised that you actually believe that?'

Rosalie shook her head, denying the temptation of his words. It couldn't be true. It couldn't. Why was he so set on convincing her of something so patently impossible?

'You barely know me.' And yet that hadn't stopped her from falling head over heels in love with him.

'I know you, Rosalie. I know you enough to want to spend the rest of my life with you.'

The echo of his words thrummed in the silence between them and she let her eyes close, allowing herself the luxury of hope.

'But I understand it may be too soon for you, sweetheart. I will give you time.' He drew her so close that she was plastered against him, her head tucked into his chest so she could hear the heavy, rapid thump of his heart. Her whole body flush with his, his legs planted wide, surrounding her. It was heaven.

'You've been treated badly in the past. You have every reason not to trust. I understand that.' She felt the vibration of his voice rumble in his chest, heard its dark liquid tones, sweet as honey. 'And I've compounded your distrust, losing my temper, awakening old hurts. I can't expect you to love me— yet. But give us time, Rosalie. You'll see that I can be more than a lover. I'll make a good husband, a loving father for Amy.'

Amy. Rosalie sucked in a deep breath redolent with his warm, spicy scent as his words struck her. He wanted to be a father to Amy! To a child whose biological father was unknown: a cowardly, violent abuser.

Arik was willing to commit himself to taking on her daughter in such circumstances?

In a country where traditions of birthright and lineage and honour were so strong, he wanted to father her little girl.

Rosalie lifted her head, blinking up at him through the sudden glaze of hot tears.

'You want to be a father to Amy?'

'Of course. She is a part of you. And she's special in her own right. So bright, so beautiful, so…Rosalie! What is it? Don't cry, my little rose. Don't cry, please.' He rocked her close against him, so close they were melded together. 'Whatever it is, I'll make it right. I swear it.'

She shook her head, knowing suddenly that it *was* right. So perfect that it was better even than her secret fantasies. What daydream could match the reality of Arik's love? So real and warm and full that she felt as if her heart were overflowing.

She rose on tiptoe, pulling his head down towards her so she could press her lips against his.

Instantly his mouth took hers, delving deeply, thoroughly in a sensuous kiss that spoke of barely restrained passion, soul-deep yearning. His embrace was possessive, almost too tight as he held her close. His body was locked hard with banked emotion, with a desire that matched her own. She felt his rigid erection against her belly and pressed up against it.

Arik shuddered, hauling her closer, hands splayed over her bottom as he shifted his weight, aligning them more intimately. The heat between them was volcanic, sparking and alive. She pressed into him and heard him groan.

'No, Rosalie. We mustn't.' He pressed his forehead against hers as he sucked in breaths so deep his chest heaved. 'Not here, not now.'

'I love you, Arik,' she whispered unsteadily.

'Rosalie!' His hand under her chin tilted her head so she met his blazing eyes. 'What did you say?'

'I love you.' She smiled through tears of happiness. 'I've loved you from the first, didn't you know? That's why I ran away. I couldn't bear to think you only wanted—'

'Shh, little one. Don't say it. Don't remind me of how shallow I was.' But already, as the stern control slid away from his features, she read the sensual intent there. The hawk-eyed intensity that told her just what he had on his mind.

He stepped forward, backing her up against the wall. 'So, you will marry me?' His hands caressed her slowly, sending delicious thrills of desire right through her. She caught her breath at the waves of sensation coiling already in the pit of her stomach.

'Say it, Rosalie. Say you'll marry me.'

That was when she saw it. The tiniest trace of uncertainty, of doubt, in his face. As if he, too, needed reassurance. She reached up and clasped his warm cheeks in her shaking hands.

'You're the only man in the world I *could* marry, Arik. I love you so much.'

The rest of her words were cut off as his mouth took hers. Sensual heat flared instantly as he pushed her back against the wall, his body a seductive weight, his hands exploring each sensitive spot, slowing at the buttons on her shirt—

'Mummy!' Tiny hands tugged at her trousers and instantly, breathlessly, Arik stood back.

They stared at each other in shocked silence, knowing that in just a few minutes more her trousers would have been pooled around her ankles and his clothes discarded in a heap.

'Why are you kissing Arik, Mummy?'

Rosalie looked down into her daughter's curious face and knew one last hurdle remained. She reached down and pulled Amy into her arms.

'Because I love him, darling. And he loves me.' She held

her breath, aware of Arik's tense stance matching her own. 'He wants to be your daddy, Amy. He wants us to live with him.'

'Really?' Huge eyes turned from her to Arik and a trickle of fear slid down Rosalie's spine. How would she handle this if Amy couldn't cope with the idea?

'Really,' Arik's deep voice answered. 'I want you to be my little girl as well. We'll all be one family.'

'And G'anma?'

'And your grandma too.'

'And Auntie Belle and Uncle Rafi and Adham?'

'They're already my family, Amy.'

'Good. I like my family.' She stared up at Arik. 'I like you too.' She blew him a kiss. 'Can we have breakfast now? I'm hungry.'

Rosalie stifled a burble of hysterical laughter at the look on Arik's face. Nonplussed barely described it.

'You go on ahead, sweetie, and we'll follow.' She put Amy down and watched her head for the door.

'The final seal of approval,' he murmured, his lips twitching.

'Except for your own family,' she suddenly remembered.

He shook his head and reached out a hand to her cheek. Her eyes closed at the tender caress of his fingers against her sensitive flesh.

'Don't worry, little one. My mother's home from her apartment in Paris and she's eager to meet you. She's been hinting for ages that it's time I settled down with one woman, but I suspect it's your painting that's really intrigued her. She's seen it and she approves. She thinks that at last I'm showing some real discrimination, choosing an artist as my woman.'

'Really?'

'Yes, really.' His hand slid down the column of her throat to the throbbing pulse at its base, drawing tingling responses from her with every feather-light touch.

'You know,' he mused, 'I was so sure it would be safe to talk to you here, with Amy present.' His hand drew lower across her skin, down to the top button of her shirt. Immediately her nipples peaked in expectation.

'I thought I'd be able to keep my hands to myself, knowing she was here.'

'You proposed to me in a stable because you didn't trust yourself to be alone with me?' Rosalie didn't know whether to be amused or horrified.

'Of course.' One dark eyebrow winged up at her doubt. 'It seemed more sensible than finding a romantic spot where I might be tempted to seduce you.'

His fingers brushed the tiny buttons of her shirt, snaring the breath in her throat.

'But you're not tempted here?' Her voice was uneven, a dead giveaway to the excitement rocketing through her.

He shook his head, slipping a button undone and pressing his lips to her collar-bone. Rosalie sighed and let her head loll back against the wall, feeling the inevitable loosening of muscles as her body anticipated his.

'I'm *always* tempted by you, my sweet rose.' He lifted his head long enough to sear her with his gaze. 'We need to marry very soon.'

Wordlessly she nodded, already sliding into the beckoning heat of his caresses, of their mutual desire, knowing that, beyond all expectation, she was utterly secure in the arms of the man she loved.

'You are everything to me,' he murmured, his lips teasing her as he followed the trail of her buttons, popping each one open. His breath hazed her skin and she reached for him, holding him as if she'd never let him go.

'Amy might come back,' she croaked as his mouth closed on her breast and she arched up against him.

'Rafiq will stop her. My cousin's no fool.' With a quick, deft movement Arik flicked open her bra and tugged it out of the way. His mouth on her bare flesh made her writhe.

'They're expecting us for breakfast,' she gasped.

'Later.' He smoothed his broad hands over her torso and down to the waistband of her trousers. She felt his smile against her breast. 'Breakfast can wait.'

IN THE
SHEIKH'S ARMS

BY
SUE SWIFT

A criminal defence attorney for twenty years, **Sue Swift** always sensed a creative wellspring bubbling inside her, but didn't find her niche until attending a writing class with the master teacher Bud Gardener. Within a short time, Sue realised her creative outlet was romance fiction. The 2001 President of the Sacramento Chapter of the Romance Writers of America, Sue credits the RWA, its many wonderful programmes and the help of its experienced writers for her new career as a romance novelist. She also lectures to women's and writers' groups on various topics related to the craft of writing.

Her hobbies are hiking, bodysurfing and kenpo karate, in which she's earned a second-degree black belt. Sue and her real-life hero of a husband maintain homes in northern California and Maui, Hawaii. Please visit Sue's website: www.sue-swift.com

This book is dedicated to Barbara McMahon,
who inspired it.

Prologue

Ten years ago

Fury raging in his heart, Rayhan ibn-Malik stomped on the accelerator. His Land Rover surged forward, churning clouds of Texas dust as he left his spread, the Double Eagle. He drove at a wild pace in through the Ellisons' open gate.

Nothing had changed at the C-Bar-C since Rayhan had put his name to the deceptive deed and purchased the Double Eagle. No hint of scandal seething beneath the broad plains. No trace of the oil riches bubbling under the surface of this peaceful ranch.

No clue to reveal the wealth Rayhan thought he'd purchased from Charles Ellison. No sign of the bounty the old man had promised.

The C-Bar-C appeared as calm and well managed as ever. Oil pumps and derricks punctuated the distant horizon. A line of trees bordered the stream meandering between the two ranches. Orderly corrals penned the Ellisons' stock.

Rayhan's heartbeat tripled as he passed the stable, nearing the main house. Brief days ago he'd relaxed in that white, balconied home, sipping beer and signing documents in apparent friendship with Charles Ellison.

Bitterness twisted Rayhan's gut. In all fairness, he couldn't entirely blame Ellison. Rayhan's own poor English and incompetent attorney had doubtless contributed to the debacle…in part.

But only in part.

Rayhan jerked the steering wheel to the left, avoiding a circle of lawn set in the middle of the wide, graveled drive. Pebbles sprayed from beneath the tires. He stamped on the brake, bringing the Rover to a halt.

As if Rayhan had been expected, Ellison waited on the veranda. Rayhan couldn't discern the older man's expression in the shadows. Getting out of the Rover, Rayhan slammed its door behind him. With no reason to censor his words, he said, "You cheated me."

Ellison smiled. But the twitch of his lips wasn't triumphant. Worse, the old man appeared patronizing. "Next time, you'll read closer, pup. A cheap lesson. You'll never get suckered again."

Rayhan flushed. *Pup.* At age twenty, he didn't need reminders of his inexperience. "Again? What again? That worthless transaction took all my money."

Ellison shrugged. "You got a fine ranch, and a beautiful herd of Herefords to boot."

"Cows?" Rayhan snorted. "Cows, and none of the oil that flows beneath the land." Without the oil riches he craved, Rayhan would have nothing to show his family in Adnan. No way to prove to his father, the king, that Rayhan was worthy of the government post he wanted and knew he deserved. A younger son, he'd long accepted he would never rule, but he yearned for the power, responsibility and respect he had earned through his birth and education.

"I couldn't sell you the mineral rights even if I wanted to. They belong to her." Old Man Ellison nodded in the direction of the patch of lawn in the middle of the drive.

Rayhan hadn't previously noticed the scruffy young girl kneeling on the grass, playing with a litter of puppies. The child's blond hair, crookedly parted, was bound into two awkward plaits. With green grass stains marring her pink overalls, the girl's unkempt appearance startled Rayhan. Nannies and nurses had always kept his sisters immaculate. This ragamuffin was a wealthy oil magnate?

Through his surprise and wrath, Rayhan struggled to grasp the situation. "The oil belongs to this child?"

"My daughter, Camille." Ellison's chest swelled with obvious pride. He walked down the porch steps and past Rayhan, who still stood on the graveled drive. The old man joined the child on the grass, continuing to speak.

"This here land belonged to her mother's family. That's why it's called the C-Bar-C, for the Crowells. My wife left everything to Cami. I manage it, of course. By the terms of the will, I could sell you the land, but not the oil rights. When she's an adult, it'll all be hers."

Rayhan's gaze locked onto the fair-haired child. Raising her head, she stared back with wide blue eyes. Thank heaven for little girls, he thought, mentally paraphrasing an old song. For they'll grow up into vulnerable young women.

Rayhan smiled. It'll all be hers, Ellison had said. *No, old man. It'll all be mine.*

Chapter One

Cami Ellison stood in front of her bathroom mirror, brushing her long hair with frustrated strokes. She glowered at her reflection as though the fierceness of her stare could zap the zit on her chin out of existence. *Nearly twenty and I still have skin like a thirteen-year-old!*

After throwing her brush onto the pink-tiled counter with a clatter, she spread sunscreen on her face and concealer over the pimple. She plaited her hair into a braid that fell below her shoulders. After securing it with a purple scrunchie, she flung open the door of her closet to survey the contents.

A strange restlessness consumed her. She wanted something—anything—to happen, like a con eagerly awaiting a planned escape. She knew her widowed father had spoiled her, but after a year away at college, Cami felt caged by the routine dullness of life with Dad on the C-Bar-C Ranch.

Since her return from San Antonio, armed with new knowledge from her studies, she'd spent every day running the ranch. But today…if she didn't get out of the house she'd start to beat her head against the walls.

She didn't know what she wanted but, jumpy and tense, she sure did want something. Maybe a good hard ride would get rid of the tension coiling in her belly, so tight and sharp it was a physical need, an ache she'd never before felt and one that she didn't know how to soothe.

She pulled on a sports bra, then covered it with a T-shirt. Tugging on stretch jeans, she tucked the pink top into her pants, then cinched on a tooled leather belt. She shoved her feet into battered cowboy boots and grabbed her old Stetson from its perch on a hook above her desk.

Though Cami loved her father and their long-time housekeeper, Robbie, the thought of exchanging pleasantries with them over coffee and toast made her want to scream. She skipped breakfast, hurrying out of the house and heading directly to the stables.

At the entrance she breathed deeply and calmed herself, at least a fraction, her shoulders settling lower and her heartbeat slowing. The warmth of the stable, the late June sunlight slanting in through its high windows and its familiar animal smells all reminded her of her childhood.

She paced down the row of stalls, greeting old friends, until she came to her buddy, Sugar. Sugar, a palomino mare, had been her mount since Cami's teenage growth spurt had retired Funnyface, her pony.

Cami opened the stall door and Sugar started forward. She tucked her long nose against Cami's shoulder to snort a greeting, as she did every day Cami lived at the C-Bar-C. Laughing, Cami caught Sugar's bridle to lead her in the direction of the tack room.

A few minutes later they were cantering across the C-Bar-C's fields. A line of bushes and trees shimmered, gray-green and dusty, in the distance. Cami remembered that their foliage hid a winding stream that divided the C-Bar-C from the Double Eagle, Ray Malik's horse farm.

The gossips in the nearby town, McMahon, said that Malik's Arabians, valued as studs and mares, had won numerous prizes, including an Olympic medal for dressage. Though they'd been neighbors for ten years, Cami didn't know Ray personally. Her father, who maintained friendships with just about everyone, had always kept his distance from Ray Malik. He'd never shared his reasons for snubbing Malik with Cami, and Cami, sensitive to her elderly father's feelings, had never asked.

Cami and Sugar entered the dappled shade of the cottonwoods bordering the stream. Cami loosened her hold on the reins, allowing Sugar her head. The mare picked her way to the water, stopping where the creek widened into a hidden swimming hole. She dropped her head and drank from the quiet pond.

After sliding off her horse's back, Cami leaned against a convenient tree to stretch her quads and hamstrings. Though an experienced rider, she hadn't been on horseback for months—not since her previous visit home. She was tight.

Through the branches, she glimpsed a flash of white fabric billowing in the breeze, Cami craned her head around the mare to see better, absentmindedly stroking Sugar's rough mane.

A rider on a big, gray horse entered the thicket alongside the creek. Catching a look at his white, fluttering head scarf, Cami wondered who on earth wore such bizarre attire. While a cynical part of her thought he looked like a refugee from an old Rudolph Valentino flick, her romantic soul was titillated by the Arabian headdress floating in the breeze.

He'd slowed the beautiful gray to a stop between the cottonwoods, allowing his horse to refresh itself in the water. Cami and her mare remained hidden behind a clump of bushes.

The man dismounted. Removing his headgear and a white shirt, he bared himself to the waist above tan jodhpurs and riding boots. His body, slick and burnished by sweat, gleamed bronze in the golden morning sunlight.

Cami's breath stuck somewhere in her throat. She pulled off her Stetson and used it to fan herself. She'd seen a man's naked torso, of course, but none of her classmates had ever struck her as…beautiful.

The man had to be Ray Malik, their mysterious neighbor. His years of hard work breeding and training Arabians showed in his broad shoulders and sinewy pecs. He knelt beside the creek, splashing the cool water onto his face and neck. When he shook his head, his longish hair scattered crystalline drops in an arc, glittering in the light.

How would he feel? Cami wondered. She'd never

stroked a man's nude chest. Now she imagined running her fingertips along those sculptured planes, rimming his dark nipples with her nails.

Her hand involuntarily clenched in Sugar's mane. Her mare shied away, snorting, then backed away from the stream, exposing Cami.

The man jerked upright. His gaze, palpable as a touch, fastened on her. Intent eyes assessed her with the attitude of a sheikh selecting a slave girl for the night. Then he smiled, gesturing for her to cross the stream onto his land.

Cami hesitated, mindful of her father's distant attitude toward Ray. On the other hand, Charles Ellison had never overtly warned her away from Ray or forbidden her to set foot on the Double Eagle.

And she'd been curious about Ray Malik for as long as she could remember. Over the years she occasionally glimpsed him in McMahon and around his ranch, mounted on one of his gorgeous Arabians. She'd heard intriguing rumors about him.

The more outlandish storytellers said that he was an Arab prince exiled from his family because of his politics. Others said he'd been a spy, now retired to this quiet corner of Texas. Some gossiped about his trysts, though none of the exotic women he was rumored to bed ever appeared in McMahon.

Well, she'd wanted something to happen. An old proverb rolled through her mind. "Be careful what you wish for…you might get it."

Cami gathered Sugar's reins, then remounted. Clicking her tongue against her teeth, she guided the mare to a narrow ford, then urged her across the stream.

Heat rose in her cheeks, but she didn't know how to hide her embarrassment. This wildly attractive male had caught her spying on him. An older man, he radiated sensuality and experience. She felt young and absurdly unsophisticated by comparison.

However, she wanted to capture his interest, prove she could attract a man more mature and worldly than the boys she'd dated in high school and college.

Cami knew she was playing with fire. Seduction wasn't on her agenda, but she realized that a man as handsome as Ray Malik probably expected more than pleasant conversation from a woman who flirted with him. She told herself not to promise anything she didn't intend to deliver.

She was honest enough to admit that although she wanted his attention, she didn't know how to get it. "Do you come here often?" or "What's your sign?" wouldn't cut the mustard. Nor would the usual opening lines that worked on campus. "What classes are you taking?" just didn't make sense here. But what did?

Cami watched the spot between Sugar's ears, the glittering water as it splashed from the mare's hooves…anything to avoid Ray's dark, keen stare.

Sugar came to the bank of the creek. She climbed the shore, and Cami halted her mount beside Ray's. She raised her gaze to meet his.

Rich and brown, his eyes glinted with a roguish humor. She was close enough to catch his scent, a spicy aftershave that hinted at mysterious souks and exotic ports of call. None of which, she glumly reminded herself, she had ever seen.

She was *such* a zero. How could she hope to interest a man like Ray Malik?

She cleared her throat. "Hi. Uh, I'm Cami, and this is Sugar," she blurted like a dork.

He smiled. Even, white teeth gleamed against his stubbly cheek. His skin was the color of wildflower honey. He had a beautiful mouth, with lips that weren't too thin or too puffy, topped by a totally adorable Cupid's bow. Her tummy did flip-flops, becoming all warm and squishy.

"I know who you are, Camille Crowell Ellison. And I know of your Sugar. She's a lovely mare. She has very good bloodlines." He stroked her horse's neck, and Sugar responded with a friendly chuff.

Cami's surprise at Ray's knowledge of her full true name was overshadowed by his interest in her beloved Sugar. "How do you know?"

"I know everything about you."

She nearly fell out of the saddle. "Why? How? No one can know everything about another person."

"I have watched you for many years."

She should have been creeped out. Wasn't he admitting he was a stalker or a Peeping Tom? On the other hand, she'd been the one spying on him as he cooled off in the water. "Why?"

"It is hard for me not to be interested in a pretty young woman, especially one who rides almost as well as do I." Ray winked at her.

She gasped. Cami, a veteran of many riding competitions, wasn't about to take a back seat to anyone—certainly not if the seat was on a horse. "Even if you do say so yourself." She was determined to deflate this man's massive ego.

His impish grin made his dark eyes twinkle. She could have sworn he was out to get her goat. But why?

"No insult intended, as you Americans might say. I am pulling your leg." Ray reached for her ankle, seizing it with one big hand. He gave it a gentle tug.

Even through her boot, she felt his strong grasp. His power remained controlled, so he didn't haul her off her mount. She figured he could have if he'd wanted. But he didn't.

What was this man's game?

She looked down at him. He released her foot, then strolled to the pile of white cloth he'd left when he'd partially stripped. He slid his arms into his shirt, allowing it to remain open at the chest, then arranged his headdress. His muscles rippled beneath satiny, amber skin.

Cami pulled her shirt away from her chest to cool down. "What's with the head thingie?" she asked.

He shrugged. "Occasionally, I miss my country, so I will dress in the garb of my people. It is very comfortable. Wrapped correctly, my *gutra* will keep dust out of my face quite well. Have you ever worn one?"

"N-no."

He gathered his horse's reins, then vaulted into the saddle in one smooth, elegant motion.

Cami had to admit to herself that she'd never mastered that little trick. "Nice horse. One of your Arabians?"

"I haven't told you who I am." His grin turned wicked.

She sniffed. "You're not the only one who knows the neighborhood. You're Ray Malik. You raise Arabians at the Double Eagle."

"Ah, so you know all about me." Rayhan sincerely hoped not. If her father had poisoned her ears with tales about Ray's anger at the oil swindle, he'd never have a chance to fulfill his long-planned revenge.

Over the years Rayhan had been careful to avoid Charles Ellison. He didn't want Ellison to have any reason to gossip to his daughter about the rancher next door. Since the disastrous land deal, Rayhan had done nothing more remarkable than raise horses and travel.

He wanted to alter the course of the conversation, and remembered a compliment always worked on women. "You sit your mare very well. Have you competed?"

She actually blushed and ducked her head. What was wrong with American males? This stunning young woman behaved as though no one ever praised her. Impossible. Ridiculous. However, Rayhan liked her modesty.

Her shirt and jeans revealed a curvy, feminine body. She still had pale hair, a mane gleaming like a halo in the morning sun. It was bound into a long, tidy braid which draped over her shoulder and curled around one round breast, like a lover's caress. He envied that braid.

Rayhan smiled. The ragamuffin had grown into a princess. Revenge would be sweet indeed.

"Yeah," she said. "Sugar and I used to compete before I went away to college in San Antonio. I don't have time to ride when I'm at school."

"San Antonio's a nice town. What classes are you taking?"

Cami's eyes widened. Her hands tightened on the reins, jerking them. For no reason Rayhan could fathom, the question seemed to astound her. Her mount turned her large head to give Cami the equine equivalent of a steely glare.

"Have a care," he said. "You sit your mare well, but she doesn't like quick movements."

"I know that. You surprised me, that's all."

"Why?"

"Your question about my classes."

"As I said, it is not unusual for a man to be interested in a pretty woman, especially if she lives on the ranch next door." Odd that Cami didn't grasp the basics about male-female relationships. Could she be such an innocent?

"You never showed any interest before."

"You were too young. A man who is friendly with a young girl is…gross, as you Americans might say."

She laughed. "I guess you're right. Well, to answer your question, I'm studying business, specifically oil."

"So, you know what you wish to do?"

"Oh, I want to stay here." Cami sounded definite. "The C-Bar-C is my home. I'll run the family oil business. I've been helping my dad for years."

"What if you married?" he asked, keeping his voice even.

"What if I did? My husband better like Texas, that's all I can say."

Rayhan decided he'd like Texas long enough to get what—or rather who—he wanted. He showed her his teeth. "Then it is fortunate indeed that I like Texas."

Confusion drifted over Cami's face before she managed a nervous smile. Rayhan realized he was moving too fast, and that he'd better back off.

"How do you jump into the saddle like that? Sugar won't let me."

She'd changed the subject, a sign she wanted to go slower. All right, he'd comply. If he could.

"It is easy, but your horse must expect the sudden weight. Try mounting Kalil." He slid out of his saddle.

"Wow, thanks." Cami dismounted and approached Kalil, stroking his nose. "He's gorgeous. Did you breed him?"

She'd drawn closer, now standing mere inches away. He inhaled her subtle fragrance. She didn't wear heavy perfume, so nothing artificial cloaked her natural, feminine aroma. He liked that. Her scent recalled the wind and the sky. Her eyes were the color of heaven.

Bedding her would be no chore.

With difficulty Rayhan reminded himself of his goal: revenge, not pleasure. He wrenched his mind back to their conversation. What had they been talking about? Ah, yes. Kalil. "Yes, he is one of my stock. I recognized early he would not be suitable for stud, so I gelded him and he has become my favorite saddle horse."

"Poor Kalil."

He laughed. "You must know that stallions make poor mounts. They are too wild and restless. You would not enjoy, for example, riding Karim, my prime stud. He would throw you into the dust in a matter of moments."

"Karim and Kalil. What do those names mean?"

"Karim means noble one, and Kalil is best friend."

"That's beautiful." Cami was entranced. The reality of Ray Malik was better than the rumors. He was handsome, he was nice and he said straight out that he was interested in her. No games. Cami liked that. She didn't like game players and she hated deception.

"So try jumping into the saddle. The trick is to use your thigh muscles."

Cami eyed Kalil. She was sure of the gelding's good manners, but he was a tall animal, at least seventeen hands. Though she wasn't short, she didn't know if she could leap into the saddle with Ray's grace. Now that he'd showed interest in her, she didn't want to mess things up by falling on her butt into the mud by the stream. "Maybe some other time."

"You are a scaredy-cat?"

Cami giggled. The child's phrase sounded hilariously incongruous coming from Ray's lips. "Am not!"

"Are too." He leaned against Kalil and regarded her from beneath lowered lids.

Bedroom eyes. That was what Ray had: bedroom eyes. Cami had never quite understood that phrase until this moment, when his smoldering glance had caught hers. She jerked her gaze away from his and fought for her fleeting poise. "You're…you're ridiculous."

"You are not up to a challenge."

With that outrageous statement, she recovered herself. "Of all the nerve! I can do anything you can do and better."

"Well, then. Let us try something less challenging but perhaps more exciting."

She turned and looked into his eyes. He stood close enough to touch, with his loose, white shirt hanging open to expose his muscular torso. He was virility personified.

Too close, too fast. Cami, don't promise what you can't deliver. She stepped back, sucking in an uneasy breath.

Mistake. His scent compelled her to draw nearer. She fought his pheromones and her instincts.

He smiled.

She was lost.

Ray ran a long, elegant finger along her jawline. Cami's flesh tingled; the tiny hairs along her skin rose. Closing her eyes, she inhaled, exquisitely aware of his exotic scent and her body. He'd somehow transformed her into a quivering mass of sensation with just one touch.

How had he done this? she wondered. She'd been touched before, but no other man had turned her on. With only one gentle stroke of the finger, Ray fanned her feminine fires into a blaze.

Her nipples rasped against the soft cups of her bra.

She didn't need to look down to see what had happened, and didn't want to. Burning with embarrassment and desire right down to her soul, she'd freak out if Ray noticed.

Part of her wanted to leave, but she couldn't let go of the challenge Ray had issued. She lifted her gaze to his.

Ray's glance shifted to her mouth, lingering there. He said, "Have you ever kissed a man on horseback?"

Chapter Two

"Sure I have."

Anger surged through Rayhan. That another man had touched his Texan princess infuriated him. She was his.

He tamped down his outrage, reminding himself that she was an American girl. Many were casual about their couplings, even loose. She's probably had sex in the saddle, he thought with disgust. His gut twisted. Could he actually marry such a female, even to seize the fortune he deserved?

Honor must be cleansed. Revenge would bring great joy, but harnessing himself to used goods repelled him.

He looked at Cami. A faraway dreaminess had entered her eyes. "When I was a little girl, my daddy would put me in front of him and we'd ride every morning."

Rayhan relaxed. She'd cuddled with her father on

horseback, not the college football team. "I have in mind something more…stimulating. Get on Sugar, and I'll show you." Mounting Kalil, he urged his horse alongside hers so they stood close.

Face to face with Cami, who was now back in Sugar's saddle, Rayhan could see a sparkling, feminine interest in her eyes. Taking a deep breath, he dropped Kalil's reins. His well-trained gelding stood rock still.

Rayhan reached for her, knowing he took a huge risk. He chanced spooking his prey. Though she shouldn't be pushed, he couldn't resist the open curiosity in her gaze. His quarry was within his grasp.

"Cami." He stroked her cheek, smooth and soft as the petals of a desert rose.

Her lips parted. He sensed her anticipation, her acceptance.

Leaning forward in his saddle, he touched his mouth to hers. Moist she was, and sweet. Better, she kissed him back with unmistakable innocence. Was it possible she'd remained untouched?

Rayhan's blood heated at the thought. He wanted more from her and took it.

Cami's world spun. She reached out and grabbed the open halves of Ray's shirt, seeking to steady herself. But deep inside she knew he didn't offer stability. Quite the contrary. He offered life in all of its tumult.

She'd been sheltered by her father's affection, but now she hungered for another kind of love, the whirlwind of falling for a potent, sexy male.

She would walk across Texas barefoot to have Ray.

Using his shirt to pull him closer, she responded when he deepened the kiss. He rubbed his thumbs along her jaw, urging her mouth open, then slid his tongue inside, penetrating her.

After one shocked, startled moment, the embers of her sexuality leaped into riotous flame. She burned from the inside out. She knew what she was doing was wrong, crazy, that Ray couldn't possibly be right for her. He'd demand more than she, a virgin, was prepared to give any man until she had a ring on her finger.

And yet, just one kiss from Ray caused her to question her deepest beliefs.

His lips curled sensuously around hers, and his tongue danced inside her mouth. She'd been kissed before, even Frenched, but the tentative caresses of the boys she knew had never felt like this. She'd never liked guys who slobbered all over her.

But Ray…Ray was different. He wasn't tentative, and he didn't slobber.

Stopping was out of the question.

Continuing was wrong, wrong, wrong. If they didn't quit, she'd let Ray sweep her away on a magic carpet of lust, and she'd give it up to him in the mud of the riverbank.

Sugar pranced back, snorting. Cami realized that her indecision must have communicated itself to her sensitive, intelligent mare.

Ray blinked at Cami. "'*Azhib.*''

"If that means wow in Arabic, I gotta agree. That was some kiss."

He nodded slowly, heavy lids lifting over those sul-

try bedroom eyes. His expression was predatory, determined. He reached for her again.

It was now or never. Moistening her lips, Cami
leaned back into her saddle, away from the temptation
he offered. "I, uh, I think you should know that I
don't do…that."

He dropped his hand. "Do what? Kiss a man?" He
didn't sound surprised; in fact, he seemed as though
he knew by her hesitation that she wasn't very experienced.

Embarrassment turned her body into one giant hot
flash. "Do, you know…it."

"It?" Now he appeared genuinely puzzled.

Good heavens, she thought. Do I have to spell everything out? Then, remembering their cultural and
language barriers, she concluded, probably.

She swallowed, and, making an effort to be absolutely clear and totally honest, said, "I don't sleep
around with men."

A pause ensued. "That is something of a relief,"
he finally said, in English as precise and careful as
hers. "That kiss would be less special if you did. But
why is this, Cami?" His words quickened. "You are,
what, twenty years of age? I remember what it was
like to be so young."

"Like you're so old. And I'm nineteen."

He grimaced as though the news were unwelcome.
"I was twenty when I came to Texas a decade ago."

"Wow. So you're thirty?" She sagged. "Dad'll
flip out."

"You are right." Again, Ray seemed to choose his

words carefully. "Your father, he may not approve of me."

"Why not?"

"I am much older than are you. To be truthful, I should not be with you at all." He turned his horse away, as if preparing to leave.

"Wait!" Cami urged her mare forward, blocking his path. "See here, I'm an adult. My father knows that I'll see who I want."

"You sound like a very disobedient daughter. This is not good. I would not cause a rift in your family." Ray's nose crinkled, giving him a comically disapproving look.

She had to smile. "Listen, I'm not going to do anything wrong. I told you, I don't...you know."

"You made this decision though other girls, um, do it?"

Cami shifted her weight. "When I was in high school, my dad watched me pretty closely. And he made me promise not to do it until I turned eighteen. He said after I went to college I was an adult and could make my own decisions." She raised her gaze to Ray's. "I keep my promises."

"And now? Are you not nineteen and released from your vow?"

"Yeah, but when I went away to school, I saw all these girls jumping into the sack with guys they barely knew just to see what it was like."

"It? Sleep around?" His eyebrows drew together into a straight, dark bar.

"Yeah, you know, sex." She shrugged. "And it didn't make them happier. Some got pregnant and had to have abortions. Some got STDs—sexually transmitted diseases. Some had to drop out because they were so distracted by their boyfriends that they failed classes.''

''So you decided not to—how can I say it—not to take that route?''

''Right.'' She bobbed her head up and down.

Rayhan couldn't have been more pleased. ''I think you are a very smart woman, Cami Ellison.'' Confident he'd seduce her, he now knew she'd be a pristine vessel for his pleasure.

He glanced at her again, taking in the details he'd missed earlier. A determined little chin. A firm mouth. Both spoke of her strong will. This woman wouldn't be easy, but she'd be worth every second of effort it took to win her.

Cornsilk hair and bluebonnet eyes—his heartbeat quickened. He'd been in America long enough to widen his tastes in women beyond the petite, dark females of Adnan. He'd come to admire American girls in all their marvelous variety.

And Cami was a Texan princess, tall, strong, smart and untouched by any other. She was perfect.

More than a little surprised, Rayhan realized that his calculations hadn't taken into account the possibility that he might actually desire Ellison's daughter.

But it didn't matter. He'd have her, whatever.

He'd tested her by suggesting that her father might not approve of their liaison; she'd reacted with a show of independence. Cami was willing to risk her father's displeasure. She was ready.

"When will I see you again?" he asked, his voice oddly husky. He cleared his throat.

Her lashes fluttered. "You're seeing me now."

"Alas, I cannot tarry with you all day." Pushing back his cuff, he glanced at his watch. "I have a ranch to manage. But tonight—tonight is another matter. Do you enjoy dancing?"

"Sure."

"Do you know Dancin' Nancy's, in McMahon?"

"Yeah."

"Come to me tonight, at about nine."

Cami's body brightened with delight. She practically danced in the saddle. Her little bounce up and down startled Sugar, who gave Cami another glare.

He'd asked her out! On a date!

With a wrench, Cami turned her mind back to the practicalities of the situation, remembering her zit and her wardrobe. Later in the week her pimple might recede. Plus, she'd have a chance to go shopping. "How about, um, Saturday?"

"I'd rather see you sooner, but Saturday is all right, too." His smile made her dizzy. He touched the side of his hand to his forehead in a mock salute. "Saturday at nine, then."

Fortunately for Cami, her salon in San Antonio had done a decent job on her face. Attired in a new outfit—a blue cotton dress with a gathered peasant neckline, belted waist and ruffled hem—Cami sat at the bar in Dancin' Nancy's on Saturday night. Ray had said nine, but Cami, jumpy and anxious, had arrived early. She figured she'd have a soda and a couple of dances before he came, just so she wouldn't be so nervous.

She kicked the toes of her favorite dress boots—black-and-white spotted calf—against the polished wood bar. A large doughnut shape, the bar occupied the center of Dancin' Nancy's. On one side of the bar a group of pool tables sat beneath hanging Tiffany-style lamps. Cowboys and oil-field roughnecks, cigarettes hanging from their lips and mugs of beer at hand, shot pool and goofed off.

A country-western band was playing on the stage that stretched the length of the other side of the room. A dance floor, where Nancy herself gave lessons, filled the area between the stage and the bar. Colored stage lights glittering off a mirror ball lit the dance floor, ringed with booths.

Cami had been coming to Dancin' Nancy's since she was a teenager. Now, seated at the bar, she listened to the ebb and flow of chatter while thinking about Ray Malik.

She had to admit to herself that little else had occupied her mind for days. She longed for his touch, craved his kiss every conscious hour. When she slept, she dreamed of loving him.

Contemplating the bubbles rising in her soda, she realized she knew little about this mysterious man.

He wasn't an American.

He was thirty years old.

He raised great horses.

He was the most intriguing person she'd ever met, and she wanted to know more about him.

Cami heard his name as though it echoed her thoughts. She raised her gaze from her glass, startled.

Around the circular bar from Cami's seat, two women were talking about Ray, their voices barely audible above the music. Cami hesitated. Then, taking her glass, she moved two seats closer. Now her back was to the door so she couldn't see who entered, but she could hear mighty fine.

One of the women, a striking redhead in a black sequined top, was finishing her story. "And he put her on a plane in Houston and never saw her again."

"A supermodel?" Her companion's eyes widened into big green lily pads. "Gone, just like that?" She snapped her fingers.

Cami shrank back into her bar stool. Yikes. This man tossed away beautiful women like empty soda cans.

She craned her head to hear more, but one of the gossips caught sight of her. After they made eye contact, the other woman turned her back and lowered her voice.

But Cami had eavesdropped enough. She repeated to herself, Don't promise what you won't deliver!

Cami heard the door behind her open. A rush of air raised the skin on her bare arms, even though the evening was warm and humid.

Ray had arrived.

She turned her head as he slid into the seat beside her. Her heart beat against the walls of her chest like a wild bird's wings. Across the bar, the chatterboxes fell silent. Cami couldn't stop herself from giving them a tiny, triumphant smile before devoting her full attention to Ray.

Tonight he wore jeans and a chambray workshirt, like many in the bar, but Ray stood out. His shirt was immaculate and pressed. Freshly washed, damp tendrils of dark hair coiled appealingly over his collar in tiny, cute curlicues. She caught his exotic scent when he leaned close to her and breathed into her ear, ''Hello, Cami.''

Playing with a lock of her loose hair, he said, ''I like your hair unbound. It looks…wild and free.''

Cami's mouth went dry. She swallowed, hoping he'd gotten the message when they'd last talked. He made her want to be wild and free, though at her own pace. Was that inconsistent? Probably, but Cami didn't care.

Ray leaned his forearms on the bar, exposing his wrists. One was circled by an expensive-looking gold watch.

Expensive was good, Cami thought. That meant he had money, so he wasn't after the C-Bar-C. When she turned fourteen, her father had started to warn her about boys who would want her for the ranch.

The sight of Ray's long-fingered, strong hands reminded Cami of the feel of those warm palms on her face when they'd kissed. Her heart tripped at the memory.

That had been the most thrilling moment of her life. She breathed deeply. She had to get herself under control.

''Hi, Ray.'' She strove to sound casual. ''How are ya?''

"Fine, now that I am with you."

Her pulse jumped, but Ray didn't seem to notice. He continued, "What are you drinking?"

"Ginger ale."

The bartender approached. "What'll it be?"

"I will have the same as my friend. And please bring her another. She is almost finished." Ray smiled at Cami.

She felt unbearably tense, yet expectant. Her skin dampened from nervous excitement. Lifting her hair off her nape to cool down, she wondered, Is this how love feels? Cami hoped not. She didn't know how much more of this she could take. She was about to explode with unexpressed emotions and barely trammeled energy.

Ray moved a warm hand to her knee, below the hem of her dress, which had ridden up onto her thigh. She wasn't wearing panty hose. He squeezed her naked flesh just above the knee.

She couldn't repress a hot quiver of desire. Picking up her glass, she gulped the icy drink, hoping she wouldn't burp out the bubbles. Please, Lord, please let me get through this evening without doing something stupid or embarrassing!

She remembered advice she'd frequently heard, that men loved to talk about themselves. All they needed was a little encouragement. "So, Ray, tell me a little more about yourself. There are…odd rumors around about you."

"Rumors? Of what sort?" His hand fell away from her leg.

She hesitated. She'd probably sound like a fool.

"Are you a prince? That seems to be the most popular theory about you."

"Yes, I am what you might call a sheikh."

She almost dropped her soda. A sheikh. A real-live, Arab sheikh here in Texas. Wow. She sought to recover her poise and asked, "What would you call yourself?"

"Rayhan," he said, smiling.

She liked that. He wasn't boastful. "Rayhan. Does your name have a meaning?"

"Yes, it does. It means that I am favored by God." His smile took on an ironic twist, turning into a rueful grimace.

"What's wrong?"

Ray rubbed damp palms on the thighs of his jeans, looking uncomfortable. He paid for the drinks when they arrived before responding. "I am the fourth son and seventh child of my father, who was the ruler of Adnan."

"Isn't that in north Africa, near Morocco?"

"Very good. Most Americans have never heard of Adnan, let alone know its location."

Cami, curious, wanted to discover the source of his obvious unease. "I take it your father didn't think much of fourth sons?"

"No, he did not. My eldest brother is now king. My second brother is his grand vizier. He trained for the position all his life. My third brother runs the military. My sisters married for political advantage."

"And the fourth son?" she asked.

"I have long believed that my chief usefulness is as a spare, ready to be slotted into position should one of my older brothers be harmed or killed.'' He gave a casual shrug, as if tossing aside his family's rejection.

"That seems unfair." Cami knew her father had spoiled her. She couldn't begin to imagine Ray's feelings when he realized he was disposable rather than valued.

"Life is frequently unfair." The harshness in his voice startled Cami, who hadn't yet seen a rough edge on Ray. Then he shrugged, and she wondered if she'd imagined his anger. He continued, "So I came to America, how would you say it, to make my fortune. There was nothing for me in Adnan. The king refused to consider his worthless fourth son for even a minor position."

Hoping to seem sympathetic, Cami nodded. "I know what you mean. In my father's bedroom he has a photograph of me next to his bed. It's ten years old. It's hard for me to persuade my father that I'm an adult when he still sees me as a nine-year-old."

Ray lifted his eyebrows. "A wonderful insight. Yes. Our parents, and others, stay in the habit of seeing us as we were, not as we are. So I came to America, as you might say, in a huff, determined to prove myself by becoming a success here."

"And so you raised world-famous, award-winning horses," Cami said. "You showed 'em, all right!"

"Yes, I suppose I did," he said, in a wry tone. "Do you know languages, Cami?"

"Only English and Spanish."

"Most useful. I wish my English had been better when I came to this country," he said.

Cami eyed Ray. She hadn't learned to read his moods, but thought that maybe the conversation bothered him. She could understand why he'd be unhappy over his father's treatment, but languages?

"Did you make your fortune? Are you happy with your life here?" She hoped he'd say yes, tell her he didn't hide a secret desire to return to his homeland. She wanted to find out what would happen between herself and Ray.

"I have done well, but I believe I may have recently discovered the greatest treasure of all." He again caressed her thigh. She tingled from the sheer pleasure of his touch.

He stood and adjusted his jeans. "Would you like to dance?"

"Yeah, sure would." She sipped her soda, then stood.

The band started to play a new tune, and lines began forming for the next dance. Cami was delighted to discover that Ray was as adept on the dance floor as he was on a horse.

And they had fun. When they did the tush push and the bump, Cami found herself turned on by his hips bouncing off hers.

The band started a slow number, and Ray wrapped her in his arms, massaging her bare back above the ruffled edge of her dress. His palm slid; she glowed from his nearness.

Spinning slowly, the mirror ball shed soft shards of red and gold light on his face, reflecting in his deep, brown eyes. Cami's world shrank to contain only Ray, the shimmering lights and the music.

He nibbled on her earlobe. "Delicious," he whispered.

She giggled. "Do you always devour your dates on the dance floor?"

"Only those who taste as sweet as the date palm's fruit." Sliding one hand down to her hip, he drew her closer.

His body pressed, hot and hard, through the layers of clothing separating them. She sucked in an exhilarated breath at his boldness. Her mind whirled.

Releasing her from his embrace, Ray took her hands, squeezing them. "I am going over there." He nodded toward the back of Dancin' Nancy's, where Cami knew a hall led to the rest rooms and an exit. "I will see you at the bar, say, in five minutes?" Lifting their joined hands to his mouth, he kissed her wrists.

"Okay," she murmured. Returning to the bar, she ordered another soda to cool down. The physical exertion of dancing made her warm, but she knew her sensual heat had another source: Ray.

She'd felt the tension in his body. Though she wasn't experienced, she sensed and understood his male need. But he'd walked away from her before he lost control.

If they continued as they'd begun, there was only one place their relationship would lead: to bed. How should she respond to him? Cami bit her lip.

She had to admit to herself that, in the past, keeping her virginity hadn't been difficult, given that she'd never met anyone who'd tempted her…until Ray.

A tug on her loose hair prompted Cami to swivel

her stool around. Jenelle Watson and her husband, Jordy, stood nearby, grinning at her.

"Hey there, Cami!" Jordy hauled her out of the chair and gave her a big, unwanted hug.

Cami pulled loose, peeling him off like duct tape. "Hi Jordy, Jenelle." After hugging Jenelle, Cami surveyed her friend. Though she'd married her high school sweetheart right after their senior class had graduated, Jenelle didn't look happy. Cami looked into her friend's eyes. They held a sadness Cami had never before seen there, despite Jenelle's pregnancy.

Why isn't she happy? Cami wondered. "Hey, let's take a booth." Carrying her soda, she led Jenelle to a quieter spot, away from the speakers. Jordy had already ordered beer. He approached, full glass in hand.

"Jenelle?" He extended the beer to his wife.

Her mouth twisted. "You know the baby and I can't have that."

"How'd you get a beer, anyhow?" Cami asked. "You're underage."

"Money talks, little honey." Jordy winked at her. He returned to the bar.

Little honey? Cami flinched. He'd never called her that. What on earth was going on? Jenelle's lips had gone tight, her jaw tense.

Cami decided to change the subject. "How's the restaurant doing?" Jenelle and Jordy operated a Tex-Mex burger franchise.

"Lousy." Jenelle nodded at Jordy, seated at the bar. "You see how he is. He drinks up all the profits."

"Oh." Cami looked around. Where was Ray?

One of the cowboys came over to their booth and asked her for a dance. She shook her head, preferring to stay with Jenelle and catch up.

Jenelle accepted the cowboy's invitation with a sidelong glance at her husband, still at the bar. Far from resenting her friend, Cami felt sorry for her. Homecoming queen Jenelle had been reduced to dancing with strangers to get attention from her husband. Life hadn't been kind to Jenelle, who was nineteen, pregnant and trapped in a lousy marriage.

The band segued into a slower beat. Cami wished Ray would come back. She missed the tremulous excitement of his embrace. Drawing an excited breath, she remembered his hardness against the softness of her body. She'd burned for him, even through his jeans and her dress. She burned now.

A few moments later, Jordy wandered by and asked Cami to dance. This time, bored from waiting, she agreed.

Within seconds she regretted her decision. An appalling combination of grease, chilis, cigarettes and beer, Jordy's aroma made Cami want to run, not walk, to the nearest door. She guessed he hadn't showered after leaving their burger joint. The green and purple lights flashing across his face added to her queasiness.

Jordy moved closer to whisper in her ear. She couldn't hear what he said since they'd danced close to the speakers. Pulling away from him, she turned her head and yelled, "What?" directly into his ear canal.

He jumped at least a foot.

Cami grinned. That would make him keep his distance. "Sorry."

"I was just saying that you're prettier than ever, Cami Ellison." Jordy glanced at his wife, dancing a few feet away. His gaze dropped to her belly. Disgust flitted across his face.

Cami realized she shouldn't have forced Jordy so far away, so soon. If he'd remained closer, she could "accidentally" step on his feet with her boots. She figured the creep deserved punishment. She didn't like the way Jordy grabbed her to dance, liked his beer breath even less and hated the way he treated Jenelle.

She looked around. Where had Ray gone? "Excuse me," she said to Jordy before walking down the hall toward the rest rooms.

Jordy seized her around the waist and hustled her out the back door.

The night air and harsh outdoor lighting struck her like a blow. She turned, blinking, then wrinkled her nose against the stink of a nearby Dumpster.

Jordy pushed her up against the wall of Dancin' Nancy's. "We ain't done yet, Cami," he said with a crooked smirk. "Don't you remember how you wanted me in high school? Well, now's your chance."

Stunned by his lies, she didn't resist when he shoved his lips onto hers and yanked down her peasant top off her shoulders, tearing it.

Braless, her breasts were exposed to the night air and to his grasp. He grabbed them, twisting one nipple hard and pinching the other as he stuck his tongue into her mouth.

Cami's throat convulsed. Jerking back, she banged her skull painfully against the wall. Dizzy, she dropped her head forward, slamming her forehead against Jordy's nose.

Something warm and wet spurted everywhere. *Blood.* She'd accidentally head-butted his nose. Miraculously, her mind cleared. She stomped on his foot with her cowboy boots as hard as she could, then jerked one knee up sharply, hoping to hit him where it would hurt the most.

Suddenly she was free, her attacker gone, and Ray was there, tossing Jordy against the brick wall. With an "oof" and a yelp, he slid down the side of Dancin' Nancy's in a heap. He curled around himself, mewling and grabbing his genitals.

Now by her side, Ray said anxiously, "Cami? Camille?"

She clutched her head. Her forehead hurt where she'd smashed Jordy's nose. The back of her skull ached at the spot she'd slammed into the wall. Her poor, abused nipples were sore. "I'm all right," she muttered.

"I do not see how." Ray helped her to her feet.

She staggered, leaning into the support he offered. He roped an arm around her, holding her up but not squeezing her hard, as if he understood that a tight grip by a man—any man—right then would have been too much.

Intending to thank him, she looked up at his face. She found his gaze riveted on her naked breasts.

Chapter Three

"Son of a gun!" Cami tried to shove him away. She scrabbled in her pocket for the truck's keys. Damn all men, anyway!

"You should cover yourself up." Ray sounded disapproving.

"What for? You've seen everything." She was overcome with the shock of what had just happened, and what could have happened if she hadn't been able to take Jordy out, or if Ray hadn't shown up. She reeled, close to falling.

Ray caught her, but this time, held her tight. "You've had a bit of a fright, yes? But now it's over." He didn't let her go and continued speaking softly to her. "Cami, you must be more careful."

She rubbed tears out of her eyes with an angry fist. "But I know everyone in McMahon! I grew up here!" She nodded toward Jordy, still limp against the wall. "I've known him since we were kids!"

"People change. Places change." Ray pulled up the tattered top of her dress, concealing her breasts. "A new well opened on the other side of town after you went away to college. There are many oil-field roughnecks and cowboys here you don't know, and who don't know you or your father. There are others who don't care." He jerked a thumb in Jordy's direction.

She sucked in a deep, shuddering breath. "You're right."

He tilted her chin so she'd have to look him in the face. "I want you to stay close to me at night, when you are in McMahon. It is not the same quiet little town you knew when you grew up."

She thought she'd never lose the chill that gripped her insides. "Okay," she whispered. She closed her eyes, letting grief overcome her. When she'd gone to college in San Antonio, she never went anywhere at night without a friend. But she thought she'd be safe back in her hometown. Now she wept for all she'd lost.

"Cami, Cami." Cuddling her close, Ray walked her from Dancin' Nancy's to a small park nearby. In the patch of trees and grass, he sat on a bench, then urged her onto his lap. "Cami, I am so sorry. I should never have left you for so long."

"Wha-what happened? Where were you?"

"Someone wanted to discuss purchasing one of my horses. We went outside to talk. He left a few moments before I saw…" After a sigh laden with regret, he slid his lips across her cheeks, sweeping her tears away.

His tenderness overwhelmed Cami's already
shaken defenses. When he touched his lips to hers,
she didn't resist, but immediately opened to him.
With adrenaline still coursing through her system, but
without a threat to overcome, she wanted him more
than ever.

She dug her hand into the hair at his nape to bring
him in tighter, to make the kiss more intimate. She
probed his mouth with her tongue, seeking his male
heat and strength. He immediately responded to her,
holding her close, his muscles taut. The barely harnessed power in his embrace shook her; she sensed
he was under control, but only just.

Ray dragged his mouth away from hers to take several deep breaths. The tension in his body eased. He
feathered kisses down her throat and along her collarbone. Clinging to him, her body quivered with
need. She tipped back her neck. A small moan escaped her.

The torn edges of cloth at her bodice caressed her
tender skin. Ray guided her back onto the bench to
nuzzle her cleavage. With a featherlight touch, he
smoothed the fabric over her breasts, then caressed
her nipples into hard points of want.

She drew in a shivery breath. His gentleness was
so at odds with Jordy's roughness that tears again
came to her eyes. Without hesitation, Ray circled her
taut flesh delicately, as if he knew exactly what she
needed. Tiny flashes of pleasure streaked through her.
She cried out.

"I want you to be my woman." His voice was low,
almost rough.

Dazed, she could only gape speechlessly at him.

"That means no contact with other men. No flirting, no dancing, no kissing."

Still she couldn't find a word to say. She looked into his eyes. The dim light shadowed them into deep pools of desire.

With slow, achingly sensual deliberation, Ray touched one long finger to the hollow of her throat, then drew it down, stroking a line of fiery want to the valley between her breasts, exposed by the torn bodice. He rolled one breast in his palm, then squeezed the very tip of her nipple. He watched her with a narrowed gaze.

Jerking upright, she gasped. Her pulse thundered in her ears. No one, not even the man who'd just mauled her, had ever dared to touch her so. Heat arced to her center.

"Or do you allow any man to handle you in this way?"

The taunting note in his voice galvanized her. She swung her free arm, batting his insolent hands aside. Shocked at her boldness, Cami shrank back into a corner of the bench, tugging her bodice high.

He smiled. "Good. A worthy mate."

"I won't be disrespected." She wiped a trembling wrist across her tingly, sensitive mouth.

Ray leaned back, spreading his arms over the back of the bench in an expansive gesture. "What is the disrespect? I want you. In return I offer myself, absolutely."

Cami stared at Ray. Never had the cultural barrier seemed so wide and deep. What was he talking about?

I want you. I offer myself, absolutely. "Oh!" He wants to be my…my boyfriend? *Boy* wasn't a word she'd apply to Ray. "This is—I didn't think this would happen."

He adjusted his jeans. "No? Never? Have you not used a mirror lately? You're a beautiful woman."

Cami flushed and turned away. She thought she looked about fourteen.

"Listen. We have much to discuss, do we not? Have breakfast with me."

A feminine wariness snaked up her back. Did Ray think she'd spend the night with him?

He smiled slightly. "Only breakfast, nothing more. In town. At Pete's." He jerked his head in the direction of Main Street.

She relaxed. Everyone went to Pete's Diner for his killer breakfasts.

"Ten o'clock tomorrow," he said. "And now I take you home."

"My truck—"

"You should not drive, not after what happened tonight." He lifted her wrist.

Her hand shook.

She curled her fingers into a fist. "I'll be all right. I'll drive real slow."

"I follow you out, yes? Do this for me, Cami. I only wish to keep you safe."

As he drove home, Rayhan watched the red taillights of Cami's truck precede his out of McMahon in the direction of the C-Bar-C Ranch.

Ten years was a long time to harbor a grudge and

plan for revenge. Rayhan hadn't been idle for those years. Far from it. Nor had he remained obsessed with his vengeance. If he had an obsession, it was for his Arabian horses, swift as the wind and beautiful as midnight. After he'd discovered he couldn't drill for oil on his Texas property, he'd turned to his first love: horses. His breeding program, now in its eleventh year, had borne fruit; his Arabians were known throughout the world for their excellence as riding and dressage mounts.

No, he wasn't obsessed, but he was a planner. Honor required him to take revenge upon Charles Ellison, but Rayhan refused to become involved in anything as messy or as inelegant as a lawsuit. Violence was likewise out of the question. In the back of his mind, he'd tucked away the intention that, when she grew up, he'd take Ellison's cherished daughter in exchange for the oil for which he'd paid, but not received. Through her, he'd get what he deserved, and his honor would be vindicated.

Wedding for reasons other than love didn't deter Rayhan. As a royal, he'd always known his wives would benefit him politically or economically. An important undertaking, marriage couldn't depend upon the vagaries of the heart.

He'd occasionally caught sight of Cami as she'd grown, changing from a little ragamuffin into an awkward adolescent. He'd never spoken with her, so he knew nothing of her character.

Now she'd matured into an adult. Instead of viewing her as a simple pawn in his plans, Ray was forced to see Cami for who she was: an intelligent young woman with an excellent mind, determined will and incisive feminine intuition.

He'd wager his finest stallion she'd seen through him when he'd tried to shrug off his father's attitude. The truth was that Rayhan had struggled all his life to prove he was someone who deserved respect, someone other than a useless fourth son.

Impressed by her insight, Rayhan concluded that, depending upon what he did, Cami would become an admirable helpmate through life or a stubborn adversary.

Tonight he'd seen her strength. She'd ably defended herself. Though distressed by the situation, she hadn't panicked.

His heart swelled. She'd be a worthy mother for his children. And as a lover—Ray smiled. He'd learned days ago her kiss was headier than fine cognac. Now he'd tasted of her ardor and her beauty. Her breasts, like peaches, had filled his hands with their heavy sweetness. He'd wanted to take her right then and there, on that park bench in the shadows, but he realized that the waiting would make their eventual coupling all the more wondrous.

Marrying Cami Ellison would accomplish many of his goals. He'd seize the oil wealth he'd wanted for so long while revenging himself on her treacherous father. He'd have a beautiful woman to warm his bed and bear his children. He'd flaunt his wealthy Texan heiress in the faces of his family in Adnan, who'd scorned him all his life.

He clenched his teeth. The last communique from his brother, the king, threatened to affiance Rayhan to a young woman from one of the ever-fractious desert tribes. The king had hinted that Rayhan would be amply rewarded; he surmised the political alliance would force the king to appoint Rayhan to a ministry. Any lesser post would insult the woman's family.

"At last, after so many years, they discover a use for me," he murmured. Bitterness twisted in his belly. Perhaps he'd obey; perhaps he wouldn't.

Could he give up his dreams of a high position in the Adnani government for Cami Ellison and everything she represented?

Cami. Full, soft and fragrant, her breasts had gleamed, pearly in the moonlight. He remembered the taste of her, the feel of her as he'd caressed her nipples. She'd hardened immediately, showing her hidden passion. The mere recollection of that stiff little tip was enough to arouse him.

But his brother claimed Adnan needed Rayhan. Was Cami worth a kingdom?

Cami clutched the steering wheel tightly to avoid bumping all over the rough dirt road to the C-Bar-C. When she approached the gates of home, she pulled into the driveway, then slowed. As she clicked the electric opener, Ray flashed his lights before he continued toward the Double Eagle.

After passing through the gate, she clicked again to close it and drove down the gravel track to the house.

Her relationship with Ray was zipping along at warp speed, and Cami wasn't sure she liked that. She wasn't sure she liked him, either, though she was physically attracted to him in a way she'd never felt.

The way he held and comforted her was beyond anything she'd experienced. She'd wanted to climb inside him, merge with him, become one with him.

But he didn't seem to have listened when she told him she wanted to go slowly. That bothered her.

Tonight he'd asked for a commitment of sorts. *I want you to be my woman.* Becoming his woman would obviously include sex.

Though he offered an equal relationship, he demanded more from her than she was prepared to give. Could she resist his kisses, his touch?

When he'd so gently caressed her hurt breasts, she'd melted. No one had ever touched her there before tonight. She hadn't known a man's comfort could be so good. He'd soothed her pain in a way that, strangely, was more exciting than a lightning storm.

How had Ray known exactly what to do?

Cami drove to her house and parked. Exiting the truck, she closed its door as quietly as she could, to avoid disturbing her father's rest.

She winced at the thought of her father. Cami knew her mom only through photographs. Dad had been both mother and father. He'd given so much to her. He'd run Cami's inheritance—the C-Bar-C—as long as she could remember, even from his hospital bed after a devastating traffic accident. Confined to a wheelchair ever since the accident, he'd lived his life for her.

After she walked to the veranda, she took off her boots before tiptoeing inside her home. Cami guessed her father wouldn't approve of her liaison with Sheikh Rayhan. Aside from the coolness between the Double Eagle and the C-Bar-C, she believed that her father would think Ray too old and too...different for her.

And he'd be right.

Sniffing the familiar aroma of lemon oil, Cami calmed. She decided she'd see Ray at breakfast and serenely inform him she just couldn't accept his flattering offer.

"I'm too young for this," she muttered as she entered the kitchen to search for aspirin and a glass of water.

But later, when she tried to go to sleep, images and remembered sensations haunted her. How good it had been when they'd kissed. Ray's hand on her breast. His approval—his *approval!*—when she'd slapped him. *A worthy mate,* he'd said.

Sounded as though Ray had big plans and she could be the star of his show. Cami rolled onto her back and stared at the ceiling.

Was Ray what she wanted? *Who* she wanted? She only had one virginity and she'd be darned if she'd give it up to just anyone.

But a real-live desert sheikh wasn't just anyone. If he really was a sheikh. But why should that make any difference?

This is the United States of America, and we don't care about royalty, she reminded herself. But if he'd lied—that was bad. She couldn't abide a man who lied to make himself into a big shot.

Cami sighed and gave up on sleep. Clicking on her

bedside light, she got out of bed and went to her desk. Opening her laptop, she pushed the "on" button.

After a few minutes of work on the little computer, she found herself staring in amazement at the information she'd discovered on the Internet.

The name of the ruling family of Adnan was ibn-Malik al-Rashad, meaning "son of the king, the leader." Their symbol was the double-headed eagle, symbolizing Adnan's dual nature as a nation of desert tribes and seafarers. Several brothers governed the country, splitting the duties of king, grand vizier, and marshal of the military.

And one of the royal brothers, according to a site she visited, lived quietly in Texas, breeding award-winning riding and dressage horses.

So he's telling the truth. But that shouldn't make any difference, Cami said to herself as she climbed back into bed. Ray was too experienced and too pushy. He wanted more than she could give.

She'd be nice about it, but this romance wasn't going anywhere she didn't choose. Sheikh or not, that was that.

On Sunday morning Pete's Diner bustled. As she entered, Cami could see all the counter stools were full. Waitresses clad in old-fashioned pink polyester uniforms topped by white aprons hustled in and out of the kitchen's swinging metal doors. They carried steaming coffeepots or huge plates heaped with fried foods: eggs, hash brown potatoes, sausage, chicken-fried steaks, biscuits and gravy.

Cami inhaled deeply. The atmosphere, heavy with

the aromas of grease and smoke, smelled like cholesterol heaven. Pete's was a bad place for a diet. Tradition, in the forms of pink polyester, high-calorie
meals and red Naugahyde ruled at Pete's.

Each booth in the row that ran down the street side
of the restaurant was occupied. Several of the patrons
still wore evening clothes. Catching the flash of se-
quins, Cami recognized one of the women who'd gossiped about Ray at Dancin' Nancy's. Lower lids
smeared with last night's eyeliner, the redhead shared
ham and eggs with a cowboy.

Ray sat in the second-to-last booth, chatting with
Billie Mae MacPherson. Dressed in pink polyester,
Billie Mae was leaning over to pour coffee into Ray's
mug while thrusting her D-cups in his face. Or had
they grown to double Ds? Self-conscious, Cami
peeked at her more modest B-cupped pair.

Billie Mae had graduated from McMahon High one
class ahead of Cami. Rumor was that she liked her
cars fast and her men faster. In order to get what she
wanted, had she tinkered with what nature had already so generously given?

Jealousy ignited Cami's innards. Snow would fall
in hot, dusty McMahon before she got beaten out by
Billie Mae, blown-up breasts or not.

Cami stalked down the row of booths, purposely
letting her boot heels clatter on the linoleum floor.
She stopped close enough to Billie Mae to be intim-
idating—or so Cami hoped. Though Billie Mae might
have an admirable bustline, the rest of her develop-
ment hadn't caught up. In boots, Cami stood darn

close to six feet. Billie Mae was barely tall enough to get on the adults' roller coaster at an amusement park.

"Mornin', Billie Mae," Cami said, nodding at Ray. "Hi there, Ray."

Billie Mae jerked upright and the coffeepot jerked with her. The breasts, however, remained unmoved— a sure sign of medical intervention.

Ray leaped to his feet, dislodging Billie Mae. "Good morning, Camille."

Cami sat and so did Ray. Something bumped against her ankle under the table dividing them. She glanced at Ray, whose eyes held that roguish glint she'd learned to welcome. Smiling, he ran his foot up and down her calf. She plucked her T-shirt away from her chest.

"Are you hot, Cami? Billie, please bring a glass of ice water." Ray winked at Cami.

"I'd like some coffee, also," Cami said.

"Menus?" Billie asked.

"Sure," Ray replied, continuing to play with Cami under the table. Her nipples rose, pushing against her bra. She couldn't believe that he could turn her on by the mere touch of his foot. Billie left and Ray asked Cami, "How went your sleep?"

"Not so hot." After switching off her laptop, she'd tossed restlessly all night.

"I am sorry. Were you unhappy about that fellow who hurt you? We can report him to the police if that is your desire." Ray pointed. "He sits there, with his woman."

Cami half rose from her seat and twisted her head to see. Ray was correct. Jordy, his nose bandaged, sat with Jenelle at the end of the counter near the door. Cami hadn't noticed them when she'd come into Pete's. She'd seen only Ray.

Neither of her so-called friends had greeted Cami. She wondered what Jordy had told Jenelle. He must have said something, given the big bandage on his nose. Cami gave them a jaunty wave, followed by a tap to her nose and a wink. Jenelle looked puzzled while Jordy glowered.

Shoving them out of her mind, Cami sat back in the padded booth and drew a deep breath. She knew that although she could make light conversation with Ray till the cows came home, she might as well just get to the point.

Her heartbeat increased. She'd spent the entire night aching to hold him tight while sure that a relationship was impossible. "Jordy wasn't on my mind." Cami fiddled with the end of her braid. "You were."

"Ah."

"I'm afraid so." She gulped. "Listen, Ray, we just can't go on like this."

Chapter Four

Rayhan's chest tightened. His quarry threatened to evade his grasp. "Like what? I was believing that we like each other."

"I like you, but...you're asking me for more than I can give you right now."

Inwardly he cursed his impatience. He wanted her badly, wanted her with all the possessiveness in his soul, wanted to make her his and keep her safe. "I am sorry. You were frightened last night. I tried to comfort you. Did I do wrong?"

"No," she whispered, dropping her gaze to the table. "You were wonderful...too wonderful."

"I do not understand how that can be. You are wonderful to me also. Cami, I hear you when you say you want to go slowly."

She lifted her head. Hope glowed in her lovely blue eyes. "You do?"

"Yes, I do. In Adnan, a man expects his lady to

remain virtuous.'' His gaze slid to Billie Mae, laughing at the counter with one of her customers. The cowboy playfully slapped at her breasts with his Stetson. Rayhan went on, ''I have been with other women in the past, but for you, I stop. All I ask is that we…cleave to each other at this time.''

''I don't understand.''

He sighed. ''I am sorry. Even after so many years, your language is difficult for me. Let me try again. We are getting to know each other. I ask that you not see other men at this time.''

''Oh!'' Pulling a paper napkin from a dispenser, Cami mopped her forehead and nose, looking relieved. ''That's okay. I didn't understand. When you asked me last night to be your woman, I thought—''

''I would be lying if I said I do not want you.'' He surveyed her mouth, her breasts, imagining the sweetness of their eventual coupling. ''But you are not ready.''

''No, I'm not,'' she murmured, looking embarrassed.

He hastened to reassure her. ''That is all right. I wait for you.''

Billie Mae came by with water, coffee for Cami and menus for them both. Cami began to pour vast amounts of virtually every condiment on the table into her mug.

Rayhan peered at her over the rim of his cup, wrinkling his nose. ''I do not understand. Cream, sugar, and what is this? Cinnamon? Why bother to drink the coffee at all?''

She grinned at him. "If they had chocolate, I'd add that, too."

He shuddered. "A waste of fine, fresh coffee."

"Don't people from the Middle East think American coffee is weak?"

"I have grown used to it. In my country, we make the coffee with the grounds in the bottom of the cup. It tastes very different, yes, but it is good. We also drink mint tea." He smiled at her, envisioning Cami, beautifully robed, by his side in the Adnani royal palace. "I would like to take you there someday... someday soon."

"I'd like that. Tell me more about Adnan."

"It is a beautiful country." Ray sat back in his booth and closed his eyes, visualizing the whitewashed houses and colorful, mosaic-clad minarets of home. "The word *Adnan* means pleasant, and it is indeed delightful."

"Why did you leave? You obviously love your country very much."

Ray opened his lids. Cami was scrutinizing him with her discomfiting blend of curiosity, intelligence and intuition. He inwardly sighed. One day, probably very soon, he'd have to tell her the truth. This woman was far too smart to deceive.

He wondered how long it would take her to discover his true motives for their relationship. He wanted her, yes, but still...

"As I explained, there was nothing for me to do there. After I finished university, I wanted a post, but my father, who was king at that time, refused to listen. I held out some hope after my brother ascended to the throne, but…'' He gave a fatalistic gesture. ''The new king was accustomed to seeing me as his useless younger brother. Nothing could persuade him to give me the responsibilities I believe I deserve.''

Billie Mae returned to take their orders. Cami ordered cereal and fruit with skim milk. Rayhan asked for a sausage omelette.

''You eat pork?'' she asked.

''Yes. I am, how can I say it, a fallen Muslim. I do not believe in very much, Cami.''

''Do you believe in God or Allah?''

He shrugged. ''I believe I am not in a position to say what, or who, dwells in the heavens.''

''Do you believe in…love?''

Rayhan looked into her eyes. Sweetly romantic, her gaze reminded him of summer evenings, the scent of jasmine and stolen kisses. ''When I am with you, I believe in love.''

Cheeks growing pink, Cami dropped her gaze to the table, rubbing her thumb along its cracked, uneven edge. He noticed she'd cut her nails short, but buffed them until they were shiny. Good. He didn't like the painted claws on some women. They looked predatory, like lizards or hawks.

He'd been with many females, but none with Cami's intriguing personality. She could, by turns, be modest and passionate, innocent and intelligent, insightful and naive.

She was really quite fascinating.

Their meals arrived and Rayhan dug into his with an appetite. He was hungry. He'd awakened early and ridden along the boundary of their adjoining properties, hoping to catch a glimpse of Cami. He'd known it was foolish, because he'd be seeing her later, but he enjoyed her and had wanted to see her as soon as possible. He told himself that the more they met, the more quickly his revenge would come to fruition.

Cami tore open a box of cornflakes and emptied them into a bowl. She picked up a banana, peeled it halfway down, and sliced it on top of her cereal. Then she poured milk over everything.

"Would you like some of my eggs? There are plenty." Rayhan waved a forkful of his omelette in front of Cami's face. Her eyes tracked it like radar. He grinned.

"N-no, thank you." She crunched a mouthful of cornflakes. "Aren't you worried about cholesterol and fat?"

"You are shy about your appearance. Why is that? You are so lovely." He thrust the eggs into his mouth, chewed and swallowed.

Cami scowled. "I have a tummy and fat thighs."

"What is it about American women? All of you are obsessed with skinny. Do you want to look like this fork?"

"No, but—"

"Of course you have a tummy. Where else would you put your food? Your thighs are not fat."

"Are so." She ate more cereal.

"Are not. I felt them last night, remember?" He grinned at the memory. He'd dreamed about lying between her splendid thighs. "I am in a position to say whether or not they are fat. They are not fat." He offered her a bite of eggs.

She blushed again, most attractively. "I'm glad you think they're okay."

"They are not only okay. They are perfect." So perfect he wanted to run his tongue over every glorious inch.

"But letting you feed me is…" She faltered, as though she lacked the right words to express herself.

"Intimate." Rayhan knew that the sharing of their meals would link them in a subtle but definite way. "But they're just eggs, Cami, not an engagement ring."

Her mouth popped open. "A ring?"

In went the eggs. She was so delightfully transparent that he couldn't stop a victorious smirk from crossing his face. He carefully withdrew the fork from her mouth before eating the last bite on his plate. "Finish your cereal. Are you going to eat the rest of that banana?" Rayhan left his side of the table to scoot beside her on the bench seat.

"I might."

He settled his hand on Cami's vulnerable nape, knowing his intimate touch was a public declaration of their relationship. She cuddled closer, easing her long, curvy body into his side. Caressing her neck, he ran the tips of his fingers up and down its length, then slid his hand down her neck to stroke her bare arm.

Cami purred, catlike. The sensuous murmur pleasantly tickled his nerve endings. Heat radiated throughout his body.

He picked up the banana with his free hand and set the peeled portion to her lips.

She drew in a breath, then opened her mouth. He smiled.

* * *

Ashamed that she'd neglected her father, Cami headed straight for their shared office upon her return to the C-Bar-C. Since she'd turned thirteen, she and her father had spent four hours every afternoon on the accounts, with few days free. The only breaks occurred when she attended college. Now, because she'd returned, they picked up where they'd left off, adding additional management responsibilities to the list of tasks Cami regularly completed.

Cami had always been aware that the Crowell oil belonged to her, though the livestock was the Ellisons'. The distribution of the ranch's assets didn't make any difference to her. She knew she'd be a wealthy woman because she'd inherit both fortunes one day. And when she graduated from college, she'd manage her holdings, leaving her father free to retire if he chose.

"Ready for work, Dad?"

Seated in his wheelchair behind his massive, dark oak desk, her father folded the sports section with a rustle. One graying, bushy eyebrow arched as Charles quizzically regarded her. "What's up, kiddo?"

Cami sighed. She should have known she couldn't hide her chaotic emotions from her father. She never could fool anyone, not even when she played a donkey in the Christmas pageant and wore a big fake head with a long nose and ears. Everyone somehow knew it was her.

Unfortunately, she didn't know how to respond to

his question. She was feeling too many emotions, all at once. Edgy with nervous energy. Excited that she had a hottie in her life. Scared her father wouldn't approve of Ray. Heck, *she* didn't even approve of her romance with Ray.

An honest person, she didn't like to evade, but this time she did. She figured Charles really wouldn't want to know if she started an intimate relationship with a man. That would just worry him, wouldn't it?

Cami searched for the right words. Her father hadn't been healthy since a traffic collision shattered his hip and his pelvis, causing numerous internal injuries, some of which had never healed right. He'd never walk again unaided, and only occasionally could use a cane to get around. Cami didn't want to say anything that would make his condition worse.

She cleared her throat. "I'm just…edgy. I guess I need to get out more. Though I went dancing last night and then had breakfast at Pete's with some friends." Darned close to the truth.

"Great!" Her father's approval made her stomach twist with guilt. "I'm glad you're stepping out. You don't need to stay home with your old dad, watching reruns and videos."

"Oh, Daddy." Cami stooped to hug her father around his shoulders. Pitifully thin, they frightened her. "I don't mean to imply I'm bored with you."

"I know you're not, darlin'." Her father paused to take a hit from his inhaler, which he kept in his top desk drawer. Charles, who also suffered from asthma, spent most of his time indoors during the summer, avoiding pollen and dust. "It's natural that at your age you want a little excitement."

"I had a little too much excitement last night." Cami gave her father a censored version of her encounter with Jordy, saying only that he'd made a heavy pass at her. Details weren't necessary and would upset her father. She finished, "I don't know what I should do. I hate to think of him cheating on Jenelle and drinking up all the money she'll need for the baby."

"I can probably take care of Jordy's drinking in McMahon with a word or two in the right ears."

"Really?" Cami slipped behind her smaller desk and flipped on switches to start her computer.

"Sure. He's underage, isn't he?" Charles reached for his Rolodex. "So, have you met a fella?"

Cami jumped a foot. So much for keeping Dad in the dark. "Uh, yeah. I—"

Her father held up a hand. "Don't tell me anything more unless you want to, Cami. I trust you to make appropriate decisions."

"But I'm not sure about him, Dad."

"What's the problem?"

"He's a lot older." There. She'd done it. She'd told her father the truth.

Her father frowned. "Is he married?"

"Oh, no!" A swell of relief lightened her. "In fact, he told me he doesn't want to see anyone else while we're dating. And he doesn't want me to, either."

Charles looked thoughtful. "That makes sense. Otherwise, how can you really trust each other?"

* * *

Her father's support buoyed her spirits, but Cami couldn't entirely excuse her conduct. She hadn't told Charles everything. On the other hand, he hadn't wanted the particulars.

Worse, Ray hadn't made a date with her after they'd finished breakfast at Pete's. He'd paid the tab, politely escorted her to her truck, then treated her to a goodbye kiss that would have curled her hair had it not been in a braid.

But he hadn't asked to see her again. Cami fretted. She didn't know what to do. Normally, with any other friend, she'd simply phone or e-mail. But Ray wasn't just anyone. He was older, and from a traditional culture. She didn't think he liked forward women. He'd made it clear that he preferred modesty, saying, "In Adnan, a man expects his lady to remain virtuous."

She wanted to be Ray's, but didn't know if she could give up the freedoms that came with being a modern American girl.

Maybe she could have it all. Cami brightened at the thought. Ray had never said anything about living in Adnan, merely visiting. Surely he wouldn't expect her to live anywhere but her beloved C-Bar-C. And if they stayed in Texas, she'd have it all: her desert prince and her home.

They hadn't planned another meeting, but Rayhan nevertheless felt serene about the situation. He didn't want to pressure Cami, so he'd decided to wait until the bird came to hand of her own will.

He made himself available, frequently riding along

the shared edge of their properties at dawn and dusk. Sundown came later in June, so often his evening ride took place close to nine at night. He enjoyed the long days; they reminded him of home.

But tonight's sunset, with its humidity and dust, its scent of horses and cottonwoods, was distinctly Texan. Tired after a long day spent training a filly to bridle, Rayhan allowed Kalil to wander as the gelding chose. Kalil picked a familiar path, the one that led to the swimming hole near the C-Bar-C.

Fed by an underground spring, its waters remained fresh throughout even the hottest summers, feeding lush greenery that protected it from the stares of passers-by. At this late hour, the hands who worked his spread were relaxing in the bunkhouse or had gone to town to have some fun. Only Rayhan, impelled by a restlessness he didn't understand, still roamed the Double Eagle.

Bands of pink and coral streaked the darkening sky. In a few minutes the heavens would transmute into a magical shade of blue that always reminded Rayhan of Cami's eyes.

Would he encounter her this evening? His pulse quickened at the thought.

Kalil poked his nose through the greenery surrounding the swimming hole and chuffed.

Rayhan, hearing a splash, dismounted to check the source of the sound.

Ah. Cami. He surmised she'd been riding hard, because Sugar stood hock-high in the water...and Cami was entirely submerged, but for her blond head. Then she rolled so she floated on the surface of the pond.

Even in the dimming light, he could see the tops of her breasts above the water. Though covered with some flimsy fabric, they swayed with the slight current.

Rayhan walked toward the water's edge.

Cami rose, standing thigh deep in the pond. The glowing sunset's light shimmered off the water sliding down the curves and planes of her body. She looked like a naiad emerging from an enchanted pool.

He couldn't speak, couldn't breathe, couldn't even think.

Even in the waning light, he could see she wore only a tiny pair of panties and a thin, cropped top. His gaze traveled down her tapering rib cage to her narrow waist. Crystalline drops nestled in her navel, inviting his tongue. Her torso flared to lovely, rounded hips and a wide pelvis, designed to carry a child.

His child. Rayhan drew a shuddering breath.

Her wet, pink panties couldn't conceal much, but the dimming light hid her secrets.

He stepped forward, deliberately crunching a branch underfoot to attract her attention. He wanted to give her the opportunity to come to him.

Chapter Five

Cami's skin chilled. Who was there?

She scanned the bank of the pond, seeing nothing in the shadows. A night bird flapped its wings, startling her.

A branch cracked. Then a dark shape emerged from the shrubbery.

Dressed in swirling robes, he appeared a wild creature born of myth and legend. He seemed not to walk but to flow gracefully as he approached the riverbank, a fey spirit of the night.

Impelled by an instinct she couldn't control, Cami went to meet him at the water's edge. She was acutely aware of everything around her: the squish of mud beneath her bare feet; the buzzing of insects; the evening scents of the foliage; her heartbeat, which had leaped to a frantic pace when she saw who stood by the stream.

Ray awaited her with the posture of a sultan who'd summoned his houri.

Yet he hadn't said a word. He didn't need to. Strong and tall, infinitely compelling and mysterious, he lured her to him without effort, the way man had drawn woman to his side since the dawn of history.

She couldn't see his expression in the dusk. Nervous, she guessed he'd dislike her spontaneous decision to strip to her undies and swim. Maybe this conduct wasn't what an Adnani male expected from a virtuous woman.

Now she stood before him. Her heart raced.

He reached forward to cup one breast in his palm. With dark, tapered fingers, he flicked her nipple through the damp silk of her camisole.

It puckered into a taut, needy point. She closed her eyes, focusing on the blissful ache. Her knees shook, and she concentrated on staying upright.

"Watch," he said, his voice soft with amazement. "See how your breast trembles in my hand."

Shy, Cami turned her face away.

He laughed.

Starch stiffened her spine, and she cut him a glare. How dare he laugh at her?

"Cami." But he didn't mock. Instead, he seduced. He bent her back over his arm to kiss her nipples, arousing first one, then the other. Excitement flared; she felt the tender flesh crinkle and tighten against the pressure of his tongue and teeth. Sucking in a breath, she pushed her breast into his mouth, chasing the pleasure.

He slipped his hand between her unresisting thighs, stoking the fire with clever, knowledgeable fingers.

Cami's moist, ready mouth, heavy-lidded eyes, her sweet gasps and pants told Rayhan she was ready for his love. Draped over his arm she lay, vibrating with need, offering herself to him, a sensual banquet.

He'd feast on her soon, but not tonight. He caressed her one last time. She writhed in his arms, his for the taking. Rather than have her on the riverbank, he set her on her feet, smoothing away tousled strands of hair from her flushed face.

She reached for him, tugging on his robes to draw him closer, molding her curves against his hardness beneath the loose folds of his *thobe*. His body jerked; he fought to master his urge to possess her immediately. When she tried to pull away he didn't let her go, palming her bottom to push her intimately against him.

"Did you think I remained unmoved?" He let his voice growl in her ear. Holding her close, he eased her along the evidence of his passion. He flicked his tongue over her quivering mouth, first testing the tender inner surface of her lip, where the flesh was so sensitive, then entering her deeper, in and out.

He licked the dainty whorl of her ear, then blew upon it.

She shivered, sinking into his embrace, as though she sought his warmth. He wrapped her in his arms, enfolding her in his robes.

With Ray Cami felt utterly safe, swathed in his silky cocoon. But his demanding kisses and virile body reminded her of the threat he posed. The tension

in his limbs signaled her that he was frighteningly
close to losing control. If he succumbed to his instincts, she couldn't protect her innocence from him.
He was too strong, too seductive, and too tempting.

"Soon," he purred in her ear.

She tugged away.

"Soon. Cami, I know how to treat a woman. I
promise. I will show you." He put a finger to his chin,
looking thoughtful.

"Show me…how?"

His smile made her every cell tingle with delighted
anticipation, even though she knew nothing would
happen. It couldn't.

"Come to the Double Eagle. Alone. In, hmm, three
days, at sundown."

"Sundown?"

"Yes. The meeting of light and dark. Male and
female." He touched her breast, again plucking the
nipple into aching desire.

Lightning streaked through her body.

"Come to me."

Come to me. Ray had the most compelling way of
making a simple dinner date sound like an invitation
to adventure. As the sun set three days later, Cami
turned the key to start one of the C-Bar-C's trucks,
wondering how he did it.

It was the sheikh thing. Shoving her foot on the
accelerator, she shook her head with exasperation.
She fell for his line over and over again. How could
she be such a sap?

I know how to treat a woman. Not that she'd find

out tonight. She'd protected herself from the possible outcome of the evening as best she could without breaking the date. No makeup; maybe he wouldn't think her attractive. But except for their date at Dancin' Nancy's and some goop over her zit, she hadn't worn cosmetics any time she'd seen Ray. He didn't seem to notice the difference. So much for facials and manicures.

Panty hose, even though Cami hated them, especially in midsummer. But any garment that encased her from waist to heels was a good idea. She would have donned a chastity belt if one existed in Texas, but had settled for an underwired bra and unsexy, brief-style panties.

Atop the restricting hose, she wore a calf-length, crinkled silk skirt, with a loose tunic top that made her look five months pregnant.

With any luck she'd have a pleasant evening, a good meal and then leave without getting in too deep with Ray Malik—or, rather, Prince Rayhan ibn-Malik al-Rashad.

With a gusty sigh she acknowledged to herself it was probably too late. She'd fallen for him faster than Juliet for Romeo. Cami just hoped her romance would turn out better.

She turned out of the C-Bar-C toward the Double Eagle. Her fingers shook slightly as they clasped the steering wheel, so she clenched them tighter, grumbling in annoyance under her breath. She was *such* a ninny.

But she couldn't stop the whirling excitement in her heart, which seemed to engender a sensual heat that spread, unwelcome and unstoppable, deep into her belly. She squirmed on the seat, feeling as though her frame, though tall, still wasn't big enough to contain her roiling emotions.

Bursting at the seams with pure sexual energy, she twitched with a restless coiling need she instinctively knew could be slaked in only one way—by taking the man she desperately wanted into her body.

She approached the Double Eagle, slowing the truck, then stopping next to a small white gatehouse at the ranch entrance. The guy inside the tiny wooden structure wore a *gutra* headdress, like Ray's. He waved her on.

Cami looked around as she drove through Ray's spread. Despite the dimming light, she could discern orderly corrals, stock, even crops. Alfalfa, she guessed, for the horses. No oil derricks or pumps, though. She wondered why. She knew a huge pool of oil lay beneath McMahon. Her land was rich with oil; wasn't his?

She shunted aside those mundane thoughts when she neared Ray's home, a big house on a rise about a half mile away from the gate. She guessed he'd built it himself. What other Texas ranch house flaunted a minaret?

She stopped at the entrance, marked by an elaborate wrought iron gate. From the outside, the house looked like an intriguing mixture of Spanish and Arab styles, with whitewashed walls and an orange tiled roof. Windows were covered with charming grillwork, seeming more decorative than designed for defense.

Though, as a sheikh, he'd be security conscious, wouldn't he? But the beautiful rose vines lacing the wrought iron belied any safety concerns.

Ray awaited her at the arched front entrance. Dressed tonight in white, flowing robes, he looked cool and comfortable as he opened her door and helped her alight.

Not so Cami. When she left the air-conditioned truck, she found the panty hose stifled her. She felt like fried sausage stuffed into a too-tight casing.

"Cami." He kissed her forehead and took her hand. She noticed he had calluses on his palms and fingers from training his Arabians, in the same spots she'd grown the tough, hard skin working with her horse.

He led her up broad, tiled steps into his home.

Ray's home.

He didn't have a front door. An elaborate wrought iron gate protected an archway, clad with mosaics. After she passed, the gate clanged shut behind her, signaling her entrance into his domain. Her pulse beat unsteadily in her ears.

She fiddled with the end of her braid. He guided her with an arm around her shoulders through a tiled walkway, sublimely cool, toward an area filled with glowing turquoise light.

Suddenly the hall opened into an enormous courtyard lined with plants and—oh, merciful heavens—the most gorgeous swimming pool she'd ever seen, glimmering in the dusk like a giant aquamarine lozenge.

Her panty hose, already uncomfortable, abruptly

became unbearable. She wanted to tear them off and run screaming like a kid into that lovely water. Sweat broke out on her upper lip.

"You look hot, Cami." Ray surveyed her with obvious concern. "Would you like a swim? The water is very nice. I keep it cool but not cold."

Looking into his eyes, Cami couldn't detect a trace of guile.

"I promise, you will remain unmolested. None of my servants would dare to touch a guest of mine." He spoke with the unconscious arrogance of a prince accustomed to total obedience.

He'd probably have anyone who dared to hassle his female guests shot at dawn. But it was Ray Cami feared. Ray, and her reaction to him. Taking off her clothes and swimming in his pool—no. No. She might as well jump into his bed.

But she couldn't bring herself to refuse. Her lips simply wouldn't form the words *No, thank you*.

"Come." He again took her by the arm and led her down the length of the courtyard, along the right side of the pool. Open to the sky, it didn't smell of chlorine but of the roses and dwarf citrus that lined his home's whitewashed walls.

A fountain splashed into the pool. Her boots clattered while Ray, barefoot, made no sound. He stopped short of the end of the courtyard before a pair of French doors. Opening them, he ushered her into a room with a bed, a dresser and closets. Though it appeared comfortable, its unused air showed Cami it was a guest room. An opulent, patterned spread covered the bed. Carpets softened the tiled floors underfoot.

Ray went to a closet to remove a white toweling robe. "Swim in your bra and panties if you wish." His rogue's smile returned. "But I would not mind if you shed all your clothes. Meanwhile, I will get you some juice to drink. Cami, you are overheated."

His nose crinkled with disapproval. She tried not to chuckle, but he was so darn cute when he did that.

He continued, "You should not let yourself become dehydrated in this weather." He disappeared, closing the French doors behind him.

Cami swallowed against her sticky throat. He was right. The enveloping clothes she'd selected, plus her boots, had been stupid choices for the triple-digit weather and high humidity of the day. Though close to dusk, the air still held an unhealthy sultriness.

She stripped down to her lingerie and noted in the mirror that her prudish underclothing hid her body more effectively than most bikinis. Picking up the robe, she donned it before leaving the cool, cave-like darkness of the guest room for the courtyard. She dropped the robe onto one of two chairs set next to a nearby table, then dived into the pool.

It was heaven on earth. The C-bar-C didn't have a swimming pool, so she occasionally swam in the creek. Fastidious, she never dipped in her head and always showered after; animals occasionally used the pool as a watering hole. She loved to swim, but hadn't used a chlorinated pool since she left college.

Rayhan entered, bearing a tray with a pitcher, a bucket of ice and two glasses. He set it on the table near Cami's robe. Sitting, he watched her splash and play. Though tempted to join her, he decided to maintain a respectful distance. He'd promised her she wouldn't be pestered.

He'd keep that promise even if he exploded with want.

Rayhan's body had gone into alert upon taking Cami's arm to escort her out of her truck. The clothes she'd selected—a colorful skirt, modestly long, with a matching shirt—suggested rather than revealed her charms, piquing his interest. Then he noticed how overheated she'd become. "Foolish child!" he muttered to himself.

When they married, he vowed to himself, he'd take good care of her. No more seminude swimming in unsanitary ponds visited by horses and cowboys. No gallivanting around in midsummer, courting heat stroke.

He hoped his nemesis, Charles Ellison, would appreciate everything Rayhan would do for Cami. Despite himself, he felt a flash of sympathy for the man. Rayhan was aware of Ellison's incapacity. Managing a willful teenager on top of severe injuries couldn't have been easy.

If all went according to plan, Ellison would be responsible for his daughter no more. Her husband would manage Cami's life—and her fortune.

The pool quieted. Rayhan glanced over to see Cami floating on her back, her bra-encased breasts thrusting above the water. Her nipples had wrinkled, and the sharp tips poked the cups, showing pink through the wet, sheer fabric.

Rayhan leaned back in his chair, enjoying the show. Grateful for his loose, concealing *thobe,* he realized tight jeans would be agony.

But this flirtation had to stop before he burst from frustration. Woman existed to satisfy man, he told himself. And Cami Ellison existed to satisfy him, whether she knew it or not. He had to convince her they belonged together.

In the meantime they both needed to cool down.

Hard, chilly pellets dropped from the sky onto Cami's unprotected belly. She opened her eyes to see Ray standing poolside, tossing ice cubes at her.

"Hey!" Cami ducked under the water, then came up by the side of the pool. She splashed Ray, nailing him solidly in the midsection. The water rendered his white robes translucent from waist to knees, sticking the fabric to his body.

She gasped. She couldn't look away from that fascinating shadowy area at Ray's pelvis.

His laughter jolted her out of her examination. He plopped onto a deck chair and howled, clutching his side.

Completely mortified, Cami ducked under the water, hoping he'd leave to change before she emerged.

No such luck. Instead, he sat at the side of the pool, dangling his legs into the water, still laughing at her.

She didn't understand. "I thought you liked modest women."

"I like *you*. Come." He held out a hand to her.

She took it and let him tug her out of the pool. He

handed her the toweling robe, still chuckling, then poured a drink for her.

Cami rubbed the folds of the robe over her face and body, then put it on, tying its cord around her waist. She took the glass and sipped, savoring the sweet, cold orange juice. "It's yummy. From your trees?" She nodded at the dark, glossy citrus trees lining the courtyard.

Ray visibly swelled with pride. "I squeezed it myself, just for you."

Hmm. She tipped her head to one side, seeing him in a new light. "You like to do things for yourself, don't you?"

He looked jolted. "What? Princes do not do... things. We are worthless creatures. Especially fourth sons." He gave her a little, puzzled frown.

Cami shook her head, remembering the calluses on his palms and fingers. "Not you. You don't have to, but you squeeze your own orange juice and train horses. You like to use your hands to accomplish goals, make things happen."

"Your insights are always surprising. Perhaps you are right." Ray shrugged. "I greatly enjoy this ranch. Of course, my Arabians are my pride. I especially love to watch the breeding mares, and dream about their foals. Whether they will be male or female, gray, dun or black, sharp tempered or easy."

This man will make an excellent father. The thought swept through Cami's mind like a tornado. She stared at Ray, noting every detail anew: wide, intelligent eyes; his hands, precise and elegant as he poured himself juice; his sensitive mouth. She quivered when she remembered how his lips felt on hers.

She evaluated the components not merely as a lover, but the way a single woman views an unattached male…as a prospective partner through life.

Then she recalled that Ray had brought up marriage at their first meeting. He'd told her she'd be a worthy mate the night outside Dancin' Nancy's. He'd mentioned a ring the next morning, at Pete's.

On top of it all, he'd admitted noticing her before they'd met. She'd dismissed all those statements at the time as flirtation, figuring he just wanted to get into her pants.

Cami sucked in a breath.

What if he were for real?

At this point, nothing about the way Ray operated would surprise her. From a different culture, she'd learned he couldn't be judged by American standards.

She eyed him. Despite his royal birth, here was a man willing to dirty his hands raising horses and even squeezing fruit for his girlfriend.

Ray topped off her juice. "Drink."

Cami examined Ray over the rim of her glass. A nurturer. That was it. Ray was a nurturer. Plus, he was so sexy she couldn't keep her hands off him. She wanted to climb inside his skin and merge with him.

One of the women's magazines she'd read advised that to get a man, a woman had to know what she wanted. She had to list desirable traits.

Cami had never bothered. At her age she'd never considered marriage.

But now she stared at Ray and tried to order her

scrambled thoughts. She didn't need a man to take care of her financially or protect her physically; she knew she could handle herself.

So what did she need?

She needed a nurturer. She needed someone who'd be a good father for their children.

That was it. She set the empty glass onto the table with a decisive clatter. If he asked, she'd say yes, and to heck with the age difference.

Chapter Six

Cami stopped her speculations short. Was she nuts? Talk about counting chickens before they hatched! Ray hadn't asked her to marry. He'd never met her father. And how long had they known each other—maybe ten days?

She needed space. "I'd like to get dressed now." She retreated to the guest room.

"There's a shower in that suite," Ray said. "You may rinse your hair if you wish."

Fifteen minutes later Cami was ready to rejoin Ray in the courtyard, barefoot, with only her long skirt and loose top covering her nudity. Her skin shivered with sensual electricity. As she moved, her breasts swayed, the nipples brushing the rough gauze fabric of her tunic.

She peeked through the French doors. The glass-topped table, now set for two, was flanked by matching, wrought iron chairs, their backs and seats padded with patterned cushions. Mellow light from enameled brass candlesticks softened the planes of Ray's face.

Absorbed, he bent over a platter, fussing with the garnish around a golden-crusted pie.

When she stepped into the courtyard, he looked up. He smiled and left his task. "Cami." Now by her side, he took her hand to kiss the palm. The tiny hairs on her arm shifted in response to his touch. Ray led her to the table where he poured a pale golden wine into two glasses.

"I don't know if I should drink," Cami said.

"I won't permit you to indulge to excess. Drunkenness is a most unflattering condition. Here is water for you, also." He lifted his glass. "To love."

Cami sipped, conscious of his intense scrutiny. Though she'd dated, she'd never been wooed, courted, *pursued* with such blatant hunger. She sensed his urgency and thought she understood its source. Men had needs. No doubt he'd try to bed her tonight. She'd tell him no, once again. She had to.

She might be old-fashioned, but she knew she'd fallen in love with this beautiful, complicated man, fallen for his Arab prince mystique and his sheer maleness.

He had a complex inner life and a mysterious past she didn't yet understand, she mused, but she'd love to unravel the intricate tapestry of everything that was Ray, even if the task took a lifetime. His secrets cloaked him with an air of mystery and intrigue, compelling her the same way hidden treasure baited a pirate.

She had to have him in her life. But if they made

love without marriage, he could easily move on, she reasoned. He'd be more likely to stick around after lovemaking if she had his ring on her finger.

If he dumped her, she didn't know if she'd ever be able to love again. Though marriage couldn't ensure happiness, she figured they had a better chance if they wed.

Cami set down her glass, remembering that when people got drunk, they got stupid.

"Let us eat."

Ray picked up a knife and sliced into the pie, releasing a cloud of aromatic steam scented with cinnamon.

Cami sniffed appreciatively. "What's that?"

"I have for you a simple meal tonight. Tabouleh salad and b'stila, a pigeon pie with almonds, egg and raisins."

"Did you cook?"

"But yes. The servants have the night off. I wished to be undisturbed."

"You cooked?" Cami couldn't get over it. Ray, a prince, had squeezed her orange juice, baked her b'stila and tossed her tabouleh salad.

He placed a wedge of pie on a blue earthenware plate, then heaped tabouleh next to it. Then he artistically arranged flat-leaved parsley nearby. He smiled at her. "Yes, I cook."

"You are not a useless fourth son."

"No, I am not. Since I came to Texas ten years ago, I have worked hard to—how would you say it—overcome the accident of my birth and make a life for myself." He served himself tabouleh and b'stila. "Eat."

Cami ate and drank. The food was delicious, almost good enough to overcome her excitement at Ray's presence by her side. And he couldn't seem to keep his hands off her. He scooted his chair close to hers, fed her choice bits of pigeon from his plate, interspersed with kisses, and plied her with wine until she pushed his hand away.

"Enough," she said. "Or I'll suspect you of getting me drunk so you can have your way with me."

"You would suspect correctly. One night I hope to get lucky with you."

"In your dreams." Cami waved her water glass in the air, feeling cheerfully loose and relaxed.

"Yes, you are, every night. But I will not push. You, Cami, must come to me of your own free will."

"Dream on."

"I know you wouldn't have just anyone, but am I still just anyone?" His eyes went wide and pleading.

"Sorry, prince." Cami balanced her last bite of b'stila on her fork. "I'm saving myself for marriage."

"Marriage! You set a high price on your love. But perhaps you are right to do so." Ray laughed softly, leaning into his chair. He angled his head back. "Look there." He pointed into the moonless sky. "Mars."

"How can you tell?"

She chewed and swallowed the last delicious bite.

"It is slightly red. Let me show you."

Taking her hand, he led her to a wooden door at the base of the minaret.

As they climbed the twisting, turning stairs, Cami felt as though she'd left Texas to ascend into a new, magical world, where mysteries would be revealed and secrets discovered. Her breath shortened, and her heart tripped as she trod the long spiral stair up the narrow tower.

It was dark, the only illumination starlight filtering through occasional slits in the minaret's walls. She couldn't see much. Her senses constricted to encompass only their harsh inhalations, the coolness of the tiled stairs beneath her bare feet and the warmth of Ray's hand on her waist, which sent tremors of longing through her.

Finally the staircase ended, opening into a large circular room at the very top of the minaret.

Eight arched apertures, unglassed and open to the night, rimmed the octagonal room. Through them, Cami could hear the twitter of birds and an occasional bark from a dog as the Double Eagle's animals settled down for the night.

The only furniture in the room was a neat desk, two stools and a large structure covered with a plastic tarp. Releasing her hand, Ray twitched aside the tarp to reveal a telescope.

"I sit up here many a night, star-watching." His voice had gone soft and a little hesitant, she thought, as if he revealed a secret, precious place within himself.

"Wow," she breathed, circling the room so she could investigate everything.

"Now, let me prove to you that Mars is truly the

red planet.'' Ray expertly twirled dials, adjusting the complex scope.

He showed her Mars, and Saturn, with its fabulous rings, then explored with her deeper into the universe. Cami saw Sirius, blazing blue-white in the night, and a double star, its two halves improbable shades of turquoise and gold, flashing in the heavens, locked together by gravity in an infinite dance.

''The colors are amazing.'' Cami looked at Rayhan with a bedazzled gaze.

''They're no more lovely than your eyes.'' He took both her hands in his. ''Cami, I brought you here to show you my heart, the deepest part of myself. I want you to have, to know, all of me.''

At the penultimate moment, doubts assailed Rayhan. What if he was moving too fast for Cami? He sensed she wanted him, yes, but she was a modern, independent woman with a strong will for one so young. She'd rarely mentioned marriage as part of her plans. What if she—

His hand closed around the box in a pocket of his *thobe*. He fingered its rounded edges and corners, taking comfort in its solidity. Don't borrow trouble, he told himself. Rayhan remembered how he'd felt at age nineteen, how desire tore at his body and mind until he'd have done anything to quench his lust.

Cami was a healthy young female. He'd caught her poised on the cusp of womanhood and deliberately awakened her sensuality in gradual stages. They'd come close the other evening at the creek; he was sure he could have brought her to fulfillment, but instead he'd stopped the seduction short. He'd intended to drive her wild, then leave her empty and needy.

He wanted all of her, not merely her body, but her heart and her soul. Nothing would satisfy him but a complete conquest.

Rayhan inhaled, letting his breathing calm. He pulled out the box.

He swallowed. "For you," he whispered. "And with it, my heart."

Cami reached for the box, her fingers quivering. She opened it. Inside, tucked into a fold of white satin, twinkled a heart-shaped diamond set in a platinum band.

She dropped the box. It disappeared into the dark shadows of the room.

"Oh, I'm so sorry!" Looking distressed, she put a hand to her mouth before peering at the floor. "It must have landed with the white side down. Will we ever find it?"

"Of course." Despite his tension and exasperation, Rayhan struggled to stay calm. Kneeling at her feet, he swept the tile with an open palm, quickly locating the box. "I did not know my proposal would so alarm you."

"I'm not alarmed, just a little surprised. I'd thought about it, and wondered if you had also. Is it for the sex?"

Her candor startled him. Though chaste, Cami's ability to discuss sex openly was uncharacteristic of women he'd known. They either evaded or flirted. Not so Cami. Her honesty about everything was her trademark. Wishing to respond as truthfully, he hesitated. Should he reveal his long-held plans? She would surely believe his calculated seduction and hidden motives deceitful.

"Well, I listened when you said you wanted to take it slow, but I do want to have you. I cannot lie about that."

She boldly touched him through his *thobe*. His body reacted to the first brush of her questing hand. "No, you sure can't," she said with a smile.

"But it is more than that." He enveloped her in his embrace, misting her forehead, her eyelids, her cheeks with gentle kisses. "You are very smart and very strong. I want you to bear my children."

She looked shocked.

He continued, "I want to care for you all the days of my life."

Cami's lovely eyes shone with tears. Sniffling, she bent her forehead so she leaned against his shoulder.

He couldn't help his urgency. He had to know. "So you'll say yes?"

Drawing back, Cami pressed trembling hands to her cheeks. Though she'd dreamed of this moment, the reality was so scary that she couldn't say yes.

But could she possibly say no? Ray made her feel things she'd never felt—wonderful, magical sensations she didn't want to do without. She'd grown to crave that marvelous tingle that ran up and down her back when she saw him. Heck, she sizzled just when she thought about him. And when they were together, the yearning ache multiplied exponentially. She hungered for it, and him, like an addict longs for his next fix.

And she wanted more.

She knew there was more. She was inexperienced, not ignorant. She'd read *Playgirl* and *Cosmo,* listened to the gossip of other women and taken sex education in school. She knew what men and women did together, and she wanted to do it, too.

Now she'd met someone she desired, respected, trusted and loved. Someone who offered her the commitment she demanded as the price for her innocence.

She inhaled a deep breath and let it out slowly while contemplating Ray.

His gaze drank her in as though she were very hot, strong coffee and he really needed his morning caffeine.

He seemed sincere. *I want to care for you all the days of my life.*

She couldn't ask for a sweeter proposal.

"Yes," she whispered.

"What?"

"Yes! Yes! Yes! Yes!" She grabbed his robe and, heedless of the diamond ring he clutched in one hand, began to twirl him around the room, laughing.

Dancing with her, he somehow managed to pull the ring from the box and jam it on her finger. "A perfect fit," he gloated.

"But of course." She imitated his accent, waving her hand in the air. The diamond caught the faint starlight, winking and glittering. "It would not dare to defy a prince of Adnan!"

He grabbed her hand and pulled her against him. His chest felt marvelously hard and solid against her breasts. He kissed her, first nibbling tenderly at her lips. After she opened to him, he made love to her mouth until he'd stolen every wisp of oxygen from her body, leaving her breathless and panting for him.

He smiled at her. "Well, then. We must get ready to go."

"Go? Go where?"

"To get married."

"Now?" She tipped her head to one side.

He stroked her cheekbone with a gentle fingertip. "Now."

"Tonight?"

"Yes, tonight."

"Why so soon?"

"I do not want you to get away or change your mind."

"Hey, I love you. I won't change." Hurt, Cami wondered how Ray could think she wouldn't be true. She'd do anything to soothe his fears, including elope. Why not? She was sure of her love.

"All right. I admit it. I wish to get lucky very soon." He gave her his rogue's grin.

Tiny shivers zipped up and down her spine. "But what should I tell my father? He hasn't been well."

"What is the problem?"

"His asthma."

Ray released her. "I know he is very important to you. What did you tell him about tonight?"

"I told him I'm having dinner out with the man I'm dating."

"Oh? And what have you told him about me?" Ray regarded her with curious eyes.

Did she detect a little nervousness? Well, that was

natural. ''Not much, just that you're older and wanted
an exclusive relationship. He thought that was okay,
but he didn't want details about, um, us.''

He scratched his ear, looking thoughtful. ''If he
does not want details, then we need not provide them,
especially if he has been unwell.''

Cami pursed her lips. ''I bet Dad wants a big
church wedding.''

''That will take a long time to arrange, will it not?''
Ray frowned.

''Yes.'' She fiddled with her braid.

''Cami, since we are sure, let's just do it. We can
have the big ceremony when your father is again
healthy. We can, what is it called, renew our vows
later, can we not?''

Chapter Seven

After Ray changed into jeans and Cami packed her still-damp lingerie into her handbag, he bundled her into the truck.

"How on earth are you going to arrange a wedding at such short notice?" Cami asked. "And where are we going?"

"Do not worry," he said, smiling. "Do not worry about anything."

They drove all night, with Cami falling asleep along the way. Arriving at the port of Galveston at dawn, she rubbed her eyes, then stared at the white metal wall of the ship looming above.

Then she understood. "We're going on a cruise, and the captain's gonna marry us! Oh, Ray, you're a genius!" She flung her arms around Ray's neck and pressed a big, smacking kiss on his mouth.

He grinned. "I'd already booked the cruise and made the arrangements, hoping you'd say yes. We will be able to marry when the ship sails into international waters."

"Where are we going?"

"It is only a short cruise, since you do not have your passport. We go to New Orleans, and visit beaches along the way to and fro."

"How long will we be gone?"

"Three days."

Cami bit her lip, worrying about the consequences of her misadventure. "I really oughtta call Dad."

"Cami, it is dawn. You cannot call your father now. He will be asleep." Ray gestured. "Let us go aboard the ship. It is early, but I will talk with the purser and see if our suite is ready. You can call home at a more civilized hour."

"Suite?"

"Why, yes. I booked the honeymoon suite, of course." He winked at her.

"Oh, my God!" Cami clapped an excited hand to her mouth.

Taking her arm, Rayhan guided Cami up the gangplank, praying she wouldn't get to a phone until after they'd left port. If she did, he bet Old Man Ellison would talk her out of the elopement. And if Ellison learned the identity of Cami's suitor before they were wed and their marriage consummated, Rayhan would wager his fastest Arabian that the union would be annulled before sundown.

No, he had to keep Cami away from a telephone until she was wedded, thoroughly bedded and, hopefully, pregnant. At the same time, he couldn't appear to obstruct her.

After talking with the two sailors at the top of the gangplank, and slipping each a fifty, Rayhan led Cami into the ship's salon, which resembled a hotel lobby. "See, Cami. If our room isn't ready, we can have breakfast. Then it should be time to call home." He pointed at a bank of phones near a rest room.

She looked relieved.

"Do not worry." Rayhan injected a good dose of reassurance into his voice. "All will be well. Your father may be surprised when he hears the news, but not displeased, I hope?"

She turned to him. "That's what I'm afraid of. I've never done much of anything without talking it over with Dad."

Fear ripped through him, the stress wrenching his gut into knots. Tugging her arm, he went to a sofa and sat with her. "Cami, if you are not sure, we shouldn't—"

"Oh, I'm sure! I just feel that I should tell him."

"Of course you should." Rayhan made a mental note to call his ranch first and arrange something—anything—to get Charles Ellison away from the phone when his daughter called, or perhaps to keep the line engaged until they'd married.

Cami looked at her watch. "It's six o'clock. Even if Dad isn't awake, Robbie will be. She's our house-keeper. She gets up early to cook for the hands." She pulled a cellular phone from her handbag and began to poke buttons.

Rayhan relaxed. He'd met Roberta Morris several times in McMahon, occasionally exchanging a few words with her. He knew she'd been hired by Charles

Ellison a couple of years after Rayhan purchased his ranch. Robbie had never shown, by word or deed, she was aware of any strain between the denizens of the Double Eagle and the C-Bar-C.

"Hi, Robbie, it's Cami."

"Cami! Where are you?" The connection wasn't great, but Cami could hear Robbie over the static.

"I'm out with a friend. Is Dad up yet?" Cami smiled at Ray, who watched her. One of his eyelids twitched.

Robbie said, "No, he had a bad night. He won't be up for an hour or so. Out with a friend? Where?"

Cami hesitated. "Hold on, okay?" She covered the receiver and said to Ray, "I don't want Dad to hear from Robbie that I'm getting married. We should tell him. So what should I say?"

"Tell her everything is all right. You had an unexpected opportunity to travel to New Orleans with a friend, and decided to go. You'll be back Thursday."

"Okay." Cami, relieved, realized that everything should be fine. She was an adult, wasn't she? Her father had raised her to make decisions for herself. Besides, he'd never gotten really mad at her for anything she'd done, not even when, at age eleven, she'd gone joyriding in one of the ranch's trucks and crashed it into a tree.

So she relayed the message to Robbie. The housekeeper said, "I'll tell your father. Thanks for calling in, Cami. Otherwise we'd worry."

After ending the conversation, Cami clicked off her phone and smiled at Ray. "Glad I got that done. Now let's go eat."

Ray had arranged a relaxing day for Cami, so after breakfast he dropped her off at the ship's spa. Following a two-hour massage and a light lunch, Cami, feeling delightfully pampered, had her face made up, her fingernails painted and her feet pedicured. Then the salon stylist washed and braided her blond hair into a coronet, the coiffure Cami wanted for the wedding ceremony.

The ceremony. Cami's heart did backflips when she contemplated what would happen at six o'clock that night. Squelching her nerves, she visited the row of shops on the ship's main deck. "Buy whatever you need," Ray had said. "Including a dress for tonight. Charge it to the room."

The *Corsair,* a fully outfitted luxury liner of the Caravel Cruise Line, boasted everything, including a bridal boutique. In a reasonably short time, Cami bought a dress, heels and a veil.

Her wedding dress. She picked a white silk sheath with a beaded, wrapped bodice. It fell straight to her ankles from the empire waist, with its long skirt skimming her hips.

Though the dress left her arms bare and plunged below her collarbones to a vee, it outlined rather than exposed her body. She hoped Ray, who she knew had a prudish streak, would like it.

A cabin attendant showed Cami, clutching several shopping bags, to the honeymoon suite. When she saw the room, her muscles slackened, allowing her parcels to fall to the carpeted floor.

A big, round bed on a dais dominated the suite. Her mouth went dry and her flesh shivered at the sight. She imagined herself and Ray, naked and entwined, on its flaming-red satin comforter.

She took a deep breath, steadying herself, then looked around the room.

Ray had apparently come and gone, leaving her a lavish bouquet of two dozen yellow roses, a gift-wrapped box and a note.

My dearest Cami,

I hope you enjoyed your day. I am told that Americans believe it is bad fortune for the bride and groom to meet before the ceremony. So we will see each other again in the ship's chapel at six.

In the meantime, please accept my wedding gift.

Missing you every moment,

R.

Cami examined the note for a long time, realizing this was the first time she'd seen Ray's handwriting. It held none of the hesitancy she supposed a foreigner's penmanship might; rather the confident strokes reflected Ray's bold personality.

Then she turned her attention to her present. She tore the silver wrapping paper from the package and discovered diamond stud earrings and a necklace that matched her engagement ring. The gifts were opulent, yet simple and modest. How like Ray, Cami thought. Better, they'd look wonderful with her dress.

Smiling, Cami fingered the platinum chain from which a heart-shaped diamond hung, glad she'd also purchased Ray a keepsake. She'd bought a chunky, masculine bracelet in gold, and had asked the jeweler to engrave the flat, square clasp.

She tried again to phone her father to share her joy, but the C-Bar-C's line was busy. Darn.

Six o'clock came. Cami, quivering with excitement, slipped her feet into her new white satin pumps and walked to the chapel. Calm but expectant, she wondered if anyone she passed in the corridors could see her pounding pulse, hear the eager beat of her heart, divine the inner joy that infused every cell of her body.

She approached the chapel's wooden double doors. A smiling woman introduced herself as the ship's activities director, then gave Cami a bouquet of yellow roses. Cami buried her face in the fragrant blooms to inhale deeply. Ray was so-o-o-o romantic.

Her resolve to wed this unique, special man, already firm, hardened into granite. Though he'd never told her he loved her, everything he did reflected his sincerity and devotion. Men didn't expose their romantic souls unless they were sure. Cami was certain she'd found the steadfast, true love she craved, now and for the rest of her life.

After helping Cami with her veil, the activities director opened the double doors. Cami blinked, dazzled by the glittering lights. She heard the trill of a sweet violin playing.

Cami's gaze traveled the length of the central aisle toward Ray, standing straight and proud against a backdrop of yellow roses, red gladiolus and white mums. He also wore white, his tux setting off his exotic, dark good looks. Her mind spun. After a few seconds she reminded herself to breathe, but it was tough. Her man was a hottie, and just looking at him sucked the wind right out of her lungs.

She practically sprinted down the aisle to stand by his side.

Chapter Eight

Champagne corks and flashbulbs popped, startling Cami, already dizzied by the brief yet solemn ceremony.

She'd joined her life to Ray's. She was married.

Playing with the stem of her champagne flute, she watched him covertly as he finished taking care of the arrangements with the captain and the photographer. Ray's broad shoulders, handsomely filling out the tux; his long, graceful hands, hands that could take her to heaven and back; his muscular, well-proportioned body, which would soon make her a woman...his wife.

When he returned to her side, her gaze traveled to his face. Though often dark and guarded, at this moment his open smile and relaxed eyes concealed nothing. Certain she'd done the right thing, Cami placed her hand in her husband's for the walk back to their suite.

At the door, Ray hefted her in his arms.

"Oh, come on," Cami said. "That's so-o-o-o corny."

"I am told it is good luck. Do you not want the best fortune can offer? Come." Ray tucked her against him with a secure grip. "Oh, Cami. I forgot. The card key to this room is in my jacket pocket."

"The side pocket?"

"No, the inner one. Get it for me, will you?"

Instead of reaching into the inner pocket, Cami shoved her hand between two of the studs of his shirt and ran her fingernails across his chest. She found his nipple and rimmed it, scratching gently.

Staggering, Ray ground out something guttural in Arabic she didn't understand.

"What did you just say?"

"Never mind. Where did you learn to do that?"

She gave him her sauciest grin and wiggled her bottom against him. Ray's grip slackened; he nearly dropped her.

Cami giggled. "In a women's magazine."

"Please get the key, Cami. Now."

She opened the door and he managed to jockey her through it without hitting her head or her heels against either jamb. "You did that very well," she said.

"I have never before done such a foolish thing. Are there many other arcane American customs which we must perform before we may get lucky?"

She shook her head. "Nope, we've done them all."

"Yes, we have, haven't we?" He swung her around. "We did it, Cami, we really did it!"

Exultant laughter burst from her chest and bubbled

through her throat, filling her with happiness. "Yeah, we sure did! We got married!"

Ray peppered her forehead, eyelids, nose and cheeks with light little kisses before carefully setting her on her feet. She kissed back, trying to take him deeper into the seduction she anticipated and welcomed.

But Ray evidently had other ideas. After slipping off his jacket, he crossed the room to tinker with the suite's music system. Soon a jazz singer crooned a sultry ballad. Ray again opened his arms to her, and she slid within his embrace, fitting there as though they'd been designed for each other.

While they danced, she feathered her lips over his, teasing and tempting, eager to truly become his. Their kisses grew deeper and more searching. Cami let her hands roam over Ray's chest, loosening his tie, plucking at the studs holding his shirt together, uncinching his cummerbund. She let it drop to the floor.

She didn't know what had gotten into her. Some wanton, sex-crazed devil-wench had taken over her body, filling it with an uncontrollable heat and need. She couldn't keep her hands off Ray.

And he sure wasn't resisting her. Instead he pressed her head closer to him when she bent to rub her face in his rough, masculine mat of chest hair. She circled one of his dark nipples with her tongue, then scraped it with her teeth into an aroused point. He moaned and murmured something in Arabic, his hand tightening on her nape.

Cami discovered she liked to turn on her husband, but she was selfish enough to want this consummation for herself. She wanted to see everything, feel everything, do everything—

A knock at the door interrupted her, startling her away from her frantic exploration of Ray's torso.

He smiled at her as he answered the door, swinging it wide. "Dinner has arrived."

Dinner! Cami didn't want dinner. She wanted Ray. She tapped her toe on the carpet as the servers unloaded the feast onto a nearby table: caviar on toast points, lobster bisque, grilled baby prawns with baby new potatoes, and a salad of fresh baby greens.

"Hmmm," she said as the servers left. "Is there a message in this supper?"

"I beg your pardon?" Ray poured two glasses of water and set them beside their plates.

"Eggs." She pointed at the caviar. "Baby prawns. Baby potatoes. Baby greens. Eggs and babies. You got an agenda here, honey?"

He grinned and dipped his head. A lock of dark hair fell appealingly across his forehead. "I am not becoming any younger, Cami. I realize in this country that women have a choice, and I believe that is right. But I hope you choose to bear children for us, to complete our lives."

She breathed in deeply, then exhaled, trying to find her center. "I don't know, Ray—"

"If you are not sure about things, then you shouldn't."

"Oh, I'm sure about us. I love you. Why do you doubt that?" Crossing the room to him, she laid her head on his chest. His beautiful, naked chest.

"I know everything has happened so fast. If you have doubts, I cannot blame you, my wife."

"My wife." She sighed. "Those have got to be the two most beautiful words in the English language, except for maybe my husband." She looked up into his face, reading anxiety in his dark eyes.

Cami couldn't bear for him to suffer a moment's worry. "I have no doubts. Let's make a baby."

Taking his hand, she led him to their bed.

Wakeful even at 2:00 a.m., Rayhan sat up in bed and glanced at his sleeping wife. Even in her rest, a smile curved Cami's lips.

He didn't want his restlessness to disturb her, so he carefully slid from between the rumpled sheets, then tugged on his jeans. He placed a single yellow rose in the dent his head had left in the pillow beside her before taking the room key and leaving the suite.

After cadging a cigarette from a sailor, Rayhan wandered over to a dark corner of the deck. Relaxing into a lounge chair, he tilted his head back to marvel at the absolute blackness of the night sky at sea, lit only by faraway pinpoints of infinite stars. Their abundant, shimmering glitter, a lavish diamond necklace on the bosom of the queen of heaven, reminded him of lovemaking with his wife.

His wife.

Everything about her shocked him, staggered him, drew him deeper into the web she'd woven with her innocent body and wise smiles, her ardent eyes and curious hands.

She'd been all maidenly modesty during their wedding ceremony. Robed in white like a virginal priest-ess, she'd spoken the words of the ancient ritual with solemnity, inspiring from him the same reverence.

Rayhan had meant every word of his vows.

Then later he'd carried her across the threshold of the honeymoon suite. Neither managed to eat much of the dinner he'd ordered. The champagne had gone flat, and the caviar remained uneaten.

They'd preferred to devour each other.

Intensely aware of the importance of Cami's first time, he'd tried to ease into sex gradually. This night would set the pattern for their lovemaking for years to come. He'd guided his wife to the peak of passion before allowing himself release into pleasure, know-ing that a bad experience for Cami would be a disas-ter.

He needn't have worried. *Lovemaking* was a mild word for what happened between them. Rayhan closed his eyes, remembering the words of the tradi-tional wedding ceremony. *With my body, I thee wor-ship.*

They'd worshipped each other the way pagans wor-ship a wild fertility goddess.

Rayhan drew deeply on the cigarette, dragging its smoke into his mouth. He touched the ring he wore on his left hand, then fondled the bracelet she'd given him. Running his finger over the engraved clasp, he caressed the incised letters: C+R. Cami and Rayhan. His heart swelled into his throat.

He looked up into the heavens, thanking Whoever dwelt there for his good fortune, for he was surely the luckiest husband in the world.

* * *

The door closed with a click, followed by the rustle of movement, alerting Cami to Ray's return. Then she felt him slip into bed, his long, cool body flowing like water next to hers.

"Where did you go on our honeymoon night?" she asked sleepily. "Bad hubby!" She smacked him lightly on one hip.

His deep chuckle rolled over her in the darkness before he grabbed her wrists and trapped them above her head. With a gasp, Cami involuntarily arched her back. She tried to pull away from his grip.

He didn't let go, but chuckled again. "Relax, my darling. Let me compensate you for my offense." He rolled, his weight pinning her hips onto the mattress.

Lips stroked her face, her neck...lower. Much lower.

Her body started to quiver with delighted anticipation. In perfect trust, Cami gave herself to her husband and his love.

They skipped the excursion to one of the beaches lining the Gulf Coast, preferring to spend the day in bed. The next morning the ship docked at New Orleans. They played tourist, first exploring a haunted mansion in the Garden District, then visiting the zoo and the aquarium. They attended an "authentic voodoo ritual" that made Cami giggle, embarrassing them so much they had to leave.

Still chuckling over the spectacle his wife had made, Rayhan treated Cami to a delicious Creole dinner. They ate crawfish étouffée and drank the wonderful New Orleans chicory-laced coffee.

After the ship left New Orleans that night, the captain announced that due to a spot of rough weather, the *Corsair* had to change course and head farther out to sea.

Cami wasn't much of a sailor, and Rayhan eyed her with worry as she collapsed onto their bed. "As you Americans might say, you look a tad green about the gills."

Abruptly, she stood, shoved past him and dashed into the bathroom. Following, Rayhan found her bent over the sink, groaning as the remains of crawfish étouffée went down the drain.

"Oh, darling." He ran the cold water tap. "Here, rinse your mouth."

Cami complied, moaning weakly. He grabbed a clean washcloth and drenched it with water. After wringing it out, he pressed it to her forehead.

It occurred to him that he'd never gone to so much trouble over another person. For his horses, yes, he sacrificed, staying up nights to watch a sick colt or a pregnant mare. But another human being? A woman?

Rayhan frowned as he led his wife back to bed. After urging her to lie down, he placed the cold compress onto her brow and hunted for a basin in case she again became ill.

He'd never troubled himself over bedmates. As a prince of Adnan, they were ever present in his youth. In Paris, where he'd attended school, the Frenchwomen kept him amused but not distracted from his studies. Later he'd enjoyed his share of American girls.

But he'd married only one woman.

Marriage has little to do with emotion, he reminded himself. Royals selected their mates for tangible qualities, not for love. He'd picked Cami because she was wealthy, intelligent and beautiful, an unsullied vessel for his seed and a worthy mother for his children.

That she was lovable hadn't entered into his decision making, and didn't have to now, or ever. That he loved her was impossible. Ridiculous. Love was a fantasy told to timorous virgins to lure them into bed or marriage. Love was a fool's dream.

He hadn't fallen in love with his wife. He'd married her to restore honor and complete his revenge upon her swindling father.

Jolted, Rayhan realized he hadn't thought about Charles Ellison, honor, or revenge for a long time.

But that didn't mean he'd fallen in love with his wife, though he quite liked his beautiful Texan princess. He'd keep and enjoy her for as long as possible.

He avoided thinking deeply about the twist their marriage would surely take upon their return to Mc-Mahon. As his wife, Cami would live at the Double Eagle. Rayhan decided she'd simply have to adjust to a more distant relationship with her father.

"What is this?" Standing at the purser's desk, Ray, brow creased, scrutinized the bill for their cruise. Cami slipped an arm around his waist and peeked over his shoulder at the paper, wondering what had annoyed her usually unflappable husband.

"I'm sure it's correct, sir." The young man behind the desk anxiously shoved back a forelock of sandy hair.

Ray turned to her. "Camille. I do not see the charges for your clothes. How is that possible?"

Cami grinned at him. Now that the storm had passed and the ship had docked, she was back to her accustomed cheerful spirits. "I put everything on my credit cards."

"You are my wife. You do not need to spend your funds."

She put her lips near his ear. "I didn't want you to think I married you for your money, honey. I'm a wealthy woman, you know." She nibbled on his lobe.

Passing a hand around her waist, he eased Cami closer. "That may be, but I am capable of clothing my wife." His fingertips drew a line up her back to her nape, then made little circles there. She shivered with renewed desire.

Glad he didn't seem to care about her net worth, she said, "Ray, I wasn't going to let you buy your own wedding present." She fingered the heavy gold bracelet circling his wrist.

He caught her hand and kissed it. "Very well, my darling. We will not argue about these trifles. But in the future, shall we not discuss these matters before-hand?"

"But of course, prince. I would not dream of dis-obeying a sheikh of Adnan." She delighted in imi-tating his accent.

He frowned and wrinkled his nose.

Cami giggled.

The ship had docked at dawn. Despite the early hour, Cami wanted to rush home to share her happi-ness with her father. She hurried Ray into his truck and didn't want to stop along the way. However, she couldn't help noticing that the closer they drove to McMahon, the quieter Ray became.

As he turned off the main road and headed toward their ranches, his hands held the steering wheel in a death grip, knuckles white.

"What's wrong?" She placed a hand over his tight fingers.

Ray sighed. "I am afraid your father will not approve of what we have done."

Her heart thudded dully. "So am I. We were pretty impulsive. But I'm sure about us. Aren't you?"

"Absolutely," he said at once. "Cami, whatever may happen, let us remember that we are sure. No regrets, all right?"

"No regrets."

Guessing her father would be at work, Cami took Ray's hand and led him through her home to the study. Sure enough, Charles sat behind his desk, talking on the telephone. When Cami entered, Ray in tow, her dad's eyes became hooded and murky. He said into the handset, "Hey, Larry. Something's come up. Talk to ya later."

Cami's father clicked off the phone and set it on the desk. An indefinable expression entered his watery blue eyes. His gaze shifted from Cami to Ray.

Cami stared. For the first time in her life, her father showed fear, and…guilt? What was going on?

Ray cleared his throat. "Hello, old friend." Acid edged his tone.

Old friend? What did Ray mean? Did her father

and her husband have a connection they'd never mentioned to her? "You two know each other?" she asked.

"Not at all." Ray's voice sounded cool, even distant.

Weirder and weirder.

"We've had some dealings in the past." Charles's glance cut to her left hand, placed on Ray's arm. "Cami, what is that?"

Cami proudly displayed her new rings. Though she adored the heart-shaped diamond, she loved their wedding set more. Of gold and platinum filigree, the flowing Arabic characters on each ring spelled out a vow of faithfulness. Or so Ray had said. "These are my engagement and wedding rings. We're married. We got married three days ago on a cruise to New Orleans."

Grabbing a cane set close to the desk, Charles stood. "Cami, why didn't you talk to me?" he croaked.

Cami could hear his tight, short, angry breaths. "I, uh, I…" She cast a desperate glance at Ray. Her father's reaction overshadowed her worst expectations. He appeared on the verge of shock, not joy.

Ray's face and eyes now looked as though they'd been carved out of obsidian. Cami had expected her suave husband to smile, shake her father's hand, maybe even ask for his blessing. Instead Ray did nothing, while Cami's tongue stuck to the roof of her dry mouth, her voice trapped by a dawning sense of horror.

"So you did it." Charles wheezed, his gaze pinned

on Ray. "You couldn't get your greedy hands on the oil ten years ago. So you stole my little girl and married her money." Limping with the cane in hand, he drew closer. "You lousy, gold-digging skunk."

Ray emitted a short, contemptuous laugh. "Gold-digging. Ha. I do not wish to boast, but I could buy and sell this town, and both of you, several times over."

"So what was the point?" Charles had hobbled to within a yard of Cami, who still clutched her husband's arm. Her father's lips had turned pale, even bluish.

Ray shrugged. "Honor. Vengeance." He fixed Cami with an enigmatic gaze. "Desire. I have need of a wife. She is most precious to you, is she not? And now she is mine."

Cami's heart forgot how to beat. *I have need of a wife.* That was cold, ice-cold. Ray had never said he loved her, and she'd let that omission slide. She'd told herself that he showed her his love by his acts, rather than by expressing it verbally.

Had she hidden the truth from herself? "What is this all about?" she managed to whisper through her taut, tense throat.

Charles raised his cane and swung it at Ray's head. He took the glancing blow on an upraised arm, then yanked the weapon from Charles's grasp, flinging it aside.

Cami's father fell against her, then toppled to the floor, limbs convulsing. He jerked a twitching hand in the direction of his desk, choking out, "My medicine!"

"Oh, my God!" Cami screamed. "He's having an asthma attack!" She raced to his desk drawer and wrenched it open, scrabbling for her father's inhaler.

Grabbing the phone, Ray punched three buttons before beginning to talk in a tight, terse voice.

Sirens screaming, an ambulance with paramedics showed up, just a few minutes after Ray called 911. They stabilized Charles, then took him to the hospital. Because she knew everyone in McMahon, including the paramedics, Cami rode along with her father. The oxygen mask over his face didn't allow conversation, so Cami's mind remained a whirlpool of questions, and her heart a maelstrom of conflicting emotions.

When Charles was placed in a cubicle, Cami lingered by his side until he could speak. Ray had stayed in the waiting room, because only one visitor at a time was allowed in the E.R.

"Dad, can you talk to me? Can you tell me what's going on with you and Ray?"

Charles sighed. "Oh, Cami. This mess is all my fault. Can you forgive me?"

"I don't know that there's anything to forgive. What happened?"

Rayhan leaned against a doorpost, occasionally sipping from a cup of the awful vending-machine coffee. He watched Cami enter the waiting room from the E.R. and approach.

For a moment he felt like a puppet on a stage, strings tugged by an invisible master. Then he reminded himself that he'd created the situation and had to live with it.

His wife had aged in the past few hours, transforming from a carefree girl to a saddened woman. Her shoulders drooped. Her feet dragged. Her teary eyes appeared red and ravaged.

He briefly closed his eyes. He'd never thought about how his actions would affect the woman to whom he'd committed his life.

He was a fool.

Finally she stood before him. He offered her the coffee.

Cami passed her nose over the rim of the cup, sniffing. She winced, then blew on the surface of the steamy beverage. "Ray, is it true?"

"What?"

"My father swindled you out of a fortune ten years ago." Her blue eyes steadily regarded him over the rim of the cup. "*My* fortune."

Rayhan breathed in and out, aware of his sighing inhalations; her eyelashes, spiky with her salt tears; the importance of the moment.

His revenge did not taste sweet but was flavored by a most bitter brew: guilt. He'd hurt her. Though that had been necessary, he wanted her to understand.

He said, "That is my opinion, yes. I was very young—about your age—and my English was not good." He gestured. "As you know, it still is not perfect. The king, my father, assigned to me the royal Adnani attorney, who did not understand the situation, either. Your father said things about the deed that turned out to be false. I could not drill for oil on my land. I still cannot.''

"And you've plotted revenge ever since." Her voice dropped to a whisper. "That's sick."

How could she think such a terrible thing? She was his wife! "We said no regrets. Did we not?" He reached out to touch her shoulder.

Cami jerked away. "That was before I learned how twisted you are." She turned and walked out of the hospital without a single look back at him.

He wanted to run after her, explain everything, but what was there to explain?

Indecisive, Rayhan shifted, back and forth, left boot to right and back again. Cami was very angry and distressed over the situation. Yes, that was it. Perhaps he would be wiser to wait. She would come back to him of her own accord, once she had calmed down and thought matters through. If she did not—Rayhan's heart froze in his chest.

Then, taking deep, even breaths, he firmed his resolve. If she did not return to him, she did not believe in their wedding vows. If so, he would not beg her. If she did not believe in their marriage, they had nothing.

Chapter Nine

Dear Dad:
I've rented an apartment in San Antonio and will start school again in September. I know I left the ranch really quickly after you got out of the hospital, and I'm sorry. But please understand why I can't stay with you anymore. I just need some time to myself to sort things out.

Cami

Syed, capital city of Adnan
Three weeks later

Rayhan's eldest brother, the king, paced up and down the tiled colonnade with jerky strides, his robes swinging. "This is a disaster!" He waved the sheaf of faxes he held. "Your wife has filed for divorce! She refuses the summons of a prince of Adnan!"

Rayhan grimaced. To Kadar, everything was a disaster. He had always been so. Cami would have labelled his brother a "drama mama," in her charming slang. "She is an American," Rayhan said prosaically. "She does not have to obey my command."

"She must." The king resumed his pacing. "The situation is very unsettled. The anti-American sentiment in the desert tribes will be inflamed by her insolence. They will seek to push us closer to the foreign extremists and their insanities."

Rayhan shuddered. No Adnani—except for the ever-fractious desert tribes—wanted their peaceful country to go the violent way of the extremists in neighboring countries. "What can be done?"

"You will not consider marrying Matana al-Qamra? Her family will be gravely insulted if you back out of the wedding. They are rumored to desire an alliance with the desert tribes to incite revolution."

"Absolutely not." Rayhan crossed his arms over his chest. "I am already married."

"Adnani law permits royal princes to take multiple wives."

"The engagement was negotiated without my agreement," Rayhan snapped. "I will not be a political pawn." He knew if he bent on this matter, his life would never be his own. Besides, he didn't want another bad marriage.

"All of us are political pawns!"

"You married for love." Rayhan nodded toward his pregnant sister-in-law, the queen, who reclined upon a chaise at the far end of the courtyard.

The king's stern face softened as he gazed at his

wife. "That is true, but Habiba and I were affianced when we were children. We grew to love each other over the years. Even if it had not been so, we would have married for the stability of the country. And that is what you must do!"

"No."

"You are refusing a direct command?"

Rayhan glared at his brother, knowing the king could have him beheaded in the central square of Syed if the monarch so chose. "*You* marry her if it is so important."

"I cannot. Habiba is in a very delicate condition. You are minister without portfolio, and already engaged to Matana. Do something!"

In the past month Rayhan had learned that his job as minister without portfolio meant that he was responsible for everything, yet had power over nothing.

"I can travel to Texas and ask my wife to visit. If she is cooperative, her presence may stabilize the situation." That would accomplish much. He missed Texas, his horses and his land. He hated the idea of begging Cami for anything, but he had to admit that he yearned for her.

Nothing had gone right for Rayhan since they'd stepped off the cruise boat. Now he wished they'd stayed on the ship and sailed away to forever.

When Cami had been near, his heart had brimmed with happiness. Without her, even the bright Adnani sunshine seemed tarnished and dark around the edges. He'd returned to his homeland to make a fresh start, but nothing worked, nothing was right.

"No, no," said the king. "You cannot demean

yourself or our family. That will damage our position with the people. I will send someone to bring her here.''

Rayhan stirred. ''She must remain unharmed.''

''But of course. She is your wife, the consort of a prince of Adnan. But she must come.''

Tucking the morning paper under her arm, Cami walked with leaden feet out of her apartment. After locking the door, she slowly made her way down the stairs and into the street. Despite her light summer dress, the August heat punched her like a fist.

As time had dragged on, she'd felt worse and worse. She prayed she wasn't pregnant, but she had the symptoms: sick a lot, couldn't keep anything down, wanted to stay in bed all day long.

A pregnancy would be catastrophic. She remembered her friend Jenelle's misery: nineteen, pregnant and stuck in a bad marriage. Tightening her mouth, Cami squared her shoulders and marched down the sidewalk. That wouldn't happen to her. She'd already filed for divorce, and if the store-bought pregnancy test revealed she was expecting, she'd deal with it.

If and when she gathered the courage to use the test.

She entered the Java Joint on the corner. She liked to drink an iced white chocolate mocha there every morning while reading the paper. Today she noticed a new employee mixing up the coffee drinks, an older fellow whose dark good looks reminded her of Ray.

She turned her head, hating anything that resembled her low-down, two-faced rat of a husband. She paid for her drink, then took it and her paper to a table near the window.

Sipping, she tried to read the paper, but her scrambled brain couldn't focus. She rubbed her temple. Her runaway train of thought would get her nowhere. She'd traveled on the same mental track over and over in the past weeks. Nothing seemed to erase the chaos running riot in her mind and heart.

Her guilt over hurting her father. Her fury toward both Charles and Ray. Her father should have told her everything years before, she reminded herself. Instead, he'd kept information germane to the sale of the Double Eagle from her.

After leaving the hospital, Cami had returned to her ranch to check the deed. A clause labeled "Grant of Mineral Rights," written in confusing language with tiny type, excluded the oil lying under both the C-Bar-C and the Double Eagle. A careless reader— or a young man with poor English—would have been misled, if not tricked.

She couldn't wrap her mind around the word *swindle* in connection with her father, who'd always cared for her so tenderly. But did Dad's acts justify what Ray had done?

Cami winced. Ray had deceived her, married her for revenge and taken her innocence for the lowest of motives. *She is most precious to you, is she not? And now she is mine.* The snake had married her only to hurt her father, as though she were nothing but a pawn for his sick games. Now he had the gall to summon her to Adnan, for some kind of royal whoop-te-do. Yeah, right.

He'd made a complete dupe of her. Every conclusion she'd reached about him—that he was honest, cared about her and not her fortune—had been dead wrong. Not only was she angry at Ray, but she was furious at herself. How could she have been such a fool?

She sucked iced coffee through the straw, hoping to cool her useless rage, then flipped through the paper to the entertainment section. She needed a diversion. A movie would do the trick.

The movie listings were printed in the tiniest of fonts. Squinting, Cami dropped her head until her nose was touching the paper, but still the words seemed to wobble and drift across her field of vision, finally growing completely dark.

Cramped and stiff, with a queasy headache reminiscent of her seasickness, Cami awakened in what appeared to be a very peculiar bedroom. Trying to ignore her nausea, she rubbed sleep out of her gummy eyes while deciphering her surroundings.

Everything seemed to have been designed for dwarves. Her long body, still clothed in her now-crumpled pink dress, had been crammed into a narrow bunk. Only a flattened foam pillow cradled her head. The odd, trapezoidal room had rounded windows sized for fairies or elves.

Cami tore off the confining sheet and thin blanket, then gasped at the slap of cool air. She became aware of a subliminal hum buzzing at the outer edges of her consciousness.

She stood. The room tipped and twirled. Stumbling

to one of the elfin windows, she saw blue sky and puffy clouds, with a sparkling ocean glittering far, far below.

''That skunk!'' She never wanted to see Ray again, but if she did, she'd skin him alive and then stomp on him with her cowboy boots. She'd ignored his imperious summons, so he'd had her kidnapped!

The timbre of the engines changed. The plane swayed, tilted, then stabilized. Cami dashed for one of the doors, praying she'd picked the lavatory.

Rayhan watched Cami shake her arm free of one of her guards. She stumbled down the ramp out of the king's private jet.

His wife looked like a ragamuffin. Her hair had escaped sloppy plaits. Though a modest calf length, her loose pink dress showed wrinkle upon wrinkle, as if she'd slept in it. It hung on her slender, wraith-like frame. Had she lost weight?

She came closer. He could see purplish crescents staining the thin skin beneath her eyes, which themselves seemed droopy and dulled.

The king's agents who'd accompanied her didn't look much better. One sported a black eye. The *thobe* of another was stained brown. As the group drew near, Rayhan deduced from the smell that the agent had been the target of his wife's morning coffee, hurled by her enraged hand.

One of the guards took her arm to help her down the ramp. Flinging his hand away, she elbowed him in the side, snarling, ''Don't touch me!''

The king's agents couldn't match her long, jerky

strides. She marched toward Rayhan, showing not a trace of the fear a lesser woman would exhibit in the same situation, finding herself abducted to a strange land. Rayhan felt his chest puff with pride. His wife had the heart of a lioness.

Now only a foot away, she reached for the front of his *thobe*. Tugging on his clothing, she drew him near, as if to embrace him. Rayhan's heart leaped. Perhaps all was well.

As he prepared to greet his wife with his heartiest kiss, she used one finger to turn his head.

He felt her lips approach his ear. His skin tingled at the puff of her breath.

"You lowdown, scheming skunk!" she screamed directly into his ear.

Yanking away, Rayhan winced. He guessed he deserved whatever punishment she meted, but at the same time, she had to understand her position in their society. Removing her hands from his *thobe,* he said calmly, "The penalty for assaulting a member of the Adnani royal family is death by beheading."

The first thing Cami noticed were the colors of Adnan. Undimmed by even a hint of humidity, utterly clear and dustless, the air shimmered with a brilliant white sun that lit everything with unnatural vividness. The sky wasn't merely blue or even cerulean, but a bright hard cobalt that hammered at her, so vibrant it hurt.

Flags were everywhere, and the national colors reflected the intense light. A field of yellow, piercing as hot curry, lay beneath a horizontal center stripe of emerald. The dazzling blue of the Adnani sky topped the yellow and green. The colors tore at her eyes, accentuating her nausea and dizziness.

The heat didn't help, either, and when Ray took her arm to lead her into an air-conditioned limousine, Cami didn't resist. Instead she breathed a gusty sigh of relief when a guard closed the doors. The sudden quiet reminded her that the airport, though small, bustled.

She leaned back against the cushions and closed her eyes, hoping to avoid the entire world, especially Ray. She didn't want to be close to him, not emotionally, not physically, ever again. She prayed he wouldn't touch her. If he did, her resolve would crumble like stale, dry cake.

Even with her eyes tight shut, keeping her hands to herself, Cami was keenly aware of his presence. When he moved, she could hear the swish of his robes and the creak of the leather upholstery. His scent, which had always reminded her of exotic casbahs and romantic, foreign shores, seemed amplified here, on his native soil.

His nearness made every cell vibrate. The tiny hairs on her bare arms stood to attention. Her skin prickled. She hated what he could do to her so effortlessly.

She was thirsty, hungry, tired, grubby, exhausted. She wanted nothing more than a shower and her bed at home.

Something cool and hard touched her lips. "Drink," he said.

Opening her eyes, she saw a glass and obeyed,

even though she didn't want anything from Ray. But fasting in protest would hurt no one but herself.

Orange juice, cool and sweet. "It isn't as good as back in Texas," she managed to croak.

"Of course it is not. The juice I gave you at my home had been freshly squeezed from my trees. This is some commercial product."

"Is it Adnani?"

"Yes. We grow citrus in a fertile region between the sea and the mountains. Beyond them, there is desert." He rolled down the window. Heat blasted into the car's interior. Ignoring it, he pointed outside at one of the banners decorating the limo. "See you our flag? The colors represent our country. Blue for sea and sky. The greenbelt. The golden desert sands."

"Wonderful." She didn't bother to keep the sourness out of her voice. However exotic and interesting this place might be, she didn't want to be in Adnan, and she swore that she wouldn't cooperate. After draining the glass of juice, she again closed her eyes, deliberately shutting Ray out.

"Cami, please. There is much you need to know. Your position—"

"Listen, Ray." She jerked upright and shot him a nasty glare. "There's something *you* need to know. Our marriage is over. I filed for divorce. I have no position here." She again turned away from him, curling her body into a corner of the limo.

The car remained quiet for the space of a few moments. She could hear only his even breathing.

"I am sorry," he said finally. "But I cannot grant you a divorce. My country is very unstable—"

"Grant me a divorce? What are you talking about?" Arrogant, too, as well as a snake. "Under Texas law, I have an absolute right to a divorce."

"We are not in Texas."

His quietly spoken words crashed down on her like an avalanche. *We are not in Texas.* The realities of her situation struck her. She was alone in a strange land, the captive wife of one of its princes. She had no pocketbook, no identification, no passport and no money.

She had nothing.

She *was* nothing.

The only thing she had was a husband she loathed. She was only someone's nameless, faceless wife.

Cami buried her face in her hands and tried not to cry from her despair and frustration.

"Camille, stop this silliness. This is no time to indulge in childish tantrums. You knew what you were taking on when we married. You knew I was a prince of Adnan—"

She jerked upright. "We never talked about it! I thought we'd live in Texas."

"I am not sure where we will live now. Much is happening here that you do not know about."

"I don't care to know." She turned away from him.

"You must. You are now Camille al-Rashad, the consort of a prince of Adnan, and that means responsibility. You are no longer pampered Cami Ellison."

Cami flinched. She scooted across the seat toward the open window, focusing on her surroundings instead of his hurtful, stinging words.

The limo was traveling through a busy part of the city. A business district, she supposed, based on the office buildings lining the streets. The wide boulevard was crowded with various kinds of transportation, from mules, bicycles and scooters, on up to Rolls-Royces. Billboards, many advertising the same products as in America, caught her eye. Most featured darkly handsome males with petite, dainty girls Cami figured were typical of Adnan.

The sidewalks were jammed; pedestrians of every age and race wore all manner of clothing.

Involuntarily fascinated, she said, "I see a lot of people in Western dress, including women. But I've heard that the Arab countries can be very repressive, especially toward females."

"Not Adnan. We were colonized by the French, you see, and are close to Europe. The European influence is very strong, especially in the cities and along the seacoast. Women need not wear the *abaya* or the veil, unless they choose."

Cami frowned. "Why would anyone want to go around wearing a black bedsheet?"

"The *abaya* is said to be very comfortable, though I would not know from experience. In the heat, the loose, thin fabrics are cool."

"Black is hot in the sun."

"In Adnan, the colors are different. See?" Leaning closer to her, he pointed out the window. "Young, unmarried women are in white to signify their innocence. Those in mourning may wear black; the long-widowed, gray. And married women choose any color they please, but the colors of our flag are the most popular.''

His nearness bothered her, grating against her already raw nerves. "What about divorced women? What color do they wear?''

He yanked away. "There are no divorced women in Adnan. Adnani understand the concepts of commitment and loyalty.'' He glowered at her, eyes smoldering.

She got right in his face. "What about honesty, huh? Love?''

"I have never lied to you!''

"There are lies of omission, aren't there?'' He was evading her question. This time she wouldn't let him get away with it. "And what about love?''

He snorted. "Love. What is it about love? You Americans are obsessed with love. I am a prince of Adnan! Princes do not wed for love. I married you because you are beautiful, smart and wealthy. Plus, you were a virgin.''

"Not anymore.'' Bitter bile flooded her mouth. She'd saved herself for marriage only to discover she'd been a pawn in her deceitful husband's game of revenge.

"No.'' A smug smile spread across his face.

She longed to smack it away, but kept her hands to herself. The fleeting satisfaction she'd get from slapping him wasn't worth death by beheading.

The limo approached a large, elaborately decorated building. Surrounded by minarets and clad in mosaics, it glittered in the sun. Ahead of the car, a dark archway loomed.

She gulped and pointed out the window. "Is that where I lose my head?"

Ray chuckled. "It is true that the penalty for assaulting a royal is death, but you are my consort. You are exempt."

"You could have said so before," Cami grumbled. The limo slid into the cool shadows beneath the arch.

"Please do not pretend you have been trembling in fear during this ride."

The limo stopped in the middle of a cobbled square beside a multitude of other vehicles, including a silver Rolls Royce and a Humvee painted in camouflage colors. "Who drives the Humvee?" she asked.

"My brother, Tariq, the marshal of the military. He has always been pretentious."

She remembered she loved to tease Ray. "I think it's cool."

"Cool. Ha." He snorted. "The grand vizier, my brother Sharif, prefers the Rolls."

"What does the king drive?"

"Kadar does not drive. He uses this limo or flies in the jet that brought you to Adnan."

She gave him a wry smile. "He'll probably find it somewhat the worse for wear."

"Why?" The chauffeur opened his door, and Ray exited, holding out his hand for Cami.

She took it. "The stuff they put in my coffee made me awfully sick."

His dark eyebrows drew together into a straight, black bar. "Is that so?" He dragged her out of the car and down a colonnade, hauling her through the parking lot and down another corridor.

She had to run to keep up with Ray's angry strides. "Well, yeah. You know I don't travel well." As they hurried through the palace, she caught bewildering glimpses of bustling offices and beautifully furnished living chambers with quiet servants arranging bouquets or polishing furniture.

"Hmmf." He urged her into a courtyard. Lush with tropical plants, it surrounded a central fountain.

Ray shoved open an elaborately carved door and immediately began shouting in Arabic to a man seated behind a large, dark wooden desk. The man, who wore white robes like Ray's, stood, yelling back. Soon the two were toe-to-toe in the middle of the room, leaving Cami, dumbfounded, by the door.

She sensed a presence behind her. She turned to see a small figure, clad in a dove-gray *abaya* with intricate embroidered trim, standing in the archway. The little lady reached up and drew back the hood of her garment, exposing dark hair streaked with silver. She smiled, her round, amber-skinned face wrinkling pleasantly.

The lady's gentleness, palpable as a mother's touch, soothed Cami's ruffled temper.

"Do not be startled. They have always been so, like oil and water." The older lady's cultured, precise tones revealed that she must have been educated in England.

"Who? Why?"

"Two of my sons, Kadar and Rayhan."

"You're…you're Ray's mom?"

"Yes. You may call me Zedda, if you wish. Everyone else does."

"Th-thank you."

"You are Rayhan's wife, yes? He did not exaggerate."

"What did he say?"

Zedda ran a gentle finger along Cami's cheek. "He said his wife was as beautiful as the dawn, with a heart worthy of a hunting falcon. That one smile from her was brighter than a beach full of diamonds."

Embarrassed and confused by the effusive praise, Cami dropped her head to examine the toes of her sandals. "Oh. And why is Ray so mad?"

"As for their dispute, the king refused to accept your marriage to Rayhan, so he had you brought here."

"The king, not Ray?"

"I believe Rayhan was aware of your journey, but not the circumstances." Zedda nodded toward the arguing brothers. "That is why he is so distressed. He is angry over your mistreatment."

"Is that the king?" Cami eyed the arguing pair. Ray didn't seem to treat his monarch with much respect.

"Yes, Kadar is my eldest."

"Why doesn't the king approve of me?"

"He desires Rayhan to wed another."

A chill raced across Cami's skin. "Who? Why?"

"The daughter of the Sheikh al-Qamra. The People of the Moon have much influence over the desert tribes, which speak of revolt against our family's rule."

Cami's head spun. What had she gotten herself

into? She was prepared to run a ranch in Texas, not meddle in Adnani politics.

Childish shrieks and giggles distracted Cami from her conversation with Zedda. A little girl, her legs furiously pumping beneath a froth of pink skirts, raced across the courtyard. She was pursued by a woman in flapping black robes. Both vanished through another archway.

Zedda smiled. "My granddaughter, Selima. Her name means peaceful."

Cami laughed.

"You are a most pleasant young woman. You will soon come to my rooms to take tea, yes?"

Cami didn't want to stay in Adnan long enough to attend tea parties, but Zedda was so kind. "I, uh, thank you."

Ray broke off his discussion to return to her side. "Zedda." He bent to kiss the lady's wrinkly cheek.

"Rayhan, your wife is tired and in need of cosseting." Zedda produced a key from a hidden pocket in her robe. "Take her to purdah."

Purdah! The word reminded Cami of secret, locked harems. She had a vision of herself imprisoned, never to see home again.

Rayhan frowned. "I had thought the old seraglio unused."

"It is maintained for the relaxation and convenience of the female members of the royal family." Zedda handed Cami the key.

"I did not know," he said.

"You had no reason to know. I will inform the servants that only you and your wife may be admitted for the next two days."

Chapter Ten

The Queen's seraglio rivaled any spa Cami had visited. Room after room of creamy marble bathing pools, each heated to a different temperature, dazzled her eyes and her senses. Elaborate, beautiful mosaics adorned every surface, with the colors of the Adnani flag prominent. The fragrances of citrus and jasmine perfumed the sultry, humid air.

Servants had evidently prepared the purdah before they arrived. Fresh towels sat in stacks near every pool. Tables loaded with fruit, meats and drink waited in each of the rooms.

Ray walked ahead of Cami toward one of the pools and, showing no trace of shyness, stripped off his robes, dropping them to the tiles. Turning, he smiled at her and held out his hand. "Come."

She stood rooted to the spot. "Ray, I don't want to fool around with you."

"Why not? It has been a long time, and we are married."

She sighed and looked away from him. She knew if she feasted her eyes on his dark, virile body, her restraint, already shaky, would shatter. Nothing would be resolved, and she'd be right back where she'd started: snared in a marriage built on revenge, deceptions and misunderstandings. She didn't want that. "Ray, we have to talk."

"Very well." He sprawled onto one of the marble benches nearby. His unabashed nakedness reminded her of the last time she'd seen him nude: when they'd made love aboard the *Corsair*. Her blood sped through her veins. She couldn't erase the memory of how his beautiful body felt joined with hers.

Rayhan grinned at Cami, hoping his casual pose and expression would hide his fiercely beating heart. The next few days would be a turning point in his marriage, his life, possibly even in the history of his country.

Alas, he had few weapons at his disposal with which to win back his bride. The frail link he'd nurtured with their lovemaking had snapped at the first sign of strain between them.

He noticed Cami averting her eyes from his body. Good. He knew from their lusty honeymoon that he did not repel his wife. She'd also tried to keep her distance in the limo. All of this meant she was afraid she'd lose her determination if she came too close or even looked at him.

The best means of reclaiming her remained seduction. Cami's wild sexuality, which he'd awakened, made her his thrall. At the same time, he had to respect her intelligence, intuition and deeply held morality.

Her anger was powerful and righteous. The peculiar obsession of American girls for true love would hamper him. Unless he explained himself with utmost clarity, Cami was bound to resent and misunderstand his motivations.

"I need to know what's going on here," she said.

At last his foolish young wife was concerned with something beyond herself. "Much is at stake. The basis for it all is the fractured nature of Adnan. You see, my country is comprised of several tribes. Generally we get along well. Sometimes we don't. There are times when the interests of one tribe may conflict with those of another. The desert people may conflict with the hill people, who think differently than do the inhabitants of the cities along the seacoast. The concerns of the farmers are unlike the problems of those who fish in the sea."

"I see." Cami's blue gaze held an shrewd glint. "From what tribe are you?"

"The people of the cities, who have long been traders, merchants and financiers, sought to unify the country under the banner of their leaders. My family." Because the conversation had taken a serious turn, he donned his robes, but allowed them to gape open up top. When they'd made love, Cami had seemed fixated with his chest. He didn't know why, but that didn't matter.

"Traders?" Cami lifted her brows.

"Yes, well, some of us were what you might call

pirates.'' He shrugged. ''In the old days. But, since the end of World War II, we have provided the strong leadership Adnan needed lest one of the larger Arab nations swallow us.''

''Is that a danger?'' Her eyes widened.

''Yes. You may have read that there is much fundamentalist, anti-American unrest in our neighbor to the east. Most of us Adnani wish to remain separate from these problems, and to chart an independent course.''

''A pro-American course?''

''Yes. We believe that trade alliances with the United States and the European Union will greatly benefit our people. But many, especially the nomadic desert peoples, disagree. Your intransigence is perceived as an insult. To complicate matters, there is the situation of my engagement.''

She looked away. ''Your mother said that the king wanted you to marry someone else.''

''Yes.'' He waited a moment or two. ''I refused.''

''What's the problem?'' Cami asked, her eyes hard and cold as blue lapis. ''I filed for divorce. You're free if you choose.''

Rayhan swallowed against his dry throat. Rising, he stepped over to a table loaded with food, drink and sweetmeats. Tugged between three competing loves—his family, his country and his wife—his heart churned.

He gave her a bleak smile. ''Divorcing one wife to marry another is not freedom.''

She followed him. ''Wouldn't it make a lot of things easier?''

"Perhaps, but it was arranged by my family without my consent. I refuse to be a political pawn. Plus, there is the issue of the oil." He poured her a glass of fruit juice, then handed it to her.

"How's oil an issue? Except for the situation between you and my dad, oil's not an issue but a benefit." She sipped.

"Oil has only recently been found in Adnan. We lack the technology to exploit our resources. The king hesitates to ally with any of the other oil-producing nations. That is where you come in." Rayhan selected a bunch of delicate, pale green grapes.

"Me?"

"My family is aware of the source of your wealth. The fact is, your oil property automatically makes you and me the resident royal experts in the subject."

She narrowed her eyes. "As you might say, I refuse to be a political pawn."

He sighed. "I will admit to you there is a slender line between political participation and...pawnship. Is that a word?"

She laughed, which pleased him beyond reason. He'd placated his wife and put her in a good humor. Perhaps there was hope for their marriage.

"No," she said. "It's probably not a word, but I understand what you mean."

"Cami, you would have more power than most Adnani brides, even the princesses. My sisters' function has been to make advantageous marriages and to produce children. You will be more."

"Just as you have always wished to be more." Cami had never experienced such complex emotions, not even during the horrible moment when she realized that both her father and her husband had betrayed her trust.

While proud that Ray thought her capable of such responsibility, she still resented the fact that he'd married her for reasons other than love. Political advantage was now added to revenge and sex. Such motives objectified her and made a mockery of their marriage and her emotions.

Underlying it all was a deep fear that she wouldn't measure up.

"My wife, I have never forced you into anything and I never will. I give you my solemn promise that nothing will happen that you do not freely choose."

She stumbled to a bench and slumped onto it, covering her face with her hands. "I don't know what to do," she whispered through her fingers. "I never guessed any of this would happen. I'm not ready for this."

His warmth brushed her side as he sat next to her. "Why do you not see yourself as you are?"

She raised her head, studying his dark, serious face. "What do you mean?"

"The woman I married is intelligent, strong and capable. She has the courage of a pride of lions and the insight of a seer."

"I didn't know you thought of me so highly." Cami remembered that Ray's mother had mentioned that he'd lavishly complimented her.

"I see you as you are. Cami, I may not choose to make romantic love the basis for marriage, but I do believe in respect." He placed the uneaten grapes onto a platter, then took both her hands in his. "I married you. I intend for you to be the mother of our children. Does that not mean anything to you?"

"It means a lot, I guess, but—"

"You need decide nothing at this moment. Why do you not take my mother's advice? Enjoy this place."

He reached for her clothing, tugging on it.

"Ray, please." She drew back and took off her dress without his help.

His dark eyes narrowed. "The implication that I would need to force you is an insult."

She felt her flush all the way to the soles of her feet. "I didn't mean—"

"No matter." He gestured with one hand, as if he didn't care, but she knew better. She'd seen the hurt in his eyes, and hated herself for it. Though he might be a snake and a skunk, her husband wasn't a rapist.

His dark gaze surveyed her.

She shivered under his thorough scrutiny. "Quit looking at me like that!"

"Like what?"

"A bug under a microscope."

"I am ever fascinated by your body. Though I do wonder whether even a scrap of food has passed your lips since I left Texas." His fingers descended the ladder of her rib cage, forcing her to recall past, happier times.

Shoving away the memories, she stood to avoid his hands, his glance. "I haven't felt much like eating lately."

"We will fatten you up here. You'll be nice and

round, like an Adnani girl. Now join me." He took two quick steps and dove into the pool.

Shining drops sprayed in a silvery arc through the air, splashing her panties. She pulled them off, kicked away her sandals, then slipped into the water.

Ray had picked a pool heated to just above blood temperature, and it felt like paradise against her skin.

Closing her eyes, Cami let herself relax.

After bathing and eating, Ray led Cami to a bedroom. Without looking around, she fell onto the mattress and slept like a hibernating bear.

Awakening disoriented, she stared through the warm darkness. From an archway to her right, shafts of moonlight slashed into the room. Where was she?

Her husband warmed the bed by her side, and for a brief moment, she was comforted by his presence. Then reality crashed down on her. Her father's sins, Ray's betrayal and her own stupidity had combined in a horrible, overwhelming vortex.

Crushed by the rubble of her trashed life, Cami clutched a pillow to her chest. She moaned at the smothering weight of her despair. The sobs choking her throat escaped.

Ray's arms wrapped around her, cuddling her close. She pushed him away as best she could. Too weak to move his rock-solid body very far, she instead found herself caressing his chest. She jerked away.

"Let me touch you. Let me help."

The raw need in his voice battered her weakened

defenses. "No, please," she managed to whisper. "I have to work this out alone."

He didn't let go of her. "No, you do not. I am your husband. You will work things out with me."

"Oh, Ray. Don't you realize you're the problem?"

"My darling wife. Did you think we would have no difficulties in our marriage?" Holding her tight, he kissed away her tears.

"Huh." Jolted, Cami realized that Ray had made a good point. She blinked.

"I married you for a lifetime. Of course there will be some bumps in the road."

"This is more than a little bump in the road."

"I realize I must struggle to prove myself worthy of you." He kissed her mouth with utmost gentleness.

Regardless of his tender caress, she let her anger shield her pain, blocking the hurt away, even from herself. Gradually she calmed enough to resist Ray when he nibbled at her lower lip.

"No, please."

"Why not?"

"It's wrong."

"How can this be wrong?" He caressed her breast, fingering the nipple. It rose, tender and aroused. "We are married."

"We married for the wrong reasons. You don't love me." She hated saying those words, hated admitting to herself she was a failure as a woman. The knowledge that her husband didn't love her sliced like a steel blade through her heart.

"So? And what of your feelings? You have said that you love me. Are your feelings of no account?"

Ray's contorted line of reasoning jarred Cami.

She still loved him. With a start she realized she'd married Ray because she loved him, and not because he loved her.

"But...but—"

"But what?" he asked. "I respect and esteem you. I am willing to care for you and our children forever."

She teared up again, using the sheet to dab at her eyes.

"You are distressed. Why will you not allow me to offer the comfort of my body? Would you not feel better?"

"B-because...because...I'm confused," she wailed. "I have so much and so little. I have everything but a husband who loves me."

"I understand that is very important to you. But what is love, Cami?"

"Don't you know? Oh, Ray!" This was worse. He didn't know what love was. How could he love anyone? He'd never be able to love her as she needed and deserved.

"Cami, I love you to the extent I am able. So, I love you. All right?"

Renewed anger flared. "No, it's not all right! You're lying."

"How can you say that? When have I ever lied to you? I'm not lying! Cami, you are making us both crazy." Ray sprang out of bed to pace up and down the room with jerky strides. "I am your husband. Whatever you need, I give. You need me to love you. So I love you! What is the problem?"

He was so over the top that the only thing she could do was utter a broken laugh.

"At least I have made you laugh," he grumbled, sitting on the bed beside her. "Rayhan, the buffoon."

"You're not a buffoon." She wiped her cheeks with the backs of her hands, then sighed.

He pulled her into his arms again. "Cami, you are exhausted. No more crying, eh? Now let's sleep."

Too tired to fight him off, she allowed him to cradle her in his arms until, at last, she slept.

Rayhan watched Cami rest, as he'd done during that most joyous of times, their honeymoon. A starwatcher, he needed little sleep. Normally he'd get out of bed and go to his minaret to stargaze, letting his imagination roam the galaxies. Here in Adnan, he'd again become a frequent visitor to the Royal Observatory, the place where he'd first learned to explore the heavens.

Tonight he preferred to watch his wife. As slumber put her tension to flight, he could see the tight muscles in her face loosen. The natural, sweet curve of her lips returned.

Rayhan took hope from that serene smile, believing it meant that deep down, in her soul, Cami was happy with their marriage. Could she look so calm in her sleep if she were truly distressed?

Despite her crazy fixation with love, he had to win her. Everything he cared about was at stake—most importantly, Cami's happiness and that of the family he craved.

When Cami awakened, she was alone in a big bed. Taking stock of her surroundings, she realized she was in someone's sumptuous living quarters. A stack of books on the chest of drawers included volumes in English, French and Arabic.

Ray's room in the palace, she figured. The massive bed bore her husband's scent beside her on the dented pillow. He'd slept with her, had held and comforted her. She appreciated that. Yesterday had left her drained.

As always, Ray had been gentle and kind. At the same time, she noticed changes in her husband since she'd arrived in Adnan. He seemed more open and emotional; she remembered what he'd told his mother about her. And he'd been incensed with his brother, the king, at her treatment.

Drawing in a calming breath, Cami realized her fury at Ray had retreated, leaving an open, bloody wound. She wanted her anger back. It had shielded her against this pain.

The two people she trusted most in the world had deceived her, and she'd been clueless. How could she ever depend upon anyone again? Why should she? And how could she trust her own judgment in the future?

Cami rubbed a fist over her chest, as though she could massage her heartache away.

She had to cling to her love, believing in the truth her heart told.

But should she settle for a one-sided sham of a marriage?

She sighed and stretched, then noticed a pile of blue fabric trimmed with gold embroidery lying across the foot of the bed. Cami got up to check it out and found clothing like the hooded garment Zedda wore. When in Rome, Cami thought.

After tossing the simple robe over her head, she left their room and went outside to a colonnaded courtyard. It rimmed lush gardens, radiating familar Adnani aromas of citrus and jasmine. The tinkle of a fountain met her ears. Squinting upward, she guessed that the clear, golden light signaled midmorning, as it lacked the intensity of noon or the colors of sunset.

Good heavens. She'd slept more than eighteen hours. Whatever the king's agents had put in the coffee had packed quite a wallop.

At the far end of the courtyard, Cami saw Zedda seated at a round table, pouring something for two little girls. One of them looked like Selima, the active toddler Cami had seen the day before.

She advanced on the tea party with hesitant steps, unsure of her welcome.

Zedda looked up as Cami approached. "Look, children! Here is Auntie Cami, Uncle Rayhan's new wife. She is from America." Zedda enunciated very clearly. "We must speak only English so she can understand us."

"Thank you." Cami walked toward the only empty chair at the table.

"Please, sit." Zedda gestured. "You saw Selima yesterday, yes? And this is Sadira, our little star. They are my daughter Leila's children."

Both girls were neatly clad in pinafore-style dresses with sailor collars. They wore white gloves on their tiny hands, which they carefully removed to eat the delicate cucumber sandwiches and drink steaming mint tea.

Cami was enchanted. For reasons known only to her, Zedda had recreated an English tea party in the midst of this wildly exotic locale. The little girls co-operated wholeheartedly, sticking out their pinkie fingers to sip the tea. They politely chatted about *Alice in Wonderland* and *Peter Pan,* which Cami gathered was their most recent bedtime reading.

She happily joined in, spreading the lace napkin across her lap and pouring tea out of the china pot for Zedda. Soon, however, the girls' nannies came to retrieve the children.

"Did you enjoy my granddaughters?" Zedda asked, sipping her tea.

"Yes, I did. A lot more than I expected." Passing a hand over her stomach, Cami wondered about her own condition.

"You are not enceinte, my dear. I would know if you were."

Cami's heart clenched. "How did you know what I was thinking? And why are you sure I'm not pregnant? I've had a lot of the symptoms."

Zedda shrugged. "It does not take a genius to discern what a young wife is thinking about when she touches her stomach while discussing children. As for your condition, I have seven children and four grandchildren, and expect that number to increase. You are not pregnant. If you have suffered symptoms—the morning illness and so forth—that is due to the stress between you and Rayhan."

Cami sighed, setting down her cup. "Zedda, I don't know what to do."

"Do you wish to talk about it? If you do not want me to repeat the conversation to my son, I will keep it a secret."

"Thanks, but it doesn't matter. He knows why I'm upset. See, he doesn't love me, and he married me for all the wrong reasons." Cami explained the situation with the land, the oil and her father.

"Hmm." Zedda fingered her napkin, a thoughtful expression on her face. "That explains much."

"What?"

"Rayhan left about ten years ago, after quarreling with his father—my husband. My son told me at the time that he needed to prove himself to Malik. But Rayhan stayed away for years, until his father had died. I now understand why he did not return. When he failed to make a quick killing in oil, he could not face Malik until honor was satisfied."

"And now it is, by his marriage to me."

"Yes. Malik would not have respected Rayhan had he returned dishonored. My husband was a strong man, Cami, but not a particularly loving one. We married for political advantage, to unify the country."

"That seems to be the tendency around here." She felt her jaw tighten.

"Yes, it is. I know it is foreign to you, but it is not uncommon, even in the West."

"I've read that boys learn how to be men from their fathers."

"That is not necessarily the case. Rayhan is nothing like his father, I assure you. Perhaps Rayhan married you for the wrong reasons, Cami, but perhaps the two of you will stay together because of the right ones.''

Chapter Eleven

"My wife." Ray's warm hand massaged Cami's shoulder. She'd been so engrossed in conversation that she hadn't noticed Ray until he'd touched her.

Turning, she scrutinized him with fresh eyes. Eyes that looked beyond the facade to the rejected youth beneath. Eyes that saw the man caught between two cultures, struggling to do the right thing by both.

"Hello, Ray." Cami caught his hand and rubbed it against her cheek.

His eyes widened, but he didn't appear displeased. "Cami, I would ask that you join our meeting. This morning, we discuss oil, your expertise."

Cami rose and circled the table to Zedda's side. Leaning over, she hugged the older woman. "Thank you so much."

Zedda stroked Cami's cheek. "You are most welcome, my daughter. Go now, until the evening meal."

As they walked together down the colonnade, Ray

said to Cami, "I am glad to see you close to my mother."

"She's a dear person."

"Perhaps you need a mother to confide in."

"Maybe. Talking with her sure went a long way to making me feel better."

Ray came to a heavily carved door. Stopping, he faced Cami. "Whatever happens now, do not be intimidated."

"I don't understand why they want to talk to me. I'm only nineteen!"

"You have been studying the oil business for years, have you not?"

"Ye-es, but—"

"Cami, listen. Oil was only recently discovered in Adnan. Few Adnani knows anything about this matter, and my brothers, especially Tariq, do not trust outsiders."

"But what am I?"

"You're family." He touched her shoulder, and even that fleeting caress was enough to distract her.

With a deep breath Cami reclaimed her focus. "I'm an American, and a woman to boot."

"We are not like other Arab cultures. Adnan was heavily influenced by the Europeans. My brothers will listen to you, just as they will consult and listen to others. They may not agree with you, but they will listen."

"But—"

"Hush." He placed a finger over her lips, and she resisted kissing it. "No more buts. You are the consort of a prince of Adnan. Remember who you are."

He pushed open the door, revealing an enormous room dominated by a big, round table.

Cami entered, heart pounding. Inside, the only person Cami recognized was the king. Ray introduced a dark man dressed in camouflage fatigues as Tariq ibn-Malik al-Rashad. She recalled that Ray's brother Tariq ran the Adnani military. Brother Sharif, also present, was the grand vizier, which she understood as equivalent to a prime minister.

An older man in dark robes, who wore a disapproving frown, was introduced as Uncle Hamid, the local mullah. He was a religious leader, she supposed. He didn't speak to her, but said something in Arabic to the King.

Kadar responded, his voice silken, "We speak in English as a courtesy to our guest, the consort of Rayhan, Prince of Adnan."

"She does not bow properly," Uncle Hamid observed, in heavily accented English.

"I'm an American, sir. We don't bow at all." Cami stared into his dark brown eyes.

Hamid sniffed and elevated his hawk nose. "How can this young woman advise us?"

Ray escorted Cami to a chair opposite the males, then sat beside her. "My wife owns and manages several thousand acres of oil property in Texas. She knows more about the oil business than anyone else in this room."

That shut Uncle Hamid up. Cami lifted her chin and looked around the table, catching each man's gaze in turn. "How can I help you out?"

The king leaned forward. "We recently received a

proposal from the OPEC to provide equipment and personnel to develop Adnani oil.''

Cami narrowed her eyes, remembering. The previous day, Ray had mentioned that the king hesitated to ally with OPEC. ''What is the price of their assistance?'' she asked.

''A percentage of the oil extracted,'' Sharif said.

''For how long?''

Her question was met by silence.

''Would training of Adnani personnel be included? Would the equipment become Adnani after a suitable period of time, say five years?'' she wanted to know.

''Those are excellent topics for negotiation.'' Sharif lounged back in his chair, eyes sparkling.

''And what about intangible costs?'' Cami ran her fingers along the carved edge of the table. ''Many OPEC nations have political agendas. Does Adnan share their concerns?''

Tariq pounded on the table with his fist. ''Exactly my point! We cannot afford to draw closer to extremists. And yet they are sure to seek our involvement in their disputes.''

''I'd negotiate a lease-purchase contract with a neutral country, or even a private concern,'' Cami said.

''And we must make certain that they train Adnani citizens to run our facilities.'' Ray finally spoke up, and she was grateful for his support. ''We cannot be dependent upon outsiders.''

''Yes!'' The king spoke. ''Rayhan, will you and your consort join us tomorrow for further discussions? You will conduct the negotiations, will you not?''

''I will, but today I belong to my wife.''

The king gestured. "Go now, but tomorrow we consult with the Royal Dutch Petroleum Company."

After inclining his head in acknowledgment, Ray led Cami from the room.

"You greatly impressed my brothers," Ray told Cami as he escorted her out of the palace.

She shrugged. "I just said what they wanted to hear."

"Very diplomatic. Perhaps they'll forgive me for marrying you."

"Are they really upset with you about that?" She pulled the blue hood of her garment over her head to avoid the intense noon sun.

"Yes, but today you have greatly swayed them, I think. Oh, the old-fashioned, like Uncle Hamid, will never approve of you, but he doesn't approve of anything. He's never liked me." Holding her arm, Ray expertly negotiated a sidewalk crowded with pedestrians, bicycles and scooters. He ducked through an archway, hauling her with him.

Abruptly the atmosphere seemed to change. Away from the road, with its noisy motorized vehicles, this area radiated a sense of the mysterious and the exotic.

A shop hung with thick, richly stitched carpets crowded the walkway to Cami's left. On her right, several men jammed a table, drinking aromatic, cinnamon-scented coffee out of tiny cups while volubly arguing in Arabic. Nearby, two silent men in striped robes bent over a chessboard, their faces serious.

The cobbles of the uneven street underfoot pressed

through the thin soles of Cami's sandals. "Where are we?" she asked.

"The old souk." Ray grinned at her. "I thought you might want to see more of my country while you decide about our marriage."

"Would we live in Adnan, at the palace?"

"Part of the time, I should think." He shouldered his way through the crowd.

She and Ray spent a relaxed, friendly afternoon wandering the narrow streets of old Syed. Cami shopped for clothes and accessories, choosing additional Adnani robes to wear.

She also bought loose, flowing outfits consisting of calf-length tunics and matching pants, with a *shayla,* a head scarf, to complete the look. Rather than haul parcels around, they arranged to have them delivered to the palace.

Ray paid for everything, showing her the curious little Adnani coins and colorful bills. A copper *birr* was roughly equivalent to a penny; *cedi* were like dimes. The major form of currency was the *dinar,* and twelve *dinarii* were equivalent to one American dollar.

"I wonder where my pocketbook is," Cami said.

"Those *hayawat* didn't think to grab your handbag?" Ray snorted. "Kadar shouldn't have sent fools to America who don't know the customs."

"We'll have to phone to cancel my credit cards."

"A nuisance. If I had known how clumsy Kadar's operatives would have been…" Ray shook his head. "I am sorry. It should not have happened."

"Yeah, and I need to call home so my father

doesn't worry. Don't you want to know how he's doing?'' Cami didn't keep annoyance out of her tone. Ray had put her father in the hospital and hadn't bothered to inquire about him.

He grinned at her as he led her past a coppersmith's stall, hung with shiny, hammered metal pans and bowls. "Why do you think I do not know the state of his health?''

She stopped to stare at him. "Do you?''

"Of course. Your father and I have spoken frequently since you moved to San Antonio.''

"You have?''

"Yes, and why not? We have had our differences, yes, but we are united in our concern for you.''

"Huh.'' Cami stared at him, flabbergasted.

He threw up his hands. "All right, all right, I admit it. I apologized to him.''

Stopping short in the middle of the walkway, she ignored the throngs of tourists and shoppers who were forced to sidestep them. "You apologized to him! But he swindled you! And what about me?''

"One question at a time, please.'' Taking her arm, he urged her to an empty table at an outdoor restaurant. "Yes, he cheated me, but I was wrong.''

A waiter arrived, and Ray, speaking in Arabic, ordered something. Cami sat, startled beyond measure by what Ray had said.

He'd realized he was wrong and without prompting from her or anyone, had independently called to apologize to her father. "What did Dad say?''

Ray shrugged. "He seemed surprised, but not as surprised as are you. And he also apologized. He explained that, ten years ago, his business had taken a downturn and he had trouble putting food on the table for you. He needed the cash I offered.''

"But it wasn't fair to you."

"Time heals much. I love the Double Eagle. My beautiful Arabians are prized all over the world."

"Then why did you pursue your revenge?"

"I was a fool, and very wrong. I did not realize how wrong I was until I saw what my vendetta did to you, my wife."

She flushed, and her anger returned. "Yeah, too bad your victim wasn't my father."

He shrugged. "I took that which was most precious to him. But I do not regret what I did. I value you at least as much as does he."

"I won't be treated as though I'm...I'm a piece of pr-property." She stood, bumping into the server, who bore an enameled brass tray with two coffees, which spilled. "Oh, I'm sorry."

Cami sat back down into the uncomfortable metal patio chair while the waiter, babbling in Arabic, cleaned up the mess.

"Your anger cloaks your love for me," Ray said. "Can you not admit it?"

Biting her lip, she turned her head. A teenager on a scooter, with tiny headphones anchored in his ears and a Walkman clipped to the belt of his jeans, zipped by.

"Cami, look at me. I need you. We are wed. Can you let go of your anger? For us? For our marriage?"

With difficulty she faced him.

He sat regarding her, worry in his eyes. "You are

thin. You haven't eaten much since we separated. Can you forgive me, for yourself?'' He reached across the table and took her hand in his, rubbing a finger on her wedding band.

She saw that he still wore his ring, and her heart split in two. Misery welled up in that empty, broken place. "Oh, Ray, I'm so hurt and mad. When I drop the wall of that rage, I'm...destroyed. How could you? Why?''

"At first, it was the revenge.'' His voice softened. "Then it became something else.''

"What?''

"I wanted you. I still do. Is that so hard to believe?''

"Yes.'' She bent her head and fiddled with her braid.

"You are the most insecure girl.'' He leaned over the table. "It was certainly not the money, Cami. My mother had given me a large cash gift to set myself up in your country. Though the transaction drained my savings, part of the problem was the shame of being outwitted.''

"None of that was my fault.''

"You are right, and I was wrong. Having you is more important than revenge.''

"Well, that's nice to hear.'' Cami met her husband's gaze squarely, and he didn't flinch away. Perhaps he's telling the truth, she thought. Perhaps there's some hope for this marriage, after all. "What did my dad say when your brother had me abducted?''

"He wasn't happy about it, so when we return to the palace perhaps you will phone him."

She bit her lip. "I should have thought of that before."

"Cami, do not blame yourself. You were exhausted when you arrived. I have already talked with Charles this day, before you awakened."

Shouting drew Cami's attention away from their conversation. Voices gabbling in English, French and Arabic assailed her ears.

Ray said something in Arabic she couldn't understand, but sounded vaguely irritable, followed by, "Here they come."

"Glad you switched to English, but what are you talking about?"

"Reporters." His eyelid twitched.

"What?"

He scratched his temple. "I am a prince, and our situation has caught the media's attention. Worse, someone leaked information on your divorce suit to the press. That has caused some anti-American feeling."

"Oh, my God. I didn't realize my personal life would cause an international incident."

A woman dressed in a navy, Western-style suit stood near Cami's chair, snapping orders in Arabic. A cameraman pointed his machine at Cami and Ray.

Speaking into a microphone, the woman said, "This is Lasca bint Wasim, reporting from the souk in old Syed, for the Adnan English Language Network. We have tracked down Prince Rayhan and his controversial American consort, Camille Ellison, in

the old souk. Are you enjoying our city, madame?''
She thrust a microphone in Cami's face.

"Ah, uh, yeah, very much." Cami's mind froze,
and she couldn't help sounding like a dork. She really
wasn't up for this princess stuff.

"Have you given up your attempt to divorce Prince
Rayhan in the Texas courts?"

Though Cami's brains might have taken a vacation,
her temper hadn't. But before she could say something unwise, she recalled something Ray had told
her. "Remember who you are."

Who was she? At age nineteen, Cami didn't really
know, but she was sure of one thing: she wasn't
someone who blabbed about her private life. "I'm
sorry, but I can't comment about that." Pulling at the
front of her hood, she tugged it over her face, retreating into its protection.

To her immense relief, the reporter immediately
withdrew, turning to the camera to finish her story.
"As you can see, Prince Rayhan's consort has
adopted the traditional garb of our country as well as
the usual response of the royal women to questions
from the press: no comment. This has been an on-
the-spot report from Syed City. Back to you, Jamal.''
The media and their cameras packed up their equipment, then left as quickly as they'd arrived.

Cami turned to Ray. "Is this going to happen often?''

He smiled. "I hope not. This is the first time the
press has paid a great deal of attention to me. They
are usually much more concerned with my brothers.
And, as you can imagine, my mother is a favorite.''

"The reporter seemed aggressive, yet respectful."

"Yes, Lasca is one of the best of the new breed of Adnani professional women. She maintains respect for our customs while pursuing her career. She knows she won't get anything out of us if she pushes too hard."

The event troubled Cami. What kind of life would she lead in Adnan, especially if she became involved with politics?

"By the way, you did very well. That Lasca compared you to the other princesses will help to undercut those who disapprove of our marriage."

"The whole thing is sorta…weird."

He shrugged. "Yes, it is a new life for you. But it is interesting, is it not?"

She laughed, realizing that nothing bad had actually happened. "Maybe I can handle the consort thing."

"There is no maybe about it. You are perfect."

Glowing with his praise, Cami found herself in charity with her husband for the rest of the day. They returned to the palace in the afternoon to rest before the evening meal.

The sound of the shower awakened her at dusk. She stretched, then followed Ray and bathed. For the evening she selected one of the new outfits she'd purchased, a pant set with a matching scarf. Then she piled her hair on top of her head with beautiful enameled combs she'd bought that day in the souk.

She pirouetted in front of the mirror in Ray's room. She loved her new tunic and pants. In a heavy cream silk with gold and green embroidery, it flowed like water against her skin. "I feel like an exotic desert princess," she said, chuckling.

"You *are* an exotic desert princess, my wife."

"We're dressed like twins." She grinned at him. He stood behind Cami and she regarded them both in the mirror.

Ray, who had selected a pale *thobe* with narrow green stripes, arranged her outfit's matching scarf around her throat.

"Not over the head?" she asked.

"I am glad you are willing to attempt our customs, especially since Western women often find them confining. But no, not at home," he said. "In the Arab culture, there is a distinct difference between the public and the private. You need not cover your head or face in the palace."

"All right." Cami knotted the scarf around her neck.

"I wonder who we will see tonight."

"The family, I presume?"

"Yes, and possibly guests, of a political nature. We entertain often."

"Will your brothers be there?"

"Perhaps, though Tariq often is away, inspecting troops or on maneuvers. Habiba, the queen, is in her ninth month of pregnancy, and she frequently takes meals in her rooms. If so, Kadar may attend her."

"I haven't met her." Cami loosened the oblong scarf and tried draping it over her elbows.

"She is a lovely person, my sister Habiba, but we greatly fear for her life. She is not—how would you say it?—she is not a good breeder."

"How many children do she and the king have?"

"None, I am afraid. She has had, alas, several miscarriages. There is no crown prince yet."

"That's not good."

"Adnani law would permit Kadar to take another wife, but he refuses to do so."

"He can have two wives?"

"All the royals can. It is the means by which the succession is secured." Her husband's voice was bland, neutral. His hooded gaze revealed nothing.

Cami swallowed past a frightened lump in her throat. What if Ray decided to… No. She couldn't. No way. Never.

She went to the door, turned and waited, giving Ray the chance to deny any plan to take another wife.

The room remained quiet.

Then she said, "Is that what you want?"

He hesitated. "I am experiencing considerable pressure from my brothers in regard to the Princess al-Qamra."

Her temper flared. Those rats had the gall to hit her up for advice while sabotaging her relationship with her husband.

But did she really want this marriage? Her innards roiled, matching her confusion.

One thing was clear. She wouldn't share Ray. "If that's what it'll take to fit in here, forget it."

His jaw worked. "I beg your pardon?"

"You heard what I said." She sucked in a deep breath, fighting the hot tears springing to her eyes. "I'll take the next plane home tomorrow morning."

Jerking open the heavy wood door, she left him.

She wanted to slam the door behind her, but controlled herself. Instead, she closed the door with a quiet click. Slamming the door would be immature. She'd learned better.

On shaky feet, Cami stepped onto the tiled colonnade surrounding the palace's inner courtyard. Evening had fallen. Despite her inner turmoil, the scent of flowers and the sounds of the fountain soothed her. Shrieking and running, small children played tag along the dimly lit pathways; Cami was sure she saw Selima pushing a small, serious-faced boy, teasing him into play.

At the far end of the courtyard, she could see Ray's brothers filling their plates at a long buffet. At a round table nearby, Zedda sat with one of the little girls, feeding her.

She couldn't face others yet and wasn't very hungry, anyway. Wrapping the *shayla* over her head to conceal her face, she wandered through the dusk until she found a quiet bench by a fountain.

Trailing a hand in the water, she prayed for calm and peace. However, she'd meant what she'd said. She didn't know how, but she had to make her way home to Texas in the morning.

Even though she adored Ray with all her heart, she couldn't stomach a rival for her husband's love.

Chapter Twelve

As he left their room, Rayhan wondered what the night would bring. Until he'd said exactly the wrong words, he'd cherished hopes that his marriage would move back onto the pleasurable course it had traveled during their honeymoon. But Omar Khayyam had said, "the moving finger writes, and having writ, moves on."

Rayhan couldn't undo the damage, made worse by his inability to express himself in English to his wife. His command of the language had faltered since he'd returned to his homeland. Now he spoke and even thought in Arabic.

He'd been struck dumb by Cami's assumption that he'd take another wife. With her sturdy notions of morality, she would never accept multiple marriage. But the al-Qamra should be brought into the royal family, for the good of Adnan.

But why did he have to be the sacrificial lamb?

He'd wanted a place in the political life of his country, but the price was too high.

He heard the clatter of Cami's heels on the tiled pavement, somewhere within the now-dark gardens. About to go to her side, he heard a familiar voice hail her.

"Young woman!"

Uncle Hamid, speaking to his wife, alone? Rayhan's fists clenched. The customs of their country limited unchaperoned contact between men and women. Why was the tradition-bound old mullah accosting his wife? And what would Cami do and say? She wasn't aware of local customs.

"Young woman!"

"Excuse me?" Cami sounded puzzled. "Hi, uh, sir."

Rayhan grinned. She wasn't sure how to address Uncle Hamid.

"It would be best for you to go back to America. The Princess al-Qamra, she should marry Prince Rayhan."

"You better clear that with Prince Rayhan." Cami's voice remained calm.

"The People of the Moon are powerful family in Adnan. They can make it werry uncomfable for the al-Rashads."

"Maybe."

"You seek to deal with me? I deal. I offer you ten thousand dinarii to give back Prince Rayhan's ring."

"Ten thousand dinarii?" To anyone but Rayhan, Cami would sound as though she was considering his uncle's offer. Cami continued, "Ten thousand dinarii? I'm not very good at math. What's that, a little over eight hundred dollars American?''

Rayhan nearly laughed out loud. Cami had probably spent more than that on his wedding gift. He knew his wife; the size of the offer wouldn't matter, even if it were ten million dinarii and she were poor as a desert rat. Though she might harbor doubts about their marriage, Cami couldn't be bought. She loved him.

He knew his wife, but did she know her husband? Rayhan, thunderstruck by the turn his thoughts had taken, considered the situation from a new perspective. Did not his Camille deserve the same confidence he enjoyed?

Rayhan put his personal concerns aside when his uncle again spoke.

''That is not enough? You are a greedy creature, even for an American woman. Twenty thousand!''

''But he's a prince.'' Cami chuckled. ''What if I want to be a princess?''

''We are royals, too. So I give you my son. He is a good boy. Twenty-five thousand!''

Cami's giggles increased to unladylike whoops. Rayhan could hear her heels erratically scraping the pavement as she staggered away from the old mullah.

She came into his view, clutching her sides, tears of merriment leaking from the corners of her eyes. He caught her before she tripped over her high heels, carefully lowering her to a bench.

''Did you hear that?'' Sucking in a breath, Cami visibly tried to control herself. ''That old skunk tried to bribe me!''

"I heard."

"Aren't you upset? You're only worth a measly two grand!"

"You are forgetting that he also offered his son."

"Oh, that's right." She turned to him, her eyes brimming with mirth. "Maybe I should meet this guy and give this some thought—"

"Maybe you should remember you'd have to put up with the, er, old skunk." Taking her hand, he led her to the buffet tables.

Cami sniffed the enticing aromas of saffron, cumin and cinnamon. She found a variety of Adnani dishes, including her now-beloved b'stila pie, as well as American and European favorites. She opted for the local food, selecting couscous with stewed lamb and roasted vegetables.

Ray guided her to a table occupied by the king, their brother Sharif, and Zedda, who dandled Sadira on her knee. Cami sat and sipped the mint tea Zedda poured for her. She noticed that some of the Adnani used forks, while others ate with their right hands, allowing servants to frequently rinse and dry their fingers.

If not for the colorful clothing and Adnani style of eating, the scene could be any family at dinner.

Despite the laughter they'd just shared, nothing had changed. Until Rayhan gave her his love without qualification, she'd never be anything but an append-age…possibly even just the number two wife. She'd bluffed Uncle Hamid only because she refused to let him force her hand. She'd make her own decisions, in her own time.

She'd still return to Texas in the morning. She didn't know quite how, but she'd find a way.

"Greetings of the evening, sister," the king said, eyeing Cami.

"Good evening, sir." She hoped she'd addressed him correctly. She didn't want to alienate him. If the king wanted Ray to marry someone else, maybe he'd help her get back home.

Sadira pulled away from Zedda and climbed up onto Cami's lap.

"Ah! You are in favor tonight," Zedda said, laughing. "One can never tell which lap a child will select."

Cami cuddled Sadira, delighted by the toddler's acceptance of her as one of the family. Even better, the king had addressed her as his sister, surely a good sign, regardless of what that hateful uncle Hamid had done. She started to relax, figuring that since this night was her last in Adnan, she'd better enjoy it.

Sadira's hair tickled Cami under the chin, making her chuckle. She asked the little girl, "Are you hungry, sweetie?" Picking up her fork, she fed Sadira a bite of lamb.

Watching, Rayhan's chest went tight. He hadn't heard Cami laugh for months. Tonight, she'd already giggled once or twice. And seeing her with his niece—he breathed deeply in an effort to dislodge the lump in his throat. Whether his wife knew it or not, she was born to bear children. His children.

Using a napkin Cami wiped a drop of gravy off Sadira's chin before feeding her more lamb. While the child chewed, his wife ate a few bites herself, then sipped some tea. "This is really wonderful. I love it here." She leaned back into her chair with a sigh that, to Rayhan's ears, seemed tinged with regret.

Rayhan started to sweat. He prayed that she hadn't meant her earlier threat to return to Texas on the morrow. He made a mental note to keep her safe in the palace.

"You do not miss your homeland?" Sharif asked.

Rayhan glared at his brother.

"Travel is always…interesting," Cami said smoothly. Her gaze slid over to the king.

"I apologize for the mode of your arrival," Kadar said, looking embarrassed.

Rayhan cut a glance to the king. Apologizing for anything wasn't like Kadar. A ruler in their father's mold, Kadar believed he could do no wrong. Perhaps his generosity of spirit this night was due to anxiety over Habiba, or maybe Kadar felt charitable because of Cami's advice on the OPEC offer.

Whatever the cause, Cami looked happier and his mother, ecstatic. Rayhan calmed. Perhaps his story would have a happy ending. He didn't know how, but he'd find a way to assure Cami of his commitment to her and their marriage.

Sadira squirmed out of Cami's lap and ran off, gabbling in Arabic. Rayhan turned to see what had seized his niece's attention.

He caught his wife's gaze. "Uncle Hamid is back."

"That's nice." Her voice was neutral.

"He has brought other visitors." Kadar arose. His gaze swept the newcomers, then shifted to Cami. "It is the Sheikh al-Qamra with his son and daughter. Yes, that is Matana, the Princess al-Qamra.''

"The al-Qamra, called the People of the Moon, are very important politically,'' Sharif said.

"Stop it, Sharif.'' Ray's tone was steely. Cami jerked with surprise. She'd never heard such cold anger from her husband before.

Sharif spread his hands. "Stop what, brother? I merely make an observation—''

"You seek to force me into a marriage that is not acceptable.'' Ray rested his hand on Cami's shoulder. "Perhaps you do not understand. This is my wife. I will take no other.''

"The al-Qamra must be brought into the mainstream of Adnani political life.'' The grand vizier eyed Cami.

"Fine. Why don't *you* marry Matana?'' Ray asked Sharif.

Sharif looked around as though searching for the nearest exit. "Oh, no. No. That girl and her interfering father are too much for me.''

"Ha. You wish to preserve your reputation as the globe-trotting playboy prince.'' Ray stood to face the king, his voice dripping with scorn. "And our brother Tariq continues to frolic in the mud with tanks and guns. But I am a man and a husband and will not permit further undermining of my marriage!'' He slapped his palm on the table.

Zedda patted his tense fingers, which relaxed. "You are right, my son. We shall have to find another way to placate the al-Qamra.''

Ray sat, as did the king, who said, "Perhaps a

string of your wonderful horses, Rayhan, will compensate for the loss of a prince.''

''Or perhaps ten thousand dinarii.'' Ray winked at Cami, his good mood apparently restored.

She smiled, buoyed by his unequivocal support. ''Why are the al-Qamra so powerful?''

''Not powerful,'' Zedda said. ''Influential. They are among the last nomadic tribes of Adnan. Every six months they complete a circuit of our nation, walking from the desert across the mountain passes to the Bay of Syed. As they are great communicators, they spread news and have much effect on opinion.''

''They could be described as…as…defiantly traditional.'' The king picked up his goblet and swirled the contents. ''Sharif is right. They must be brought into the mainstream of Adnani life and into this millennium.''

''I understand.'' Cami stood, drawing back her shoulders. ''Ray, please introduce me to our guests.''

He took Cami's hand and led her to the gate to greet their guests. She narrowed her eyes at Uncle Hamid, that snake. She'd bet her ranch that he'd deliberately brought her rival here just to bait her. By Hamid's side stalked another man. Dressed in brown robes, he wasn't as elderly as the mullah but appeared older than Ray and his brothers. Probably Sheikh al-Qamra. Bringing up the rear was a slight figure, a young man, in black. The son, she guessed.

And Matana, a small, delicately formed girl, clad in pearly white. As she drew back her hood, Cami could see that Matana was exquisite, with high cheekbones that reflected the moonlight, enormous dark eyes and full red lips.

Cami wanted to run all the way back to Texas. She remembered something Ray had said yesterday, when he'd criticized her body: "You'll be nice and round, like an Adnani girl." Matana epitomized the Adnani ideal of beauty. She was a nice, plump pigeon, ready for his plate…or for his bed. Sick with jealousy, Cami felt her stomach wrench.

Besides, Matana was the daughter of a sheikh, the woman Ray's family had selected for him. Regardless of what he'd said at the dinner table, it was Ray's duty to marry for political advantage.

Cami refused to share Ray, but Adnani law and custom allowed him to take Matana al-Qamra to wife, as well. And if the marriage would be good for Adnan, did Cami have the right to stand in his way?

Suddenly her husband was by her side, the warmth of his hand on her elbow. He leaned close. "Remember who you are," he whispered into her ear.

Breathing deeply, she forced her body to relax while straightening her spine and stretching to her full height. In the heeled gold sandals she'd purchased that day, she towered over little Matana, who tilted back her head to look at Cami.

Hamid introduced Matana as Prince Rayhan's fiancée, his voice edged with malicious glee. By her side, Cami sensed Ray stiffening.

"Former fiancée," he said, his tone icy. "May I present to you she who will be my only wife, Camille Ellison al-Rashad."

Cami turned her head and looked into her husband's eyes. He met her gaze without flinching, while giving her arm a comforting squeeze. The tension in her stomach loosened and fell away.

"Yes, as you well know, Uncle Hamid, since we talked earlier today," she said, smiling, even though she wanted to smack the cruel old man.

Matana, with a bewildered expression, looked around and met the gaze of the slight young man standing behind her. He bent his head toward her ear and spoke to her in rapid Arabic. Her eyes widened, and she skewered Hamid with an outraged glare from beneath her impossibly long lashes. If looks could kill, roast Hamid would be served at dinner along with the b'stila pie.

With a nervous gulp, Cami continued. "I am Prince Rayhan's wife and consort. I'm pleased to meet you, Matana, though I wish the circumstances weren't so awkward. No one informed you?"

Her brother again spoke before Matana said, "N-no," in hesitant, careful English. She pressed her lips together.

Cami loosened her arm from Ray's grip to take Matana's elbow. "I'm sorry," she said, her voice soft. "Now that your engagement is over, what are your plans?" She gently led Matana over to the buffet tables for a more private chat, with the young man following.

Rayhan wanted to pump his fist into the air and shout out an American-style cheer.

Smiling every second, his wife had coolly and calmly chopped off his uncle's political legs at the knee. Based on Matana's reaction, Rayhan believed

that none of the al-Qamra would ever trust Hamid
again. The People of the Moon maintained a nomadic
lifestyle, so the word would spread, and in a few short
weeks, Hamid would find his power and influence
greatly reduced among all Adnani.

Sheikh al-Qamra didn't look any too happy, either.
Rayhan's mother, no doubt responding to her impec-
cable political instincts, moved quickly to the sheikh's
side.

Ray edged away, allowing his mother to work her
magic. But he believed that even Zedda's smooth di-
plomacy couldn't alter the inevitable.

Though Cami had used a friendly tone of voice,
Rayhan had seen the dangerous glitter in her eyes. He
reflected that Hamid was most fortunate that Cami
wasn't wearing cowboy boots. She looked as though
she wanted to stomp on Hamid's toes for creating the
situation. Rayhan was equally infuriated. What was
the wily mullah's game?

It didn't matter. After glowering at his uncle, Rayhan looked for Cami. He hoped that he could quickly
extricate his wife from the situation. With her help,
he was sure he could untangle the thicket of emotions
that had twisted his heart into confused knots. He desperately wanted to be alone with her.

Near the buffet table, Cami wore a supremely self-
satisfied smile as she chatted with Prince al-Qamra,
who'd translated for his sister. Cami offered him a
plate and gestured to the buffet. A few steps away the
king now played diplomat, no doubt exerting himself
to soothe Princess al-Qamra's ill humor.

Rayhan eased his wife away from Prince al-Qamra, who bowed and nodded.

"You appear pleased with the world," Ray said to Cami.

She stuck her straight little nose into the air. "I think I'm quite good at this princess thing."

"I told you, you are perfect. Why do you doubt yourself, my wife?"

She nodded in Matana's direction. "Ray, Matana's a peach. Why'd you turn her down?"

He shrugged. "Oh, Matana's not a bad sort. But we have little in common. She doesn't speak English. She doesn't love Texas. And she's not you."

Her cheeks flushed a most charming shade of rose, visible in the lanterns lighting the courtyard.

"Shall we now retire?" He offered her his hand.

She stiffened, and didn't take it.

He sighed. "Cami. You do not understand. Most couples do not have what we have, my darling."

"What?" She didn't resist when he pulled her to his side.

He must have piqued her curiosity. "It is good between us. Very, very good. Think you any other man's touch would pleasure you so well?"

Cami looked at Ray. She had to admit, if only to herself, that even the slight caress of his fingers on hers as he escorted her to their suite was enough to thrill her to her toes and bring her to her knees...if she let that happen.

But she wouldn't.

Or would she? Her body quivered. Heat pooled in her belly.

He'd publicly claimed her as his only wife. He said she was perfect, describing her in complimentary terms to everyone he met. Although she'd filed for divorce, he refused to accept the death of their marriage, even though a lovely consort was available.

Ray opened the heavy, carved door to his—their—bedroom and ushered her inside, kissing her even before the door was partially open. He kicked the door shut while pulling her close.

She couldn't suppress her response to the tender brush of his mouth. When his fingers fumbled at the buttons securing her tunic, she didn't resist. She couldn't deny the excitement thrilling through her body. Everything that had happened—their blissful honeymoon followed by weeks of deprivation, then days of frustrating, unfulfilled closeness—had combined to stretch her control to the breaking point.

She wanted him.

She needed him.

She loved him.

Opening the halves of her garment, he exposed her naked breasts to the moonlight streaming into the room. He cupped and lifted them to his mouth, tonguing her nipples into ecstasy.

Ray raised his head. Her breasts, deprived of his warm caress, cooled, the tips hardening into stiff little nubs that ached for his love. She moaned with suppressed passion.

He feathered delicate kisses up her neck until he came to her ear. "Do you remember our first kiss?"

Sighing with remembered pleasure, she murmured, "Oh, yeah."

"And then later, when we again met at the pond."
She shivered in his arms.

"Like a river goddess, you walked out of the water
and into my heart." His voice had dropped to an intimate whisper. "It was the most erotic moment of
my life."

"Me, too. Not even our honeymoon—"

"I know. But our loving is so wonderful. Can we
not try to find again the reasons we married?"

Spearing her fingers into his hair, Cami dragged
him close for a long, deep kiss. His big hands dropped
to her hips, kneading her buttocks through her clothes.
The heat of his touch pervaded the layers of heavy
silk, inflaming her desire.

While they kissed, he walked her over to his bed.

After they'd loved, Rayhan eased his weight off his
wife and stared at the ceiling, trying to compose his
disordered thoughts.

As usual, Cami quickly divined his mood. "What's
up, Ray?" She stroked his side.

His flesh rippled with renewed need. He rolled to
face her. "I have had many women. And yet, the act
of love takes on a unique and magical quality with
you. It has never been so good for me."

"Me, neither." She grinned at him.

"I think perhaps you do not understand how special this is because I was your first." He wove a
strand of her hair around his fingers. "And, I pray,
your last.

"But believe me, my Cami, when I say to you that
the act of love is rarely so pleasurable. It is not com-

mon for a man and a woman to find paradise at the same moment. Yet you and I have climbed the heights together more than once. It is not only physical. It is because we are true mates."

Rayhan clasped her face in his hands, framing her cheeks with his palms. He became vividly aware of every aspect of his wife: her wide, wondering eyes, which masked her sharp intellect; the texture of her flushed skin; her lips, soft and sensual with their love-making.

He thought about everything they shared. Their love of horses. Their ranches in Texas, which would join, as they had, into one perfect whole. She had even developed a fondness for Adnan; had she not said she loved the place, despite the harshness of her treatment by some members of his family?

"You have captured my heart, seized my soul. Everything about you fascinates me," he said, his voice husky. "Your beautiful face, which shines with your inner light. Your mouth, which always, with complete honesty, reflects your feelings. Your lovely, strong body, which I hope will bear us many healthy children.

"When we were apart, the world turned gray and dead. When we are together—even when we argue— my world is brilliant again with color and light.

"I cannot happily live without you, my Camille. If that is not love, then what is it, this love you crave?"

Her exquisite eyes filled with tears. "You...you love me."

"Yes, my beloved. I love you. I am yours forever."

"That's all I needed to know," she whispered, slipping her arms around his neck.

"Then we will stay together?" Rayhan couldn't stop the choke of need in his voice. He didn't have to stop it. Cami was his true mate. She could see every flaw and still love him. He was sure of that.

"Together, forever."

"Forever."

Epilogue

One month later

His wheelchair pushed by one of the royal servants, Charles rolled down the ramp of the king's jet. By Cami's side, Ray chuckled. "Your father looks as though he had a much better flight than did you."

"Amelia Earhart had a better flight than mine." Cami pushed back her hood. The noontime sun of Syed beat down on her head, but she didn't care. She wanted her father to be able to spot her blond hair among all the dark Adnani.

Behind her, and to her right, scores of reporters, camera operators and onlookers clustered behind a yellow barrier patrolled by the local police. Since they'd announced their plans to renew their vows in a lavish public ceremony, Cami and Ray had been relentlessly shadowed by the press.

Now, the day before the rituals would begin, Adnani excitement had attained Himalayan heights. None of the royals could poke a nose outside the palace without a horde of media demanding interviews.

As minister without portfolio, Ray had decided that allowing full press access to certain events would quell the antiroyal, anti-American rumors. The arrival of Cami's father was the beginning of four days of media madness. Cami, gritting her back teeth when she heard the news, had resolved to grin and bear it.

Wearing a white *abaya* embroidered with the Adnani national colors, she stepped away from Ray's protective aura and advanced to the end of the ramp. She met her father and bent to kiss his cheek. "Hello, Daddy."

"Kiddo, I wouldn't have recognized you in that get-up except for your hair. You've gone native on me!"

Cami laughed, then edged aside to let Ray greet her father. Ray shook her dad's hand, saying, "Relax when I do this." He quickly kissed Charles on both cheeks in a traditional welcome.

Dad stared at Ray, Cami giggled, and the crowd erupted in cheers.

Hand in hand, Cami and Ray accompanied Charles to the king's limo. After they were comfortably seated, Cami asked, "So is it true? Have the two of you really buried the hatchet?"

Ray lounged against the cushions on the right side of the luxurious car. "You doubt my word, my princess?" His teasing smile belied the seriousness of the question.

"No, but—"

"Everything is fine." Her father patted her hand. "It was my fault, anyhow—"

"No, no." Ray poured orange juice into a glass and handed it to Cami. "The blame is entirely mine. I was a fool—"

"I was a cheat." Charles's tone was somber. "We were looking at some tough times, Cami, and I couldn't bear for you to go without. But I was ashamed of what I'd done for the next ten years."

"That is all over, is it not?" Ray asked.

"If you can forgive me, it is." Charles extended his right hand to Ray, who took it, smiling.

Three days later, as Cami sat next to Ray at a banqueting table, she said to him, "I think we're well and truly married."

"Yes, and do not ever forget it, my wife." Lifting her hand, he kissed her wedding ring.

Because of the diverse religious groups in Adnan, their wedding lasted three days and included three ceremonies, Islamic, Christian and Jewish. Protocol required them to attend scores of parties all over Syed from dusk until dawn.

Finally Cami, dressed in a traditional white dress— her twelfth gown of the three-day period—had circled Ray seven times, part of the ancient Jewish ceremony, the last of the wedding rites. The feast that followed, attended by numerous international leaders, lasted until midnight.

Cami nibbled on a stuffed grape leaf, trying to enjoy herself, though she was exhausted by the countless social gatherings. She wondered if she'd ever return to her beloved ranch again.

Pushing aside her homesickness, she counted her blessings. Not only did Ray adore her, but the men in her life—her father and her husband—seemed to be getting along famously.

Cami looked across the table at her father. Resplendent in a tuxedo, with servants waiting on him day and night, Charles appeared to be having the time of his life. The palace children had adopted him as a kind of surrogate grandfather. He delighted in teaching them how to play poker and checkers.

Beside her Ray put his hand on her knee under the table and squeezed. "This has all been very much fun, but when are we going back home?"

She turned to him, smiling. Did he mean what she hoped? "Home?"

"Yes, home. To Texas. I am—how do you say it? Housesick for my ranch, my home and my horses. Do you not miss your Sugar?"

Her amazing husband had virtually echoed her thoughts. "Oh, Ray!" She flung her arms around his neck. "Let's leave tomorrow."

He laughed. "If that is your wish."

"But what about your job?"

"Minister without portfolio? I'll resign."

"But you always wanted a high government post."

He shrugged. "It is less than it is supposed to be. I have already discussed the matter with Kadar. He agrees to appoint me—us—as special envoys to the United States in regard to oil. It will be our responsibility to manage the oil trade between Adnan and the United States."

"Hmm." Cami sipped mint tea. "That sounds… interesting. We'd have to shuttle back and forth from Texas."

"Yes, with visits to Washington, D.C. So how about it?" He took her hands in his.

A score of flashbulbs popped as the media immortalized the moment. Cami winced, but Ray appeared oblivious. He continued, "Will you share this crazy life with me, my wife?"

"Hmm." She fiddled with her wedding ring, pretending to mull over his proposition. "There's only one problem."

His face fell. "What is it? Tell me. You know that together, we will solve our problems. True love overcomes all obstacles, does it not?"

"Yes, it does." Cami smiled. Never had she such confidence in her husband's devotion. Since that wonderful night when he'd openly declared his love for her, their marriage had strengthened, growing strong enough to endure any adversity life might cast at them. "We'll just have to be careful about the planes we choose. I'm told that flying in unpressurized cabins is bad for pregnant women."

Ray drew in his breath in an audible gasp. "Do you mean—"

"Yes, I do." Cami adored the expression of joy and pride on her husband's face. She drew his head down to hers for a passionate kiss. "Consider our baby another wedding present."

*   *   *   *   *

SHEIKH SURGEON

BY
MEREDITH WEBBER

Meredith Webber says of herself, "Some ten years ago, I read an article which suggested that Mills & Boon were looking for new Medical™ romance authors. I had one of those "I can do that" moments and gave it a try. What began as a challenge has become an obsession—though I do temper the "butt on seat" career of writing with dirty but healthy outdoor pursuits, fossicking through the Australian Outback in search of gold or opals. Having had some success in all of these endeavours, I now consider I've found the perfect lifestyle."

CHAPTER ONE

KAL watched the bird spiral upwards, riding the desert thermals higher and higher until it was a black speck against the impossibly blue sky. The bird's flight lifted his spirit until it seemed his soul soared with it, released from the imprisonment of his body. Only here, alone in an endless sea of sand, did he experience the lightness of spirit that was close to happiness.

As close as he would ever come…

Suddenly, the black speck dropped like a stone, down and down and down, wings tucked back to add destructive power to the speeding descent. It disappeared from sight behind a sand dune, and Kal whistled then held out his arm for the bird's return.

It had missed its kill and he wasn't sorry—he had food enough for himself and the bird. But the falcon's failure reminded him how long it had been since he'd spent time with his birds—flying them and training them. His men exercised them regularly, but they didn't have the same touch and the birds knew it.

But what was more important? Training falcons the way his ancestors had for thousands of years, or bringing modern medicine to his country—providing the best medical services for his people?

He slipped the bird's hood over its head and set it on a stand, his hand lingering on the shiny dark feathers, feeling a tight bond with this living creature that could fly so freely, yet returned willingly to its captivity. Just as he would return to the hospital, for to do anything else would be unthinkable.

But not until tomorrow…

He walked back across a sand hill to where he'd left his big four-wheel-drive, and brought out a bundle of sticks. He'd build a fire and camp out beneath the stars—forget the world he was escaping, if only for a night. But though the stars shone like a scattering of bright diamonds in the velvety night sky, and the wind across the desert sands soothed him with its song, he couldn't recapture the lightness he'd felt as he'd watched the bird soar, and his mood turned deep and heavy—his soul now a weighted stone within him.

The plane dropped beneath the clouds and there, spreading to the horizon, were the desert sands, just as Kal had described them—a golden sea, with wave upon wave of wind-sculpted dunes. Kal had spoken of their beauty, but the longing in his voice when he'd mentioned the desert had told Nell more than words ever could have. The man she'd loved had loved this arid country with a bone-deep passion bred into him over the thousands of years his ancestors had roamed those sands.

Now, seeing them for the first time, Nell clasped her hands tightly together, the photo of Patrick—Patrick with hair—before the cancer—squashed between them. It was like a talisman, this photo, and she'd held it tightly throughout the twelve-hour flight, so now the outer plastic cover was sticky with her worrying and a crease was developing across her son's finely aquiline nose.

Patrick was well—she'd phoned home twice from the plane, the first time because she'd been intrigued to find all she had to do was swipe her credit card in the receiver then dial, and the second time to hear Patrick's voice one more time before they landed.

This remission would last. She had to be as positive as he was. Yet here she was about to land in a foreign country, just in case being positive wasn't good enough.

Just in case…

'Safely down,' the comfortably plump woman beside her said, and Nell registered the jolt she'd felt and opened her eyes. The woman and her husband had been kind and undemanding travelling companions, so Nell smiled at them and wished them all the best for the rest of their journey.

They knew part of her story—the part where she was travelling to this desert country to demonstrate the use of spray-on skin for burns victims. It was something that had been developed in the burns unit where she worked and fate had played into her hands when the hospital here had requested information on the innovative technique for their new burns unit and had asked if perhaps someone would come and demonstrate it.

A month, that's all Nell had—to both explain the treatment to the staff at the hospital and to find Patrick's father. To somehow tell him, at the risk of her own hard-won emotional security, that he had a son—a son who might, one day soon, need his help and the help of his people…

She closed her eyes again—the magnitude of *that* particular exercise all but overwhelming her. It would be all right, she promised herself as the plane taxied towards the low, well-lit terminal. It *had* to be all right!

But once out of the safety of the plane, nerves began gnawing at Nell's stomach. Through passport control—purpose of visit to this desert kingdom, business—and customs—no, nothing to declare—the gnawing grew stronger and stronger until she wondered if people could develop stomach ulcers in such a short time.

A door at the far end of the customs hall spilled her out into a wide foyer, crowded with people clamouring for a glimpse of their returning loved ones. And at the back of the crowd, a small sign held aloft. DR WARREN was all it said, but the woman in the headscarf who held it was smiling so warmly Nell felt the panic in her stomach ease.

'I'm Nell Warren,' she said, pushing through the crowd and holding out her hand to the smiling woman.

'Yasmeen,' the woman offered, shaking Nell's hand and drawing her further from the jostling crowd. Then a screeching, rending, tearing noise, so loud and fearsome it conjured up images of other worlds, rent the air, and people began to scream and scream so when the sirens started, they were like a continuation of the high-pitched sounds of terror.

'Something has gone wrong.' Yasmeen stated the obvious, but she was already moving with a purpose. 'All hospital staff take part in simulated airport emergencies,' she said over her shoulder. 'I must go. You can stay here and wait.'

'If it's an emergency, the more hands you have the better,' Nell told her, dropping her small suitcase beside a pillar and hurrying after the woman through a crowd that was now in full panic mode despite what were probably reassurances echoing from the public-address system.

Ducking and weaving, they finally reached a deserted corridor on the ground floor, and Yasmeen pushed through a door into a large room, glass windows on the far side of which reflected the angry red glow of a fierce fire. Going towards the windows, Nell saw the fire engines racing across the tarmac, some units already in place, sending streams of snow-like foam onto the angry conflagration.

Yasmeen was murmuring to herself—a prayer, Nell guessed, for her own heart was praying for whoever was trapped in the burning plane. The door behind them opened and more people swept in, some wheeling trolleys, others carrying first-aid equipment. Two ambulances pulled up outside, the public-address system issued what had to be instructions, and Nell felt the tension build as emergency crews awaited the order to move.

'We will wait here and treat the injured as they are brought in,' Yasmeen said to Nell. 'As the first doctors on the scene, we must do what we can. The hospital will be on full alert by now and more ambulances will be here shortly. The worst cases we'll send straight to the hospital where emergency teams will have more facilities to treat them.'

Nell looked at the burning aircraft and wondered if they would have any patients to treat. Surely no one could escape so fierce a fire.

'Do you know what happened?'

Yasmeen shook her head.

'From what people are saying around me, it seems the plane was coming in to land—praise be it wasn't your plane—when it skidded on the runway. Maybe the wheels didn't lock, or some oil made it skid. It slewed off sideways, hit a stationary plane, and then burst into flames.'

Nell shook her head, imagining the horror of those on board. How many had there been? She couldn't tell how big the burning plane was, but her flight had carried over four hundred people.

'Look!' Yasmeen grabbed her arm, and there, black against the leaping red and orange flames, were small figures, fleeing across the tarmac.

'So some have survived,' Nell murmured, watching as airport vehicles stopped by the small figures, collecting them, then speeding towards the room where she and Yasmeen waited with the other emergency staff.

It was her last rational thought for some hours. The first victims had been lucky—not badly burned—so the job was to clean the wounds and dress them, to wrap blankets around shaking shoulders and treat them for shock. But as the room filled with the less badly injured, the scene of operations moved outside onto the tarmac, where arc lights lit a scene from hell.

'Cover wounds with clean dry cloth, intubate if their airways seem undamaged—if there are no burns on their face or throat—but otherwise provide oxygen through a mask. Remember a lot will have lung damage from inhaling the heat and smoke. Get fluids flowing in,' Nell said to Yasmeen, who had hesitated beside her as the more seriously injured began to arrive. 'Raise the injured parts and treat for shock, don't attempt to treat the burns, don't peel off clothes, don't puncture blisters, don't raise their heads as it could compromise their airways,' Nell added, aware she probably had more experience in burns first aid than the other doctor. 'Tell the other people here to do the same. Would you like me to do the triage? Sending the worst cases to hospital first?'

Yasmeen nodded and though Nell could feel the other woman shaking beside her, Yasmeen pulled herself together and gave orders in a crisp clear voice.

Mobile medical supply vans had appeared from nowhere, the sides of the vans opening up to reveal an abundance of equipment. As she checked patients and tagged them in order of the severity of their injuries, Nell marvelled at the organisational set-up of the airport that it had these vans on standby.

She worked as if controlled from somewhere outside herself, checking, treating, passing patients on, until at last more and more of the bodies being pulled from the plane were already dead and the grim task of handling them could be turned over to someone else.

'Come on,' she said to Yasmeen. 'We'll be needed at the hospital.'

The other woman's face was black with soot and grime from the clothes of the patients they'd treated, and Nell guessed her own was just as bad, but Yasmeen's smile lit up her darkened face and she shook her head at Nell's suggestion.

'You're a guest here and you've already done enough to help,' she protested. 'I will take you to the quarters we've arranged for you where you can clean up and rest.'

Then it was Nell's turn to shake *her* head.

'No way! This is what I do, Yasmeen! I'm a specialist burns doctor. How many of them does your hospital have? I also know the uses of the spray-on skin—that's why I'm here, remember. Take me to the hospital. I can help in either your emergency room or wherever else I'm needed.'

She smiled at her new friend.

'I'll clean up first,' she promised.

Yasmeen smiled again, then led the way back through the airport and out the other side to where cars jammed the roads, news of the accident having sent panicking relations racing to the airport.

'It's a gridlock. We'll never get away. Perhaps we should go back and hitch a ride with an ambulance,' Nell suggested, but a clattering noise drowned out the words and she looked up to see a helicopter descending towards the far side of the terminal building.

'Come on—that's the best ride for us. The chief's own personal helicopter. He's been talking about getting one for the hospital, but until it happens, he's willing to use his own for emergencies.'

Yasmeen grabbed Nell's arm and hurried her back the way they'd come.

'I was wondering why he hadn't turned up earlier, then remembered he'd taken some rare time off and had probably gone out to the desert.'

Yasmeen was talking of this 'chief' with a mixture of respect and affection as she led the way through the milling crowds, and from the words she used—'chief' in particular—and her accented English, Nell guessed she'd trained, for a time at least, in the United States.

'This chief? Is he a department head? Or the hospital

CEO?' Nell asked, and Yasmeen turned to flash another smile her way.

'Chief surgeon, head of the hospital, and also a member of our ruling family. Khalil al Kalada is a great man who was not only born to greatness but has lived up to the finest of his family's traditions.'

Khalil al Kalada.

The words seemed to come from a great distance, echoing through space, closer and closer until they hammered like drumbeats in Nell's head.

Cold fear clutched at her heart while panic spread through her body. Not yet, her mind yelled. I'm not ready yet! But though her feet faltered Yasmeen urged her on, racing her headlong towards a meeting with the man she'd come so far to find.

As Kal brought the helicopter down, he saw the wreckage of the still smouldering plane in the distance, his father's helicopter parked a little to one side of it, but the medical action would be where the arc lights lit up a makeshift emergency room.

Still cursing the fact he'd taken his vehicle, not the chopper, out to the desert so his response time to the emergency call had been slow, he hovered for a moment, taking in the traffic jam beyond the terminal building, picking out the flashing red lights of ambulances and other emergency vehicles stuck in a seemingly impossible tangle of cars. Police vehicles were clearing the road, forcing cars to the verges so ambulances could get through. It was making the tangle of civilian traffic worse, but at least the ambulances were moving.

His father's pilot would be at the controls of the helicopter on the ground, awaiting orders. Kal radioed him, telling him to take off and offer assistance to the police vehicles, advising clear routes and using a loudhailer to get non-essential vehicles off the road. He'd have liked to have called police headquarters as well and suggest they arrest any non-emergency personnel on the roads, but that might be a little extreme…

A light touch on the controls brought him lower. He'd check the situation on the ground then head straight back to the hospital. By now a call would have gone out to all staff, asking them to report for duty. The facilities would be stretched to the limit—he'd have to contact nearby states and ask if they could take patients. Could some be airlifted to hospitals further afield? His father's private plane had as much medical equipment as a state-of-the art emergency room, while his family's business interests were spread like tentacles throughout the world. There'd be contacts who'd smooth the way for the repatriation of foreign patients…

He landed in the darkness beyond the arc lights, left the cabin and ran, bent low to dodge the slowing rotors, towards the centre of the activity. As ever, some people stopped work to nod or make a tentative bow towards him, unable to prevent themselves offering this small acknowledgement, but a tall man in smoke-blackened robes stepped forward to greet him with a handshake.

'I'm head of airport security, Highness,' the man said, giving his name as he grasped Kal's hand. 'All we know is that the plane skidded off the runway, hit a stationary plane and burst into flames. The worst cases are on their

way to hospital, minor injuries and people still shocked
are being treated by our staff inside the building, and now
we are getting ready to transport those deceased to the
mortuary.'

He waved his hand towards a line of shrouded bodies.

'So many dead!' Kal murmured, pain for the waste of
life biting into him even while he accepted the deaths as
God's will.

'More would be dead but for the doctors from your hospital who were here on hand to help the injured and tell my
staff exactly how to treat them.'

The man paused then added, 'More will die, Excellency.
Many on the way to hospital are very badly burnt.'

'Then I must go—they'll need me there,' Kal told him.
He'd have liked to have added that he didn't need the royal
terms of address—didn't use them himself—but he sensed
the man needed the formality and ritual—needed to know
some things didn't change and that while a member of the
ruling family was present, all would be taken care of.

But as Kal turned back towards the helicopter, a voice
called his name, and he turned to see two women hurrying towards him.

'Sir, Yasmeen—I'm Yasmeen Assanti, Ward Six. I was
here, collecting the woman from Australia who was coming to show us the spray-on skin. I told her not to help but
she knows burns better than I do. She's been like an angel
of mercy, sir. We'd have lost more people without her.'

She turned, apparently to introduce the 'angel of
mercy', but the second woman was now crouched on the
ground, holding a shroud high and peering at the person
lying beneath it.

'He's alive!' she called, her voice so hoarse it came out like a croak.

Kal dashed towards her, kneeling on the other side, calling for lights to be directed on the patient, checking the man who'd been left for dead.

'Get him into my helicopter,' he yelled, beckoning to two men who were lifting bodies into the mortuary van. 'Yasmeen, get fluids and something clean to cover him. You…' He glanced at the woman across the stretcher. 'Stay with him. Do what you can.'

She nodded, her hands still busy checking the patient, feeling for first a radial then a carotid pulse.

'Oxygen, too, Yasmeen,' she said, lifting her head briefly so Kal had an impression of pale eyes in a blackened face. But it was her voice, although raspy with the smoke and soot she'd inhaled, that sent a shiver down his spine, and out of nowhere came an expression he'd heard while studying in Australia—something about a ghost walking over a grave.

He stepped back to make room for Yasmeen, then two men were lifting the stretcher, and the stranger was walking beside it, holding an oxygen mask in one hand, just above the injured man's nose, and the heavy oxygen bottle in her other hand.

Kal raced ahead of them to open the doors of the helicopter and prepare it to receive the stretcher, then, after giving orders to the men about how to strap it into place, he climbed forward into the pilot's seat and prepared to take off, checking with Air Traffic Control that he was cleared to take off.

Above them planes would be circling, unable to land.

Most would be diverted to nearby airports, or turned back if they were on short flights. He had no doubt one of his brothers would be in the control tower, making sure everything was being done efficiently up there, while another brother would be handling questions from the media as news of the disaster spread beyond the narrow confines of his country.

But as the little helicopter rose easily into the air, staying below the level of the circling planes, he turned to look back into the cabin, where a dirty, dishevelled woman knelt beside an injured man.

It couldn't be…

'I can't get a tube in,' Nell muttered to Yasmeen. 'His airway's compromised. Hold the mask just slightly above his mouth and nose so it doesn't stick to his burnt skin. I've got pure oxygen flowing out so whatever he manages to breathe in— No! Damn! He's not breathing by himself at all now. This is what can happen—suddenly his airway collapses altogether or oedema closes it.'

She switched tubes so she could bag the man, forcing air into his lungs while Yasmeen held the mask, but the man's chest failed to move.

'He needs a tracheostomy so we can insert a tube into his trachea, but because of the oedema and because the lungs might have suffered major damage, the pressure of pumped oxygen could…'

She was thinking out loud, but knew the tracheostomy was the only way to go, although it carried severe risks for burns patients. Yasmeen had brought a medical kit out to the helicopter, and Nell found a packaged scalpel and another package with tubing in it.

Yasmeen touched her hand.

'Do it,' she said, but the man's clothing had burnt to the skin on his neck and Nell's fingers faltered as she sought the tracheal rings through which she could plunge the scalpel.

In the end she took a chance on the position and was relieved to hear a release of air. Once a small tube was in place to keep the gap open, she saw the man's chest rise and fall.

He was breathing by himself!

She took a deep breath herself, then Yasmeen leaned close to talk above the noise.

'That's the hospital up ahead. We'll land on the roof. Strap into a seat.'

And leave this man who'd been left for dead once already?

'I'll hang on tightly,' Nell told Yasmeen, taking the oxygen mask from the other doctor and holding it close to the tracheostomy tube, still worrying about the extent of lung damage her patient might be suffering and whether too much oxygen would exacerbate it. Lungs were delicate—pressure could burst them. Inhaled heat and particles of noxious gas would already have damaged the fine tissues…

At least worrying about her patient stopped her worrying about the man flying the helicopter. His glance had done no more than pass over her earlier, and for that she was sincerely thankful.

OK, she had to talk to Kal some time—that was why she'd come. But exhausted from travel, shaken by the emergency and covered with soot and ash? Hardly!

The little craft touched down lightly, then he was there again, kneeling right beside her.

'A tracheostomy on a burns patient—contraindicated surely,' he said, his voice stern with disapproval.

'He wasn't breathing and we couldn't force air into his lungs,' Yasmeen said. 'Dr Warren tried. She tried everything before she resorted to cutting him.'

The fluid catheter was leaking along the patient's arm and Nell's head was bent, trying to find a new site, while this conversation took place. It was a measure of her involvement with the injured man—of her determination to keep him alive—that she could stay focussed on what she was doing, aware of Kal only on the periphery of her conscious mind.

Or maybe her concentration was a coping mechanism.

She felt the slight pop as the needle entered a vein and, holding the catheter in place, she reached with her free hand for tape. Long slim fingers pressed what she needed into her hand—not Yasmeen's fingers, which were blunt and slightly chubby. The touch was cool—impersonal—and though her conscious mind had lost the battle to keep Kal at bay and her body was quaking with an apprehensive dread, she calmly taped the catheter into place and reattached the drip tube.

'We can move him now,' she said, keeping her back to the man who knelt beside her, looking instead towards the group of people gathered at the open door of the helicopter.

'Dr Warren?'

Kal's voice, familiar enough to send shivers up her spine although her name was unfamiliar on his lips.

'I'll go with the patient,' she said, fussing with the tube, battling for emotional control. Deliberately rude, but so tense she feared she'd shatter into a million pieces if she turned to face Kal now.

Then an image of Patrick's face rose up in her mind. She couldn't risk getting off on the wrong foot with Kal.

Her heart hammered with panic, a thousand butterflies fluttered inside her, and her knees and fingers trembled with uncertainty, and fear, and dread, and some other emotion she didn't want to think about. But she was a grown woman, with a son who needed help, so she lifted her head, met his eyes, forced a facsimile of a smile to her lips, and said, 'Hello, Kal.'

But before he could reply the man on the stretcher gave a convulsive lurch and became the focus of her attention once again. She leant across him, holding him still, checking that the incision she'd made in his throat was still open.

'Yasmeen?' The woman had come to the opposite side of the stretcher as it was lifted, and Nell spoke across the patient. 'Do many of your staff speak English? Will the nurses understand me if I ask for things?'

'Yasmeen will stay with you to translate until a nurse who speaks English can be found. It shouldn't take long as most of our staff are bilingual.'

So much for not getting off on the wrong foot. His voice would have frozen fire!

He delivered this reply then strode away, a stranger in a smoke-grimed white robe, pulling off his headdress, grabbing scrubs from a trolley as he passed, turning from the desert chieftain she'd seen emerge from the helicopter into a doctor once again.

Why, after fourteen years would she turn up in his country?
Coincidence?
He didn't think so.
But he couldn't think of any reason for her to have come. She'd assume he was still married so it couldn't have been some mid-life crisis to reclaim her youth.

Could it?

No, not Nell, who was sensible and pragmatic and who'd understood his position from the start.

Besides, she was married, too—her name was Warren, not Roberts—though she wore no rings...

Kal shook his head as he ducked into a side room and pulled off his robe, seeing sand from the desert spill on the floor, staring at the last reminder of his hours of freedom as he tried to get his head back on track. He pulled on the loose scrubs. He was a doctor again—a doctor with a huge emergency in his hospital and a strange feeling in the pit of his stomach. No way could he let his thinking be distracted by Nell's presence in his hospital. If anything, he should be grateful—the Dr Warren he'd expected was a burns expert and if ever one was needed, it was now.

Dr Warren!

She must *have married...*

Why ever wouldn't she?

He had.

But pointing this out to himself didn't make him feel any better about Nell marrying, though he knew it was irrational to be thinking about Nell at all—let alone about her marital status...

'We've sixty-two victims in the ER so far.' Lalla el Wafa, his A and E nurse-manager, met him as he came out of the elevator on the ground floor. 'The doctors on duty haven't been able to do more than check their status, make sure their airways are patent and that they're getting fluids and electrolytes.'

'We take one patient at a time and do what we can. What we don't do is panic,' Kal told her.

They'd paused in the passageway and now had to stand against the wall to allow the wardsmen wheeling the injured man Kal had transported to pass. Nell was still beside him, bending over him to hold a mask close to the tube in his throat.

Was she worried about lung damage that she hadn't attached the tube directly to the oxygen tank? He must ask her later. Since the explosion at an oil well three months ago that had prompted him to open a burns unit at the hospital, he'd been reading up on treatment of burns victims. It had changed so much since his training days when he'd dealt with an occasional burn in ER, and he still didn't know as much as he needed to know. Neither had he been able to find a suitable specialist doctor to employ as head of the unit.

Maybe he could persuade Nell to stay.

Are you going mental?

The group disappeared through the doors at the end of the corridor, but Kal still stared in that direction. As the doors had slid open Nell had lifted her head to speak to Yasmeen and he'd noticed the clean-cut profile, with a long straight nose.

A nose Nell Roberts had always thought far too long for her to ever be considered beautiful…

A nose he'd kissed a thousand times…

CHAPTER TWO

HE CAUGHT up with Nell as the man was wheeled into a curtained alcove, but the sight of sixty-two—no, sixty-three now—patients in the ER stopped him following her—*and* demanding answers to all the questions in his head. Blackened, blistered, wailing with pain, the injured lay against the wall, and were slumped on chairs, while those tagged more urgent were on trolleys, which were in lines four or five deep.

'Have they been sorted into priorities?' he asked Lalla, who had followed him and was still hovering by his side.

'Someone at the airport toe-tagged them and we're working off that classification.'

Kal guessed who the someone was. He looked at the patients lying on makeshift stretchers along the far wall—tagged less urgent but they'd be in pain, and would be suffering shock. A young doctor was yelling for more fluids, while another was lifting an injured man in his arms, obviously desperate to get him to a treatment room, but they were all full, with staff rushing in all directions—a scene from hell.

He and his staff could handle burns cases—they had before and they knew the current emergency procedures—but they usually handled one person coming in with burns—six with the oil fire. Not sixty-three, a lot of them foreign, and a lot of them so severely burned he wondered if they'd live.

'Kal, I don't want to be telling you your business, but you have to do this systematically.' Nell emerged from the curtained alcove and stopped in front of him, delivering this opening foray without a hint of apology in her voice. 'Staff should calculate the total body surface area burned using the rule of nine. Any patient with more than twenty per cent TBSA should be given fluids—Ringer's lactate for the first twenty-four hours. We'll work out electrolyte balance later. They should be catheterised and their fluid output measured. Ideally it should be evaluated for haemoglobin, which would show a breakdown in red blood cells and could lead to kidney failure. At the first sign of red blood cell breakdown, they'll need a diuretic to clear the fluid faster to protect the kidneys.'

Kal stared at the woman standing in front of him, telling him what to do, as if this was the most natural thing in the world. Did she feel nothing of the emotional chaos he was suffering? Or was she just far more capable of separating her emotional self from her practical one?

'Tell them to dress the wounds with whatever sterile dressings you have available—we've time later to do excisions and skin grafts and fancy stuff. That can wait at least twenty-four hours post-burn—even up to five days if necessary—but right now we have to stop fluid loss through bleeding or wound seepage and stabilise the patients as best we can.'

'Pain relief?' he asked, as the crying, wailing and moaning broke through the turmoil in his mind. Of course Nell should be telling him what to do—it was her field of expertise. And, of course, he too could separate his emotional self from his practical one—hadn't he been doing it for years?

'Morphine's the best. IV. They'll all be getting fluids anyway. Then I need someone—you, probably, as Yasmeen says you're a surgeon—to check the wounds for bands of eschar—circumferential burns on the chest or extremities.'

'Cut through them?' Kal asked, pleased to find he was able to talk to the suddenly reappeared Nell as if she was just another doctor.

His body didn't think she was just another doctor, though why his body should be responding to anything but the medical emergency he had no idea.

She nodded.

'You won't need anaesthetic. It only happens in third-degree burns and the nerve endings in the skin have all been destroyed so it doesn't hurt the patient, but you'll be opening up more surface area to infection, so a topical antibiotic and a clean dressing should be applied.'

'Will one cut suffice?'

The pale eyes studied him, a frown gathering between her neatly arched brows.

Frown lines—she's got frown lines!

'It usually does, but you'll be able to tell if one cut's enough. With extremities—eschar on the arms or legs—you'll get a pulse in the wrist or ankle once you're done. With chest constriction, you might need two cuts—one midclavicular and one transverse. You'll see the chest rise and fall once it's free.'

Yasmeen called to her and she turned away—then

swung back to call after Kal, 'Don't tie off bleeders on the limbs immediately. Let them bleed three to five minutes to release pressure, but holding the extremity above heart level. Then tie them off or coagulate. And tetanus prophylaxis—conscious patients will be able to tell you their tetanus status. And nil by mouth on all of them—paralytic ileus.'

Kal nodded, knowing that, but also knowing she was right to remind him—to remind them all—of the basic treatment. One burns patient coming in would be treated quickly and efficiently, with all these reminders Nell had issued in the forefront of the ER doctor's mind, but, faced with so many patients, it would be easy for a doctor, anxious to do everything for everyone, to forget something of the basics.

Kal moved away, aware of Nell going not to the man they'd airlifted to hospital, but to check a very small patient on a trolley by the far wall. Yasmeen was bent over the trolley, talking anxiously to Nell, but Nell's frown told Kal it was too late. That he was looking at the first of the hospital casualties.

'Even if we could have saved him,' Nell told Yasmeen, 'he wouldn't have survived very long. Look at his little body—can you see a bit of it that isn't burned? Adults with more than sixty per cent burns to their bodies have little chance of survival, so what hope would this tiny soul have had?'

She put her arm around Yasmeen's shoulders and led her away, reminding her they had living patients to tend. Reminding herself of the same thing. Her mind argued that she shouldn't have spoken to Kal as she had, giving orders, but although all ER doctors knew the routine for treating burns patients, she'd been in emergency situations before and was aware that the sheer volume of patients at a time like this threw normal thinking into disarray.

She moved on to the man who'd been left for dead, catheterised him then sent a urine sample to the lab for testing, checked the oxygen level in his blood—still too low—fiddled with the oxygen valve to produce more flow, then knew she had to move on. There were too many patients for her to be spending time with one man.

'You've always got to be aware of carbon monoxide poisoning with burn victims,' she explained to a young doctor who seemed mesmerised by a patient with the telltale cherry-red colouring. 'The blood carries carbon monoxide far more easily than it carries oxygen—for some reason haemoglobin has an affinity with the carbon monoxide molecules. So, as well as the patient breathing in the deadly fumes, the blood's too busy shunting the wrong gas around the body to be bothered with oxygen.'

'Is that why the patient's unconscious? Carbon monoxide poisoning rather than burns?'

Nell looked at the patient, reassessing the percentage of injured body surface area.

'Most probably. Pump one hundred per cent oxygen into him, but watch for a change in his level of consciousness. Do you have a hyperbaric chamber?'

The young doctor looked puzzled. 'Like we use for divers with the bends?'

Nell nodded.

'Yes. We have a lot of tourists coming here to dive, so we've always had one in the hospital.'

'Well, if he's still unconscious in, say, an hour, we should put him in there. The situation is similar to someone with the bends. We need to get the carbon monoxide out of his blood using pressure, then force oxygen in.'

She glanced up from writing this advice on the chart to see Kal had joined them.

'We've others affected by carbon monoxide. I'll make sure all the staff know to check the level of consciousness of their patients.'

He disappeared again, but from time to time, as she worked, Nell was aware of him nearby. Sometimes he'd ask a question or direct her to a particular patient.

Nell moved among the doctors and nurses fighting for the lives of these badly injured people, aware of how different this type of doctoring was. No one was taking records of past illnesses, and in a lot of cases they didn't know the patient's name or nationality. It was enough to know a human being in terrible distress lay on the stretcher in front of them, and to do everything possible, firstly to save that person's life then to ease their pain and keep infection at bay.

A couple of times Yasmeen dragged her away to a small sitting room, where exhausted staff sat silently as they refuelled on coffee and biscuits. Sandwiches appeared and were eaten on the run, staff aware they had to eat but their minds always on the patients.

At some stage Kal walked past and she remembered something else that needed checking.

'Eschar on joints, too,' she said to him. 'Sometimes you need to cut along the outer surface of a limb at wrist, elbow, knee or ankle joint. Mobility is a huge problem for burns victims later, and sometimes we can prevent problems by releasing burnt tissue early. Again, the wounds will bleed a lot but cauterise them this time.'

Kal nodded and walked away, and Nell knew every patient in ER would be checked for any burnt tissue that might be constricting movement of a limb.

Uncountable hours later, the scene in the ER looked less like a vision of hell, though torn wrappings from dressings and instruments still lay ankle deep on the floor. They had transferred fourteen critically injured patients to the new burns unit, two of these to the burns ICU, and another eleven were in wards throughout the hospital. Twenty-one less badly injured had been treated and either sent home or put up in hotels, and another ten, who were members of a football team from a neighbouring country, had been flown home in the ruler's private plane, to be treated at the main hospital in their capital city.

The small child had been the first of six patients they hadn't been able to save and Nell was still in the ER, still fighting for the life of the man who'd been left for dead.

'Let someone take him up to the ward,' Yasmeen pleaded, her face cleaned of soot but now grey with exhaustion. 'We can make room for him there and the nurses are fresh—they can watch him for you.'

'I won't move him till he's stable,' Nell muttered, checking again on the test results she'd just got from the lab. 'His acid base status is all over the place. It *has* to be to do with inhalation injury, although his lungs show clear on the X-ray. He's not pink so it's not carbon monoxide, and with a tube in place it can't be swelling to his lower trachea, although that rarely happens because the vocal cords effectively stop heat going further.'

Once again she found herself thinking out loud, but if she expected help from Yasmeen she was disappointed. The other doctor simply repeated her advice that Nell should hand the patient over and get some rest.

'But—' she began, then another voice cut in.

'We're taking him up to the ward.'

Nell glanced up from the infuriating puzzle that was this patient to see Kal standing in the opening of the curtained-off treatment room, and though his statement had been an order, not a suggestion, she had to argue.

'He shouldn't be moved.'

'He has to be moved,' Kal said firmly. 'You've done all you can and you're so close to exhaustion you could make the mistake that kills him.'

Shocked by his blunt words, Nell opened her mouth to continue her argument, then read the implacability on his face and closed it again.

'Yasmeen,' Kal continued smoothly, 'I'll find someone to go with him and make sure he has a nurse to watch him. You go home and get some rest. I'll see Dr Warren to her quarters as soon as I've arranged the transfer.'

Nell opened her mouth again, this time to protest that she could find her own way—a protest so stupid it was just as well no sound came out. Not that Kal would have heard. He'd disappeared.

'Come on,' Kal said roughly, returning minutes later. He took her arm and guided her firmly away. 'You're dead on your feet.'

Realising resistance was futile, Nell plodded along beside him, her legs apparently understanding what he'd said, as they became so heavy she could barely lift them.

Beside her, Kal muttered words that seeped dimly into her consciousness—angry words from the tone.

Was he telling her she was a fool? He used to tell her that when she meekly accepted the worst shifts during in-hospital training stints. Or when she'd lent her notes to friends who'd skipped lectures.

'You're smiling?'

His voice was so incredulous she couldn't stop her smile from widening.

'It must be tiredness because I rarely think about the past, but I was remembering how you used to call me a fool,' she said, turning to face him and looking into his eyes for the first time, scanning his face for similarities and differences, seeking something of the serious young man she'd loved to distraction in the tired, hard, angry, unshaven face.

'A long time ago,' she added quietly, then, because the young man *was* there and because her heart told her she *still* loved him, she turned away before he could read it in her eyes and her quest became more complicated than it need be.

She continued down the corridor beside him with no idea of where they were. Still in the hospital, she assumed, although they'd walked along a high, windowed bridge from one building to another.

'Were your bags sent up here?'

The question didn't make sense.

'My bags?'

'Suitcase! Belongings! I assume you came with spare clothing and a toothbrush at least.'

Nell stopped walking and looked around vaguely. She had her handbag over her shoulder, having slung it across her chest as she'd run to help, managing to keep hold of it until Yasmeen had put it in a locker while she herself had been in ER.

'I left my suitcase at the airport when the siren sounded. Yasmeen wanted me to wait, but I knew I should help.'

Kal made another exasperated noise.

'You never did have any common sense,' he grumbled, walking on again so she was forced to follow. 'Tucking lame ducks under your wing, taking in strays—you'd give away your shoes if someone needed them.'

'Well, now I have, I suppose,' Nell said, trying to lighten Kal's angry mood, although she was feeling so exhausted she wondered why she bothered. 'That's if the person who picked it up did need them and didn't just take the case for the sake of it.'

Kal made a growly noise under his breath and stopped at a door. He pulled a ring of keys from his pocket and fitted one in the lock.

'This is a master key and I can't give it to you, but if there's no key on the table inside, I'll get someone to bring one to you in the morning.'

In the morning?

'Isn't it already morning?' she asked.

'Tomorrow morning,' Kal said gruffly. 'It's close to midnight, local time. You've worked through a night and day.'

He opened the door on a pleasantly furnished living room with a small kitchen at the far end. 'Bedrooms and bathrooms through there.' He waved his hand towards a door off to the right. 'You'll find toiletries in both bathrooms and bathrobes in the bedroom cupboards.'

'First-class hotel stuff,' Nell said lightly, wondering how soon he'd leave. Tiredness swamped her and she wasn't sure she'd have the energy to shower before she collapsed into bed.

'First class doesn't begin to describe the job you've done for us since you arrived,' he said, and a gruffness in his voice made her turn to look at him. The pain in his eyes hurt her heart and she swayed towards him, wanting more than anything to hold him and ease away that pain.

He caught her shoulders and held her away, still looking at her, his face hardening, the pain shrouded behind his heavy eyelids.

'Unfortunately we'll need more help from you—at least until we can get some other burns experts here—so get some sleep.' He spoke harshly, as if he resented the fact she was needed, and in her exhausted state this attitude confused her.

'I don't mind helping,' she offered.

'Get some sleep,' he repeated, then his hands dropped and he turned and walked away, swinging back to face her as he opened the door.

'If you need anything lift the phone and press one for the apartment block's reception office. They'll send up food now if you want it, or when you wake. Press four for me. My apartment is next door but if I'm not there, the call will be switched to the office, and whoever answers will page me.'

The door closed behind him but, tired as she was, Nell

couldn't move. For a long time she stared at the door—at where he'd been—then with a shrug of her shoulders she headed not for the bathroom but for the phone. With a six-hour time difference, it would be early morning in Australia. She'd stolen time from patients and phoned from downstairs to let the family know she'd arrived safely and to assure them she hadn't been involved in the accident. This time she needed to phone to check on Patrick before she had a shower.

Patrick!

She turned and stared at the door again, while a shiver of presentiment feathered along her spine.

There's a reason she's here and I'm not going to like it.

The words echoed in Kal's head as he made his way back down to the ward to check on the patients one last time before he, too, grabbed some sleep. The other thing he didn't like was the way his mind seemed to be producing a running commentary on the situation, not the accident situation—he was handling that quite well—but the Nell situation.

Why shouldn't it be that she was simply the best person for the Brisbane hospital to send? Or that their relationship had prompted an interest in his country and curiosity had brought her here?

Not for one minute do you believe either of those explanations! the voice in his head said, and a queasy feeling in Kal's stomach told him his instinct agreed.

But this wasn't the time to be looking a gift horse in the mouth—Nell was here and from what he'd seen of her at work today, they couldn't have had a better person helping out.

* * *

Yasmeen arrived only minutes after the breakfast Nell had ordered—laden with bags and parcels.

'The chief sent me to the shops,' she said in an awed voice. 'He said I was to get you clothes. He said good quality and to get you slacks so you wouldn't feel out of place in the hospital, but some loose dresses for you to relax in at home, and some nightclothes and underwear. I bought different sizes and can take back what doesn't fit.'

Nell shook her head as a porter followed Yasmeen into the apartment, with more parcels in his arms and carrier bags dangling from his fingers.

'It's a wonder he didn't bring the whole store to me,' Nell muttered.

'Oh, he was going to,' Yasmeen said, totally serious, although Nell had been joking. 'But I said I didn't think you'd like it. That you'd be embarrassed. So he phoned a place and got it to open early, and I was the only person there.'

'That must have been fun and, yes, I would have been embarrassed,' Nell assured the anxious woman. 'But I can't try on all this stuff now. I've slept for hours longer than I intended. I need to be in the burns unit.'

'You've slept for about six hours,' Yasmeen reminded her. 'Same as me. But I didn't have a long flight from Australia before the accident sent us into chaos.'

'Good thing we're doctors and used to lack of sleep,' Nell said, emptying parcels onto the lounge and fishing through them for clothes that might be suitable. 'It's underwear I need. I can just wear scrubs until my suitcase turns up.'

'It won't turn up,' Yasmeen told her, handing her a bag

with underwear in it. 'And if you don't wear the clothes I bought, the chief will blame me.'

'Blackmail?' Nell said, but yesterday's emergency had forged a bond between them and she smiled as she said it, then grabbed a pair of navy slacks and a loose fitting T-shirt, took the bag of underwear and headed for her bedroom.

The female staff she'd seen yesterday had been in navy slacks and tunic tops, and she'd realised that was acceptable dress code for women who when they went out in public would probably wear long robes over their house clothes. She should show respect for their customs by dressing the same way.

'You can't have slept for six hours if you've done all this shopping,' she said, pulling her hair into a tight knot behind her head as she came back into the living room, dressed and ready to go.

'I left the hospital before you,' the other woman said, then she smiled and Nell knew she, too, felt the bond between them, a bond that had bridged the boundaries of nationalities and cultures.

They walked swiftly back across the other bridge—the one between the living quarters and the hospital—Yasmeen leading Nell to the new burns unit, where the state-of-the-art equipment made Nell feel envious.

'The fifteen we have here will all need grafts. I've taken uninjured skin from some of them and the lab is already working on growing it. We've two types of interactive burn dressings we can use in the meantime—the new ones that promote wound healing of the body tissues—but we've been waiting for your advice on which patients to treat with which dressing.'

Kal delivered this information. He was standing right in front of her, a trolley laden with equipment by his side.

'We have a treatment room, a small theatre and bathing facilities here in the unit, and rooms where family members can stay. We're arranging to fly in a family member for all the patients who aren't local so they have emotional support.'

One look at him was enough to tell Nell he hadn't slept, although he was clean-shaven now except for the very short, neatly trimmed beard and moustache around his mouth.

Traditional, she knew, from the time long ago when she'd tried to persuade him to shave it off so she could see how he looked without it!

'You've done well,' she assured him, then, not daring to suggest he needed sleep, she said instead, 'With your permission, I'll take over now. I'll check the status of each patient and prioritise them again for surgery.'

She glanced at the trolley.

'You've pressure bandages as well as the artificial skin, but will there be enough?'

'More of everything is being flown in, and a group of Spanish doctors and nurses should be on the way this afternoon or tomorrow.'

Nell nodded. It was now common practice for specialist doctors from other countries to help in medical emergencies worldwide.

'I'd like to see all the patients,' Nell said, because although she'd suggested it earlier, Kal had not agreed. Now *he* nodded.

'Yasmeen and I will accompany you. I have surgeons standing by if you want to start debriding burnt tissue.'

'It will depend on the patient's status,' Nell reminded him. 'Some will be able to withstand the trauma of surgery but with others we might have to wait. Three to five days post-burn is still acceptable for surgery, although current thinking is to get it done as soon as possible.'

Yasmeen led the way, and they went from bed to bed, Nell impressed by how efficiently the patients were being nursed, with one staff member to every patient and computerised records up on a screen beside each bed.

'I've removed blisters on this and several other patients,' Kal told her when they stopped by the bed of a teenage girl with severe second-degree burns to her face. 'I know it's a contentious issue, whether the blistered skin aids healing, but my experience suggests the prostaglandin in the blister fluid promotes deeper burns, and on her face—'

He broke off, obviously anxious, and Nell was quick to agree she'd have done the same for the girl. She checked the computer screen.

'The dry dressing is great and I see you're using aspirin for its anti-prostaglandin effect. I'd have gone the same way. What is important is that nurses know to keep cutting back the dressing as the wound heals so the patient isn't tempted to play with a loose edge or pull at it to peel it off. The same goes for the dressings we'll put on grafts, although the dressings on them are harder to get to as we have to immobilise grafted areas.'

While Nell explained this to Kal, Yasmeen was talking to the patient in her own language. As tears welled up in the girl's dark eyes, Nell turned enquiringly to Kal.

'Her parents and brother didn't make it,' he said, his voice hard with frustrated anger. 'We're looking for other relations, but it's difficult with just the plane's manifest to work from. Many people book their seats over the internet these days and although the airline company has contact phone numbers, the number, as in this case, is often of the family home.'

'And no one's there to answer,' Nell said quietly, touching the girl's bandaged hand.

She moved on, knowing there were patients who needed more of her attention. She had to decide which ones might be stable enough to begin the lengthy, painful business of debriding burnt flesh and attaching skin grafts.

'Tell me about the grafts,' Kal said, as they looked at the legs of a woman who had severe burns on the fronts of her legs, particularly around her knees. 'This woman has good skin on her back and buttocks we can use, and we can mesh the skin to make it go further, but we can't use mesh on some places, can we?'

Nell studied the patient, thinking of the instrument called a dermatone that could divide the skin into infinitely thin layers, and how these layers could then be meshed—cut and stretched to go further.

'We never use mesh on the face because it doesn't heal as well.' Nell answered part of the question while examining the woman's arms. 'Generally, we use split-thickness skin grafts on the face or neck or areas where it's in the patient's interests to have a cosmetically good result. Skin from the back or buttocks is good for grafting, but I wonder if in this case we shouldn't take skin from her arm. Could you explain to her I want to push her sleeve up?'

Kal spoke to the woman, taking her hand and looking into her eyes as he introduced Nell and explained.

The woman patted his hand, as if she'd been done the favour, and pushed up the long sleeve of the hospital gown.

'The problem is,' Nell said, running her finger over the woman's smooth, unburnt skin, 'that the graft site—where we take the skin from—is always more painful during recovery than the wound site and just as susceptible to infection. So if we take skin off her back and immobilise her legs to stop the grafts shifting, how's she going to lie?'

Kal shook his head, and smiled ruefully at Nell.

'I knew it was a specialist field, but that's common sense. I should have thought of it.'

'You can't think of everything, but now you know, I think you can start with this woman. She's fit enough in herself to stand an anaesthetic and while you've got her under, you can take off all the burnt tissue, do a small graft from her arm to this area here above the knee. Because the knee needs flexibility, you're better going with a full-thickness graft which has more elasticity. We use epinephrine and thrombin to control the bleeding from the donor site, and xeroform gauze and heat-lamp treatments to help heal the site.'

Kal nodded and spoke to the woman again, then smiled at Nell.

A smile shouldn't make me feel as if the sun's come out, she thought, especially here and now, but before she could pursue this reaction, he was questioning her again.

'Now, if we're taking all the burnt tissue off and only grafting that small area, what's best to use on the rest of the wound?'

'An allograft—false skin—or one of the new preparations that promote wound healing, or maybe, if it's suitable, some of my spray-on skin.'

She smiled at him.

'You didn't think I'd let you go into Theatre without me, did you? I'll be with you and whatever other surgeons you can muster through this first op, though there are other things more important than surgery for me to do after that.'

'Other things more important than surgery!' he grumbled, and this time Nell's reaction was one of remembered pleasure. She and Kal had worked well together all those years ago. It had been their shared dedication to the job that had brought them together—that and an attraction that Nell had never felt before.

Or since, she admitted honestly to herself as Kal spoke again to their patient.

A nurse was sent to get an anaesthetist and a young resident told to prepare the patient for surgery, while Nell moved on, seeing the rest of the patients in the special unit.

'I know it was set up for this reason,' she said to Yasmeen, 'but you could hardly have expected to have to ever deal with this many burn-injured people at once.'

Yasmeen told her about the oil fire and Nell understood that it was for a large-scale emergency Kal had started the unit.

Just in time, as it had turned out…

The patient she thought of as 'her' man was the last she saw. Tucked into a corner of the ward, with mobile equipment monitoring him, Nell almost cheered to see him still alive. But she forgot about cheering when she saw his respiratory function was still poor.

'I'd like to do a fibre-optic bronchoscopy to check his upper respiratory tract, then a proper lung scan. There might be pockets of air trapped in his lungs by obstructions of some kind.'

'I'll arrange it,' Yasmeen told her, giving orders in her own language, though Nell had realised by now that most of the staff spoke some English. 'They must be ready for you in Theatre.'

Nell glanced at her watch but, though she'd set it to local time on the flight, the time didn't seem to mean anything to her. She'd work and then she'd sleep and eventually the days and nights would sort themselves out and her body clock would adjust itself.

But as she was shown into the theatre area by a young nurse, and she saw Kal scrubbing up on the other side of the room, she wondered about his night and day—his body clock.

'You haven't slept—are you up to this?' she demanded, and heard a gasp of what sounded like shock from the theatre sister who was holding out Kal's gown.

Kal turned and grinned at her, the smile lighting up his exhausted face.

'You've shocked Sister Aboud,' he chided. 'Sister Aboud thinks very highly of me and would never speak to me like that.'

Nell smiled at the sister, who was now looking extremely embarrassed.

'When I knew him, he was a fellow student—a post-grad surgical nobody just like me,' she explained, having known from the gasp the woman could understand English.

But the woman didn't seem appeased, and throughout the operation, which was watched by half a dozen other surgeons, she cast doubtful glances Nell's way, as if wondering what the intruder was doing in her theatre.

'Thanks,' Kal said quietly, when they'd done all they could at the moment for the woman. 'You've set me on the right track for future ops.'

'Once the Spanish team gets here, you'll have specialist burns surgeons,' Nell reminded him. 'But in the meantime, that's enough for one day. If you don't get some sleep, you'll collapse on top of a patient and then he or she will sue for injuries sustained in hospital and—'

Kal had pulled off his cap and mask and looked down at her, and the flow of light banter stopped, the words dried up by the expression in his eyes. They burned into hers, seeming to see past all her defences, deep, deep down into her soul.

'I will go and sleep,' he said quietly, 'when I am satisfied all is well in my hospital.'

Uh-oh! Nell thought as he swept away. Was I just put in my place?

But 'mind your own business' hadn't been the message in his eyes. That message had been personal.

Scorchingly personal!

At least he was gone and she could relax and do her job. She stripped off her theatre gear and headed back to the ward, ready to take up where she'd left off, but when she entered the procedures room, ready to insert a nasogastric tube into a patient, Kal was there.

'You need to sleep,' she told him yet again, cross because, at a time when she needed to be fully focussed on her work, Kal's presence was proving a distraction. Physically, because her skin burned—bad analogy—when he was near, and mentally because parts of her mind kept thinking of why she was there—the why that had nothing to do with the burns unit.

'I'm a surgeon and I'm needed here,' he snapped back. 'Now, let's get to work.'

'Kal, there's nothing the doctors here can't handle at the moment. None of the other severely burned patients are well enough for major surgery. The rest of today's jobs are medical, getting patients stabilised, working out their nutritional needs and starting tube feeding. Even those well enough to take food by mouth probably won't be able to eat enough to take in the calories they need—we're talking 3000 to 4000 calories a day. I need a dietician up here to work out their caloric intake and the individual formulas for each patient.'

'Working on the weight of the patient and the severity of their burns?' Kal said. 'Do you use the total body surface area affected in the figuring of their requirements?'

'Yes, it's one of the most important factors, because the extent of the injury determines what the body is losing, particularly in protein.'

'And the problems associated with tube feeding?'

Was he testing her? He would know this stuff. She studied him for a moment before answering, but looking directly at him made her heart feel fluttery so she turned back to the patient on the table.

'Aspiration's the most dangerous—the head of the bed needs to be elevated at thirty degrees and gastric residuals measured frequently—then, too, the tube placement needs to be checked.'

She managed a smile.

'It will drive your head of nursing mad but I think these patients are going to need one-on-one nursing for some time to come.'

Why was he testing her? Kal wished she hadn't smiled. And how the blazes was he going to get the staff to provide one-on-one nursing for any length of time?

He couldn't think straight. He *must* be tired, but he wasn't going to have Nell erupting back into his life and telling him what to do. Though he knew he'd be better off getting some sleep now, and working when she was sleeping. That way he didn't have to go through an experience like the one he'd had in Theatre, where working next to her had been so distracting he'd wanted to swear long and hard.

Which really would have shocked Sister Aboud!

'I'll make sure we have the nurses,' he said, dragging his mind back to the issue at hand. 'There are two small private hospitals, mainly used by expats, and both have offered to lend us staff.'

Nell smiled again, but he knew it was with the pleasure of knowing that the staff would be provided. Then the smile warmed as she ordered gently, 'Go, Khalil. Go and sleep. By tomorrow we'll have more patients well enough to begin excision and grafting, and once that starts it's an ongoing process as we can only do small areas of burn every two to three days.'

No one had ever said his name as Nell said it. Perhaps she was going through a mid-life crisis and was revisiting a lost love.

Reviving a lost love?

Renewing a lost love?

Excitement soared as the falcon had soared, then dropped like a stone as he told himself not to be fanciful. Even if Nell was no longer married, she'd always known of his commitment to family and she'd certainly assume *he* was. Hadn't he told her that's how things worked in his country? One married for life. Sometimes more than once, that was allowable, but marriage was for ever.

Most of the time!

Nell worked through the day and into the night, with Yasmeen and with doctors she didn't know, trying to keep patients alive being the first priority, stabilising them so they'd be well enough for surgery the second. At some stage Kal came back and ordered her to leave the ward, but when she returned the following morning and saw him there, dishevelled and unshaven, she knew he'd stayed on in her place.

'Get some sleep,' she said to him, realising from the way other staff treated him that no one else would dare tell him what to do, although she seemed to be making a habit of it. 'You won't be any use in the state you're in, and there are other surgeons willing to work on any patient well enough for surgery. Skin grafting takes a clear head and a steady hand, Kal, and you've got neither at the moment.'

For a moment she thought he was going to argue, but then he turned and walked away.

'You know him from before?' Yasmeen asked, having watched this small interchange with wonderment.

'We met while he was studying in Australia. Out there he was just a fellow student, not the Grand Poo Bah or whatever he is here.'

'He's not a Poo Bah, or whatever you said, but a sheik,' Yasmeen protested, and Nell regretted her attempted levity. Yasmeen had already demonstrated that she held Kal in some kind of awe. 'His family, they've been our rulers for generations. It is unusual he became a doctor, but he's a good doctor and he's made the hospital what it is, insisting on the best of everything.'

'He's certainly got that,' Nell agreed, but uneasiness stirred within her. She'd always known Kal's family had some kind of standing in this country, although he'd never boasted about them in any way. It was something she'd guessed from his bearing and sometimes from his attitude.

But the ruling family?

Oh, hell! Would that complicate things?

She didn't need, or even particularly want, them to acknowledge Patrick, but she might one day want some of their bone marrow…

Damn!

'Dr Warren, could you come?'

A young nurse drew her towards a patient with twenty per cent burns to his body.

'Here!' The nurse pointed, showing her a small area of redness near the patient's thigh, the first sign of an infection.

Thanking the woman, Nell turned her attention to the task of fighting this invader before it took over the man's body. All thoughts of Kal and his family were forgotten…

CHAPTER THREE

IT WAS late afternoon, and she was unlocking her apartment when Kal emerged from his, refreshed from the sleep but more confused than ever about Nell.

'Do you keep an apartment here because the hospital demands so much of your time?' she asked. 'Wouldn't you have been better going home and having a proper break?'

'This is my home,' he said, looking into the eyes of the woman he'd thought he'd never see again, seeing the dark rims around the irises of her clear grey eyes and tiredness in the bloodshot whites. But the question wouldn't wait any longer.

'Why are you here, Nell?'

She hesitated, just long enough for him to suspect she was going to fob him off.

'I don't want some tale about spray-on skin!' he growled. 'I want the truth.'

The pale eyes pleaded with him.

'I want to tell you, Kal,' she whispered, what little colour there was in her face draining from it. 'But now?'

'Now!' he said, listening to the voice in his head suggesting again that this woman was up to something, and ignoring common sense which reminded him that the hospital desperately needed her expertise.

But she was antagonising him just by being here—making him want to touch her, to take her in his arms and hold her, remembering her body, kiss her, remembering her lips...

'I need a coffee,' she said, walking into her apartment but not shutting the door in his face.

He followed her, and saw the bags and parcels strewn across the couch. He should at least let her unpack. And when was she going to eat?

After she's told me what's going on—that's when!

'Coffee?'

No smile accompanied the offer but that was just as well.

'Please.'

He didn't smile either, but he watched her move as she filled the kettle, her litheness and economy of movement unchanged by the years they'd spent apart. He noticed her hands as she spooned instant coffee into mugs. No rings, but she'd just come from the ward and few staff wore rings at work as they could tear the fragile rubber gloves.

She concentrated on the simple task, not looking at him, not even glancing up to ask him how he liked it.

She pushed a cup towards him, then put sugar on the table.

'There doesn't appear to be any milk anywhere, but I don't mind drinking it black.'

He heard her speak but the anguish in her eyes suggested they weren't the words she wanted to say, so he waited, sipping at his coffee. The old Nell would weigh things up, practise what she wanted to say, but usually, in the end, it would all come out in a rush, as if she was afraid if she stopped to sort the words into the practised order, she'd lose them.

Her parting speech to him had been testimony to that. 'I'll love you for ever—that's all I can say.'

The words had burst from a throat constricted with tears, but the letter she'd pressed into his hands—a letter he'd read and reread on the trip home until it had fallen to pieces in his hands—had contained the rehearsed speech, with words like 'always knew it couldn't be for ever between us' and 'totally understand' and 'admire your loyalty and devotion to your family and your commitment to your promise'.

He watched her struggle for a moment, then it came, a statement so abrupt he had trouble processing it.

'We have a son.'

There was a deafening silence before he could answer.

'We have a son?'

He knew the loudly spoken echo had been his—it was his voice—but the sentence still made no sense.

'A boy. I was pregnant when you left. I didn't know at the time and when I did find out I couldn't tell you because you were going home to get married—you were probably already married by then. It was part of the bargain with your parents, and I couldn't ruin that for you or have you torn between two loyalties or spoil your marriage with that kind of news, and I thought you'd never need to know—'

Kal halted the flow of words the only way he could, by grabbing her shoulders and giving her a little shake.

'Stop right there!' he ordered. 'Right now!'

His voice was rising with his anger. No, his anger was rising much faster, hot and dangerous as the flow of new lava spewing from a volcano.

'I have a *son*? You were pregnant and you didn't tell me? By what right did you make that decision? You, who knew my feelings about family! About blood ties! *My* son, and you kept him from me? How could you? How dared you?'

Nell felt the heat of his rage burning through her T-shirt, as fierce as the flames she'd watched on her arrival. She stared into the furious face of the father of her son and imagined she could see a thousand generations of Bedouin warriors ranging behind him in defence of the family honour.

'Kal—' she began, anxious to explain—aware she'd made a hash of it. But he thrust her away, so roughly she had to catch the bench to stop from falling.

'Kal!' His name was a plaintive plea on her trembling lips, but he'd moved away, striding towards the door, though when he'd flung it open he turned back to glare at her, anger still reverberating in his deep voice as he spoke.

'And where is he now, my son? If he's stuck lib some boarding school...'

An unspoken threat hovered in the air, but Nell ignored it, desperate to calm things down so she could get to the really important part of this revelation.

'He's with my parents. We've always lived with them so they could be there for him while I worked.'

'Which was, of course, important for your fulfillment, no doubt, and your self-esteem and all the other palaver you so-called liberated women go on about.'

That was too much altogether for Nell. Forget calming him down.

'I'd say at least half of the doctors I've met in your hospital are women, so don't make this a women's lib issue,

Kal! I've worked to support my son, and to provide him with a good life.'

'And I couldn't have done that?' Smooth as silk, his voice now—smooth and somehow scary. 'Couldn't have given him far more than your puny salary would ever have provided for him? And what's his name, this son of mine? Warren, after some man you married to gratify your own desires?'

'Get out of here!' Nell ordered, clinging desperately to the last vestiges of control. 'Now!'

She should go after him—try to explain—but she was so exhausted, both from work and the debilitating effect of the fierce confrontation, that Nell sank down onto the lounge amidst the parcels Yasmeen had brought, and buried her face in her hands.

The worst thing about it was he was right. She *had* known how he felt about family. She *had* known that if she'd told him, he'd have returned in an instant and insisted on marrying her.

But what would that have meant to his family? Just how badly would they have taken it, and what damage would it have done to Kal's position within it, when family meant so much to him? Family and honour! Honour was a word not often used in her life but to Kal it was the backbone of his existence. And Nell had known that Kal not marrying the woman to whom he had been betrothed would have brought dishonour both on the woman and on his family…

She heard the sound of a key in the door and raised her head.

He was back.

'And your parents? Are they still in the same place?'

Nell struggled to her feet.

'Why? What are you going to do?'

'I'm sending someone to get my son.'

Fear for Patrick propelled Nell across the room. She grasped Kal's arm.

'You'd kidnap him?'

He shook off her hands

'Don't be so melodramatic. I'll merely send a plane and some of my people to take care of him on the journey. You'll phone your family to let them know what's happening.'

Nell couldn't believe she was hearing this.

'You can't do that. You can't just fly into a country and take a child out of it.'

'If he's my son, he's hardly a child.'

Nell gasped at the implication of his words, but she didn't have time to protest. She had too much to explain.

'Kal, we need to sit down and talk rationally about this. There's so much you don't know—so much to explain—but I can't talk to you when you're in this mood.'

'Then don't talk to me. The time to talk was fourteen years ago, Nell. You've left it too late.'

He saw the pain of his words etching lines down her cheeks, deep as acid burns, but the rage within him was too hot and strong to prevent him hurting her.

'Kal?'

She touched his arm again and for a moment, hearing his name on her lips, feeling her fingers on his arm, he almost weakened, then he remembered this woman had denied him his son for thirteen years.

He could *never* weaken.

He walked away instead—out of her apartment. She hadn't answered his question but the hospital would have records of Nell's address, and the boy would be there. The plane was always on standby. One phone call and it would be ready to roll by the time his staff reached the airport. The new jet would make good time, and with the time difference they'd arrive late afternoon in Australia. The Spanish burns team was due to start work at the hospital in the morning so he'd have time to go to the airport and meet the boy.

He'd take Nell—there'd be awkwardness and he'd need her to smooth things over on this first meeting…

He lifted the phone to call the airport then heard the knock on the door. He knew it was Nell and hesitated, then put down the receiver and crossed the room.

Nell looked around. The apartment looked very similar to the one she was using, except that books were stacked on the low coffee-table and on the end tables beside the couch. Stacked, too, on the kitchen divider—the books the only sign someone used the place.

She looked at Kal, wanting to ask why he needed so many books in what had to be a place he used only occasionally, but what Kal did or didn't need in his apartment wasn't her concern.

And he'd always had books—always been reading—not only about medicine, but about anything and everything.

It was a trait Patrick had inherited…

Thinking of Patrick steeled her for the confrontation. She studied Kal's face desperately seeking some kind of softening, but it remained implacably set against her, granite hard, while his eyes still burned with anger.

She took a deep breath and rushed the words towards him.

'Patrick has cancer. He's in remission right now, but he needs constant monitoring.'

Just saying it brought back the nightmare of the last eighteen months—the initial diagnosis, then the treatment, the joy of the first remission so soon after treatment and then the devastation of the relapse. She could feel her heart beating erratically and a hard lump growing in her throat, but if she showed weakness for one second, Kal would pounce.

He watched her swallow and wondered what it had cost her to say those words. Pain was squeezing *his* rib cage and he didn't know the boy.

'He has cancer and even then you didn't think to contact me?' he asked, the pain confusing him because it seemed to be dampening his anger, and he needed his anger to handle this situation. 'What kind of cancer?'

'Leukaemia. T-cell ALL. He's in remission at the moment, but it's the second remission and if it fails he'll need—'

And suddenly it all became clear.

'A bone-marrow transplant! You keep a son from me for thirteen years and now you're here to beg me to help him?'

He flung the accusation at her then frowned.

'But parents are no good—you need a sibling for a match.'

His eyes narrowed.

'Are you telling me you want another child? A child of mine? You've come here for, what, a month, hoping to get me to father another child which you'll then take away from me. And is this fair to this child—?'

Nell stopped him, which was probably just as well. His

head was all over the place and he had no idea how he felt about any of this.

'It's not about another child, Kal. I didn't even think of that. Anyway, there's only a thirty to thirty-five per cent chance of a sibling being a perfect match. But the procedures are much better for mismatched bone-marrow transplants these days. Parents usually have a three out of six HLA match—the human leukocyte antigens that are the genetic markers on the white blood cells—and that's really not enough. Not yet, although if we can't do better, the specialists are willing to go with a parent's bone marrow. The problem is, although he's on a register for donors, he has some HLA antigens in his blood that aren't found in Australia. Apparently…'

She stopped, as if she found the rest of the bizarre explanation impossible to continue. Well, he wasn't going to help her, not one little bit. The more she talked, the more his gut twisted at the thought of this son he didn't know suffering so much. T-cell ALL—acute lymphoblastic leukaemia with involvement of the T-cells. His mind was recalling all he knew of it, considering the damage it did, and the worse damage the treatment could cause.

'Apparently these antigens are found more frequently in a specific ethnic group and though he might not need bone marrow—this remission might last, he might be cured—I couldn't take the risk, Kal. I had to find out if you had a bone-marrow donor programme over here, and if maybe someone on it… Maybe you or someone in your family even…'

Kal stared at her, seeing the strain in her pale exhausted face, hating her yet wanting to hold and comfort her.

Dangerous thoughts, dismissed immediately.

'Don't expect me to feel sorry for you,' he snapped. 'There was no need at all for you to have gone through this on your own. And where's Mr Warren? Where does he fit in? If you are married, why are you still living with your parents?'

He stepped towards her because anger had returned a thousandfold, though this time it was a different kind of anger—jealous anger—so unexpected it drove him beyond all bounds of decency and common sense.

'Have you left him, too? And why's that, Nell? Did he not kiss you like this?'

He seized her by the shoulders and dragged her towards his body, bending his head and capturing her lips in a hard, possessive kiss.

Tasting Nell again! He didn't drink but could there be more intoxication in alcohol than there was in kissing Nell?

Her lips parted, perhaps in protest, but he refused to release her, feeling her body soften, then slump against him, feeling her lips respond and a faint puff of air as she murmured his name.

One hand moved from her shoulders, his finger trailing downwards to the soft mound of a breast, teasing at the nipple through the clothing she wore, his mind gloating as he heard her sudden intake of breath.

'Did he not make you whimper when he touched you, Nell? Is that it?'

She broke away so suddenly it shocked him back to some measure of sanity, but regret at his behaviour was all mixed up with regret that the kiss had ended. Until he saw her face—saw disappointment etched into it and deep shadows of sadness in her lovely eyes.

'Nell!'

She turned away from him and walked towards the door, and though he followed and caught up, he didn't dare touch her to stop her leaving, for fear he'd need to hold her close again.

'Let me know if you think you can help.'

She threw the words over her shoulder, but he heard the thickness of tears in them and his heart ached for her—yearned to comfort her—but how?

'Nell?'

She turned now and he saw the tears, not streaming down her cheeks—oh, no, she was far too strong for that. But they were pooled in her eyes, valiantly held back, and fear joined anger in his heart.

Had his rash words and harsh behaviour ruined any chance they might have had of being friends again?

You don't want her for a friend but for a lover!

This idea spun him even further out of his orbit, and Nell was standing there, looking at him. Waiting for what he had to say?

For an apology?

She's the one who should be apologising.

'We have a fledgling donor programme but I can look into expanding it. And of course I'll have the test,' he said, aware how lame the words sounded, and knowing it wasn't what he wanted to say.

Or not all of it.

Nell nodded, then turned away, continuing on to her apartment. She knew her back was straight but inside she felt as if her bones were crumbling and all the soft parts of her melting.

With anger *and* desire.

How dared Kal kiss her like that? That was the anger talking.

But why had she been so stupid as to pull away? That was desire. A desire so fierce and strong, so easily rekindled even after fourteen years, that she *had* very nearly whimpered in his arms. How *could* she have been so weak? This wasn't about her, and physical gratification. This was about Patrick.

'But there'll be some conditions!'

She was halfway through the door when she heard this rider, and she spun around, aware he was close—probably too close—but needing to see his face, to see if he could possibly mean he'd attach provisos to an act that could save his son's life.

His eyes, their colour still a fascination to her—pale brown like good brandy—challenged her to defy his statement, challenged her to ask what kind of conditions. But she'd had enough of Kal and the emotion-entangling games he was playing.

'Whatever!' she said, and shrugged carelessly, although her heart was breaking. This man wasn't the Kal she'd loved and whose memory had shone so brightly in her life for the last fourteen years, but there was no way she'd let him witness her distress.

'Marriage!' he growled as she turned away once again. 'We'll legitimise my son!'

This time she couldn't face him. Here was an offer she'd fantasised about so often over the years, although now it felt repugnant.

'As your second wife?' she snapped, angry because with

that one word he'd killed the dreams she'd had. 'Or would it be third? Or fourth, perhaps? Changed your mind about monogamy since your idealistic youth?'

She continued walking into the apartment as she spoke, but heard his footsteps on the càrpet behind her so when he put his hand—just one hand this time—on her shoulder and spun her around, she wasn't as startled by his touch as she'd been earlier.

'My only wife,' he snapped right back at her. 'My other wife and I divorced. Our marriage never worked out. All I did was make her unhappy—too unhappy even to conceive a child. I blamed myself—I blamed that destructive, intangible, idiotic concept you westerners call love—for the whole debacle. Remember love, Nell?'

'Yes, I do remember love!' she retorted. 'And it's not some destructive, intangible or idiotic concept, but emotion, Kal. Real emotion! Remember emotion?'

'Emotion?' he queried, stepping closer. Dangerously close. 'Emotion, Nell, or sex?'

And once again he put both hands on her shoulders, only this time he didn't drag her closer, but stepped to narrow the gap between them, so that their bodies were all but touching, so close Nell could feel the desire between them, like static electricity arcing in dry air.

She knew he was going to kiss her again even before she saw his head bend towards her, and although his hands were non-restraining on her shoulders, she couldn't move.

If he kisses you again you're gone, her head yelled at her, but her body burned for a touch it should have forgotten long ago, and her breasts ached for his hands to hold them.

He kissed her again.

This time he'd seduce her, Kal decided. He gentled his lips so they tempted and teased, the harsh demands of the earlier kiss hidden behind this provocative flirtation. He drew her closer, feeling her body melt against his, fitting his contours as if they'd been designed as one then split apart into male and female.

Her lips seemed to swell in lushness, her tongue touched his, timidly at first, then teasing and enticing. He knew his arousal would be hard against her belly—knew she'd be aware he wanted her—his desire matched in intensity by hers, if the small gasping noises she was making were any indication.

Then she whispered his name and whatever restraint he might have been clinging to gave way altogether. He swept her into his arms and carried her through to the bedroom, tossing her on the bed, then pulling off her shoes and throwing them aside, running his hands up her legs until he came to the waistband of her slacks, unfastening, unzipping, reefing the long trousers off her.

'Kal!'

If it was a protest it was a half-hearted one, not strong enough to stop his calm, deliberate task of undressing her.

'It is our custom for the bride to be in layers of clothing—a wedding gown, a cap and breastplate of gold, then black robes, covering all her clothes, and veils covering her face. We unwrap our brides as we do a very special parcel.'

The words penetrated the fog of desire that had wrapped around Nell like the veils he spoke of.

'But I am not your bride!' she answered. 'And neither—'

He stopped the words with another kiss, stealing her

breath and making a lie of her attempts to stop this unbelievable seduction.

But now that she was sitting, it was easier for him to peel off her T-shirt. Still kissing her to stifle further protests, he unfastened her bra, releasing her breasts. Nell knew she could stop him with a couple of well-chosen words. Although maybe she couldn't! She would have been able to stop the old Kal but this man, intent now on undressing himself, coldly preparing to make love to her—this was a man she didn't know.

So why not stop him?

Shame forced her to admit it was because she wanted him. She wanted to lose herself in him—to forget the last few years with the strain of Patrick's illness, and to escape, if only momentarily, the horror of the fire and the pain and mutilation of the patients she must tend.

Kal was naked, his body hard and lean. He sat beside her on the bed then turned, his eyes unreadable, his lips set in a thin line.

'Are you ready?'

It was such a bizarre question she couldn't answer it. She frowned up at him, but then he put his hand flat on her stomach and her heart lurched at the touch. His hand moved lower, his fingers tangling in her pubic hair, seeking out the aching centre of her womanhood, while his head bent so his tongue could tease her breast.

His fingers explored, his lips nuzzled and sensation transported Nell to a place where thought was impossible, her body a quivering mass of nerve endings, responding to Kal's as if hard-wired to it all those years ago. Electricity tingled in her toes, and her head buzzed with sensation as he drew her with unrelenting mastery to a gasping, shattering climax. Then he entered her, driving deep into the hot, hungry centre of her being, again and again until the waves of orgasm broke once more, swamping her so she had to cling to him, whispering his name into the smooth skin of his shoulder, feeling his own tension build to a final release.

His body relaxed and she wanted to hold him, to feel his weight on top of her, to keep the closeness for ever, but he rolled away, once again sitting up on the side of the bed, his back towards her.

'There'll be papers to sign, of course, to formalise things, but we're married, you understand.'

It was a statement, not a question, and so coldly uttered Nell shivered, then gathered her scattered wits and sat up herself.

'Married! Don't be ridiculous, Kal. We had sex, nothing more. Two people hungry for each other. Seeking satisfaction and release. Marriage? The very idea of it is ridiculous.'

He turned towards her, his face all hard planes and angles, no sign of post-coital softness despite the shuddering climaxes they'd shared.

'Why did you marry this Warren man if not for sex? Did you love him? Did he leave you? I'm assuming you're not still married to him. You couldn't have changed so much you'd cheat on your husband, and you could have stopped me at any time during that little performance.'

That little performance? Was that all it had been? A performance to show how easily he could dominate her? Of how easily he could manipulate her feelings?

Well, two could play that game! She could be just as cool and detached as he could. It didn't matter that her insides were aglow with satisfaction and her body all but twitching with the hope that it could happen again.

Soon!

'Garth Warren was a good man—a close friend. We'd known each other for a long time, and I thought maybe it would be good for Patrick to have a male influence in his life.'

'I'm glad you didn't use the word father!' Kal growled. 'So what happened to this paragon?'

'Garth? We parted within six months. It wasn't fair to have married him in the first place because I didn't love him, and as things went on I knew I never could. He's remarried to a lovely woman and I'm godmother to their twins.'

'How civilised you westerners are!' The derisive retort was so unlike Kal, Nell wondered if she'd ever really known him. 'Love or no love, if you were my wife, I'd have chained you in a cellar before I let you go.'

'But you did let me go,' Nell reminded him softly.

'You were not my wife, though you would have been if you'd told me of my son.'

He stopped abruptly and turned to her again, his face now puzzled.

'My son. His name is Patrick?'

Nell nodded, wondering if this, too, would make him angry, but all he said was, 'Why?'

'I remembered you telling me of the tutor you'd had, and how it had been his influence that had made you decide to study medicine.' Nell shrugged. 'He seemed to mean a lot to you…'

Kal stood up and left the room. He was forty years old, yet his emotions were as tumultuous as the most raw adolescent's. This woman had thrown his life into total chaos.

First she'd fired his body to such an extent he'd behaved like the barbarian she probably believed him to be. Then she'd fired this rocket into the congealed mess that had once been his mind.

She'd called his son Patrick! Named him after the man who'd given Kal so much. His love of books—the inspiration to do medicine—the strength to break from family tradition by studying something apart from business—and the confidence to bargain with his father to make it possible.

His son was called Patrick.

He left the apartment, aware in the part of him that had always been true to the manners and decency and moral behaviour instilled in him that he had behaved very badly towards Nell. So what if the sex had been unbelievable?

He groaned to himself as he entered his apartment, and, pleased to be diverted from his thoughts, picked up the phone to retrieve the messages signalled by the red flashing light.

The Spanish team was definitely due to arrive the following morning. One of the burn victims in the ICU had died. Two of the less critical patients in other wards were being repatriated to their home countries and Lalla had organised nursing staff to travel with them. His mother would like him to phone her when he had time, and a Mrs Roberts had phoned from Australia.

Mrs Roberts? Nell's mother?

Patrick! Something was wrong with the boy and Mrs Roberts didn't want to tell Nell directly.

He dialled the number that had been left, not thinking for a minute of the time difference, though when a cheerful voice answered the phone he realised it would be morning in Australia.

'Oh, Kal, I am so sorry to bother you, but I've been trying to phone Nell and can't seem to make the receptionist at the hospital understand me. In the end I thought of you. Could you, please, ask her to phone me?'

'Is it Patrick? Is he ill again? Should we come?'

There was an audible gasp, then Mrs Roberts said, 'Oh, she's told you already. I'm so glad. And so sorry, too, Kal, for the way things turned out. You, her, Patrick—but no, he's fine. He's staying over at a friend's place for a couple of days—they're studying together for a chemistry exam. But Don, Mr Roberts, he's been on a waiting list for a kidney for a long time and they phoned last night to say there was one available. I wanted to let Nell know and to tell her I'd be in touch as soon as the op was done, and also that I've arranged for someone to look after Patrick because I'll want to stay at the hospital as much as possible. My sister, Mary, is arriving this afternoon.'

Maybe it was the distance between them, but Mrs Roberts sounded remarkably calm for a woman whose husband was about to undergo major surgery and whose grandson was in remission from leukaemia.

'Has Mr Roberts been seriously ill? Shouldn't Nell be there? Won't you want her support?'

'I'd like nothing better,' Mrs Roberts said, 'but you don't know Nell too well if you think she'd leave her patients to come home and hold my hand. She knows her dad has the best doctors available, and she knows how much he wanted this—to get off the dialysis—so she'll be worried but she'll be pleased as well. But I don't want her to worry about Patrick.'

'I'll look after Nell, and Patrick, too,' Kal heard himself say. 'She probably hasn't had time to tell you, but I'm thinking of bringing him over here. It seems like a good idea to get to know him while Nell's working in the country.'

Kal knew this was toying with the truth, but found himself driven by something beyond rational thought or reasoning.

'Oh, Kal, that's wonderful. I've been so worried about him—about how he'll handle seeing his grandfather when he comes home from hospital. Patrick has always thought that his grandfather is ten feet tall and bulletproof. He understands about the operation, of course, and knows Don will need time to recover, but to see him weak—I've been worried about the effect that would have on Patrick.'

Mrs Roberts hesitated and though anger was racing through Kal once again—it should be *he* Patrick looked up to—he knew he had to sound calm and in control.

'Then it will be good all round if he's here,' he said, and was congratulating himself on his composure when Mrs Roberts raised another doubt.

'But what about his tests? Patrick's blood tests and regular check-ups? His medication?'

'Mrs Roberts, I'm a doctor, I live at the hospital, we have some of the best pathologists and oncologists in the world here. You can be very sure that Patrick will be well cared for. Now, let's get the main things sorted out. When is Mr Roberts being admitted and where?'

'We're leaving in ten minutes for All Saints Private.

Nell knows the number, but tell her not to keep phoning. I'll be sure to contact her whenever there's any news.'

Kal assured her once again that he'd look after Nell, then offered his private number and his mobile number.

'If I can't take the call, it will switch to a paged message so call me any time—day or night—and leave a number where I can call you back.'

Mrs Roberts said goodbye, and Kal hung up and stared out the window at the bright lights of the city, and beyond them the blackness that was the desert.

He'd done it! He'd made a commitment to see his son. *Not in a particularly honourable way!*

Anyway, honourable or not, it was for the best, though, of course, Nell might not agree.

Nell. Over here, helping his people, working at his hospital, while at home her father was about to undergo major surgery. He felt the first stirrings of guilt. His conscience reminded him of his recent behaviour towards her. He even felt a pang of anxiety for her—a wish that he could spare her the pain and worry he knew this news would cause.

Would she be sleeping now?

If so, should he let her sleep? Tell her in the morning, by which time her father's operation might be successfully completed?

Wouldn't that be better than having her lying awake all night, worried and anxious, as she waited for her mother's call?

Though her mother would call him first, not Nell. For some reason he hadn't given Mrs Roberts Nell's direct number. Was it so he could shield Nell if the news was bad? Tell her himself rather than have her hear it over a telephone?

Maybe some of the gentleness Kal had always believed made a man a better person remained, though he'd shown precious little gentleness to Nell earlier.

Still debating whether to tell Nell or not, he walked out of his apartment, his bunch of keys dangling from his fingers. He knocked quietly on her door, a strange thought rising unbidden in his mind.

If she's awake and I tell her and she's upset, then the obvious thing to do would be to stay with her to comfort her through the long anxious hours. He could lie with her, hold her...

He refused to listen to whatever else might be suggested, but quietly unlocked the door, aware of his invasion of Nell's space but needing to see her.

She was sleeping soundly, a sheet across her naked body, her shoulder-length dark hair splayed across the pillow, her lashes black on cheeks so pale he again felt a pang of guilt about what had transpired earlier.

He wouldn't wake her, but he'd sleep close by, his phone set to vibrate rather than ring, so when the news came—and, please, God it would be good—he could tell her straight away.

That decision made, he should move. He knew he should. But the sight of the sleeping woman held him in thrall, and he stood and watched her breathe and thought of all he didn't know about her—and of all the time they'd wasted.

Surprised by what seemed like regret, he searched around inside himself.

No, the anger hadn't gone, and why should it? She'd been wrong not to tell him she was pregnant, but right now her family was in trouble and she was far from home. He backed away into the living room, where he swept all the shopping bags off the lounge and tried it for size. Pulling one of the cushions down for a pillow, he settled on the floor. He slept better in the desert with just the sand beneath him. Sleeping on the floor was no hardship.

It wasn't exactly a snore, more just heavy breathing, loud enough for Nell, when she stirred in her sleep, to notice it.

The sound wasn't close enough to bother her, but she slipped out of bed and was about to go and investigate when she became aware of her naked state. She really should have gone through the clothes Yasmeen had left—the ones in the living room, where the noise was.

She pulled off the top sheet to wrap around her body and tiptoed out. Moonlight lit the room, as it had her bedroom, but in its glow she could see nothing to explain the noise.

Maybe it was just the water pipes…

No, that was definitely a snore. Not a loud snore, more a kind of snort, but definitely a noise made in sleep.

She crept towards the couch, thinking maybe a very small person might be curled up on it, then she saw the figure on the floor.

Kal?

Why had he returned to her apartment?

And what was he doing, sleeping on the floor?

She couldn't think of a logical explanation to either of the questions, but felt contrarily glad that he was here. Oh, he'd spoken harshly—acted harshly too—but she couldn't believe the gentle man who'd lived inside the arrogant one she'd first met in Australia could have disappeared altogether.

She stared at him, bemused by the very different sides of Kal. It had been the arrogant man who'd made the loud noises about marriage.

But the gentle man *was* still there inside him. She'd seen him in action on the ward. Maybe it was only in personal relations that the arrogant man held sway.

She made her way quietly back to bed. She was too tired to consider what Kal might or might not be doing on her floor, or to work out how much or little he'd changed since she'd known him before.

It had been fourteen years after all. Didn't everyone change with time?

Not Kal! her heart prayed, but her body burned with memories of their love-making and she was forced to admit that, yes, he'd changed. The old Kal had been a wild, exciting lover, demanding, yes, but always—well, lover-like. Tender in his whispered words, warmly loving and affectionate in the afterglow of love. Tonight's Kal had been ruthlessly competent, bringing her an almost unendurable pleasure but remote from her—detached—so unemotional she'd felt his coldness sweep across her when he'd drawn away.

So why on earth was he sleeping on her floor?

Penance?

Kal?

Hardly!

Nell went back to bed. Against all common sense she was strangely comforted by the sound of his breathing and she slid quickly into a dreamless sleep.

Less comforting was his news next morning. He was in the kitchen when she came out—again wrapped in the sheet as she needed clean clothes from the parcels in the living room. Beyond him, through the windows, she could see the city, and as she grew closer she could see the parkland surrounding the hospital, gardeners way down below working on keeping it neat and trim.

Why was she thinking about parkland?

So she didn't have to think about Kal being in her apartment?

Or about her reaction to his presence?

'Nell.' His voice was gentle as he stepped towards her, and her heart leapt. He was going to apologise for last night. They could start again. Try to bridge the gulf between them. 'Your mother phoned last night.'

He was close enough to grab her as she whispered, 'Patrick?' Close enough to pull her to him and hold her as he explained.

'Not Patrick, but your father. It's all right. He's OK. Your mother phoned to say they'd found a donor kidney for him and he was going straight in to have the operation. I didn't wake you because she said she'd ring again as soon as it was over. I've just spoken to her—it went well, and he's conscious.'

Nell pulled away and looked up at the man who'd given her this startling news.

'Is that why you slept on the floor?'

Kal nodded, not able to explain the need to be near her.

'Thank you,' Nell said, so formally he knew he'd somehow made things worse, not better, between them. 'I'll phone home now—or phone the hospital. And I'll have to ring Patrick, too. He'll have been worried sick.'

'He's at a friend's place and didn't know until your

mother rang to tell him it was successful. Someone called Mary is going to stay at the house with him so your mother can be at the hospital.'

Until I get there, Kal should have added, but he knew Nell would fight him on this. If she'd wanted Patrick to meet his father, she'd have brought him with her on this trip.

He told Nell the name of the hospital he'd written down and waited, but she turned away from him, heading straight for the phone. He could see her fingers trembling as she dialled the numbers, but he couldn't find anything to say to comfort her.

You set the parameters of this relationship with your be-haviour last night, the voice in his head reminded him, and he swore under his breath and left the room.

CHAPTER FOUR

ONCE satisfied all was well at home, and buoyed by news that the surgeons were delighted with her father's progress, Nell ordered breakfast, then showered and dressed for work while she waited for it to be delivered.

Concern about her father's continued recovery was keeping other thoughts at bay, and for that she was grateful. But when she entered the burns unit a little later, the first person she saw was Kal, and her body surged with remembered passion, while her heart fluttered with what couldn't possibly be love. How could she still feel love for Kal after his behaviour last night?

You responded last night!

The accusation, silent though it was, reminded her, and remembering made her blush.

'Where will we start?' she said to Yasmeen, anxious to get her mind focussed totally on work. In the past—when Kal had left—she'd used work to blot out her emotions. Now, older and stronger, surely she could do the same.

'With the patients who need surgery?' Yasmeen suggested, and Nell followed her to the bed of the first of these, an airport worker who'd been one of the first onto the burning plane and who, in trying to rescue people, had been badly burned himself.

He had enough unburned skin to take some both for growing new and for grafting. Again, the good skin could be sliced into very fine layers to make it go further.

'The worst burns are on his arms.' Kal had been at the patient's bedside and now he moved a little away to point this out to her.

'Which means if we excise the injured tissue right down to the fascia, taking off the underlying fat, we'll get good blood supply to the graft so a better chance of it taking, but he'll be left with bad disfigurement as the fat layers never grow back and his arms will look so thin they'll be stick-like.'

She looked at Kal.

'Will that matter to him, do you think?'

'He's a young man and good-looking. I think it might,' Yasmeen said, her voice tentative, giving Nell the impression she was shy in Kal's presence—or unused to working closely with him.

'Yasmeen's right,' Kal said, smiling gently at the other doctor, as if he, too, had sensed her diffidence. 'We are a proud people, and perhaps too conscious of our looks. Do you think the risk of performing a shallower, tangential excision and grafting onto the superficial fat is too big to take?'

Nell thought about it for a moment, her gaze straying back to the patient in the bed. He *was* a good-looking young man.

'OK, here are the facts. We'll get more blood loss with the tangential, so we have to be sure he's strong enough to cope with that. We also need to have extra blood on standby in Theatre. And if the graft doesn't take, we'll have to try again, and each time we lose a graft and have to try another one, the wound gets bigger. But I'm happy for you to go that way if you both believe it's in his best interests long term.'

Kal nodded then looked at Yasmeen again.

'Let's ask him,' Yasmeen suggested, and she turned to the very ill young man lying in the bed. She spoke briskly in the fluid-sounding language, and though Nell had found a tutor to teach Patrick Arabic from the time he'd been a young child, she understood very few of the words herself.

'Least scarring,' Yasmeen confirmed. 'I'll stay here and do the paperwork to get him to Theatre. The patient in bed six is the one you should see next.'

'You're sure you're all right to be working?' Kal asked as he accompanied Nell to the next patient.

'Better working than brooding,' Nell assured him. 'At least here my mind is fully occupied with patients and I don't have time to worry about Dad.'

'Fully occupied, Nell?' he murmured, sending a frisson of reaction through her body.

'*Fully* occupied!' she lied, glaring at him. 'Are you so vain as to believe that with these patients to tend and my father just out of Theatre, I'd be thinking of you?'

Kal smiled, a knowing smile that said he knew she'd lied, and that simple shifting of his lips and the glimpse of strong white teeth turned the frisson into a tremor.

'Your mother will let you know if anything goes wrong, and one of my family's jets is on standby should you need to fly home.'

Nell turned to him, the words not really making sense. Common sense while she was still frissoning and tremoring? And *one* of the jets? How many could one family have?

'A jet's on standby?'

Kal frowned at her.

'You're a guest in our country and doing a great service for us—greater than was originally intended. Of course we will see you get home as swiftly as possible, should it be necessary. I arranged for the crew to be on standby as soon as your mother phoned last night.'

I should thank him, Nell thought, but somehow the words wouldn't come. Being near Kal was confusing enough, battling the physical stuff even more debilitating, but kindness? No, she really couldn't handle kindness.

She forced her mind firmly back to the task in hand—first, deciding which patients were well enough for surgery, then working out treatment and procedures for the others.

They listed four patients for Theatre, then Kal headed off, as he'd be operating. Nell demonstrated to the nurses and junior medical staff how to gently slough off burned skin in the special bath. She then, with Yasmeen translating, reiterated all the information already given about barrier nursing, clean gowns and gloves, careful hand-washing—all the extreme measures staff had to take to prevent the spread of infection in the newly revealed wounds—and demonstrated how the spray-on dressing could be used to close them.

Her last patient was the man who'd been left for dead, and to her dismay he was no better. She'd been present when a specialist had checked his lungs, so she knew there was no damage, yet with only second-degree burns and with those only on about twelve per cent of his body, he should be picking up.

Was it because he had no family—he hadn't, as yet, been identified—that he was making so little progress? Not even certain of his nationality, Nell still talked to him all the time she examined him, seeking the smallest sign of infection beneath the charred skin, checking his obs and test results again and again in search of some underlying problem that might explain his continuing decline.

In the end she knew no more and had to leave him with his nurse and make her way to the doctors' office. She was already late for her meeting with the dietitian to discuss the IV feeding of individual patients. The secretary someone had found for her translated the medical information on the computer from Arabic to English and, working with the dietitian and the computerised observations, patient weight and the urine and blood test results of each patient, they worked out the necessary nutritional needs for each individual.

'Should we change this daily?' the dietitian asked, and Nell shook her head.

'Maybe every second day, though if the obs show any deterioration in a patient's status I'll call you straight away.'

Two patients, they decided, could try oral feeding. Both had family support, and with encouragement should be able to manage the high calorie intake required to rebalance their bodies.

'No tea or coffee,' the dietitian reminded Nell. 'Just high-protein supplements for drinks. I'll write it up and make sure both the nurses and the kitchens understand.'

'And speak to the family members too, perhaps,' Nell suggested. 'They're the ones likely to bring in things that their relative might enjoy, without realising that everything he or she eats should be going towards their "good calorie" tally.'

The dietitian smiled as Nell put the two important words into inverted commas with her fingers.

'We do that, too,' she said, and Nell laughed, always pleased and surprised to find how little difference there was between her and the women with whom she now worked.

She felt the same bond with the physiotherapist and occupational therapist who followed the dietitian into the office. Both were aware the needs of burns patients differed from other hospitalised patients, but neither had had experience of dealing with them or of organising the special programmes they needed.

'It's important for us—the doctors—to watch for any change in the patient's sensory perception. Facial swelling can distort vision, or wounds might prevent patients wearing glasses or hearing aids, but we can miss things that the nurses or you therapists might pick up on, so be extra-vigilant.'

The young male physiotherapist assured Nell they would be, then asked questions about the advisability of patients exercising when they were in so much pain.

'The pain does make them reluctant to move any part of their bodies,' Nell agreed, conscious as she spoke that Kal had entered the room. 'But the wounds cause contractures so they need to exercise. Part of the problem with burns patients, more so than with, say, post-op patients, is irritability and agitation. This makes it harder to persuade them to try even gentle movement. Sometimes family members will help by encouraging the patient, but of course you then get the family member who tells you not to bother their son or brother, so you're battling on two fronts.'

They discussed the disorientation of patients in hospital and the necessity to always explain to the patient exactly what was happening. The OT would work with

establishing good self-care routines with those well enough
to undertake simple tasks for themselves, while the phys-
io had a number of ideas for exercise that could suit even
the most badly burned patients.

'You shouldn't have to be putting in extra time, teaching other people their jobs. Surely all the information is in
their textbooks or on the internet,' Kal scolded. 'You're
doing more than enough on the medical side.'

The secretary had departed with the two therapists, she
to get some lunch for Nell and the other two to return to
their jobs, so she and Kal were alone in the room. She
looked at him as he sat down across the desk from her and
tried to read his mood.

No chance! His face betrayed nothing, and the eyes that
had once softened when he'd looked at her stared resolutely
at a point somewhere beyond her left shoulder.

'The information *is* available, but if you haven't worked
with burns patients before, you could be tentative, and the
patients need certainty and firm, though caring handling.
They've suffered a terrible psychological blow as well as
the insult to their bodies, and need all the help they can get
to make it through these initial stages of hospitalisation.'

She paused for a minute, thinking back over her early
experience in burns.

'Actually, they need even more psychological support
later, when they realise just how long term their treatment
is going to be. There's no quick fix with burns, unfortunately. Speaking of which, how did the ops go?'

This is good, the voice in her head congratulated her.
You stood up to Kal and now you're talking to him professional to professional, and hardly quaking at all inside.

'They went well,' he said, and Nell was sure he'd added a little prayer under his breath. But he was doing the 'professional to professional' business far better than she was. There was absolutely no indication in his face, or voice, or bearing, that last night he'd decreed they would be married, or that he'd then made her breathless with his love-making.

Love-making?

Unfortunately, while her head was querying the word he was speaking again, and she missed the first part. Something about the Spanish team.

'The team is made up of two plastic surgeons and two teams of theatre nurses. Naturally, they have more expertise in this field than I have, so although I want to learn whatever I can, I have to return to my own duties and my own surgical patients and will be here less often.'

Yes? And that means what? Nell was totally confused. Professional to professional was all well and good, but what about the personal issues yet to be resolved?

Was he being kind? Avoiding upsetting her further while she was concerned about her father's health?

Or did he intend to continue with this marriage idea and come to her apartment every night? Coolly professional by day, hot but emotionless lover at night?

Nell shuddered.

'Are you all right? Did you eat breakfast? Have you had lunch?'

Another switch in mood, but before Nell could reply, the secretary returned with Nell's lunch on a tray. The young woman bobbed a kind of bow to Kal, put down the tray and scampered away.

Nell was about to make a comment about the subservience many members of the staff showed him when he sighed.

'Ever since I started work at the hospital, it's been like that,' he said, his voice heavy with what sounded like genuine regret. 'I try to tell them that I'm just another doctor, but our people—the locals, not the staff who've come from other lands—still insist on some form of acknowledgement. It must have been bred into them with their mother's milk.'

He sighed again.

'Does it bother you so much that you sigh over it?' Nell asked, then realised it was hardly a professional-to-professional type question.

He looked directly at her, his usually alert gaze turned inward.

'Yes, it does,' he said then his eyes narrowed and he focussed on her. 'But, then, a lot of things bother me. Isn't it the case with everyone? You, for instance. Aren't you bothered by the fact you kept my son's life a secret from me for so long?'

The question was so unexpected, coming as it had when Nell had been lulled into a false sense of security by talk of work, that she couldn't answer it immediately. By the time she was ready to tell him that it wasn't a question that could be answered with a yes or no, he'd left the room, walking out as quietly as he'd walked in, leaving only his aura, haunting Nell like a wounded ghost.

A wounded ghost?

Hadn't she been just as wounded?

Don't start feeling sorry for him—he's hard as nails, as tough and deadly as the desert he loves so much.

She reached in her pocket for the card with the phone number of her father's hospital on it. It would be evening at home, and right now what she needed was to touch base with her family. To ground herself with their voices—maybe even speak to her father if he was well enough. Then she'd phone home and talk to Patrick. Her family were her life—her reality. All this other stuff that was happening was like a story—something out of *Tales of the Arabian Nights*, only with darker overtones…

She picked at the pieces of cut fruit on the lunch tray as she waited for her call to go through to the hospital, then nibbled at some salad while she was put through to her mother.

'He's terrific—here, you can speak to him.'

Nell couldn't believe it. She knew people came out of major surgery far better these days, but to be able to speak to her father when he was less than twenty-four hours post-op?

'Dad!'

'I'm fine, honey. Tired but fine. Patrick came by earlier. He's looking good. He was in great spirits because he'd cut his hair.'

Her mother took the phone and explained how delighted Patrick had been to have enough hair to cut it back to a number one—the favoured, almost shaved look all his friends wore.

It was such a normal, innocuous conversation, Nell smiled. Yes, family definitely grounded one! They talked some more about nothing in particular, then said goodbye, Nell assuring her mother she was looking after herself.

It wasn't until she'd hung up that Nell realised there'd been no mention of Kal. Was her mother being tactful or had the conversation she'd had with Kal meant little to her?

Not that it mattered, although Nell felt a little niggle that her mother hadn't said it had been nice to talk to him or asked how he was—asked anything…

'What do you mean, I've no operations scheduled?'

Kal wasn't exactly yelling at his secretary, but his voice was probably a little louder than it needed to be.

'You were busy with the accident victims and I assumed you would be for some time, so when Dr Armstrong offered to do your list, I checked with all the patients to see if any of them minded, and they didn't, so he's operating here today and again tomorrow.'

She looked doubtfully at him.

'I could tell him you're free to do tomorrow's list, but then he might think—'

'That I think he's not competent,' Kal grumbled. 'Which isn't the case at all! He's a top surgeon—we've worked together often.'

Telling his secretary something she already knew! Of course she wouldn't have thought twice when Bob Armstrong had made the offer. The pair of them worked as a team on complex cases a couple of times a month.

None of this made him feel any better.

'So what am I supposed to do?' he demanded.

'Go back to the burns unit?' The tentative suggestion made him scowl. Working close to Nell was having an exceedingly detrimental effect on him, turning him into a person he didn't like at all, while at the same time it was giving him thoughts he shouldn't have—thoughts about how soon he could get her back into bed.

Never!

He was so certain he'd blown his chances with Nell that he felt depressed.

But thinking of Nell gave him an idea.

'I'll take a day off,' he announced, and his secretary looked so startled you'd have thought he'd suggested he was taking up needlework.

'But you had a day off last week,' she protested, her voice faint with shock.

'And two days off in how long—six months? Is that too much to ask?'

'Of course not.' She was scrabbling to recover her composure. 'Of course it isn't. I'm always telling you you should take more days off. It's just…'

'Unusual?' Kal offered helpfully, then he decided this conversation had gone on long enough. 'I'll see the Spanish team before I leave, and make sure they're settled into their accommodations and have everything they need. After that, I'll be contactable on my mobile.'

He walked out of the room, wanting privacy. Then he'd see his hospital administrator and give him the task of looking after the Spaniards. God or Fate or some kindly juxtaposition of the planets had given him this free time and he wasn't going to waste it. He was going to Australia to get his son…

The pretty, suntanned blonde at the car-hire counter in the main airport terminal building laughed when he said he hadn't been in Brisbane for fourteen years.

'You'll find it very different—especially the volume of traffic—but there's a street directory in the car so you should be able to find your way.'

She handed him the keys, explained where the car was parked and wished him luck.

Not that he needed it. The roads were still familiar and he drove to the Roberts' house with only one wrong turn. It was late afternoon and no one was at home, but he was content to sit on the front steps of the neat brick house with its wide, tree-shaded verandas and think about the past—about waiting here for Nell—until someone returned.

Mrs Roberts? Or the aunt called Mary? Kal couldn't recall her but, then, Nell had had a multitude of relations. Perhaps that had been part of what had attracted him to her—because her sense of family was as strong as his.

Family!

He really hoped it would be Patrick who came first, but when he thought of Patrick—of this stranger who was his son—his heart crunched into a tight hard lump.

Instead he had thought of Mrs Roberts again. She'd always been kind and welcoming—both of Nell's parents had been. The fact he was of a different race and culture had meant nothing to them, content that Nell was happy with him, pleased to think he could give her happiness.

'For one whole year!'

He spat the words out bitterly, wondering at the arrogance of his young self who'd outlined the 'rules' of the relationship to Nell, telling her from the beginning it would only be an affair.

Later, loving her, he'd explained why. Explained the pact he'd made with his parents. He could break tradition by studying medicine—even do a year's post-graduate study in far-away Australia—but he'd promised he'd then return and marry in the traditional way, marry the wife he didn't know but to whom he'd been betrothed since he'd been sixteen.

'Hi! Can I help you? Are you looking for my grandparents? I'm afraid Gramps is in hospital at the moment and Gran's up there, making sure the nurses look after him properly.'

The tall young lad had stopped a couple of feet in front of Kal, who stared at him, shaken, bewildered and tongue-tied as he drank in his son's appearance. Anger that this should be his first meeting stirred turbulence into an overwhelming rush of emotion at seeing him.

'Aunt Mary should be home soon. She said she'd do a run up to the hospital with some clean clothes and stuff, so I guess that's where she is.'

There was another awkward pause, the result of Kal's continued inability to speak, then the boy stuck out his hand.

'I'm Patrick, anyway.'

Kal stood up and took the hand offered to him, feeling the fragile bones in the thin fingers, knowing the boy's lanky leanness was a sign of recent illness, not a growth spurt. More anger rushed through him. He should have known— he should have been here! What if his son had died?

Realising he was probably freaking the boy out with his silence, he blotted the anger from his mind, swallowed hard and introduced himself.

'Kal,' he said, with gentle pressure on the bony fingers. 'I'm Kal.'

'My father's name is Kal,' Patrick said cautiously. 'His whole name is Khalil al Kalada—he's a kind of prince in a foreign country.'

The stream of information stopped abruptly and the boy

stared at Kal, his gaze going from the top of Kal's head, down to his feet, then back up again. Then the colour drained from the lad's face, and Kal reached out to grab him, scared the shock might prove too much.

But Patrick stepped away, straightening his shoulders, and though Kal could see the tremors in his son's limbs and the dryness of the lips Patrick licked and licked again, he didn't touch him—just waited—and watched the realisation dawning across the teenager's face.

'You're him, aren't you?'

Patrick stared at him, as if transfixed, but try as he might, searching desperately through his muddled mind, Kal could find no words to say, his throat closed tight with emotion, his mind focussed on this tall, gangly youth with eyes the colour of good brandy.

The boy recovered first.

'Does Mum know you're here? Is this OK? Did she ask you to come? Send you? Is it OK to be talking to you? I don't know the rules about this kind of stuff.'

He rubbed his hands on the sides of his shorts, as if embarrassment had made them sweat, then he grinned at Kal, though his eyes were filmed with tears and there was a suspicious tremble on his pale lips.

'Sorry, but Mum's never got up to what to do when I meet my dad, not in any of the talks she's given me. But I know some Arabic.'

He put his hands together in front of him and greeted his father with the traditional words his tutor had taught him.

'*Salaam alaikum.*'

Peace be with you.

Kal tried to speak but couldn't. His chest was bound

tight with emotion, his voice lost somewhere in the tidal wave of love that had swept over him when this Australian boy had greeted him in his own tongue.

He shook his head and stepped closer to his son, putting his arms around the boy, hugging him tightly and holding him, feeling the trembling tension in the too-thin frame, feeling it slowly abate and the boy's body slump against his.

His own emotion broke like a wave on a rocky shore, flooding in then sweeping back, leaving him drained and depleted.

Then Patrick broke away and looked at him.

'You *are* him, aren't you?' Then he frowned. 'Look, I know it's rude, but should you show me something saying who you are? You see, I should ask you in—will ask you in—but stranger danger and all that stuff…'

Overwhelmingly proud of this boy-man, Kal pulled his passport out of his pocket and handed it to Patrick.

'You're right to be cautious,' he finally managed to say, while in another part of his mind gratitude to Nell for raising Patrick so well momentarily blotted out the anger he felt towards her for depriving him of so much.

Patrick looked at the photo in the passport, then at the man who stood before him. Kal felt his scrutiny and grew anxious that further inspection might stop the boy from liking him. But all Patrick did was rub his finger gently over the photo a few times, then he looked up at Kal and said, 'This is so weird, meeting like this. I didn't think we ever would meet, you see. Not after Mum explained about your other wife and everything. I've never blamed you. I understood. Maybe, when I was a kid and went to things like soccer and a lot of the other boys had dads there and I only had Mum and Gramps, I'd think about it, but Mum told me about your promise and I understood that things were different where you lived and promises and honour and all that stuff were really important to you.'

Kal turned away so the boy wouldn't see the tears in his eyes. Was it going to be like this all the time? Would everything the boy said overwhelm him with emotion?

And what of Nell? Could he continue to be angry with a woman who had produced a teenager with so much guts and understanding?

By God, he could!

'So if you want to come in?'

He'd missed the first part of the invitation but, still holding the passport, Patrick was now walking up the front steps.

Seeing the passport reminded Kal of why he was here. Enough of this sentimentalism—it was time to be practical.

'Do you have a passport?' he asked, and Patrick, who'd reached the veranda, turned to smile at him.

'Of course. I got one a couple of years ago when I went to New Zealand with the soccer team. Before I got sick.'

He stopped suddenly and frowned.

'I suppose you *have* talked to Mum, and that's why you're here.' His frown deepened and for the first time Kal saw a resemblance to Nell—perhaps because just about all she'd done recently had been to frown at him! 'I talked to her after she phoned the hospital last night and she didn't say anything about you coming, but she'd probably have been upset about Gramps.'

Kal shook his head. Love, wonder, anger, love—far too

many emotions for one man to handle, but the boy was waiting for an answer.

'I explained to your grandmother when I spoke to her. It seemed a good idea, with your grandfather recovering from the operation and your grandmother being busy for a while looking after him, for you to come and visit me. After all, your mother's over there. So what do you think?'

Patrick stared at him, delight warring with doubt in his open face.

'I don't know about leaving Gran,' he said, putting the doubt into words first.

'Your grandmother thought it was an excellent idea, but you shouldn't take my word for it. I can take you up to the hospital to see them both and you can ask them what they think.'

The doubt gave way to tentative excitement.

'Would I be able to see your falcons?' Patrick asked, then, before Kal could answer this totally unexpected question, he darted away, returning seconds later with a book he pressed into Kal's hands.

'It's my favourite book—well, almost favourite. I've got so many it's hard to choose but I read this one again and again.'

Kal looked at it, his fingers tracing the title—*The History of the Sport of Falconry*—unconsciously echoing his son's movement on the passport.

'Did your mother give you this?' It took a while but he finally managed to force the words out through his tightened vocal cords.

'Of course. She said it was your favourite sport—better even than soccer—so I thought I should learn about it, just in case...'

'You ever met me?'

Tears filmed the boy's eyes again, and Kal saw his son's Adam's apple bob as he swallowed hard, but he couldn't speak either, so once again he hugged his son, the book squashed between their bodies.

This time he broke away.

'Go and pack—the weather's warm. Will you need schoolbooks? Do you have any important exams coming up?'

Patrick seemed to welcome the shift in conversation, and grinned.

'Schoolbooks? No way! I've missed so much school, this year is a catch-up year and I'm repeating a lot of work I've already done. Mum says if I find any of it a struggle, she'll get a tutor, but I've just done a chemistry test and I think I did OK.'

He disappeared into the back part of the house, returning seconds later.

'I'm sorry—would you like a cup of tea or something to eat?'

Kal had to smile. Mrs Roberts had always welcomed him to this house like that.

'No, I'm fine,' he told Patrick, and as the boy turned away again Kal looked around, feeling unaccountably at home in this house he hadn't visited for fourteen years.

Patrick returned within minutes, a huge canvas bag slung across his shoulders.

'I hope this isn't too much?' he said, the anxiety in his voice betraying his youth and a desire to please.

'Not at all,' Kal assured him. 'You've got your tooth-brush?'

'Actually no.'

The bag dropped to the floor, making a dull thud that suggested much of the contents were books, and Patrick disappeared once more, reappearing with a sheepish expression and a tartan toiletries bag.

'Haven't got my tablets either.'

He headed for the kitchen and pulled a plastic container down from a high shelf. Then, as if struck by a sudden thought, he turned to Kal.

'I know you're a doctor—do you know about the leukaemia? Know I have to have blood tests all the time?'

The question was so matter-of-factly asked that Kal choked with emotion again.

'We'll do the tests,' he managed to assure his son, then the two of them left the house, Patrick running back inside to leave a note for Mary, then locking the front door and bounding down the steps with barely a backward glance.

CHAPTER FIVE

'HE's doing what?' Nell yelled into the phone, unable to believe what her mother was telling her.

'I thought you knew. He said he'd talked to you about it—about it being a good opportunity to meet Patrick and get to know him while you were over there—and to be honest, Nell, I thought it would be for the best. It's far better for Patrick not to be around while your dad convalesces.'

That made sense, but the effrontery of the man, to go flying off to Australia without so much as a by your leave and pick up *her* son and fly back here with him.

The hide of him!

'Nell?'

Her mother's anxiety travelled over the thousands of kilometres between them and, hearing it, Nell hastened to reassure her that, of course, she'd done the right thing in letting Patrick go with Kal and, of course, it would be better for Patrick, and probably much easier on everyone to have him out of the house.

But where did that leave her? She all but whimpered as she put down the phone, then anger swamped the panic.

That manipulative man! Taking off like that, kidnapping her son and presenting the whole deal as a *fait accompli*.

And he'd lied to her—telling her he had to return to the surgical ward and his surgery duties, and flying off to Australia instead.

Consumed by rage, Nell paced the apartment and though she told herself it would be good to see Patrick, an uneasy fear overlay even that small glimmer of pleasure.

Fear?

She stopped pacing, wanting to explore this new emotion further, but the phone interrupted her.

'Mum! It's Patrick. I'm ringing from Kal's jet. Just like you phoned me from the plane on your flight. Kal said to tell you we're due to land at about ten in the morning your time, and he'll bring me straight to the apartment at the hospital. Isn't this exciting?'

As exciting as walking on broken glass with bare feet or swallowing fire! Nell thought, but the joy in Patrick's voice stopped her saying anything negative. He'd been through so much and had had precious little to be excited about lately. What she had to say would be said to Kal. It would keep!

'It will be lovely to see you,' she said lamely, then added a goodbye and hung up. No need now to think about where the fear had come from—it had found a focus. 'Kal's jet', 'Kal said'—oh, yes, the fear was that this man would steal her son. Not only physically, as he'd done already, but emotionally—and then where would she be?

Fuming with frustration that she couldn't immediately tackle Kal about his duplicity, she took another turn around the room, then realised just how clever he had been. She couldn't tackle him in front of Patrick, or do or say anything to make Patrick think what Kal had done was wrong. No, right from the start, she'd been determined that Patrick should grow up thinking his father was an honourable man—bound by his promises and beliefs.

How could she betray that conviction now?

Back and forth she marched, her mind in turmoil, though now one small ray of light shone tentatively in the darkness. Patrick's presence would prevent Kal seducing her with his touch and kisses—there'd be no more passionate love-making in either of their beds.

Contrarily, this thought didn't bring the solace it should have, so she went back to being angry with the man's behaviour as far as Patrick was concerned.

She was at the furthest point from the phone when it rang again. Thinking this time it might be Kal himself—with an explanation or even an apology—she shot across the room and grabbed it.

'It's the burns unit, Dr Warren. Could you come?'

Nell didn't hesitate. Whoever had rung might not have had enough knowledge of English to explain why Nell was needed, but she knew she wouldn't have been disturbed as she glanced at her watch one in the morning if it wasn't an emergency.

She met Yasmeen, who had also been summoned, in the corridor outside the ward.

'It's your man—the one we can't identify,' Yasmeen said to her. 'BP dropping, oxygen sats in his blood right down—he's dying, Nell.'

'He can't die!' Nell stormed, pleased to have an outlet for her anger. 'Not now.'

Yasmeen said nothing, and Nell understood. These

people accepted death with far more composure than she could. As far as they were concerned, death was simply an extension of life and the timing of it was the will of God.

The man was comatose but, then, he'd never been more than semi-conscious at any time since he'd been in hospital. Or as far as they knew, he hadn't. Unable to speak because of the tracheostomy, they had encouraged him to respond with movements of his hands or eyelids, or by writing on a pad they had tied to his bed, but no matter what language they used to speak to him, there'd been no sign that he heard or understood.

'He has to have some underlying illness!' Nell said. 'We've been testing his blood but only to see what's happening inside him, not for any signs of disease. He's got oxygen flowing into his lungs through the tracheostomy tube, his red blood cell count has been OK—not marvellous but not terrible—so why aren't those cells picking up oxygen? Is it a disease that destroys their carrying capacity? Is that what we're missing?'

She was thinking out loud and didn't expect Yasmeen to answer, but the other woman was staring at her as if she'd asked a million-dollar question. Silence for a moment, then Yasmeen smiled—the kind of smile that went with a million-dollar answer.

'Maybe all along he had heart problems. Maybe he has some kind of transposition of the arteries—only not a total transposition but the pulmonary veins aren't feeding their oxygen-rich blood back into the heart for some reason...'

'Not arteries but valve problems—a leaky valve.' Nell felt as if a bright light had been turned on. 'The oxygenated blood is slipping back and being recirculated through the lungs.' She thought about the function of the heart for a moment, then shook her head.

'No, that wouldn't work. But it could be some kind of hole between the ventricular septums. Maybe he had weakness there that has worsened with age. Didn't you, or Kal, or someone, tell me that the ex-pats' hospital was getting a wonderful reputation for its success with heart patients and people were flying in from all over the world to be treated? Heart disease and cardiac surgery—two things for which the hospitals here are famous!'

Yasmeen nodded, then walked across to the desk and lifted the phone. She turned towards Nell, obviously thinking, then put down the receiver without dialling.

'There won't be anyone there at this time of night who can help us, but we should phone first thing in the morning and ask if they were expecting a patient for a heart operation. In the meantime, what do we do?'

'Get hold of a heart specialist. Do you have one here or do your heart patients go to the other hospital?'

'We've got consultants who work here, but…'

Yasmeen hesitated.

'You don't like calling them out at night? Too bad,' Nell said. 'You can blame the crazy Australian doctor. Let's get someone here to take a look at our man. In the meantime, I'm going to increase the oxygen flow. Some oxygen is getting into his blood. Maybe with a higher concentration, enough will get through to keep him going until we find out what's wrong.'

Yasmeen went back to the phone, and Nell returned to her patient's bedside. She didn't know why this man had become so important to her, but she had no intention of giving up on him now, or letting him give up either.

She adjusted the flow meter, checked his IV lines, speaking firmly to him about hanging on all the time, telling him he owed it to his family, although she didn't know if he had one. Certainly no one had come forth to claim him, although by now details of this so-called mystery man had probably been printed in newspapers all around the world.

But if Yasmeen thought calling in a consultant in the early hours of the morning had been a bad idea, the consultant himself thought it an even worse idea, though he apparently—he communicated only with Yasmeen—considered their tentative diagnosis a possibility and agreed to do an exploratory cardiac catheterisation in the morning.

Glaring at Nell, he said something more to Yasmeen then departed, leaving Yasmeen to explain the situation to Nell.

'Bother the man!' Nell muttered. 'He was here—already awake—so why couldn't he do it now?'

'He needs equipment and staff,' Yasmeen said lamely, and it was Nell's turn to glare.

'You're telling me someone else might be using the equipment now? And what staff? A radiographer to follow the progress of the tube up into the heart? Surely there's a radiographer on duty.'

She was about to say more, but noticed Yasmeen's look of distress and realised she was taking out her own bad temper on the woman who'd been nothing but helpful since they'd first met. She put her arm around Yasmeen's shoulders and gave her a hug.

'I'm sorry, it's not your fault. And now that we've at

least got something organised to happen, why don't you go back to bed? I'm happy to stay here with him. In fact, there are a few things I want to check on some other patients, so I might as well be here.'

Yasmeen argued but in the end she relented, but it was only after she'd gone that Nell wondered whether she lived in the hospital apartments or had to travel some distance to her home.

In fact, she knew nothing whatsoever about Yasmeen, except that she was an excellent doctor and her English had an American accent. Was it that the accident and doing the best she could for so many patients had made Nell incurious, or was it because Kal occupied all the spare edges of her mind so there were no brain cells left for normal musings about a colleague's life?

Tomorrow she'd find out more about Yasmeen. No, tomorrow had already become today and today Patrick would arrive, flown in by his father in a private jet. Damn Kal! What thirteen-year-old kid could fail to be impressed by such a display of wealth and power?

Nell's patient stirred, saving her further anguish as she concentrated on the readouts on the monitor. The increased oxygen flow wasn't helping and the drugs she'd given him to raise his blood pressure had lifted it slightly, but not enough to give her hope that he was improving. The young nurse who was specialling the man said something, and Nell, looking at her, realised the girl was praying. She had taken the man's hand, carefully holding it so she didn't touch the burn wounds on his wrist, and now her head was bent towards it and soft, liquid words slipped from her lips.

Nell remembered Kal telling her that his people had always used prayer as a part of the healing process. They had remedies for illnesses, but every cure, even in these days of modern medicine, was offered along with prayer, for was it not God's will that the patient lived or died?

Could prayer do what medicine couldn't? Nell wondered, turning her attention back to the monitor.

No change, but the young nurse's faith touched Nell, and she sank down in the chair on the other side of the bed and added her own quiet prayer for the man's recovery.

Together they watched over him through the remainder of the night, and by morning, Nell was pleased to see, he had picked up slightly, so when the consultant returned, Yasmeen was able to report that the patient was well enough for him to do the cardiac catheterisation and, if it looked possible, even to try a balloon valvuplasty to close the defective septum.

'*If* there is a defective septum,' Nell muttered to herself, certain the solution to her patient's problems couldn't be that easy.

But it was, and the surgeon emerged from the small operating theatre so triumphant he forgot he'd been pretending not to speak English. He gave her an inch-by-inch description of his masterful catheterisation, then detailed the skill he'd shown in fixing the defective wall, finishing with the intimation that if the patient didn't improve now, it would be Nell's fault, not his.

Nell thanked him and followed the wardsmen wheeling the patient back to the unit. Tiredness was swamping her now, dragging at her feet so she felt as if she walked through mud, but her mind was on the man—wondering what changes she should now make to his treatment, considering possible reactions between the drugs the heart consultant had prescribed and the antibiotic and pain-relief regime he was on for his burns.

'Nell!'

The sound of her name, spoken as if it was being repeated, made her turn, and there, ten metres behind her in the corridor, was Kal.

Kal!

Patrick!

'Where's Patrick?' she demanded, too tired and confused to even begin to say all the other things she wanted to say to this man.

'He's in your apartment. I left him there and came to find you. I'd have thought you would have been waiting for him.'

The slight hint of reproof in Kal's voice was enough. Nell took off down the corridor, fury blotting out her surroundings and making her want to strike out at this man who was turning her life upside down.

'How dare you speak to me like that?' she raged, lifting her fists to pound them on his chest, only to have him seize them in his hands. 'And how dare you sneak off and take my child? Of all the underhanded, horrible things to do, and while I'm here working at *your* hospital!'

'He's my child, too,' Kal reminded her, his voice as hard and smooth as steel, his hands imprisoning her struggling fists with effortless ease. 'And if we're talking underhanded or horrible, wouldn't keeping him from me for thirteen years fit that description?'

'I *couldn't* tell you!' Nell snapped. 'Do you think I didn't want to? Wouldn't have given anything to have you back? But at least I acted from honour! Something you pretended to uphold. Honour! Ha!' she scoffed. 'Was this honourable behaviour, Sheik Kalada, sneaking off behind my back? Taking my child?'

'Our child!'

And at that moment she hated him. Hated him as much as she had loved him. Because he was right! Patrick was *their* child.

'It was still the wrong thing to do!' she muttered, hanging onto the anger as this proximity to Kal, his grip, less tight now on her fists, was turning wrath to attraction.

'It was wrong, but would you have agreed without a lengthy argument?' he asked quietly. 'It turned out a friend had taken my surgery list so I had time to go and come back. Your mother seemed relieved that Patrick would be out of the way while your father convalesced, and it's not as if you were in some other country. I flew out to Australia to bring Patrick to back to be with his mother.'

The effrontery of this bald-faced lie pushed attraction aside.

'You brought him back for your own reasons,' Nell stormed, 'so don't make out like it was some Scout good deed for the day.'

She snatched her hands out of his and stormed away, intending to go straight to the apartment but aware she'd have to hide the anger she was feeling. Patrick would be excited by his adventure and think it was the greatest fun for all of them to be together. She couldn't dash that excitement or throw a dark cloud of gloom over his delight.

'Nell, Nell!'

Yasmeen's voice followed her up the corridor, and she

turned back to see the other woman explaining something to Kal, her hands moving swiftly as if demonstrating what was happening, her face, even at a distance, anguished.

Nell hurried back.

'It's your man,' Yasmeen told her. 'His BP's dropped again—dropped drastically.'

'Damn!' Nell muttered, and headed off with swift strides back towards the ward. She sensed Kal following, and was reminded of where things stood. She stopped and turned.

'Kal, I have to go to this patient. Could you explain to Patrick?'

Kal looked at her and for the first time saw the grey tinge of exhaustion in her usually clear skin and the dark circles under her eyes.

'Have you slept at all?' he demanded, and she found a small smile to offer him. The kind of valiant smile that made his heart ache.

'Not recently,' she said, then she touched him on the arm. 'But I have to go and I can't leave Patrick on his own.'

Her fingers tightened on his muscle, and she looked into his eyes as she added, 'Please?'

Of course he'd go to the boy! So why was he hesitating? Why was he making this woman almost beg?

Guilt, compunction and an overwhelming sense of emotion he was sure couldn't possibly be love swept over him. He leant forward and, ignoring Yasmeen, who'd been standing beside Nell, obviously fascinated by the byplay, kissed Nell gently on the cheek.

'I'll take care of Patrick,' he promised. Then he walked away before he could hug her and apologise for all the things that had gone wrong between them since they'd met again, and tell her how wonderful their son was and congratulate her...

She'd disappeared from view by the time he got that far in the list of things he wanted to say, and he hauled his mind back, reminding it that what she'd done had been wrong—that he was the injured party here, and she the one who should be apologising.

He went back to Nell's apartment, ready to explain the emergency. As a doctor's son, Patrick would surely understand. But he didn't have to explain anything. The lad was stretched out the couch, sound asleep, although the television was on, blaring out some rock video.

Kal studied him, seeing resemblances to himself and to his brother's children. Not much of Nell. Had it worried her that her son was so much *his* child in looks? She'd obviously been at such pains to ensure Patrick never thought badly of the father who'd deserted them, he doubted she'd have worried much about his looks.

Kal went into the kitchen and poured himself a glass of cold water. He should go to work—check out what was happening, not only on the ward but in the hospital as a whole. But he wouldn't leave Patrick on his own. Even had he wanted to, he'd promised Nell, so he picked up the phone and called his secretary, explained where he was and checked on what was happening.

'We can survive without you for a few hours—or even days,' she reminded him. 'That's why you chose good deputies. You've just never believed they could run things as well as you do. Have faith.'

Kal smiled at her admonishments, but he'd been brought

up to take responsibility, not only for his own actions but for his people. It was a hard habit to break.

He noticed the pile of books Patrick had unpacked and stacked on Nell's dining-room table. A few more piles and the apartment would look like his. He picked out the one on falconry and sat down to read, smiling when he saw the fine marks Patrick had made beside some passages and the star he'd put against Kal's grandfather's name. Yes, the boy's great-grandfather had been a master in training birds, and this had obviously appealed to the lad.

Nell returned to the ward, where the registrar and a junior doctor were already by the bed.

'Has the heart consultant been called?' she asked Yasmeen, taking in the grey, depleted look of her patient.

'He's on his way,' the registrar replied, and Nell nodded at him. He was always happy to try out his English on her.

The first place Nell checked was the area of the groin where the catheter had been inserted, but though the dressing showed some blood, there wasn't enough to explain the man's condition.

'Internal bleeding seems the most likely scenario for such a sudden collapse,' she said. 'We need a scan. Will the registrar have to order it or—'

But at that stage, with not even a sigh or murmur of protest, the man stopped breathing while the monitor showed his heart had stopped.

'Resuscitation?' the young doctor asked, and Nell considered it—thought about the shock paddles, the man's injured body leaping on the bed—and rejected the option with regret. Even when he had seemed conscious, the man had shown no will to live, and though she'd fought for him and urged him to fight, it had been plain he hadn't wanted to undertake the battle.

Sheer stubbornness on her part had kept him alive, but now she wasn't going to push him further.

Her explanations for this decision, however, should be medical, not emotional, and she said quietly, 'If we shock his heart and the leak is in there, or in the vessel the specialist used in the catheterisation, all we're doing is pumping more blood into his body cavity, giving the lungs even less room to expand. Instead of saving him, we'd be killing him again.'

The others nodded, seemingly satisfied with her theory, but her heart ached with the loss of this man she didn't know, and she stayed in the room when the others left, helping the nurse prepare him for his move to the mortuary. She'd like him autopsied but didn't know if that would be done as a matter of routine for all deaths in hospitals in this country. She'd have to ask—

Kal. She no longer had an excuse not to go to Patrick, but Kal would be there, and the thought of seeing the two of them together—father and son—was almost too much for her to contemplate.

She found Yasmeen instead and asked her about autopsies.

'It should be done,' Yasmeen said worriedly, 'but—'

The heart consultant appeared out of the doctor's office and Nell understood the 'but'.

'I've signed the death certificate. Given the seriousness of his burns, it's no wonder he died. It really was a waste of time my operating. No need for us to do an autopsy.'

He was so certain—*and* so obnoxious—Nell dug in her heels.

'His family might want details. They might ask for a full report.'

'He has no family,' the consultant told her.

'Of course he has—we just haven't found them yet.'

Yasmeen was tugging nervously at Nell's arm but Nell found it was good to be getting rid of a bit of accumulated ire on this man.

'And when we do, how do we explain?'

'He died of burn injuries,' the man snapped, then he strode away.

'Can we go above his head?' Nell was aware she was being stubborn but she still asked Yasmeen the question.

'Only to Kal. The man's a consultant so he's not a hospital employee, but Kal still decides what does and doesn't happen in the hospital. You could phone his office.'

Nell nodded, although she knew, unless Patrick was being inducted into the running of a hospital, the CEO wouldn't be in his office but in her apartment.

'I'll track him down but, in the meantime, can we hold the man's body somewhere? I don't want action being taken on the death certificate just yet.'

'We have to hold him anyway and keep trying to find his family,' Yasmeen reminded her, 'although if he's of our faith he should be buried within twenty-four hours.'

She was frowning, as if the complications were too much for her, and Nell put her arm around her.

'Kal will sort it out,' she said, and though she was still so angry she could spit over Kal's behaviour, she had faith that he would indeed sort it out.

She gave Yasmeen a hug and departed, assuming Kal would still be with Patrick in her apartment. But the skip of excitement her heart gave at the thought of seeing her son was soon damped down by memories of her patient's death.

'I should have thought of heart problems,' she said, talking in a low but anguished tone to Kal. They were in the kitchen of her apartment and, having feasted her eyes on her sleeping son and assured herself he had good colour in his cheeks, she'd drawn Kal into the kitchen to explain the problem. 'But even so, once we realised it, we should have been able to save him.'

The anger she felt towards him had softened when he'd taken her hand then put his arm around her shoulders as he'd told her how sorry he was that the man who meant so much to her had died.

'There was no reason for you to think of heart problems,' Kal now assured her. 'Look, the man had a pad on which to write. He was conscious enough some of the time to have responded to questions, and we'd asked him in—what?—a dozen languages if he had any underlying health problems. And he heard the questions because he looked away when we asked them—ignoring us.'

Kal turned her to face him, and tucked a lock of hair behind her ear.

'No one could have done more for him. Remember, if you hadn't stopped to check him, he'd have been delivered to the mortuary that first day.'

Disturbed by Kal's gentleness and also by the abatement of her anger, Nell backed away.

'Can we have him autopsied?'

Kal thought for a minute.

'Why?'

'I don't think he died of his burns. I think he haemor-rhaged internally, possibly as a result of the operation.'

'As a result of the consultant's carelessness? Is that what you're saying?'

'No. The man is probably a very competent surgeon, but if it was a mistake, shouldn't we know about it? Doesn't the patient deserve that much from us?'

Kal shrugged, but his reply was less casual.

'Yes, he does. We'll autopsy him. If nothing else, find-ing the cause of death might save the hospital problems later should some family member turn up.'

Nell was pleased but knew someone who wouldn't be so excited. For a moment she considered not saying any-thing, but knew it wouldn't be fair to embroil Kal unknow-ingly in a problem.

'The heart consultant is against it.'

Kal raised an eyebrow as if to say, So? and Nell had to smile. The arrogant Kal was back.

But her smile faded as she remembered it was the arro-gant man she needed to fight—the Kal who'd gone out to Australia and, without her permission, taken her son out of the country. She was reasonably certain there were illegali-ties involved, although she had no intention of pursuing them.

No, it was the principle of the thing that was bothering her.

'The boy's awake.'

From the warning note in Kal's voice he'd guessed what she was thinking, and frustration with the situation meant she had to force a smile as she turned towards her son. But the pretence didn't last long. Seeing him, hearing his happy shout of 'Mum' and feeling his long, thin body in her arms as he hugged her fiercely brushed away all her anger.

'This *is* a surprise,' she said finally, holding him at arm's length so she could look at him. 'Did you remember your tablets? Did you think to phone the hospital to get them to send your records?'

She saw the happiness in his face fade slightly and gave him another hug.

'Of course you didn't. How could you think of everything with Gramps in hospital and with your…with Kal whisking you away in his plane? It's OK. I can email them to send the files direct to me and I'll print them out for whichever doctor your…Kal chooses for you while you're here.'

Beyond Patrick's shoulder she saw Kal's scowl. Was he annoyed because she couldn't bring herself to say the word 'father' or because she'd intimated this was only a short visit?

But of course it was—so he'd better not be thinking any different.

She scowled right back at him, then wondered if she'd guessed wrongly when he said to Patrick, 'I think it's time you tasted local food. Your mother's been up all night but I doubt if she's eaten, so how about you go off and forage?' He dug in his pocket and drew out a roll of notes, peeled off several and handed them to Patrick. 'If you go down to the ground floor in the elevator and turn right, you can't miss the canteen. It's self-service so choose a few plates of whatever looks good, put them on a tray, bring them back up and we'll share it.'

Patrick looked as if Kal had given him a gift rather than a job to get him out of the way.

'Will they have felafel? And hummus? And shish ke-babs? And Mum does a fruity kind of rice as well, but I forget its name.'

'Go check it out,' Kal said to him, leading the way to the door then standing there while Patrick strode towards the elevator.

'He's a fine boy,' he said, coming back towards Nell, his eyes and the gravity in his voice making the words even stronger praise. 'You've done a wonderful job with him. I'd like—'

'I don't want your compliments on Patrick's upbringing,' Nell snorted, although she'd gone just a little teary to hear Kal say those words. 'I want an explanation for your behaviour, and I want to know what you intend doing now you've disrupted Patrick's life like this.'

Kal stiffened, drawing himself up to his full height and looking down at her with hard, unyielding eyes.

'I intend to get to know my son, and then, when I judge he will be easy with them, I intend to introduce him to my family.'

'Introduce him to your family?' Nell knew her words were faint, but so was she. 'You'd introduce him? Acknowledge him?'

'He is my son!' Kal said, his voice as cold as wind off snow. 'They are his family. Of course he should know them.'

Nell felt for the chair she knew was somewhere behind her, pulled it out from the table and sat down with a bump.

This is what you want, she reminded herself. OK, it hasn't happened as you planned, but if they meet Patrick surely they'll all be willing to be tested as possible bone-marrow donors.

But if they meet Patrick…

Her mind tried to grasp the ramifications—to work out where this family reunion might lead. Surely Kal couldn't think Patrick could stay on in this country. It had been all very well for Kal to have talked of conditions—and even, ridiculously, of marriage—but Nell's life was back in Australia, and Patrick's place was with her.

Her heart scrunched with momentary panic.

Wasn't it?

CHAPTER SIX

'WHAT would you like? A cup of tea? Coffee? Have you had anything at all to eat? Don't you know about looking after yourself?'

Kal's voice was brusque, but as Nell shook her head in answer to any or all of his questions, she was relieved he thought her sudden subsidence into the chair was to do with hunger or over-tiredness.

Although now, with Patrick gone, she should be talking to him about this family idea he'd suddenly dumped on her.

He beat her to it, but with talk of her family, not his.

'I saw your father. I took Patrick to the hospital before we left. He—your father—looked remarkably well and the doctors are apparently delighted with his recovery.'

Pleased by this diversion, Nell looked up at the man looming over her.

'And Mum? How's she holding up?'

Kal smiled—the warm, genuine, lighting-up-his-face smile that had always made Nell's heart race.

And still did.

'She's exactly as she always was. A spaceship could land in her back yard and as the little yellow and purple spotted aliens poured out, she'd greet them with a smile and offer tea or coffee. She's sitting up there by your father, knitting brightly coloured scarves, and has a large bag of wool so the nurses can choose what colour scarf they'd like her to knit them. Needless to say, she has them eating out her hand and they can't do enough for your father.'

Nell had to smile. Yes, that was her mum!

And though she'd cut out her tongue rather than admit it, Nell knew that not having to worry about Patrick with his meals and tests and doctors' appointments would ease the strain on her mother right through her father's convalescence.

'So, with your family all tidied away, that leaves us,' Kal said.

'There is no us,' Nell reminded him. 'There's you, there's me and there's Patrick. And now you've finessed him here, you can get to know him, but you'd better be able to take some time off work to keep him entertained, because I'm not only here to do a job, I'm needed in the burns unit. I can't just walk away from that to show Patrick around.'

She paused, realising something she hadn't considered before.

'Even if I knew where around was! I came from the airport to here, and that's it.'

'I'll show you both around,' Kal said. 'Now the Spanish team is here, it will be easier for you to get away.'

'The Spanish team is surgical,' Nell reminded him. 'They're taking the jobs you and other surgeons were doing, not working on the ward. It could be weeks before things stabilise enough in the unit for anyone to take time off.'

'Everyone needs time off,' Kal argued.

'That's not what I've heard about you,' Nell shot back at

him, knowing this argument about work wasn't the issue. Patrick was the issue. She took a deep breath and tackled it.

'I mean it, Kal. You'll have to take time off to be with him. You can't bring him over here then just dump him in my apartment and go back to work. He needs company, and he'll want to see the city and the surrounding country. And don't think you can ask one of your minions to do it and palm off your responsibility that way. No, you brought him over here, it's up to you to look after him.'

But having taken this stand, Nell realised just how dangerous it was. Thrown into his father's company for any length of time, Patrick, at a vulnerable age, couldn't help but be impressed. Nell knew, none better, the magnetic charm Kal could weave so effortlessly. He'd cast a spell and Patrick would be caught in it.

'That's ridiculous, and so's your attitude to work.' Kal's remonstrance interrupted her thoughts. 'You should be seeing the country also. You can work in the mornings and in the afternoons we will all go out.'

All go out?

Like a family?

She erupted into protest.

'Just like that! You're going to organise *my* life now, as well as Patrick's! Well, thanks but, no, thanks. While I'm needed on that ward, I'll stay there.'

'You forget it is my hospital, Nell,' he said, with cold, implacable logic. 'I can forbid you working at all!'

'You'd do that? Put those patients' lives at risk? Just to get your own way? Or is it to pay me back for not telling you about Patrick? Is this spite, Kal? I'd have thought you'd be above that!'

Silence greeted her outburst. A silence that went on for so long she was forced to look up at him.

He looked puzzled, an expression she wouldn't have associated with Kal, and as his eyes searched her face, she felt her antagonism dying away, killed by what seemed like genuine regret in his expression.

'Nell, do we have to argue? Shouldn't we be rejoicing in our son? I— All the way back on the flight all I could think of was seeing you again—seeing you to tell you how grateful I am for the way you've brought him up and how proud I am of that fine boy. But here we are, throwing harsh words at each other. Is there no middle ground where we can meet? No amnesty possible, for the boy's sake if for nothing else?'

Nell stared at him. Of course there should be an amnesty—or something—but if she showed weakness in front of Kal he'd ride straight over the top of her, moving in on her son—on her life—taking over both their lives as if it was his right.

'I'm too tired to talk about this now,' she said, knowing it was a coward's way out, but in part it was true, for exhaustion was weakening her defences and for a moment the thought of having someone take over her life—and the responsibility for Patrick—had seemed exceedingly appealing.

'Food for a starving mother!'

Patrick came through the still open door with a tray of food, but he wasn't alone. A sweet-faced young woman followed him, another tray in her hands.

'I explained I couldn't carry enough for three people— for me and Mum and you, Kal,' Patrick said, putting down his tray then turning to take the second one from the woman, thanking her in English then Arabic. She bobbed her head towards him then departed. 'So the man in charge of the counter down there sent the woman with me.'

He turned towards his father.

'My Arabic must be OK because they seemed to understand me, although they went right off the planet when I said I was your son. Are you a big cheese in this hospital, Kal?'

Nell hid a smile as she looked at the 'big cheese', wondering just how he'd explain his position, both in the hospital and in this country, to Patrick.

'I'm the hospital boss,' he said, and Patrick nodded.

'I thought it must be that,' he said easily, lifting dishes off the trays and setting them in the middle of the dining table. 'Plates, Mum?'

Nell looked around, taking a moment to work out what Patrick was talking about.

'Somewhere in those kitchen cabinets, I guess,' she said, waving her hand towards the cupboards. 'I've only been eating breakfast here and that's sent up from downstairs. All my other meals I've had on the ward.'

Kal knew from his own apartment exactly where the plates would be, and he turned to find them and get cutlery for the three of them, the small task masking his annoyance at himself that Nell had taken on so much virtually since her arrival in this country and he'd done nothing to stop her.

They'd needed her in the burns unit—that was undeniable—but surely he should have seen she was working herself into exhaustion.

He put the plates on the table then took one up in his hand, serving a little from each of the dishes onto it, then placing it in front of Nell.

'Have something to eat then go to bed,' he said, trying hard not to make it sound like an order. 'Your mother's been up all night with a patient,' he explained to Patrick. 'So after we've eaten, I'll take you for a drive around the city so you can get your bearings.'

He hesitated, eyeing Nell, waiting for a comment. But her head was bent above the plate he'd given her, and all her attention seemed to be on scooping food onto her fork.

'Once you get to know your way around, you can do some exploring on your own. I'd like to show you all I can, but there'll be times when I'll be working.'

'That's OK,' Patrick said easily. 'Mum's always encouraged me to do things on my own, though I would like to learn more Arabic. I can get by with speaking it fairly well but I'm not so good at reading and writing it.'

'I'll find someone to teach you,' Kal said, then he hesitated again, worrying about the boy this time, not Nell. 'That's if you really want to be doing lessons when you're supposed to be on holidays.'

'I don't mind that,' Patrick assured him. 'It'd give me something to do while you and Mum work.'

Nell lifted her head and threw Kal a look that would have shrivelled grass, but Kal knew she couldn't argue and drove home that point, saying easily to Patrick, 'Well, if you're sure that's what you want.'

Conversation then turned to the food, Patrick keen to learn what each dish was called so he knew what to order in future.

Was I so self-confident at his age? Nell wondered, then shook her head. Of course she hadn't been. When she'd been Patrick's age she'd been a mess, embarrassed in adult company, squirming in discomfort with boys, and only secure and confident when surrounded by her girl friends.

Patrick's illness had matured him—she knew that—but seeing him with Kal, the two so alike in manner as well as looks, she wondered if confidence was a genetic thing. She couldn't imagine Kal had ever been a tongue-tied adolescent or known a moment's embarrassment in his life.

'So tell me about your medical tests. What do you have done and how often?'

Nell watched as Patrick turned towards his father, calmly outlining his medication and the regular blood tests he had to have.

'They look for low blood cell counts with the blood tests but I have to watch for other things. Do you know it's T-cell ALL? We found the cancer when I hurt my ribs playing soccer and had a chest X-ray. It showed a shadow in the space between the lungs and they found it was an enlarged… What do you call it, Mum?'

'Thymus. That's where the T-cells are made. You had an enlargement there and in the lymph nodes.'

'Thymus, that's it.' He patted his chest. 'It's in here, in some bit they call the media—something, but of course you'd know that. But with T-cell, other lumps and bumps can grow. It's like…'

He stopped again and looked at Nell.

'Lymphoma,' she offered, not interrupting because it pleased her that Patrick had taken the trouble to find out so much about his illness.

'Lymphoma. More like that than leukaemia, in fact. With the first relapse we found a lump in my neck, which was good because it meant we saw it almost straight away.

We hadn't been expecting it because the first lot of treatment—you know how they hit you hard with the drugs at first—'

'Remission induction,' Kal put in, and Patrick nodded.

'Then remission consolidation, then maintenance. Well, in the first stage my white cell count dropped very fast, which is usually good news for a cure first time round, but then we found the lump straight after the consolidation and we had to do stage one again. So now I look for lumps and bumps or swellings anywhere and everywhere, including in embarrassing places, as well as having the blood tests every week.'

Kal was frowning and Nell wondered if he was again thinking he should have been there for his son, although personally she'd have given anything not to have had to go through that dreadful time again.

'How did you manage when they found he'd relapsed?' he asked her a little later when Patrick had returned to the canteen for sweets.

'I was thinking about that just then,' she admitted. 'Most people ask how I felt when Patrick was first diagnosed, but there's so much to do, so many specialists to see, all the different drugs and the effects they'll have on his body to learn about and then to explain it all to him. So I was too busy to think of anything but getting him treated and keeping him positive, but the second time…'

She couldn't speak as the remembered horror of that news flooded over her.

'That's why I had to come,' she said at last. 'I had to know there was some hope ahead of us should that dreadful day ever come again.'

Then, without looking at Kal, she stood up, pushing her

chair back with her legs, holding onto the table as if she were eighty years old.

'I need to sleep,' she said, and turned away.

Then Kal was there, his arm around her, supporting her, offering comfort she didn't want to accept.

'I'll take care of him,' Kal said, his voice gruff but not with anger this time.

Nell nodded, though she had no idea whether he was talking about the bone-marrow test or looking after Patrick that afternoon while she slept.

And right now she wasn't sure she cared, until Kal kissed her on the top of her head, then turned her in his arms so she was held in his embrace.

This time the kiss wouldn't be on the top of her head. She knew that but she couldn't move away.

'Sex in the afternoon? *Come on*, guys!'

Patrick's comment spun them apart and though Kal's face was thunderous as he turned towards his son, Nell touched his arm.

'Teenage humour,' she said quietly, though to Patrick she said, 'You watch your mouth, young man!' Then she headed for the bedroom, too tired to be bothered what happened between the two of them.

She woke four hours later. It was dark outside and the silence in the apartment told her she was on her own. She turned on the bedside light and noticed for the first time that someone had been in and unpacked the parcels Yasmeen had brought to the apartment—how long ago?

She rubbed her face with her hands, unable to work out quite how long she'd been here—wondering if perhaps this was jet-lag.

Whatever! She could see toiletries on the dressing-table, and through the partially opened wardrobe doors noticed clothes hanging neatly.

But the light also revealed a note on the bedside table and she picked it up.

'We're in my apartment, thinking in terms of dinner at about eight. If you wake up, come and join us, otherwise make sure you get something sent up for yourself.'

It was signed 'Kal', although she'd have known his strong, upright writing anywhere.

Had he brought it in himself and put it there? Had he wanted to look at her as she slept, as she'd looked at him the other night? Or was that just wishful thinking, prompted by the hope that their love-making might have meant something more to him than sex and a display of his dominance over her?

She laughed at her fantasies and got out of bed. It was seven-thirty and she'd already missed hours of Patrick's company. She had no intention of missing more of it, even if it meant putting up with Kal's company as well. She opened the wardrobe, wondering exactly what Yasmeen might have purchased for her that would fit into the 'going out for dinner' category.

Nell was confident that whatever Yasmeen had chosen wouldn't offend the sensibilities or go against the dress code of the local people, but in her heart she hoped the clothes wouldn't be too sensible. Fool that she was, she'd like to look good in front of Kal.

Look good? What she'd really like would be to wear something that would knock his socks off, which was about as likely as all the burns patients miraculously getting better that day.

She ran her fingers past the dark shirts and neat slacks, then over long, all-encompassing garments in black and navy, finally coming to a dress in midnight blue. It had sleeves, and looked long enough to cover her down to her ankles, but it seemed to have some shape about it and she knew the colour suited her.

She pulled it out and threw it on the bed, then searched the drawers for underwear that might be more inspiring than the neat cotton bras and panties she'd already un-packed and worn.

Nothing to start a red-blooded male's heart racing, not that any red-blooded male—or one in particular—would be seeing her underwear, but there was one set in black. It would look better under the blue than the white she'd been wearing.

She showered, washed her hair and blow-dried it, pleased that it behaved for once and sat down neatly around her head. She'd had moisturiser and some make-up in her handbag which she'd miraculously managed to keep hold of during the emergency, and for the first time since her ar-rival in Kal's country, she used eye-liner and mascara—un-derstated but enough to make her eyes look bigger—then added lipstick in an effort to make her face looked less tired.

All done, she slipped on the dress, surprised to find it so light she felt as if she was still naked. A plain garment but not a cheap one! She fingered the fabric—a fine-woven silk, she guessed. But it wasn't until she looked at herself in the mirror that she realised just how special the garment was. She looked beautiful—not an adjective she could ever remember using to describe herself. But something about the colour, or the cut, or the combination of both, made her look tall, slim and elegant, while at the same time the dress shimmied down her body so her curves looked curvier, and going in and out in all the right places as well.

'Wow!' she muttered at her reflection.

'Wow!' Patrick echoed when he opened the door of Kal's apartment a few minutes later. 'New dress, Mum?'

But it wasn't Patrick's reaction she was after and although she answered him, she was watching Kal, feeling as well as seeing his scrutiny, so when his eyes met hers, his hot with desire, Nell felt a surge of triumph, then immediately squashed it.

The last thing she needed was Kal desiring her!

Wasn't it?

CHAPTER SEVEN

SHE was beautiful, and Kal ached to tell her, ached to hold her, but so much had gone wrong between them he couldn't find the words.

Couldn't say them either, in front of Patrick.

The reminder aggravated him and he realised for the first time just how awkward having a teenage boy around could make things.

Should have thought of it earlier when he caught you about to kiss her.

Yes, he should have, but he hadn't and now he wanted to tell Nell she was beautiful, but it wasn't only Patrick inhibiting him. No matter how attractive Nell was or how attracted he, Kal, was to her, in the back of his mind all the time was the fact that she'd cheated him, and the more he saw of Patrick the more he felt how much he'd lost in not seeing his son grow up and the more his anger at Nell grew.

'So, where are we going, Kal? Do you mind me calling you Kal?'

Patrick grinned at him, then added, 'I'm sure you'd like it better than me calling you Pops!'

'Pops?' Kal echoed weakly, then as Patrick fell about

laughing he realised it was a joke and smiled. Nell was smiling, too, a small smile, though the glint in her eyes suggested she'd thought it just as funny as Patrick had but didn't want to laugh.

And seeing her, with the smile on her delicately painted lips and the light glimmering in her amazing, cool grey eyes, his body stirred with a desire so deep and strong it startled him.

How could anger and desire co-exist, so both were equally fierce emotions?

'Kal's fine,' he said, then realised he'd spoken too abruptly when Patrick, who'd been heading for the elevator, turned back towards him. 'Really!' Kal added in a gentler tone, reminding himself of the sensitivities of adolescents.

He took Nell's elbow and guided her along the corridor behind Patrick, who was now loping along, bowling an imaginary cricket ball.

'Does he play cricket as well as soccer?' Kal asked Nell, inwardly congratulating himself on his outward composure, given the state of his mind and the problem desire had caused in his body.

'He did,' Nell said. 'He's sports mad, although his one great desire has always been to learn more about falconry.'

She turned towards Kal and smiled—at him, not Patrick this time—causing him more discomfort.

'I should never have told him about your birds.'

'I'll take him to see them, of course,' Kal told her, then realised Patrick had stopped bowling and was waiting for them to catch up.

'To see your falcons? You would? Cool! When?'

Nell laughed.

'There's a certain immediacy at that age,' she told Kal, who could only look at this beautiful, laughing woman and shake his head.

He considered himself something of an expert where women were concerned. Admittedly, as the hospital had grown and his responsibilities had grown with it, he'd had less time for dalliance, but when he and his wife had divorced, he'd discovered a single man was in great demand, particularly with the ex-pats who lived, worked and played in the burgeoning city. So he'd had no trouble at all finding women with whom to enjoy a pleasant, relaxed, no-strings-attached relationship.

But Nell? He had no idea where he stood with her as far as a relationship was concerned.

Not a clue! Most of the time they'd spent together had been in argument, which had put distance between them, but earlier today, when he'd been about to kiss her, she hadn't moved away.

And that night—he'd lost count of how many nights ago it had been—she'd responded to his love-making with so much ardour she must still feel something for him—even if it was only physical! So how could she be so cool? How could her body not be burning for a repeat session, and how could it not be tied in knots of frustration over the situation with Patrick being there?

The anger bubbled to the surface again. He scowled at her then regretted it as her laughter faded.

'What now?' she demanded quietly, as Patrick stepped into the elevator ahead of them.

Kal shook his head, then offered a smile himself. It would definitely lack the radiance of hers, but right now a partial, forced stretching of the lips was the best he could do.

'So, where are we going?'

Patrick repeated the question he'd asked earlier, and Kal, relieved to have something other than his libido to think about, answered him.

'There's a restaurant on the top floor of a new building on the seashore. Remember as we came in to land I showed you how the Gulf of Arabia curls into the land?'

'And you said you used to go fishing where all the sky-scrapers are now?' Patrick replied. 'Cool!'

Nell watched her son interacting with his father and felt an ache in the region of her heart. Not only had she denied Kal the opportunity to see his son grow up—a denial she was certain he would never forgive—but she'd denied Patrick a father.

Had she done the wrong thing all those years ago?

'Mum goes off into a fugue state like that now and then,' she heard Patrick say, and wondered what she'd missed of the conversation.

They were exiting the elevator now, not on the ground floor where she'd been before but into a well-lit basement. Kal led the way to a big, black, four-wheel-drive vehicle, and the lights on it flickered as he released the door locks.

'Kids in the back,' he said to Patrick, who accepted the decree with only a token protest, although, as Nell settled into the front passenger seat, she wished she'd had the foresight to grab the back seat for herself. Admittedly the car was wide, but Kal was still too close, the energy his body seemed to radiate buzzing against her skin, while his aftershave—a musky tang she wouldn't have said she liked had she sniffed it in a shop—permeated all her senses, firing her body to an agony of desire she hadn't felt for fourteen years and had never thought to feel again.

'Comfortable?' Kal asked.

'No!' came out before she'd considered the repercussions.

Kal smiled as if he knew exactly why she'd said it, but of course Patrick had to ask.

'It's the dress,' she told him, which both was and wasn't a lie. She was reasonably sure it was the feel of the silk brushing against her body that was making whatever Kal was doing to her worse, but the excuse she offered Patrick had nothing whatsoever to do with the fabric. 'I lost my luggage when I arrived and Yasmeen, a doctor I work with, was kind enough to go out and get me some clothes, which is just as well as I haven't had a spare moment to myself. And though the dress is beautiful, you know me, Patrick, more at home in jeans and a cotton shirt.'

'Or a miniskirt,' Patrick reminded her. 'You've still got great legs, Mum,'

'Tha-ank y-o-u,' Nell said, making her voice sound old and croaky, concentrating on Patrick so she could ignore the questioning look Kal was throwing her way.

'Mum used to wear a miniskirt to cricket matches in summer until all my friends started getting older and whistling.'

Why had she brought up her son to be so open and forthcoming? Why couldn't he be like the teenagers she knew who were content to sit silent and slightly surly in adult company?

'But I guess women don't wear miniskirts much in this country,' Patrick continued, 'though you'd see Mum still had good legs if you took us swimming.'

A ripple of apprehension feathered along Nell's spine. Was Patrick's conversation more than idle chatter?

Surely he couldn't be trying to push them together? And, if so, why?

Nell shook her head at her own stupidity. So he'd have two parents instead of one, of course.

But he had that now.

Kal had made some reply to Patrick's comment but Nell had missed it, and, thankfully Kal was now pointing out landmarks they were passing, probably to her as well as to Patrick, though she wasn't listening. She was working again on sorting out a few priorities in her head. Number one was Patrick's health. She'd have to speak to Kal again about the bone-marrow tests. Number two had always been Patrick's emotional well-being—in fact, until he'd got sick that had been number one.

And as he'd never had an on-the-spot father—he'd been too young to remember much of Garth being around—why should he want one now? Fathers were all well and good, and this father in particular would be very useful for Patrick to have in his teenage and young adult years, but a permanent fixture in *both* their lives? Nell couldn't see that it was necessary at all.

'They call this building the big rig,' Kal was saying when Nell tuned back into the conversation. 'People think at night, when it's lit up as it is, it looks like one of the oil rigs out in the desert. Before oil was discovered, this was such a poor country the symbolism of the rig is very important.'

He paused then he added, 'To some.'

'You don't sound very certain about that,' Nell said to

him as they pulled up in a well-lit entry and an attendant appeared to open her door.

'Oh, it's been good for the people in many ways,' Kal told her, remaining in his seat although the door on his side had also been opened. 'The hospital is just one instance. But we're losing so much of the old way of life. Patrick spoke of miniskirts. Our young girls are not going that far, but it is the loss of values that comes with change. That bothers me.'

He got out, leaving the attendant to park the car, and joined Patrick and Nell on the pavement.

'Values?' Patrick queried, as they were walking through the foyer of the hotel. 'What kind of values, Kal?'

'Family values first and foremost,' Kal told him, and Nell wondered if some of what she'd been thinking might have gone out in thought waves into his head. 'It's the structure of the family that has held my people...' He punched Patrick lightly on the shoulder and amended, 'Our people together. You will have heard tales of the male being the head of the household and as such entitled to respect, well, that is so, but it's the women who have held the tribes together, who know all the family history. They know who's related to who and how, and they teach the young children the importance of loyalty and honour and integrity because these are the things that helped the Bedouin tribes survive the hardships of the desert through thousands of generations. They allow we men to think we have the power, but in truth it is the women who run our lives.'

'Same in our family,' Patrick told him gloomily. 'Gramps and I might have great ideas about weekends away—going off fishing for a few days—but he always has to ask Gran and I always have to ask Mum!'

Kal laughed and put his arm around his son, and Nell, seeing the two heads so close together, felt her heart bump about in her chest. Kal was telling Patrick that wasn't quite what he'd meant, but over his son's head his eyes met hers, and the message in those eyes reignited the deep throb of desire she'd felt earlier.

Forget it. With Patrick there, it was impossible to do anything about it—which was a *good* thing because seductively delicious sex with Kal would only weaken her defences against a man who was used to getting his own way.

'We go up to the top floor,' Kal was saying, but his eyes continued to tease hers, as if he knew exactly the effect he was having on her.

The elevator took them swiftly upwards and spilled them out into a restaurant that looked out over the city to the south and darkness to the north. A bowing waiter led them to a table by a window, and Patrick, who'd at least seen something of the city that afternoon, now wanted some landmarks pointed out so he could get his bearings.

'Wait!' Kal said, settling opposite Nell and turning to the waiter to order drinks and a platter of finger food on which they could nibble while they decided on their meals.

'Now, see the building with the blue light on the top?' he said to Patrick. 'That's the hospital. This afternoon we drove from there down to the docks so if you look to the right you'll see the lights along the darkness of the Gulf. That's where cruise ships berth and container ships carrying foodstuff and goods. If you look further down there you'll see the lights of the bunkers where the oil tankers take on their loads.'

The waiter returned with a tray of different-coloured drinks.

'So many!' Nell gasped as the man unloaded the tray onto the table.

'Different fruit juices and combinations of juices. I didn't know what you and Patrick might like, so I ordered a selection.'

He smiled—at her, not Patrick—and she felt again the shimmy of attraction in her skin and the heat of it warming her body.

'This is one you should try. Persimmon juice.'

He passed her the glass, his fingers brushing hers, oh, so casually, yet deliberately, Nell knew.

He was seducing her right in front of their son!

Why?

To prove Patrick would be no barrier to their relationship?

What relationship?

Nell sipped her drink, only half listening to Patrick's chatter as he tried different drinks, giving them marks out of ten for drinkability.

The persimmon juice was both sweet and tart at the same time—not unlike the man who'd offered it—although it had been a long time since he'd been sweet to her.

No, he'd been sweet today when she'd told him of the man's death—

'Did you do anything about an autopsy?' she asked, pleased to have something to take her mind off obsessing over Kal.

'Yuck, Mum! We're out at dinner. No autopsy talk, OK?'

Kal smiled at Patrick's complaint but nodded to Nell.

'It was being done this afternoon. Results will be on my desk in the morning—'

He stopped suddenly and smiled at her.

'Actually, they'll be on my desk by the time we get back to the hospital. And since Patrick is obviously averse to such things, we could drop him back at the apartment then go across and take a look. You haven't seen my office yet, have you?'

Nell couldn't believe this was happening! Oh, the conversation was OK—on the surface it all made perfect sense—but there was no way Kal was talking about autopsy results. He was teasing and tempting her—challenging her, in fact—to be alone with him. He'd been sending seductive vibrations her way since she'd turned up at his apartment door, and now he was upping the ante—offering a way they could do something about the attraction that was simmering between them, without in any way affecting or offending Patrick.

'Here!'

Now he'd lifted a small round ball of food and was offering it to her in his fingers, leaning across the table, his eyes holding hers.

'Try it, Mum, it's delicious. And after that you can try this little pastry thing. What's its name again, Kal?'

Kal replied to Patrick's query but his eyes still held Nell's, daring her not to take the food into her mouth. She opened her lips and his fingertips brushed against them, fanning the flames of desire she was feeling right through her body.

'Great, isn't it? I told Kal not to tell you if any of the things that went into the food were particularly gross, but he said most dishes are made of meat or beans or nuts, not sheep's eyes and things like that.'

'Sheep's eyes?' Nell echoed faintly, nausea easing a little of the desire. 'Tell me I didn't just eat a sheep's eye.'

Patrick laughed, but all Kal said was, 'Would I do a thing like that to you?'

I don't know, Nell wanted to reply. You're doing plenty of other stuff I'd rather you didn't!

But with her body feeling more alive than it had in years, she knew that wasn't entirely true. She didn't want Kal seducing her with his eyes, and his smile, and his tempting fingers, but that was because any kind of relationship between them would complicate things, not because she didn't like what he did to her.

Not only would it complicate things but she'd end up hurt. Losing Kal once had been bad enough—but to lose him twice? No, she couldn't handle that.

But he talked of marriage?

Marriage without love, the hard-headed bit of her brain reminded her. He'd talked of love, too, and not with any affection for it or belief in it!

'She might be asleep, sitting up with her eyes open!'

Patrick's comment made her realise she was missing something.

Missing something? The evening was turning into a nightmare. She was eating food and sipping her drink while her mind argued about love relationships and her body hummed with...

What?

Lust, the hard-head offered, but surely it was more than that.

'I'm sorry,' she said, finally responding to Patrick's continued teasing. 'I must be more tired than I thought. But I'm with you now. What were you talking about?'

'Kal was pointing out more landmarks,' Patrick told

her. 'See over there, at the edge of the city lights, there's a big square of lights with a scattering of lights inside it. That's his family's compound. It's kind of like a small suburb because his father and brothers and some other relatives all have their own houses inside it. Kal has a house there, though he uses the apartment at the hospital because it's easier for him to get to work if he's needed urgently.'

Had Kal explained all that while she'd been lost in thought?

Ashamed to have been so inattentive, Nell peered obediently towards the square of lights.

'They have bright lights around the outside of the compound to keep the djinns away. Djinns are spirits—they can be good or bad, but usually they are mischievous more than bad and though these days people don't really believe in djinns, they don't exactly not believe in them either, Kal says.'

Nell glanced towards this oracle her son was quoting.

'I think maybe my man who died had a bad djinn,' she suggested, but looking at Kal wasn't a good idea so she turned back to the window, determined to get with the conversation and put all thoughts of desire and seduction firmly out of her mind.

'Is the compound on the water? Is the blackness beyond it a branch of the Gulf?'

'No, the blackness beyond it is the desert,' Kal said, and something in his voice—the way he said the words—brought desire and seduction right back, not only into her mind but into her body as well.

Not long after they'd met they'd gone to stay on South Stradbroke island, taking a water taxi with a group of

friends to camp there for the weekend. The others had
teased Kal about the camping, telling him he should be the
expert, and expert he was. But late that first night, when
their friends had been drinking around the fire, she and he
had walked across to the ocean side of the island and sat
on the top of a high sand dune, looking out over the water.

It had been a moonless night, and Kal had turned to her.

'It looks like the desert. In the darkness, the soft ridges
of the waves could be the dunes,' he'd said quietly. 'It
looks like home.'

She'd heard the depths of his homesickness in those
words and had put her arms around him, offering comfort,
letting him talk.

'It even sounds the same. When the wind whips the
sands across the dunes, you hear that shushing sound the
waves are making. I'd love to take you to the desert, Nell.
Love to show you all the places that mean so much to
me—to have you share them with me. But I can't do that.'

He'd turned to her and kissed her then held her hands
and told her of the bargain he'd made with his parents, and
how his values meant he had to honour it.

'So, nothing can be between us but friendship, my
lovely Nell,' he'd whispered, tangling his hands in her hair
and looking deep into her eyes. It had been then that she'd
known there would be more, because a little love and joy
and rapture shared with Kal would be better than none.

She'd told him so, and that night, in the dunes, with the
ocean making desert noises beside them, they'd made love
for the first time.

Turning back from the window, she glanced at him, and
knew he'd been thinking of that time as well. Just so had

their thoughts always matched, but back then there'd been love to bind them together—a love that had been deeper and stronger and more desperately passionate because they had known it wouldn't be for ever.

the full penalty always exacted, but back then there'd been love and that, from Clementine's POV that had had an impact — a huge one and unpredictably mysterious dimension they had known it was often the case.

CHAPTER EIGHT

OR SO she'd thought. Maybe she'd just imagined he'd felt as she had. No matter what had happened back then, here and now was a different matter. Here and now he only wanted marriage because he wanted Patrick, and he was using the undeniable attraction he knew still existed between them to tempt her into it.

'So what are we going to eat?'

She asked the question of Patrick who'd been perusing the menu, comparing the English side of it to the Arabic and pointing out to his father the words he knew.

Patrick rattled off a list of incomprehensible dishes, assuring Nell she'd enjoy all of them, then he looked at Kal.

'Is that all right? It won't cost too much, will it? Mum always likes to pay our share, but she took leave to come over here to show the skin spray, so I wouldn't like her to use up all her holiday money on one dinner.'

'I will pay for dinner,' Kal said, in a voice that forbade any further discussion on the matter, and this time the look he turned on Nell was the angry one again—all hint of seduction or remembered love-making burnt away.

Fortunately Patrick, with the insouciance of youth, failed

to notice the change in the atmosphere at the table and chattered blithely throughout the meal, questioning Kal about the dishes, about the city and about the way his people lived.

Nell found the food delicious but she couldn't enjoy it as she should have, aware the whole time of the difference in the man across the table, puzzling over how such an innocuous remark of Patrick's could have turned him back into the arrogant Kal.

She was thankful when the meal was finally over and they left the building, but although she tried to slip in front of Patrick into the back seat, telling him he'd see the landmarks he now knew better from the front, it was not to be.

'No way, Mum, you sit up front with Kal. I'll sit back here and pretend we're a family. Mum, Dad and the kid in the back. Glad I've got beyond kiddie seats.'

Patrick was just rattling on, Nell told herself, but one glance at Kal's grim profile told her the words had done more than rattle *him*—they'd made him even more angry than he'd been earlier. In fact, if she hadn't known better she'd have been sure he was muttering expletives under his breath.

Though maybe, not being used to adolescent company, he was praying for patience.

He pulled into his parking space in the basement car park. Patrick got out and opened Nell's door, waiting for her to get out then giving her a hug.

'I'm having the best time,' he whispered to her, and Nell felt guilt swamp her again, this time for being so ungracious about the attention Kal was paying the boy.

'That's great,' she said to Patrick, wanting to add, Make the most of it. But he'd ask why and things might get very sticky.

'So, Patrick, have you checked out the channels we get on TV? There are two local channels in Arabic and all the rest are cable, so you get mostly US or UK programmes.' Kal asked the question as they went up in the elevator.

Patrick assured Kal he'd got it figured, then yawned.

'But I don't think I'll be watching much TV tonight. If feeling like you've been run over by a bus is jet-lag, I've got it.'

'Run over by a bus?' Nell went into immediate panic mode. 'Were your last tests OK? When were they? Have you missed one? Any lumps?'

Patrick put his hands on her shoulders.

'Relax, Mother-worrier. I'm just tired from the flight. I know I slept this morning, but that couldn't have been enough.'

He leaned forward and kissed her on the cheek, then gave her a quick hug, while Kal, his face unreadable, held the elevator doors open, waiting for the exchange to finish and the pair of them to exit.

They walked up to the apartment together but as Nell made to follow Patrick through the door, Kal held her back.

'You're forgetting the autopsy result will be in my office.'

Nell looked at him, but the desire that had tempted her earlier was gone from his face, replaced by an unreadable mask.

'I'm tired, too. I'll read it in the morning.'

'By morning it will be filed away and if, as you believe, that consultant had something to do with your patient's death, you'll never know.'

He was not quite blackmailing her but definitely daring her to accompany him to his office. Why?

She glanced towards Patrick who, although he'd

pleaded tiredness, was using the remote to flick through the television channels.

'Go and read the horrible thing,' he said to her, without taking his eyes off the screen. 'I've already unpacked in the second bedroom and if I can't find anything to watch for a while on TV, I'll go to bed and read.'

But Nell still hesitated.

'Scared, Nell?' Kal whispered, so only she could hear, and although she knew it was a goad to make her do something she didn't want to do, she fell for it, determined he wouldn't guess just how confused she was.

'Of you? As if!'

She turned back to Patrick and blew him a goodnight kiss.

'That's in case you're asleep by the time I come back. If you're still sleeping in the morning, I'll leave a number where you can call me when you wake up.'

'Oh, don't worry about the morning. Kal and I are leaving early to go out to the desert,' Patrick said cheerfully.

'Oh! Well, have fun!' Nell managed to say, although her throat was tight with anger. She shut the door and faced the man who, not content with seducing her with his eyes across the table, was now seducing her son away from her.

'And just when was this little expedition arranged?' she demanded, so furious with Kal that once again she wanted to beat her fists against his chest. Only last time she'd tried that he'd captured her and his touch had done weird things to her anger…

'This afternoon. Patrick did mention it at dinner but you might not have been listening.'

'And how long is this desert jaunt going to last? Will he miss his blood tests? Will you make sure he takes his tablets?'

Kal put his hands on her shoulders and looked down into her face.

'Do you think I wouldn't make sure he took his tablets? Could you believe I am so insensitive I could find my son only to lose him to a disease? Can you think so badly of me, Nell?'

Nell tried to move away but his grip tightened.

'I don't know what to think of you!' she snapped. 'Your arrogance, your attitude, your changing moods, I don't understand any of it. Like tonight—come and see the autopsy report now or forget it! That's close to blackmail, Kal. Why? Why couldn't a copy have been left for me in the office on the ward? Why push me like you did to come now?'

'You don't know?' he asked, his eyes blazing into hers, not with the desire she'd seen earlier, but with something she didn't understand.

Something that made her feel uncertain—not afraid exactly, but certainly wary.

'No, I don't know!' He'd relaxed his grip and she managed to slip away. 'But now I'm here, let's get it done.'

She walked away, back the way she usually went to cross the pedestrian walkway to the hospital, assuming his office was somewhere that way.

His long strides soon overtook her quick angry ones, but he didn't stop her, neither did he speak. He simply walked along beside her back to the elevator, pressed numbers into a keypad to take it up, then guided her out and along another corridor.

Eventually he stopped at a door, pulled out his keys, unlocked the door and held it for her to go inside. She entered what must have been an anteroom to his office, set up, she imagined, so he could hold small staff meetings in comfort, because over by the windows there was a long couch and several armchairs grouped around a coffee-table, while closer to an inner door was a desk with all the usual paraphernalia of a secretary or personal assistant.

He herded her into the anteroom then pointed to an armchair.

'Sit!' he commanded.

Nell moved towards the chair, but turned back before she lowered herself into it.

'Should I beg as well?'

Kal looked at her for a moment, then the mask cracked and a smile that sent shivers down her spine lit up his face.

'Later,' he said, silky smooth! 'Much later. For now, we need to talk. Do you want a tea or coffee? An alcoholic drink perhaps? I keep some for visitors.'

Nell shook her head. She was twitchy enough about what was going on here—alcohol would surely make her even more uptight.

Apparently satisfied he'd done his duty as a host, Kal took the chair opposite her, then leaned forward so he was barely two feet away, not quite invading her personal space but close enough to make the twitchiness worse.

'Do you deliberately set out to make me angry, Nell? Is it some kind of punishment because I left Australia? Because you were pregnant?'

He paused as if waiting for a reply, but Nell couldn't make sense of the questions, let alone fashion a reply.

'When have I made you angry?'

With that question, apparently, from the frown on his face! Kal caught himself before he exploded and contented himself with a glare at the infuriating woman who had turned his life upside down.

'You do it all the time,' he told her, letting a little of his fury bubble in the words. 'You've come over here on *leave*—that's what Patrick said. You're not even being paid! Do you think that doesn't make me feel terrible?'

'But Patrick told you that, not me,' Nell protested. 'And I took leave to come over because part of why I was coming was personal—in fact, to me, the biggest part was personal—so it was hardly fair to expect to get paid.'

Kal couldn't believe anyone could be so naïve. He stood up to stop himself from reaching out to shake her and strode across the room to relieve some stress.

'Everyone in the universe does personal things on their fully paid-for, work-related jaunts. You must know that. You must have been to conferences where half the attendees are out playing golf when they should be attending lectures and the other half are usually getting over hangovers.'

'I don't go to many conferences,' Nell said quietly, and realising she probably didn't go because of Patrick made Kal even angrier.

'This is what I mean. That boy thought you should pay for half the meal, and he was worrying about what it would cost you. It was my responsibility to see you and he never wanted for anything—that you never had to worry about money. How do you think I feel that you've taken that away from me and struggled to juggle work and bringing up *my* son?'

She looked at him, her eyes wide, her expression puzzled.

'Kal, it was my decision to go through with the pregnancy, and that made Patrick my responsibility. I've never regretted it and, yes, at times it's been tough, but he's never wanted for anything vital and at the same time he's not been spoilt. He knows the value of money and that he can't have everything he wants just because he wants it. If it's something I won't buy, he has to save for it. Would you throwing money at us have made a difference to how I brought him up? I don't think so!'

Good, she'd stopped looking puzzled and was angry now, but not as angry as he was, although he couldn't pin his anger down to one single point.

'That still doesn't alter the fact you're not being paid—you're working at my hospital for nothing.'

'I'm a doctor, it's what I do, but if it's going to make you feel better and stop this ridiculous conversation, then pay me. Put me on the payroll and pay me whatever you pay Yasmeen. Now, shall we look at the autopsy report?'

'Do you really believe I brought you here for that reason? If the report is on my desk, there'll be a copy of it on your desk, too. It will be marked private and for your eyes only, although you can discuss it with Yasmeen as the senior local doctor in the ward.'

'Well, in that case, I'll be off,' Nell announced, ignoring his question and standing up, her departure, as far as he could see, imminent.

'Nell?'

She looked at him and sank back down into the chair.

'OK,' she said. Faint colour was rising in her cheeks but she held his eyes with a defiance he had to admire. 'When you first talked about coming here to see the autopsy report, I thought it was a ploy for the two of us to be together, and I'd be a liar if I didn't admit that the physical attraction between us is still strong, and the thought of us being able to do something about it was very appealing. But during dinner I was thinking about where our relationship began—thinking about love, Kal. I think you loved me then—I certainly loved you—but I've made the mistake of going into a relationship without love once before and I'm not going to do it again, no matter how enjoyable the sex might be.'

'Love! You talk of love? What is it, Nell? Quantify it or define it for me. Oh, I fancied I was in love back then, but if what I felt for you was love, then let me tell you it's an emotion I never wish to experience again. Not for what it was at the time, but for the fallout, which proved more deadly than nuclear waste. Shall I tell you what love did for me, Nell?'

She didn't answer but he told her anyway. Told her of the sweet young bride who'd cried into her pillow night after night, unable to conceive because of her unhappiness and made more unhappy by that inability.

'I was kind to her, and gentle, and tried everything I could to make her happy, Nell, but some part of me was locked away from her. She knew that instinctively, and though she never probed, she felt lessened by it and in the end she returned to her father's house, causing pain in both our families, shame in mine. Now she studies and hopes to teach eventually at the university. Philosophy, Nell! Does it encompass love?'

So bitter, Nell thought sadly, but she wasn't going to let him get away with that.

'Everything encompasses love, or it should,' she told him, tilting her chin so he'd know she had no intention of giving in on this point. 'Love isn't just something between people—it's a warm feeling inside you. Maybe if your ex-wife enjoys learning and teaching, she'll find the warmth and comfort of love in her job. Maybe the marriage wasn't any more right for her than it was for you. But don't knock my belief in love, Kal, don't even try. Love has given me the best memories of my life and a beloved son. How could I not believe in it?'

She stood up again and walked towards the door, and this time he didn't try to stop her. Neither did he say anything, which was just as well because Nell's heart was pounding so rapidly she doubted she could have answered. Opening the door, she was tempted to look back at him, but looking at Kal was a dangerous occupation so she continued right on out.

'We'll still get married!'

The words echoed down the corridor and she spun back towards him, forgetting she didn't want to look at him.

He was standing in the doorway, leaning against the jamb, a look of implacable determination on his face.

'You've *got* to be joking!' she snapped.

'Not for one minute,' he said. 'Patrick's my son, you will be my wife!'

'Just what century are you living in, Kal?' Nell demanded, coming back towards him so he couldn't fail to see how serious she was. '"You will be my wife," indeed? What will you do next? Fling me over a camel and ride off with me into the desert?'

'No, but I'll fight you for my son. I'll fight you in any court in any land, and I'll prove I can give him a better life. More than that, he's nearly fourteen. The judge will ask his opinion. And you've given me the task of looking after him while you work. Do you think he will want to go back to a tame life in Australia when he sees what I can offer?'

Pain so great she wondered if she was having a heart attack squeezed Nell's chest and she reached out to the wall for support.

'You'd do that? You'd do that to me?' The words sounded like a pitiful mew, even to her own ears, but Kal wasn't moved. If anything, he looked more fiercely unyielding.

'You've kept him from me for all these years,' he reminded her in the cold, remote voice she found so unsettling. 'Yes, I'd do it.'

Nell turned and walked away. She'd have liked to have kept a hand on the corridor wall for support but she was damned if she was going to let him see—again—just how devastated she was. She reached the elevators and leant against the wall for a moment, wondering what to do next, too upset to think straight.

She couldn't go back to the apartment—if Patrick was still up, he'd guess she was upset. There'd be coffee in the canteen, although she wasn't certain it operated twenty-four hours a day, and coffee might make her more uptight.

The ward! She needed to see the autopsy report some time. She'd go down to the ward, sit quietly in the doctor's office and read it.

Or pretend to read it while she sorted out her head.

All was quiet on the ward, although several of the patients, as she went from bed to bed, unable to be there without checking on them, were awake, their injuries making sleep difficult.

She picked out the three new post-op patients because the limbs that had received skin grafts were splinted and swathed in bandages to prevent movement. The young girl with the facial wounds was sleeping, but a woman all but covered in the now-familiar black veils sat by her side, the rubber gloves and medical face mask she wore looking out of place with her traditional dress.

Nell smiled at her, and the woman's eyes smiled back above the mask.

'Her skin is healing,' Nell said quietly, peering at the girl's cheek. The woman nodded, then touched the girl lightly on the arm.

'Her heart will take longer,' she said, her English clear and understandable. 'I am her aunt, but an aunt can't replace a mother and a father, though I will try.'

Nell felt tears well in her eyes and though she knew they were probably to do with her own emotional trauma, she touched the woman on the arm.

'I am sure you will do a wonderful job,' she whispered, then she left the ward, afraid that if she encountered any more emotionally fraught situations she'd end up crying like a baby.

The autopsy report—had Kal had it translated into English for her?—was on her desk, and she slumped into the chair and looked at it, not really reading the words.

Until she came to 'gross internal bleeding' and had to start at the beginning again. The heart consultant had inserted the catheter into the man's femoral artery and through it to the left ventricle, where he'd closed a slight hole in the ventricular septum. But somewhere along the line, maybe as he'd withdrawn the instrument on the end of the catheter, he'd nicked the wall of the artery, so small a hole it had gone unnoticed both by him and the radiographer.

Blood had begun to seep from the artery, then, as less blood had reached the man's leg and his brain had told the heart to pump harder, more blood had escaped, enlarging the hole until the volume of it in the chest cavity had constricted the lungs until it virtually squeezed the heart to death.

Accidents happened in medicine, Nell reminded herself, but that didn't stop her anger building at the consultant who'd been so pleased with himself. Not that anything would happen to him. With no relations to fight for his rights, the patient's death would be recorded, the autopsy report filed, and that would be that.

Unless *she* sued on his behalf!

And bring trouble on the hospital? Yasmeen would be involved. Did the friendship she'd offered Nell deserve to be repaid that way?

Kal, too?

Was she thinking of this as some kind of payback to Kal?

Nell shook her head. She didn't have a vindictive bone in her body—though she did feel anger towards the consultant.

But realistically she didn't know much about medico-legal law in her own country, let alone in this one, so how would she go about getting justice for her patient?

And what would it achieve?

She was pondering all these questions and getting absolutely nowhere when the door of the office opened and Kal appeared.

'I thought I might find you here,' he said, waving what was apparently his copy of the autopsy report towards her. 'I'll need legal opinion, of course, but the consultant is definitely responsible. I'll suspend him from working in this hospital immediately and find out what other course we should take against him. The patient not having a family makes it difficult, but his death shouldn't just be pushed aside as an unfortunate accident.'

'But if you take legal action, the hospital will also be included in the responsibility for the man's death,' she reminded him.

'So?'

Nell stared at him, unable to believe what she was hearing. This was the Kal she'd once known, the man to whom truth and honour had been so important—important enough to be pursued even at the risk of hurting the hospital. So maybe it was truth that had made him hurt her by denying love. Maybe he really did believe the emotion she called love was nothing but a destructive force.

'Are you listening to me?' he demanded, and she shook her head.

'Not really,' she admitted. 'I got lost after you said we shouldn't push his death aside as an unfortunate accident. I was thinking the same thing when you came in, but didn't know what to do about it, or even if there was anything we could do.'

'I'll do something,' he promised, then his gaze moved over her, and for the first time since things had fallen apart in the restaurant his face softened.

'You spent your first few days here telling me to go to bed. I'm telling you that now, Nell. You look exhausted.'

He paused, then allowed a rueful smile to flick across his lips.

'Beautiful, but exhausted.'

He held out his hand towards her.

'Come, I'll take you up to the apartment. Your apartment, not mine, though that discussion isn't finished!'

Nell took his hand and let him pull her to her feet, then found herself glad of his supporting arm as they made their way back to the apartments. Emotional as well as physical exhaustion was dogging her footsteps now.

And weakening her resolve…

Having someone to lean on, literally as well as figuratively, was a very seductive thought…

CHAPTER NINE

KAL glanced at the boy who sat by his side, looking out of the window, asking questions about the buildings they were passing. He tried to see something of Nell in the profile or in the face when Patrick turned towards him, but all he saw was his own young self.

Then the city slipped away behind them and the long straight road stretched out into the desert.

'Wow! It really is desert,' Patrick said, and Kal smiled.

'Wait until we turn off this road—you won't believe civilisation can be so close.'

He drove swiftly, Patrick talking and asking questions, constantly surprising Kal with his perception and intelligence, then the small marker came in sight and Kal pointed it out.

'Can you make out tyre tracks running away from the main road?' he asked Patrick, who peered obediently through the window.

'Only just,' he said. 'In fact, they seem so faint I might be imagining them.'

'It's because the sand shifts all the time,' Kal told him.

'Desert sands are like the sea, always on the move. We'll get out.'

They walked around to the front of the car where he showed Patrick how to feel for the hardness of a much-used track beneath the soft top layer of sand, then pointed out how the 'road' ahead could be seen as slight indentations in the sand.

'But that's for those who don't know the desert,' he explained when they were back in the car. 'Those of us who have lived here know always where we are. Do you know how to find compass points from the sun?'

'I've a vague idea—something about pointing your watch towards the sun? But my watch is digital, so that wouldn't work.'

Kal stopped the car again and, using his watch, showed Patrick how to do it.

'So, in this desert,' he added, when they were driving again, 'all you need to do is to remember the main road runs directly east-west, and we went south off it, so as long as you keep driving north, you'll hit it again somewhere.'

It was basic desert lore and the first of many things he taught his son, although later, when Patrick asked what he'd do to find the north at night, Kal laughed and showed him the compass in the front of the car.

'And this is a GPS—a global positioning system—which gives you the co-ordinates of where you are at all times. It has some locations set into it. See, go to menu—you've got town, oasis, beach and camp. We're going to camp so choose that one.'

Kal drove on while Patrick worked out how to follow

the GPS direction, and shouted with delight when they came to where a black tent had been erected.

'The camp?'

'It is,' Kal assured him, feeling so much pleasure and delight in his son's company it was almost painful.

But not as painful as his head, which was throbbing with unrelenting persistence. He knew it was from lack of sleep. He'd spent the night in his office, dictating letters and messages for his secretary, leaving notes for the various unit managers at the hospital and more lengthy notes for the legal people.

Fortunately his men had set up the tent and the cook had prepared food and put it in the refrigerator in the car, so all Kal would have to do was forage in it for lunch and light a fire to cook the meat for the main meal this evening. Not camping out the way Patrick might have expected, but Kal had wanted to spend as much time as he could with the boy.

He walked into the dark coolness of the tent and saw the carpets spread across the floor and a pile of white clothes in a corner.

Patrick had followed him in and was looking around, marvelling at carpets spread on sand.

'Out here, I shed my western clothes,' Kal said to him. 'Will it bother you if I put on a kandora—the long dress—and suffra—our headdress?'

'Great. Can I wear one, too? Or do I have to be a full sheik or something special like you are to get to wear one?'

Kal laughed and went to the pile of clothes.

'You could wear the kandora and, if you like, a coloured suffra—red and white, or black and white check—but I have only white here because that's what I wear. So let's see you as a sheik.'

It was the start of a busy but exhausting day, Patrick wanting to know so much about how Kal's people had lived before oil had changed their lives, wanting to learn to drive, then tearing up and down the sand hills in the big, safe, automatic vehicle, wanting to cook the dinner over an open fire, assuring Kal he was a barbecue expert.

And Kal let him cook, for the headache, which had persisted all day, was now joined by some kind of fever, and though he hid the tremors he was feeling from the boy, he knew they should drive back to town.

Maybe after dinner, although he knew Patrick would be disappointed...

Patrick carried the plate of meat and vegetables he'd cooked on the heavy grill over the fire towards the carpet Kal had spread in front of the tent. Kal had explained that this would be where they ate—cross-legged on the carpet, using their fingers instead of cutlery, an initiation into the Bedouin way. But though Kal was there, he was lying down, and when Patrick spoke to him, he didn't answer.

'Kal!'

Frantic, Patrick shook his father's shoulder, then common sense returned and with it the basic teachings of first aid he'd learned at school. He pressed his fingers against the vein in his father's jaw—and almost cried with relief to feel the throb of a pulse. Kal's chest was rising and falling, too, so he was breathing.

Patrick left him there and ran to the car, remembering the easy steps of starting it, then putting it into gear. He drove it towards his father, praying he wouldn't do something stupid and run over him.

Then, with the back door open, he heaved the man's heavy body up, surprising himself with his own strength, his heart pounding with exertion and fear, a little 'Please, don't die' prayer fluttering continuously on his lips.

Somehow he got Kal in. He looked at the fire and kicked some sand on it, though he doubted it could set light to anything out here, then he ran back to the car and turned it, praying again—this time that he was heading in the right direction to meet the main road back to town.

As he crested the first sand hill he saw a glow on the horizon. Relief flooded through him. All he had to do was drive towards those lights, for that was surely the city.

He hit the main road twenty minutes later. From time to time Kal had mumbled something, but he'd not responded when Patrick had spoken to him so, determined to save his father, Patrick drove on.

The city drew closer and, aware he wasn't very good at steering yet and knowing he'd never handle the big vehicle in traffic, he began to work on a contingency plan. At the first of the big roundabouts on the approach to the city he stopped the car on the verge, turned on the hazard lights and got out, taking off the white robe he'd been wearing so he could wave it to attract attention.

A huge semi-trailer pulled up in front of him, and the driver ran back towards Patrick. He spoke far too quickly for Patrick to understand him, so he grabbed the man's arm and led him to the car, pointing to where his father lay, his breathing now so loud and raspy Patrick was terrified Kal might be dying.

Fortunately the man seemed to understand for he hurried back to his truck then returned a few minutes later, saying the English word 'ambulance' over and over so Patrick would understand.

And an ambulance it was, siren blaring, lights flashing, pulling up beside the truck within very few minutes, paramedics tumbling out.

'It's my father,' Patrick said, relief making his voice tremble and building a huge lump in his throat.

But the men had obviously recognised Kal as an al Kalada, for the name was whispered reverently and the attention became even more urgent.

'Come,' one of the attendants said to Patrick as Kal was loaded into the back of the ambulance. 'Come with us.'

Abandoning the car, Patrick climbed in, only too pleased to have other people in charge—*and* doing the driving. Besides, the ambulance would take Kal to the hospital and Mum was at the hospital. Everything would be all right.

Not wanting to go back to an empty apartment, Nell had stayed on in the burns unit office, checking on test results of all the patients, changing dietary orders where needed, working out which patients might be able to take food by mouth. The office had a wide window in one wall, and some change in the flow of staff traffic past the window made her look up. Staff were gathering in small groups and clusters, talking excitedly and waving their hands.

'What's going on?' she asked when a young ward aide came in with some supper for her.

The girl started to explain in Arabic, then stifled her

words with her hands, thought for a few minutes then spoke slowly, as if translating every word she needed into the English she would have learned as a second language at school.

'The sheik, he sick in desert. A boy drive him to town, now ambulance bring him here.'

In this hospital there was only one sheik.

But Kal sick and a boy drove him to town?

Patrick?

But Patrick couldn't drive!

'Where are they now? Where's the boy? What's wrong with Kal—the sheik? What kind of sick?'

The young girl shrugged, Nell's barrage of questions obviously beyond her limited English.

Nell got up, determined to find someone who would understand, but no one she spoke to knew any more than she'd already heard.

Ambulances took people straight to A and E, she reminded herself, and with only a few wrong turns she made her way back to where she'd spent so many hours on the night of her arrival.

Patrick was sitting on a bench by the wall, looking so lost and alone she thought her heart would break.

'Oh, Mum!' he cried as she came towards him, then he stood up and put his arms around her, holding her close while his whole body shook with the release of tension. 'I tried to get someone to phone you, but they didn't seem to understand your name or didn't know what apartment you were in, and I couldn't leave Kal here on his own and go and find you.'

He broke off with the choke of a sob, and Nell held his

long, thin body against her own while anger that Kal would put him in this situation gathered in her belly.

Although Kal hadn't done it deliberately.

He was sick?

She patted Patrick's shoulder and held him a little away from her.

'What kind of sick is Kal? What happened, Patrick?'

Patrick's lips began to tremble, as if remembering brought on a panic he hadn't been able to exhibit earlier when Kal's life might have depended on him staying calm.

'He just collapsed, Mum. He'd said earlier he had a headache and I asked why he didn't take something for it, and he said he'd rather wait and see if the desert air cleared it. He said the city often gave him a headache. Then I said I'd do the barbecue and when I brought the meat across he was lying there.'

'And you drove him back—how?' Nell demanded, although her heart was full of fear for Kal. A sudden collapse—a stroke? A brain tumour? Possible diagnoses raced through her mind, but Patrick needed her now—needed to talk through the trauma he'd experienced.

He was explaining how Kal had taught him to drive that morning, and how he'd practised on the sand hills.

Nell hugged him again, praising his courage and his good sense in getting help as soon as he'd got close to the city. Then, as she released him, she saw a group of people sweep through the doors into the ER. A tall, imperious-looking man in a white robe led the way, a small, veiled woman clinging tightly to his arm. Behind this pair were other white robed figures and a gaggle of black-robed women, their faces masked behind the fine veils that fluttered around their heads.

Hospital staff appeared from nowhere, greeting the new arrivals with reverent salaams.

'Let's go, Mum,' Patrick said, and Nell heard panic in the simple words.

She put her arm around his shoulders and led him back the way she'd come in, so he didn't have to pass these people, who were obviously members of Kal's family.

'They will want to see you some time,' she said carefully. 'If only to thank you.'

'Maybe, Mum,' Patrick said, the break in his voice showing the strain he'd been under. 'But I've just got used to having a father—I don't think I'm ready for more relations. And Kal might not have told them about me. He told me he's not married any more, and hasn't any other children, but whether...'

Nell knew exactly what the 'whether' was—Kal had mentioned introducing Patrick to his family but Nell doubted it would happen any time soon...

Although if they were to get married...

We're not, she reminded herself as they made their way back to the apartment.

'What could be wrong with him?' the boy asked, as the elevator rose towards their floor.

'I don't know, but he's in the best place and in good hands.'

'But you'll find out how he is, won't you, Mum? You'll find someone to ask?'

Nell promised she would, but once inside the apartment she realised Patrick hadn't eaten so she phoned down to order food, then for the first time it struck her that all her son was wearing was a pair of shorts.

'I'd been wearing a kandora—the white gown thing they wear,' he explained. 'But I took it off to wave it at the cars. Must have left it by the road. It's one of Kal's. I hope he won't be angry.'

'I'm sure he won't,' Nell soothed. 'But maybe while we wait for dinner, you could have a shower and get into your pyjamas. You've had a big day, one way and another.'

So Patrick was in the shower when the knock came on the door. Nell opened it, thinking it was their meal, to find the tall man in the white robe she'd seen earlier in ER.

He had a string of amber worry beads in one hand and she heard the clicking noise they made as he moved them through his fingers. Apart from that, she could only stand and stare, sure this was Kal's father—an important man, a ruler—unsure what he wanted of her.

'I thought you would like to know Khalil has regained consciousness. It seems he has a recurrence of a fever not unlike malaria which he picked up in Africa some years ago. But thanks to the boy's prompt action he was able to be treated swiftly, and though he is very weak and will be kept in hospital for a few days, he will recover.'

Relief from a terror she hadn't fully realised she'd been feeling flooded through Nell.

'Thank you for coming. For telling me,' she said, uncertain whether to ask the man in or not—uncertain what he knew and didn't know.

But the man didn't seem discomfited by her silence. He stood there, clicking through the beads, staring at a point somewhere behind her, his eyes thoughtful. Then finally his gaze turned back to her.

'He is Khalil's son, this boy?'

Oh, hell! Did Kal want his family to know?

Did it matter what he wanted?

Yes, it did, but so did Patrick's birthright.

Nell nodded and the man nodded back at her.

'He told me he had things to discuss and that he would do it soon. I knew of you, of course, from long ago, but not that there was a child.'

There was no reproach in this gently spoken statement, and the lack of it made Nell feel weepy. She swallowed hard, and did her best to explain.

'Kal didn't know either,' she said. 'I knew he was to marry—it seemed unfair to tell him and spoil something that had been arranged and to which he was committed. I knew how much his marriage meant to his family—and how much his family meant to him—so how could I tell him and cause a rift between them?'

'You chose a hard road, but for the boy to have done what he did today, you have raised him well.'

Nell shrugged, not sure she could take too much more of this extraordinary conversation. At that moment Patrick erupted out of the hallway, asking her if she had a spare toothbrush as his was in his bag back in the desert. He stopped when he saw her visitor, hesitated for a moment, then came more quietly towards her.

'Have you heard how Kal is?' he asked, nodding to the visitor but directing the question at his mother.

'He's regained consciousness,' Nell told him, 'and is getting all the treatment he needs. Apparently it was a sudden recurrence of a disease he picked up in Africa some years ago.'

She was aware she was repeating, parrot fashion, what

her visitor had said, but although she guessed the man was Kal's father he hadn't introduced himself so she couldn't introduce him to Patrick.

Fortunately he took the matter out of her hands, bowing low to Patrick and touching his hand to his forehead.

'I am your grandfather,' he said in his precise English. 'I am sorry it has taken us so long to meet.'

Patrick, much to Nell's surprise, bowed back, but lower, as if aware of some distinction in obeisance.

'I am Patrick,' her suddenly mature son said. 'I am honoured to meet you, sir.'

And with that he came forward, his hands together, and the other man grasped his shoulders and drew him close, touching his nose to Patrick's nose in what Nell knew was a traditional greeting between male relatives and close friends.

'You did well to get Khalil back to the hospital. Do you drive so young in Australia?'

Patrick grinned at this new relation.

'No, but Kal gave me some lessons this morning and the car's an automatic—it could have driven itself. I'd have been lost without the lights of the city, though. Kal had shown me the GPS but I didn't really know how to work it.'

'You did well,' the man repeated, his voice deeply sincere. Then he turned back to Nell.

'I thank you for the gift of this boy. I will return in the morning.'

And with that he walked away, his back ramrod straight, everything about his bearing betraying his rank.

'Wow!'

Patrick put Nell's reaction into words, but as she was

about to close the door she saw a member of staff coming down the corridor, wheeling a trolley she knew would hold their meal.

Patrick was still asleep when Nell was ready to leave for the ward the next morning, but his overnight bag had been delivered and was just inside the door of the apartment. She checked inside to make sure his tablets were there and left him a note, reminding him to take them and giving him the phone number where she could be reached.

'Phone me when you wake up,' she added as a PS on the note, then she took it into his bedroom and left it on the floor just outside his door, where he couldn't fail to see it when he came out. She stood and looked at him for a moment, his gangly, adolescent frame flung with such abandon across the bed.

Weird that she'd come here to get Kal to help Patrick should help be needed, yet it had been Patrick who'd helped Kal.

This would strengthen the bond between them, she knew, and as she left the apartment and saw Kal's father coming towards her, she felt a quailing in her heart. Another bond—another person tying Patrick to this country…

'You are well?' the sheik enquired politely.

'I am well,' Nell responded, 'but Patrick is still sleeping.'

'I have spoken with Khalil this morning and know of Patrick's illness. He will be tired after the excitement of yesterday. With your permission, I will sit in your apartment until he wakes up. Khalil tells me you are needed in the hospital and the boy is his responsibility. I will take that on. He will be safe with me. You need have no fear.'

Nell had no fear—neither did she have a clue how to respond. All she could manage was a feeble 'That's very kind of you', then she rallied and added, 'But there's no need for you to put yourself out. Patrick is used to taking care of himself.'

'Khalil tells me the boy wishes to learn to read and write in Arabic—it will be good for me to be a teacher. You have no objection if we drive? He will learn to read more quickly if he sees road signs and billboards with words he recognises.'

Khalil says—Khalil tells me! It was Patrick all over again. Nell agreed it would be all right and excused herself with the explanation of being needed on the ward, but what she really wanted to do was find out where Khalil al Kalada was and rip his head off. He knew she didn't want this arrangement between him and Patrick to be anything other than a 'getting to know your father' one—not that she'd wanted that!—but even from a hospital bed Kal was weaving a web that was entangling Patrick and drawing him closer and closer into his family.

Patrick should know this other family, conscience reminded Nell, but she was too mixed up to listen to that namby-pamby voice.

Though she'd have to leave ripping off Kal's head until later. She'd left the unit office last night before finishing the jobs that needed doing and would have to get them done now. She also needed to liaise with the Spanish team and make sure the post-op treatment they wanted for their patients was taking place.

Down in the ward, Yasmeen greeted her with the news that Khalil was deathly ill in this very hospital, and Nell nodded, hoping he wasn't really deathly ill while she was feeling so uncharitable towards him. But knowing Yasmeen's opinion of Kal was close to god-like, she decided her friend was probably exaggerating, though as she worked through the morning she was aware of a nagging concern for the man nibbling away at her anger and her determination not to have anything more to do with him.

So at six, after a phone call from Patrick—the fourth of the day, each reporting on where he was and what he was doing—to say he was having dinner with his grandfather, Nell casually asked around and discovered Kal was in a private room on the top floor of the hospital.

'It's all private rooms up there,' the young nurse added, with the kind of wonder usually reserved for talk of heaven.

Nell thanked her and departed, then was foiled as the elevator wouldn't take her to that floor, needing a code of some kind to get her past the penultimate one.

She thought for a moment, remembering Kal's office had been on the top floor. She'd watched him key in some numbers and had thought nothing of it at the time, but now she closed her eyes and tried to recall his actions.

One seven zero nine—her birthday, now she thought about it. She smiled to herself as the elevator rose obediently up to that final floor, although it was hardly likely Kal had even set the code—and if he had, why choose *her* birthday?

A very officious-looking sister came towards her as she walked in what she assumed was the direction of the ward. Kal's office had been to the left and they certainly hadn't passed any private rooms, so she'd turned right along the corridor, pushing through some swing doors before seeing the woman.

'You are looking for someone?'

Nell held up the hospital ID she'd been given on her first day in the burns unit and the woman looked at it and frowned.

'We have none of your patients here,' she said.

'No, I'm here to see Dr al Kalada,' Nell told her, trying to sound just as officious herself.

But the woman wasn't swayed by officiousness. She frowned at Nell and said in tones of great disdain, 'He is seeing only family.'

At that moment a veiled woman in black robes, beneath which a lilac skirt peeped demurely, came out of a room further down the corridor. She said something and the sister turned away from Nell, answering then hurrying to do the woman's bidding.

Uncertain if it was one of the women who'd accompanied Kal's father into the ER, Nell moved forward hesitantly. The woman watched her for a while, then ducked back inside the room, returning a few seconds later with a second black-robed figure. This woman came towards Nell, her feet seeming to glide somehow above the floor so smoothly did she move.

'You are Nell,' she said, holding out her hands and taking hold of Nell's in a warm clasp. 'Khalil is sleeping now, but he has been worried about you and the boy. He begs your forgiveness for not looking after the boy and putting him in danger with the drive back to the city.'

The woman's face was masked, but her eyes, keen with intelligence and so like Kal's she had to be his mother, were smiling anxiously at Nell.

'Patrick is fine,' she assured the woman. 'By now it will

seem a great adventure, and think how he'll be able to boast about it to his friends when he returns to school.'

Wrong thing to say apparently, as the smile faded from the warm brown eyes, which now looked puzzled.

But Nell felt tiredness wash over her. Perhaps relief that Kal was all right might have caused it—or lack of sleep the previous night from wondering how he was! Whatever, she couldn't handle trying to figure out why the woman now looked puzzled, so she asked if she could see Kal, and was led into his room.

Five women sat around the bed, all quiet, although three of them appeared to be praying. Only one wore the trousers and tunic top that was the uniform of a nurse, so the rest must be family. Nell glanced at the masked faces. Was one of them his ex-wife? Would she still have the right to sit by his bed?

Then his mother introduced them. This one was her sister, Kal's aunt, this one and this one sisters-in-law and the other his mother's friend, like an aunt but not so closely related. Nell said a weak hello to all of them, her mind more on the figure who lay motionless on the bed.

She looked at the nurse.

'He *is* sleeping?' she asked. 'It's not a coma? Have you done brain scans? It's not something worse than the recurrence of an old illness?'

The nurse beckoned her to come outside, then introduced herself. Her name was Annie, and she was English, working in the hospital because her husband worked here for one of the oil companies.

'I'm glad you got me out of there even if it's only for a short time,' she said. 'Yes, he's sleeping naturally. Last night he woke briefly and became so agitated the doctors put him into an induced coma, but just while they did brain scans and got his temperature down. At about eight this morning he came out of that and was alert. It *is* the old illness, nothing more sinister, but it's left him drained and he'll probably sleep for twenty-four hours.'

'But you're in there with him—he has a nurse with him all the time? Why, if he's OK?'

'The family!' Annie explained. 'You *do* know who they are? They're a bit like gods around here, they're so revered, so of course the doctor treating Dr al Kalada has insisted he have round-the-clock nursing care, although the doctor knows his relations will also stay with him. It's the custom here—but if you're the Australian doctor working in the burns unit, you already know that.'

She finished her explanation, then looked enquiringly at Nell.

'I guess you met him through the plane crash,' she said, but as far too many people in this hospital right now already knew of her relationship to Kal, Nell had no intention of explaining anything. She thanked the woman for the information and walked away, but as she made her way back down to the level where the bridge crossed to the apartments, she regretted not talking more to the English girl…

Anything would have been better than this sense of being very, very alone that she was experiencing right now…

CHAPTER TEN

PATRICK'S next phone call was to say he was back at the hospital, but as Kal was now awake he would call in and see him before coming back up to the apartment. And though she assured Patrick that would be all right, for the first time in her life she was jealous of him. That he would be able to see Kal and hear from his own lips that he was feeling better…

To see him with his eyes open, not deadly still and pale…

But to see him with all those people around? What could you say? Tell him you love him?

Yeah, right! And listen to another dissertation on the destructive elements of that particular emotional state…

Nell paced the room, passing and repassing the dinner she'd ordered, unable to eat as the depths of her anxiety about Kal tied her stomach into knots, while her mind began to wonder if perhaps what he was offering—a loveless marriage—would be better than not being with him at all.

No, half a loaf of bread might be better than no bread to a starving man, but hers was an emotional hunger, and she suspected it wouldn't be satisfied with half-measures.

She had made this decision—for about the hundredth time in the last few days—when a knock sounded on the door. Thinking it was Patrick, she strode towards it and flung it open. It wasn't Patrick but the small woman she had assumed was Kal's mother—accompanied by one of the other women, though Nell couldn't be sure which one.

'Patrick and my husband are with Khalil so I came to speak to you,' the woman said, her voice slightly hesitant but her English clear enough to be easily understood.

Nell ushered the pair inside and waved her hand towards the couch.

The two women sat, then Kal's mother pulled some sheets of paper from a pocket in her robes.

'We have one hundred and fourteen names on this already, and that is only what we have achieved today,' the woman said, handing the sheets of paper to Nell. 'I am sorry they are in Arabic but I do not write in English, but the names are there and already these ones have been registered, although the testing seems to take a little time.'

Nell looked at the pages with the graceful curves of Arabic script across them. They told her nothing and, try as she may to make sense of the conversation, nothing clicked.

'I don't understand,' she said softly, not wanting to offend this woman.

'Khalil told us last night about the boy's illness and the bone—bone marrow?—Patrick might need. He was disturbed he had not done something about it earlier and cursed his selfishness in wanting to get to know his son. He was so upset I assured him I would take care of it, so this is where we are now—the people on the list you have are all relatives, but by the end of the week my husband says we will have ten thousand more people on it, and more again the week after that. Khalil says he will get more specialists to do the tests so it does not take too long, and someone else to set up all the results on a computer. He says our country might become known as a donor bank—is "bank" the right word?—for all the world.'

Nell looked at the sheets of paper in her hand and shook her head. Last night this small robed woman who, Nell had no doubt, rarely ventured from her home had first heard of Patrick's plight, and now she was talking of a bank of thousands of would-be bone-marrow donors, all tested and listed there, ready to give something of themselves to save the life of a stranger.

'Thank you.' She said the words, but knew they were inadequate.

The woman waved away her thanks, then added, 'We pray that Patrick will not need it.' Her light brown eyes, so familiar to Nell, were soft with understanding. 'But I know why you had to come and ask us this thing, although it must have been a hard decision for you to make. Hard for you in your heart.'

Nell nodded, for that's where it *had* been hard—where it was hurting so much now.

They sat for a little while, Nell aware she should offer hospitality but too torn apart by conflicting emotions to find the necessary energy. Then the women rose, Kal's mother taking Nell's hands between hers and pressing them together.

'The road ahead might seem dark now, but it will lighten. I can see the glow of it ahead of you.'

Nell thanked her again, rising to her feet and following the two women to the door. She doubted anyone could see into the future, but the image of some glow ahead of her was a comforting one—though maybe the glow was the hot summer sun back in Australia, and somehow the thought of that glow wasn't nearly as enticing as it should be.

Kal was released from hospital the following day, and predictably Patrick begged to be allowed to accompany his father to the house in the family compound where he would convalesce for a few days.

'Well, I can hardly say no,' Nell said, a trifle tetchily. 'I can't expect you to hang around here all day on your own.'

Patrick ignored her mood, hugged and thanked her, then packed his bags and headed off, accompanied by a white-robed man who had been waiting in the corridor.

'This is Ahmed, one of Kal's men,' Patrick told her by way of introduction, then they left, Nell watching from the door of the apartment, more and more aware of the growing affection between her son and his father, and the growing attraction to Patrick of the life his father—or his father's family—led.

'So I bring him up, fight for his life, then lose him, not to cancer but to his father?'

The thought pained her so much she felt like crying, but she'd already shed her bucket of tears over Kal, and more than a bucket over the possibility of losing Patrick, so she refused to shed any more. She phoned home instead, speaking to both her parents, explaining why Patrick wasn't there to talk to them, telling them about the donor register getting under way, hearing their delight.

She had just hung up when the phone rang again.

'You didn't come to see me in hospital.'

Just hearing Kal's voice was enough to make her heart thud erratically, but the accusation in his voice steeled her against any weakness.

'I came,' she said. 'You were asleep, and well protected against the wiles of casual women visitors.'

Kal laughed.

'Too well protected,' he said. 'I felt like a child again, living among the women. My father shooed them all out when he and Patrick visited.'

'Where's Patrick now?' Nell asked.

'He's out at the stables. Some of my younger cousins and their friends were playing soccer with him for a while, and now they're going riding. The trails are well lit and they know to keep a watch on him without him knowing it. They won't let him get too tired.'

Playing soccer, going riding, driving cars—what wasn't on offer for Patrick in his father's life?

There was a pause, then Kal said, 'It is ironic, isn't it, Nell, that you came here looking for insurance in the form of bone marrow in case it was needed to save Patrick's life, and it turns out he saved mine. Without prompt drug treatment, the encephalitis could have caused brain damage and even death.'

'Encephalitis?' Nell breathed, her grouchiness over Patrick's fun forgotten. 'You had encephalitis? No one mentioned that to me.'

'They didn't tell you?' Kal sounded puzzled. 'I thought my father—'

'Your father said it was a recurrence of something— I thought some minor virus—nasty and fast-acting, but encephalitis?'

'You should be careful, Nell.' His voice almost purred down the phone. 'You're sounding as if you care.'

'Of course I care,' Nell snapped at him. 'I've always cared. I love you, Kal. You're angry that I didn't tell you about Patrick. You feel denied and cheated. Well, I've done my penance for whatever wrong I might have done you—loving you has been my penance, and now look where that has led me.'

She slammed down the phone.

It rang again and, although she knew she shouldn't, she answered it.

'Where has it led you, Nell?' Kal asked, as if they hadn't been interrupted.

'It's led me to the point where we are now—the point you threatened me with—the point where Patrick gets to choose whether he stays with your fabulously wealthy and important family, where he gets to ride horses and probably camels and drive cars and go camping in the desert, or to go back home with dull old Mum. You've even got what will probably end up being the biggest bone-marrow donor register in the world happening, so you can use his health as an added enticement for him to stay. That's one that will play well in court.'

'Nell, stop! It needn't be like this. You must know I still have feelings for you, feelings that could well be love.'

'You wouldn't know love if it got up and bit you on the backside!'

She slammed the phone down again and left the apartment, not certain she'd be strong enough not to answer it a third time. She headed for the ward, then decided she hadn't the will to be as cheerful and positive as she needed to be for the patients she would see, so went down to the lobby instead. She'd been outside the hospital only once—the evening Kal had taken her and Patrick to dinner. She'd go for a walk. From what she remembered of the drive to the hotel, there were parks spread through the city like emerald-green oases.

'Taxi?'

The cab edged up behind her as she came out the front doors, and suddenly she had a better idea.

'Could you drive me out to the desert?' she asked.

The driver looked puzzled. Maybe he didn't understand English.

'To the desert? You want to drive out to the desert?'

His English was OK, he just didn't understand the request. Nell smiled at him.

'I've been here for nearly two weeks and I keep hearing about the desert, but I haven't seen it. Would you drive me out there—it needn't be too far—then wait for me while I look at it for a while?'

'It is night-time, lady,' the driver said, no doubt sure she was mad.

'But there's a moon,' she pointed out. Then she opened her handbag and counted out how much she had in local currency. Patrick had got her some from an automatic teller machine on his first day in town when he'd asked for some change and she'd realised she hadn't any money. Now she offered the man her collection of notes.

'Would this be enough?'

'To drive you to the desert and wait there for you? It is far too much.'

He named a sum and, although he continued to shake

his head, he allowed her to climb into the back of the cab, and he took off slowly out of the hospital grounds, speeding up as they reached the main road, but still driving carefully, as if he needed to be fully alert should his passenger show further signs of derangement.

Eventually they left the city and drove along a wide highway, lined on either side with what Nell assumed were date palms. She was reasonably sure the darkness beyond the palms was desert, but the driver seemed to understand she needed something more. Eventually he turned off the highway, drove a little way, then stopped.

'My car is not made to cross the sand,' he said, turning in his seat to look at her. 'But up ahead is the first of the sandhills that run east-west across the country. If you walk up there, you will see them ranging into the distance, though not as well, of course, as if you'd come during the day.'

'Night is fine,' Nell told him, but didn't add that night was what she needed, because night would hide the tears she knew she'd probably shed.

'I will leave the headlights on so you can see the way and find the way back, and, lady, please, do not go beyond my headlights, or I will get very worried about you.'

'I won't leave the lights, and thank you,' Nell said, then she opened the car door and got out, slipping off her shoes so she could feel the texture of the sand beneath her feet, her mind a muddle of so many things that for a while she was content not to think at all.

The warm night air wrapped around her, a slight breeze lifting her hair and brushing against her skin. After that first time, she and Kal had often camped at South Stradbroke, walking across to the dunes at night, finding a special magic in the sand and sea and moonlight.

And if ever she'd needed magic, it was now. Kal's mother saw a glow in her future—a glow from the fiery conflagration that would be her fight with Kal, because no way would she let her son go easily.

Even if life here would be better for him? Not only financially, but in every way? Not even if he chose to live with his father?

Nell crossed her arms across her chest as if the action might stop her heart from bursting. Who was she kidding? As if she could ever put Patrick through the emotional agony of making a choice between her and Kal.

Knowing Patrick, she knew he wouldn't stay without her blessing, but his choice, given one, would be to have her stay, too. And being Patrick, he'd make sure Nell's parents were included in whatever arrangements were made— Kal would probably send the jet over to bring them to visit whenever they wished!

The bitterness of that last thought made her shiver. She'd think about Patrick's likely first choice—her staying on.

She'd reached the top of the dune and sat down, not so much to look out over the desert as to consider her future.

She'd have a job—Yasmeen had said they'd been advertising for a specialist to head the burns unit, without success.

But there'd be Kal...

'Nell.'

No wonder the taxi driver thought I was mad. Now I'm hearing voices.

'Nell, I'm coming up the sand hill now. I didn't want to startle you.'

Nell turned in disbelief.

'Are you having me followed?' she demanded. 'And what do you think you're doing here when you're just out of hospital? Have you no sense at all? How do you think Patrick would feel to find his father, then have him drop dead because he didn't look after himself?'

Kal reached her side and dropped to sit beside her.

'Stupid, I know, but I didn't drive. Ahmed brought me. Well, he took me to the hospital and I saw you getting into a cab and I did that "follow that car" thing for the first time in my life, then when we stopped beside the cab, the driver seemed prepared to defend you to the death until Ahmed and I managed to persuade him it was a lovers' tryst. I told him who I was, and eventually he agreed to drive back to town.'

'You sent my cab away?' Nell knew this wasn't the point she should be arguing but it seemed a stable point she could latch onto in the morass of her emotions.

'But I hadn't paid him.'

Kal laughed and moved a little closer, putting his arm around her shoulders and giving her a little hug.

'I paid him,' he assured her, but although that issue was settled, something else had occurred to Nell. She moved away from Kal's arm so she could make the point more decisively.

'And it's definitely not a lovers' tryst!'

'It could be,' Kal murmured, but he didn't touch her again. Instead, he drew up his knees and rested his chin on them, looking out over the rolling sands of the desert.

'Did you think of the island when you came here?' he asked.

Nell nodded, unable to lie about memories that were so precious to her.

'I, too, think about it whenever I am in the desert. Maybe that's why I spend all my days off out here, usually alone, though sometimes with my birds for company.'

He was silent for a long time, then he spoke again.

'Do you think that's love, Nell? Fourteen years of coming to the desert to sit on a dune like this and think about the island? To think about you?'

Nell couldn't speak. Her throat had closed up so tightly she felt she might never speak again. And Kal didn't seem to need an answer, though he moved slightly and rested one hand lightly on her shoulder.

'I can hear your laugh when I'm out here,' he continued quietly. 'In the city there's too much noise to hear it, but out here I see you running down the sand hills, laughing at the sky, and I can hear the joyous sound of it. Is that love, Nell?'

Nell shrugged, not to move his hand but in answer to his question. She had never been able to return to the island, afraid memories would overwhelm her there, but if Kal really did come out here and think of her—was it love?

'I thought it was obsession.' His words hovered in the air. 'A kind of madness I should be able to shake off. "Physician, cure thyself"—that's what I used to quote, but there was no cure, and that was bad. I am not a man who should have obsessions. Then one day you were there, bent over a dead man in a disaster zone, calmly taking charge, turning to me and saying, "Hello, Kal," as if we'd parted yesterday.'

His hand grew heavy on her shoulder, but Nell knew he hadn't finished, while in herself she wanted to be sure she was more than an obsession.

Would he get to that?

'So that was bad enough, then you sprang Patrick on me, and although I knew in some part of my mind you'd acted in what you saw as my best interests at the time, I was angry, Nell, so angry, yet bereft as well, with grief that I had lost all those years of my son's life. Can you understand that?'

This time Nell nodded, although Kal was still looking out across the desert, not at her.

'But even though I blamed you, I needed you. I looked for you and sought you out and felt better being near you, even when we were fighting all the time.'

He turned towards her now, and lifted his hand to move her chin so she was facing him.

'Is that love, Nell? Does love hurt when you are arguing with the object of that love? Does it make us lash out to hurt the loved one in return? I can't believe it can be, Nell. I can't believe if I really loved you I would threaten to take away your son. Is love so irrational? Is it so confusing we do wrong in its name?'

Nell stared at him, seeing his familiar face, made young by moonlight, in this unfamiliar setting.

'I don't think love's about hurting people, Kal, but neither can it protect anyone from hurt. Love's about being there for each other when hurt happens—that's when love is needed, sharing the hurt as well as the joy. It's like the desert, stretching endlessly to the horizon—limitless. As hard to quantify as the grains of sand we're sitting on.'

She turned away, looking out over the play of moonlight on the rolling sand hills.

'Can I apply for the job as head of the burns unit?'

'You'll stay?'

The joy in his voice was unmistakable.

Pity she had to kill it…

'If Patrick decides he'd like to live here then, yes, I'd like to get a job so I can be near him. That's what I came out to the desert to decide. What would be best for Patrick. I won't fight you over him, Kal, or have him made to choose between us. He's been through enough lately and doesn't need that kind of pressure from people who supposedly love him.'

'But you'd stay with me! We'd be a family! Of course you can work if you want to. We couldn't hope for a more qualified surgeon to head the unit, but you talk as if—'

'As if we'd be apart? Wouldn't we, Kal? Even if we shared a house, for form's sake or for Patrick's or your family's, wouldn't we still be apart?'

'You don't believe I love you.'

The statement fell between them, flat and somehow ugly.

'How can I, Kal, when you're still not sure yourself? When you still think of me as an obsession, and look hopefully for a cure. We could share a house, even share a bed, and, yes, that part would be good, but inside I'd be dying, Kal. If that sounds dramatic, I'm sorry. But love can't live in a vacuum. It needs to be nurtured, not with gifts and promises but with love returned.'

He stood up and walked away, down the sloping face of the sand hill—not towards the car but away from it.

Then he turned and raised his arms towards the night sky.

'What do we do when words are not enough?' he said, asking not her but the stars and moon. 'Here we see the magnitude of nature, but how to show the magnitude of love?'

He turned around, the white robe whirling around his

body, then he walked back towards her and knelt in front of her.

'Yes, it's an obsession, but I don't want a cure, Nell. Because it's love as well. A love so deep and strong and all-consuming you might call it an obsession. But however it's labelled, I hope it will remain with me for the rest of my life.' He took her hands and lifted them to his lips.

'As I hope you will remain with me for the rest of my life…'

Her heart tap-tapping against her rib cage and hope tap-tapping in her head, Nell spoke his name, knowing her uncertainty and disbelief would be echoing through the word.

'Kal?'

He drew her closer, and silenced any further questions with the lightest of butterfly kisses.

'I love you, Nell,' he said, his voice gravely deep—desperately sincere.

'I was really sure all along. Right from when I saw you again at the airport,' he added quietly. 'But some stubborn streak kept getting in the way of admitting it. Yet the more I denied love, and derided it, the more certain I was inside that it was what I felt for you.'

He cupped her face in his hands and looked deep into her eyes.

'I'm a man who is used to being in control,' he said, 'but with you I lose it completely, and that's a very scary thing for an al Kalada.'

'So you'll stay scared for as long as we're together?' Nell teased, high on happiness now she was certain that the miracle of love had embraced her once again. Embraced her and Kal and, within that magic circle, Patrick.